FIFTH ESTATE

BY

Jason Blacker

ISBN-13: 9781927623756

For the freedom of the press without which democracy's foundation is fractured.

CHAPTER ONE
TRASH CAN

JOSEPH Severn knew he was onto something. This was going to be his biggest break yet and it might even land him in the fourth estate. That was a rung up the ladder from working the lowly fifth estate jobs. It might not have sounded like much to his friends but it was the pinnacle of his profession. Almost. A Pulitzer would be the icing on the cake. And who knew, this might lead to that as well. But, baby steps. First he had to make it to the Washington Chronicle.

Arguably the most revered paper in the country. Some would say the New York Times, but he thought it was the Washington Chronicle. They'd excelled lately at breaking news. Big stories. Like the one in Syria they'd coined General John. About generals paying for and keeping a stable of Syrian women as prostitutes to be doled out as rewards for soldiers with the most kills. It was a barbaric practice. But what he was about to uncover was bigger than that. It would rock the nation to its very core.

But let's get back to the very beginning. Or at least a

beginning of where this started. It was four weeks ago when his editor had come to him at his desk in the Bronx where he was still working at TrashCan. TrashCan's slogan was "Digging in the deep webs for the ugliest stories nobody wants you to read". It was long and cumbersome. Not like the Chronicle's "Shining Light on Democracy's Dark Corners". But it was true. Both the name and the slogan summed up pretty perfectly what they did. They looked for dirt. TrashCan was a tabloid. Joseph had no problem admitting it.

TrashCan was the kind of Web 2.0 media that had grown into a large tentacled monster. They had websites writing about pretty much everything and anything. From Android to Zombies, well zombies from TV anyway. But TrashCan was the masthead of this ungainly monster that Webswum Inc. had become.

"I want you to interview this kook who keeps calling," said Rufin Flatter.

Rufin Flatter was the Editor-in-Chief of TrashCan. He was an older guy in his mid-fifties. That was to say that he wasn't hip to Web 2.0 and other technologies. But he had been an Editor at The World Post which, at its height, had a circulation of over 300,000. That made it a top 25 newspaper in the US and it was based in Brooklyn. Now it was struggling to stay afloat.

Rufin Flatter reminded Joseph of J. Jonah Jameson. He was the Editor of the Daily Bugle which was the fictional newspaper that Peter Parker, aka Spider-Man, worked at. Rufin Flatter had the same brush cut hairstyle with gray sides and a lampshade mustache. He had bushy eyebrows and he had no idea who J. Jonah Jameson was. The top of his head was dirty dark brown leaning towards dark gray hair and the sides were more silvery. His eyebrows and mustache however were the chestnut brown of a man twenty years younger. Rufin was also found carrying an unlit cigar around, always ready to light it up if he got the chance.

"C'mon Rufin," said Joseph, "I'm working on this post about police brutality against seniors. It's something, I swear."

Rufin Flatter's nickname around TrashCan offices was Ruffian. Only because it looked similar to his name. He was grumpy and acerbic but hardly a ruffian. His name, Rufin was happy to let everyone know, was pronounced "Raff-in".

Joseph was actually working on a story about police brutality against seniors. He'd uncovered it when visiting his grandmother at the senior's home she lived at. It had been a long story in the making primarily because none of the seniors wanted to talk about it. This is what was happening. The particular home his grandmother was at also housed several mothers and fathers of current NYPD police officers. Some of these men, and a policewoman too, were abusing their elderly parents in secret. Not beating them black and blue you understand, but certainly abusing them and taking their frustrations out on their elderly folks.

Joseph thought it was a good story. Better than the churn he had been putting out lately. This story at least had some bite. He'd even come up with what he thought was a catchy title. "Police Brutality: NYPD Beating Up Pensioners!" He was particularly fond of the exclamation mark at the end. That gave it the air of gravitas it deserved.

"Listen, I want you to talk to this fella and that's it. He's probably got no story. Thinks he saw something that's not gonna be interesting. Maybe he was pissing at a urinal next to Mayor Vistaysky and the Mayor said something about a budget and he figures it's a big conspiracy."

Joseph let out a big sigh. He'd been writing at least three posts a day for over a year now that never gave him much satisfaction. He thought been a journalist was going to be a great job. Something that helped protect the pillars of democracy and contribute to a knowledgeable world. What he'd found out instead was that every blogger in their mommy's home was masturbating about fake news, and what it was doing instead was undermining the very fabric of this democracy with the stain of this sinister mental ejaculation. Yeah, he felt pretty strongly about it.

He realized that what he needed to do was to get into the fourth estate. He needed to get into the big leagues where real journalism was hard at work. Working in the blogs, or the clogs, as he liked to call it, or more specifically the fifth estate, was doing nothing but contributing to the problem. It was all about massive amounts of content rather than digging deep into real issues.

"Ok. Is he gonna call back or what?"

"He's on the phone already. Take line 3 and you'll get him."

"What's his name?" asked Joseph as he picked up the handset, but Rufin had already left his desk.

"Joseph Noah Severn."

"Hello?"

"Hello, this is Joseph Noah Severn."

Joseph had taken to using his full name lately. He thought it added an heir of seriousness to the work he wanted to do. Plus, he'd liked the reason his parents had given him that middle name.

"Who are you?"

"I'm a journalist with the TrashCan. You called. Who are

you?"

There was a long pause on the other end of the line.

"Hello?" asked Joseph.

"Yeah. I've got a story," said the voice whispering so that Joseph could barely hear it.

"That's what my Editor told me," said Joseph.

"Your name really Noah?"

"My middle name, yes."

"Like Noah of the Ark?"

"Exactly like that, yes."

"That's a good omen."

"I've never thought of it like that. What's your name?"

"Shem's my middle name," and then in hushed tones, "shit, I've said too much."

"I've heard you've got a story for me Shem," said Joseph.

"Call me spiderman," said Shem, "one word and lowercase, not like in the comic books."

"Uh.. OK," said Joseph.

"What have you got for me spiderman?" asked Joseph.

"I want you to get a burner. Then put the app Pressage on it and then text me at 555-497-7978. The text must say 'Ark of the Covenant' or I won't answer it."

"Why?"

The line went silent on the other end.

"Hello?"

"Hello Shem, I mean spiderman?"

It wasn't like in the old days when you could actually hear the line getting hung up on you with a quiet click. Now the line just went dead. Joseph looked at the phone's receiver for a minute. Then he put it back to his ear, but there was nothing there. He hung it up.

He wrote the number down on a piece of paper quickly

before he forgot. He sat at his desk for several minutes. One thing was certain. This Shem or spiderman was a kook. That was for sure. But Joseph was intrigued enough. Even the guy's name was intriguing. He searched Shem on the internet. He learnt that Shem was the oldest son of Noah. The Noah of Noah and the Ark's fame. Not him, not Joseph Noah Severn. Joseph Severn was a gangly twenty-something without a girlfriend, and without any kids he knew of, but with a mess of curly blond hair. Shem was also blessed by Noah for covering up his father after his father got into the sauce a little too much and ended up naked in a tent. They don't tell you what was going on in that tent.

What were the chances that he, Joseph with the middle name Noah, would make conversation with someone crazy named Shem? But he was intrigued, and that very same day he went to the closest convenience store and picked up a burner. His number was 555-365-9936.

CHAPTER TWO
PRESSING PRESAGE

OVER the previous four weeks, Joseph and spiderman had conversed through texts and talk. Pressage, Joseph had learnt, was a private messaging app that also allowed for voice calls. Everything was encrypted through it. Spiderman swore by it. Joseph found the naming of this app to be quite intriguing. If you took away an 's' you had presage which Webster had informed him meant 'something that foreshadows or portends a future event'. Kinda like an omen. If you kept the word as it was, it was actually French for 'pressing'. Perhaps they were both coming to understand a pressing omen as Joseph liked to think. Spiderman being a little crazy seemed to like that too.

But over these weeks Joseph hadn't received anything substantial from spiderman. And he felt that heavy rains were coming. If he was to survive the floods he needed the tools and materials to build his ark. And this ark was gonna be an investigative piece of journalism the likes that no one had ever seen before. At least that's what spiderman kept promising him in vague terms.

As Joseph sat in his car, ten minutes early for their first meeting, he scrolled through some of their texts.

Me: Ark of the Covenant

That's how it had started. The Ark of the Covenant, Joseph had learned, was made according to God's instructions as given to Moses after the Israelites had left Egypt. It was said to contain the two tablets that held the Ten Commandments as well as, at least by some accounts, Aaron's rod and a pot of manna. Everybody needs food for the journey. But manna, Joseph learnt, is more than that. It's special food that God provided to the Israelites on their journey from Egypt so that they wouldn't starve. Problem is, like most biblical myths, if you read too deep into it they start to fall apart. Like the fact that manna stored "was full of maggots and began to smell..." That's from Exodus 16:20 Joseph learnt. He wondered why, if it was food from God, it rotted like everything else.

Aaron's rod, incidentally, was a simple staff imbued with miraculous power, because... God, or magic or mythology. Joseph didn't particularly care. The thing was, Joseph wasn't religious. His parents had named him after Noah Webster, the dude who's dictionary he had consulted on the word 'presage'. His parents highly regarded education and language. That was all. That was why he was given the middle name Noah. He'd never stepped into a synagogue or church in his life. That was true. Joseph was just a name his parents had liked. Yeah, it was full of religious history, but the honest truth was that his parents had just loved the musical Joseph and the Amazing Technicolor Dreamcoat, and that's why they'd named him Joseph.

spiderman: hello

Me: Hello

spiderman: ground rules. we never text or talk except through this app

Me: OK

spiderman: i have to get comfortable with you first

Me: OK

I mean what else could Joseph say? Spiderman went off on tangents about conspiracies, miracles and truth. It seemed to Joseph that spiderman, or Shem, was your garden variety religious whacko. But like a journalist or a bloodhound he thought he smelled a story. Or maybe he just hoped there was one here.

spiderman: if you lie to me you'll never hear from me again. lies will be found out. the Lord detests lying lips, but he delights in people who are trustworthy. proverbs 12:22

Me: I won't lie. Now is probably a good time to tell you that I'm not religious

spiderman: the righteous hate what is false, but the wicked make themselves a stench and bring shame on themselves. proverbs 13:5

spiderman: you can be righteous but not religious. you cannot be religious and not be righteous

Me: Proverbs?

spiderman: spiderman... right now ;)

It seemed that under all that craziness was someone with a subtle sense of humor. He also seemed pretty easy going, at least through texts, for someone so devout. At least he seemed pretty devout and religious to Joseph. As Joseph scrolled through the texts it was peppered throughout with biblical quotes, especially Proverbs and Psalms. And also a real angst about doing the right thing. Telling the truth or being quiet.

Me: Who are you?

spiderman: i've struggled a long time with this. but the truth must be set free. if we claim to have fellowship with him and yet walk in the darkness, we lie and do not live out the truth. 1 john 1:6

Me: Is it really that difficult for you?

spiderman: yes. you have no idea what i have. what it will do to our country

Me: Maybe you should be going to the CIA or the FBI or something. Not sure I'm the one to help

spiderman: you are. it's a sign. God works in mysterious ways. you are not religious yet your middle name is Noah. my middle name is Shem

Me: Yes, but it sounds like you might be in danger

spiderman: resist the devil, and he will flee from you. james 4:7

Me: OK

This was the kind of thing that intrigued Joseph. He admired spiderman's faith. But would spiderman not take responsibility for his own safety. Faith alone will not heal broken bones. That's where you gotta get help from science and medicine. But about this issue, whatever it was to come, spiderman felt that God would protect him.

spiderman: i sometimes fear they're onto me

Me: Maybe you should go to the police and get real help? I can't protect you, especially as I know nothing about it.

spiderman: in time Noah, in time. but you, Lord, are a shield around me. psalm 3:3

Spiderman preferred to call him by his middle name. Joseph didn't care. In the blog comments of the TrashCan he'd been called a lot worse.

Me: If you tell me what it is you know, you might be

protected. If we get the truth out it'll be harder to quash

spiderman: your trials and tribulations will soon be over. better a patient person than a warrior. proverbs 16:32

Joseph thought that perhaps the better approach was to fight a proverb with another proverb. At this stage he was starting to get a little frustrated and impatient with the lack of disclosure.

Me: When justice is done, it brings joy to the righteous but terror to evildoers

spiderman: ;)

spiderman: proverbs 21:15. i think it is time to meet

And so here Joseph was at a dingy bike bar in Hoboken called The Rattlin' Chain. It was almost nine pm on Thursday November 23rd. It was Thanksgiving Day. It wasn't like Joseph had anywhere else to be. His parents were in Ashland, Ohio. He'd told them he was too busy to make it out, but he'd see them at Christmas. His sister and her husband would be there too. And his niece. So here he was sitting outside a dingy bar as snow fell from the bruised sky like manna. Spiderman better have something for him.

CHAPTER THREE
RATTLING CHAINS

JOSEPH walked into the bar. It wasn't the kinda place he'd seek out all by himself. It was dark. It was also littered with big dudes with the arms torn from their denim jackets. They had beards and some didn't have hair. Joseph counted six of them in the bar. They gave him the once over. A couple continued playing pool. The rest went back to their drinks. On the back of their jackets was their crest. These guys were the Seventh Sons. A small outlawed motorcycle gang that was usually up to no good. Their logo was of a skeleton holding a 7 that was also a stylized scythe. Around the skull's neck was a chain that carried seven 7s.

Joseph looked around quickly but didn't see spiderman. None of the bikers were spiderman because Stanley said he'd know him by the camo baseball cap he'd be wearing. None of the bikers wore baseball caps. Joseph found an empty booth in a dark corner of the bar. He sat down.

"Hey, new guy," yelled the bartender.

Joseph looked around.

"Yeah you."

Joseph looked at him.

"This ain't no fancy Manhattan lounge. We don't do table service. You thirsty, you come to me."

Joseph smiled uncomfortably. He got up and walked over to the bar. He figured he needed to order a couple of drinks at least or risk getting kicked out.

"Couple of beers," he said, trying to sound tough, but he felt like a child.

"Coors Light for the lightweight," said the bartender.

A biker seated at the bar laughed at that.

"Just give me a couple of Buds," said Joseph.

The bartender who looked like he fit right in with the Seventh Sons cracked open a couple of bottles and put them on the counter. He didn't offer glasses and Joseph didn't ask. He paid and took them back to his table. He sat down and took a sip from one of the bottles. He started to wonder what the hell he was doing in a place like this waiting for a kook.

A few minutes later at about five minutes after 9 the door to the bar opened. Joseph looked back towards it and saw a lean young guy walking in. He carried a black backpack and he looked to be around Joseph's age if not a half dozen years older. He was hard to make out from where Joseph sat, but he was about average height and skinny like Joseph. He had on a hoodie and camo pants. On his head was perched a camo baseball cap that looked like it might fall off if he kinked his neck. Even from this distance Joseph could see his curly hair was plentiful and red.

Joseph raised his beer to him. Thank God, about time, he thought. Spiderman nodded at him. Spiderman stood still for a moment and looked around. Then he walked up to Joseph and slid into the opposite side of the booth. The two of them got a couple of looks and then everyone went back to their own business.

"Spiderman?" asked Joseph.

He hadn't been told if there was a secret passphrase for this meeting or not.

"Yeah, you Joseph Noah Severn?"

Joseph nodded.

"I need proof."

Joseph pulled out his Driver's License and showed it to him. He also pulled out his media ID that Webswum Inc. had issued him. It had TrashCan Media on the top and underneath that it said "A Webswum Inc. Property". Both had his photo on them.

Spiderman looked at them for a long time and then pushed them back to him over the table.

"Do you have your phone here?" asked spiderman.

"Yeah."

"Put it on the table."

Joseph put his burner phone on the table. Spiderman fished his own phone out of his pocket and punched in some numbers. Joseph's phone came to life with a notification that said "spiderman: testing"

Spiderman nodded. He opened up his phone and took out the battery. He placed the two pieces on the table. He took a look at Joseph's. He tapped away at it for a while.

"What are you doing?"

"Making sure it's not recording us," he said.

After he was satisfied he placed it on the table.

"Do you have your other phone with you?" asked spiderman.

Joseph nodded.

He pulled out his iPhone and put it on the table.

"Shit," said spiderman. "I was worried about this."

"What's wrong with it?"

"It doesn't have a removable battery. Can you unlock it?"

"I don't feel comfortable doing that," said Joseph.

"Look man, I don't want to look at your porn, I just want to make sure it's not recording us."

Joseph looked at spiderman for a while.

"OK," he said and placed his thumb on the sensor.

Spiderman picked it up and tapped away at it until he was satisfied. Then he put it back down on the table.

"Happy?"

"Not yet," said spiderman.

Joseph watched as spiderman opened up his backpack and took out some plastic self closing bags and a roll of heavy duty aluminum foil. Joseph frowned at it. Spiderman placed them on the table. He took Joseph's iPhone and put it in a Ziploc bag and sealed it. Then he triple wrapped the phone inside the plastic bag with the foil.

"Can you call your phone?" said spiderman.

Joseph picked up his burner and dialed. He put the phone to his ear. Then he pulled it away and offered it to spiderman.

"It's gone straight to voicemail," he said.

"Good," said spiderman.

Spiderman took the phone from Joseph and took out the battery. He placed them in another plastic bag and wrapped it in foil. He did the same with his own burner phone and battery. Joseph looked on quizzically.

"What was all that?" he asked.

"Home brewed Faraday cage."

"A what?" asked Joseph.

"It prevents these devices from receiving signals so that we can be spied on. They can turn smartphones on from a distance without you knowing. Then they can record and take pictures."

"I don't believe you."

Spiderman looked around nervously and fidgeted with the quick on his thumb.

"Are you a cop?" he asked, whispering.

Joseph frowned, shook his head quickly like he heard a mosquito close by and pinched his lips together.

"Fuck no," he said.

"You could probably lie anyway. Doesn't matter. If you were a cop I'd probably be dead."

"I'm not a cop. Jesus, have some beer and relax dude," said Joseph.

Spiderman was as nervous as a wounded bird in a cage of alligators.

"Can you not use the Lord's name in vain?" said spiderman.

"Yeah, sorry."

They sat in silence for a few moments. Both sipping beer.

"I suppose if they got malware onto your phone they could remotely access it," said Joseph, coming around to the first part of the conversation.

Spiderman shook his head.

"Nope. Don't even need to do that," he said.

"I don't believe you," said Joseph. "You're telling me that Google and Apple have backdoors to allow for this shit?"

Spiderman shook his head again. His cap almost came off, so he took it off and put it on the table. His hair reminded Joseph of an Afro. A red Afro with loose curls. It wasn't as neat either.

"No, they're doing what they can to offer secure OSes.

What I'm saying is that they can access a phone remotely because of their ninja skills man. These guys aren't messing around. That's why I only uses burners."

"Who are 'they'?"

"We'll get to that."

"I don't know man. I'm pretty skeptical."

"I'll prove it. After we've done here I'll install it on your iPhone and then you'll believe me."

"You could have done it already when you were tapping away at it before."

Spiderman shrugged.

"I wasn't."

"Anyway, if what you're saying is true, then this is a huge story. So why didn't you go to the Times with it or the Chronicle?"

"I did. They told me to pound sand. Didn't believe me."

"Probably because they thought you were a little cray cray, am I right?"

Joseph didn't know why he said that. He'd been thinking it. This guy sure sounded like a crazy conspiracy crackpot. A triple C as he had called it when speaking to his buddies at TrashCan.

"I'm sorry dude, I didn't mean it like that," said Joseph, sipping on his beer. Spiderman was taking to pulling the label off of his. He shrugged.

"Not the first time I've heard it. At least you're honest with me and you're sitting here listening."

Joseph nodded.

"You've gotta understand where I'm coming from. What you're saying is literally insane. If people knew about this they'd go ape shit. There'd be riots in the streets."

"Dude, this isn't even half of it. But I think you're wrong.

The ISPs are spying on us already for advertising purposes and nobody's doing anything about it. In fact it's only getting worse. We think we live in this great free country. We laugh at the Brits who have a camera on every street corner. Man, we've got cameras in every pocket, in every hand. We are literally plugged in 24/7 and just about everything about us is known. The only problem for them, which is a small help for us, is that they can't sift through it fast enough. That and a lot of them are just plain incompetent."

"OK. So tell me how you know all of this. If I'm gonna write a story I need to be able to verify the veracity of it."

"I work for an international organization that you've never heard of."

"And what do they do?"

"They're working towards the coalescence of world power under the authority of a central power."

"And that power?"

"That power will be the Bilderberg Consortium. They are our future leaders, though despots is probably a better term."

Joseph chuckled and drank some beer.

CHAPTER FOUR
BUILD A BERG

FUCKING guy, thought Joseph. He is a crackpot. If nothing else this should be entertaining. Joseph knew about the Bilderberg conspiracies only very vaguely. I mean come on. Yeah the rich probably had aligned goals but that didn't mean they were actively trying to overthrow democracies and centralize power. I mean shit. We lived in a country that had gone to war with itself just to give everyman a literal chance at freedom and equality.

"Man this is gonna be good," chuckled Joseph some more. "Just give me a sec I've gotta get us some more beers."

Joseph stepped out of the booth and went over to the bar. Spiderman frowned at him. He had hardly touched his beer. He didn't like beer much. In fact, he hardly ever drank. But he waited patiently for Joseph to return.

"Here you go," said Joseph, not noticing that spiderman had hardly touched his first beer. Joseph finished his first in a large gulp and put it aside. "So you were gonna tell me about the Bilderbergs."

"You think I'm a conspiracy nut, don't you?" asked Spiderman.

Joseph nodded, finding it hard to stop grinning.

"Yup, I ain't gonna lie."

Spiderman shrugged.

"I shoulda known," he said. He fiddled with the label of his first beer. "Maybe I made a mistake."

"Listen man, I'm here aren't I. Let me hear what you've got to say. Worst case I still think you're a conspiracy nut and I won't write the story. Best case, you get to tell your story to the world and maybe we do uncover a big New World Order. Isn't that what they call it?"

Spiderman looked at him from a sideways face. Then he shrugged.

"Yeah, OK," he said.

"Look, I'm gonna listen. Doesn't mean I'm gonna believe it, but I'll let you try and convince me. I'm just trying to be honest with you."

Spiderman nodded.

"So you know what the Bilderberg Consortium is?" Spiderman asked.

"Not really. I only know it as this group of rich and powerful people hellbent on taking over the world. At least that's the conspiracy I hear. I haven't paid it much attention."

"That's a pretty accurate description actually. They meet every year and they're known as the Bilderberg Group officially. To us in the inside the organization is known as the Bilderberg Consortium. It doesn't really matter what you call them, the fact remains their agenda, which is never made public, is always the same."

"And that is to create a new world order."

Spiderman nodded.

"Right, the New World Order."

"And what is the purpose of this?" asked Joseph.

"Well, to create order for one thing. That's in the name. They want to do this by eliminating all state actors and creating a planned economy. But how they're gonna do that is the horrible part."

"Before we get to that, who are these people?"

"The official list is always made public before their meetings every year, but they're the puppets. The real leaders are a group of 13. All men representing every continent. And you've never heard of them and they're the richest men in the world."

"Like Warren Buffett and Bill Gates you mean?"

Spiderman shook his head in annoyance.

"No, not the public faces of the world's richest people a la Forbes. That's just for show. Who do you think owns Forbes anyway. These 13 have a combined wealth of 7 trillion dollars. That's trillion with a T. These guys are off the charts. They're consolidating power and they're gonna have the world by the tail by mid-century with a backup plan for the end of the century latest."

"Dude, seriously. They'll all be dead by then. I mean they've gotta be old men already."

"Yeah, the youngest I've heard is in his mid-fifties. But you don't understand. This the long game. The Bilderberg Consortium was only started in 1954 a little after the end of the war. It was started by these guys' fathers. They don't care if they don't see the realization of their goals. Their kids will. They're like fanatics. It's the end goal which is so important to them."

"Honestly Spidey, a peaceful world wouldn't be too bad," said Joseph. Spiderman was telling a mesmerizing tale and

Joseph was enjoying it. He didn't buy it, but he was enjoying it.

"Yeah sure, but the way they're gonna go about it isn't gonna be nice and peaceful, and in order to maintain that so called peace," and spiderman put air quotes around it, "they're gonna rule with an iron fist."

"I dunno man, we've got bigger problems than some white dudes trying to create a new world order. I mean the terrorists, for example, will kibosh their plans if nothing else."

"Dude, that's exactly my point," said spiderman, getting more animated than Joseph had seen him. "Who do you think's controlling those terrorists. The Bilderberg Consortium."

"That's why people don't take this shit seriously, man. I mean c'mon. There's no proof. Soon you'll be telling me that the Pope's not Catholic he's a Bilderberger."

Spiderman smiled and shook his head.

"No, the Pope's not a Bilderberger but he tows the line. That attempted assassination on Pope John Paul II was a shot across the bow to all the world religions to get in line."

"Right, and you're gonna tell me that Marilyn Monroe and JFK were all Bilderberger murders," said Joseph grinning from the other side of his beer bottle as he took a sip.

Spiderman nodded.

"Now you're getting it."

Joseph frowned.

"Dude, I was joking with you."

"I'm not. I'm serious. There are very few suspicious deaths or even outright murders since the 50s that haven't been orchestrated by the Bilderberg Consortium."

"OK. So tell me why they'd kill someone like Marilyn Monroe. Maybe I can understand a head of state like JFK, but an actress. Please."

"I know exactly why they killed Marilyn and JFK. The two are intertwined. I have the records."

"Then enlighten me."

"Because JFK wasn't towing the line. In actual fact, he was getting too trigger friendly with the nukes. You can't have a New World Order if there's no world to put order to. JFK was getting too comfy with the idea of nuking the Russians. He thought he could get away with it with very little blowback on us. He had bad advisors. As for Marilyn, she was interfering with JFK. You know they were close. They were having an affair and he was giving her too much secret info that she shouldn't have had access too."

"I see," said Joseph, not sure what he believed.

"And the thing with Kennedy which not a lot of people know is that he was too aggressive in Vietnam. You see, the biggest obstacle for the Bilderbergers has always been to keep Russia and America, and now China, in a sort of equal power and respectful struggle. JFK was taking that too far, pushing the Russians too hard in Vietnam. That's why he was killed."

"What about Johnson? He continued on with that war?" said Joseph.

"Yeah, but he played it how they wanted it to be played."

"What about James Dean?" asked Joseph, just putting out a random celebrity death to see if spiderman had anything to say about it.

"He was killed by the Bilderbergers," said spiderman.

"Why?" asked Joseph, rolling his eyes.

"He was a pretty smart guy," said spiderman, "and he

started to poke around where he shouldn't have been. Let me put it in simple terms seeing as you aren't really taking me seriously. All the entertainment franchises, like sports, and art, music, movies etc. All of that is part of the Bilderberger plan to keep us docile and compliant. What's the biggest thing we get upset about nowadays? It's when our team loses or a ref makes a bad call. It's like Noam Chomsky said in Manufacturing Consent, and I'm misquoting, but it was along the lines of 'either you repeat the same doctrines everybody else is saying, or else you say something true, and then you sound like you're from Mars'. He also said that 'propaganda is to democracy what the bludgeon is to a totalitarian state.'"

"There's a classic example of why most people don't believe you," said Joseph. "Noam Chomsky is saying a lot of things that if true..."

"They are true."

"OK, if true, surely he should have been murdered by now by the Bilderbergers. But here he is in his eighties or nineties, cruising around like a doddering old man. Why haven't they put him down?"

"They've looked into it, but he's not considered a threat. Yeah he talks about some really dangerous things, but you'll notice he never gives a name to those things. He never identifies the Bilderbergers. When asked about them he dismisses it as conspiracy theory. That's why he's never been murdered, he's not seen as a threat. In fact, he's helpful. He talks about propaganda and the elites' control over media and government but it's always the United States that's mentioned. The US is just a puppet of the 13 as are the other governments. I mean, we can talk about our current president. Nobody thought he'd get into power."

"You're talking about David Troll? The lunatic we have as president?"

Spiderman nodded.

"Yeah. Nobody thought he'd win it. In fact, he was considered an outside hope at best. And what happened? The billionaire is now in power. Just as the Bilderbergers had planned. I knew before Troll was running that he would win the presidency. He's an ideal candidate."

"How so?" asked Joseph. He was warming to spiderman now that they were onto the current president who Joseph despised. It had literally shaken him to his core when he learnt that the asshole had made it into power.

"He's easy to manipulate and control. He's got a fragile ego which we've clearly seen, but there is so much dirt on him he'll never be able to shake it off. That stuff with the Japanese geishas. That's nothing. The man is truly despicable and the Bilderbergers know without a shadow of a doubt he'll do whatever they require. He's their man."

"But do you have any evidence?"

"Yeah, I've got plenty, that's why I've come to you. I've seen the videos of him with the geishas and other prostitutes. I've heard some of the wiretaps. He's not wrong about that, it just wasn't the previous president that's been doing it. You see what they're doing don't you?"

Joseph shook his head and drank his beer. This guy had an answer for everything. It was intriguing and a lot of it sounded legit. But that's because we like to fill in the gaps when we don't have all the information. We've got great imaginations.

"They're playing us against each other and against our governments. This is just diversion. The manipulation is so obvious I'm surprised people can't see it."

31

"So you have actual records to prove what you've been saying?" asked Joseph.

Spiderman nodded, and then nervously looked around the bar. Nobody was paying much attention to the two of them.

"OK. Tell me a little bit about the work that you do then for the Bilderberg Consortium."

CHAPTER FIVE
Spinning a Yarn

"BASICALLY I'm like an IT specialist for them. Anything they want done I do. I manage their network and servers here in North America. This is new, because for the longest time, everything related to the Bilderbergers has been paper and very little of it for obvious reasons. But just in 2010 I was hired as they decided to transition to digital record keeping. They've been looking into it since the sixties."

"Why has it taken them so long?"

"Bad encryption and bad digital design technologies for the most part. Doing technology with the foremost priority being privacy is hard. Encryption is hard, but they've managed it now. For example, our very government requires that companies selling encryption services, software or hardware, overseas do it with weakened encryption so it's easier to spy on."

"I thought that ended in the nineties," said Joseph.

Spiderman shook his head.

"No way. Listen man, if an official from the government is

speaking or offering up written records to the public they're lying. You'd do well to use that as your base."

"I know they might keep certain things from us or manipulate the truth for security reasons, but lying all the time, c'mon."

Spiderman shrugged. He'd pulled off pretty much all of the label from his first beer. He took a sip of it and went to pulling the label off his second.

"I'm just telling you how it is. 99 times out of a 100, they're lying, plain and simple. They're putting backdoors into everything they can or else they're trying to spy on us whenever they can. But like I said, the NSA, the CIA, FBI, whatever, those aren't the organizations you need to be worried about. I'm with the organization you need to worry about."

"Because they can install software onto our phones without us knowing about it?"

"That's a small part of it. Listen. They have a quarter of a trillion dollars at their disposal. That's the budget for the Bilderberg Consortium's work. And the department I work at uses eighty percent of that."

"That's a pretty big budget. So you get to play with 200 billion dollars a year?" asked Joseph.

"Yeah, the department I work in. There's only a handful of departments. It's a huge budget. 200 billion dollars is almost as much as Apple's revenue for the whole year. And Apple's the biggest company in the world at the moment. And unlike Apple, all of the 6 Bilderberg Departments have about a quarter of the employees that Apple has. There're about 25 thousand of us."

"What are these departments?" asked Joseph.

"IT, Finance, People, Marketing, Production and

Purchasing."

"That doesn't sound threatening at all," said Joseph.

"Of course not. That's by design. IT, though, is the catchall department. That's where the R&D happens, the planning of the world order and the mechanisms that are put into place."

"I'm thinking though, 25 thousand people doesn't seem like a lot to get a new world order in place."

"It isn't. But we use hundreds of thousands of others. For example, during the Vietnam war, we bought people to instigate atrocities and turn the war as we wanted it to go. The Tét Offensive was our doing. Tens of thousands of people killed and wounded and we instigated it."

"Why?"

"Because the Bilderbergers felt that the area had been destabilized enough and wanted to turn towards the Middle East as an area to destabilize. You see, all these wars are oftentimes started by the Bilderbergers to destabilize a region. Of if they're not directly started then we manipulate them to get the result we want."

"And the results you want?"

"The results the Bilderbergers want is to get people scared enough and docile enough that they'll welcome their leaders of the New World Order eagerly. It's a long game like I said."

"I see, and you have proof of all of this?"

"Not everything they've been up to, but a lot of it. I've managed to get 2 Terabytes worth of evidence out, but I think they might be onto me so I've stopped now."

"And why are you doing this again? I mean if what you're saying is true then you must be making some good coin?" asked Joseph, finishing his beer. He was getting tired of the stories now. If what spiderman was saying was true, he didn't know how people would take to the information. I mean people were mostly struggling with just getting by in Troll's new 'America, Back to Basics' bullshit.

"I make 250K a year. My manager makes 1.2 mill. They pay well and I could be a manager in a few years. The reason I'm doing this is because they're killing people. That's what's gotta stop. I can't in good conscience keep working for the devil. For false Christs and false prophets will arise, and will show signs and wonders, in order to lead astray…"

Joseph had been waiting for a quote from scripture the whole evening. And that sounded like one.

"Who's that?"

"Mark 13 verse 22. I feel like I've been led astray by the devil masquerading as a disciple. They said we were working towards a more peaceful world. A world as promised when Christ comes again. What they really are is the Four Horsemen of the Apocalypse. And I believe they're leading us towards the Last Judgement and I want to die knowing I did Christ's work. That I tried to live a Christian life."

Spiderman looked up at Joseph briefly before looking back at his beer bottle where most of the label had already been taken off.

"Why haven't you just disclosed this to Wikileaks?" asked Joseph.

Spiderman shook his head sadly.

"Dude," he said, looking back up at Joseph, "what has Wikileaks been leaking lately. Nothing but stuff about America and American government agencies and military. Wikileaks is part of the Bilderberg agenda. I need a real journalist. And now that I think about it, I might have been misled to try the Chronicle and the Times, I'm sure they're easily swayed by the Bilderbergers. That might have been a mistake. We're gonna have to get new burners tonight. And you're gonna have to leave your iPhone at home when we meet."

"So now you're saying that two of our most venerable newspapers are owned by the Bilderberg Consortium?"

Spiderman shook his head quickly.

"No, but I'm pretty sure if the Bilderbergers don't want a story published by them it won't get published. Plus, they're probably tapped into the papers' network. Darn it, I should have verified that. It was a mistake of mine not to..."

Spiderman stopped picking at the label and got lost in thought for a moment.

"You OK?"

Spiderman nodded slowly.

"Yeah, I think so. I used a different burner and I used a different name so I'm probably difficult to trace and associate from the Chronicle to you. But I still think we should get new burners every few weeks or month."

"I don't mean to be a whiner, but that's gonna start adding up. I'm not making a quarter of a mill a year."

"I understand, I'll reimburse you. But you've gotta do it. It's important."

"Listen, spidey," said Joseph. "I want to believe you, I really do, and you spin a good yarn, but if we're gonna move forward I need a little bit of evidence."

"All I've got is my ID and business card," said spiderman.

"That's a start. Show me?"

CHAPTER SIX
RADIO SEES YOU

SPIDERMAN opened up his backpack again and pulled out a little card. It was a plain white business card. He passed if over to Joseph.

"It's not gonna help you," he said.

Joseph looked at the card. It was plain white on both sides and of average card stock. The back was just white. The front only had two lines on it. The first one was the company name, "Pipe Dreams Plumbing & HVAC". The second line had a telephone number. Joseph turned it back and forth to make sure. Then he looked at Spidey.

"You work for a plumbing company," he said.

"That's the cover."

"And no address, no name?"

"That's right. It's about giving out the least amount of information."

"So it's not legit?"

"It's legit," said spiderman. "If you call it a woman will answer it. She'll sound a little surly, quote you about fifty percent higher than what a real plumbing company will charge you and she'll tell you that we're fully booked for the next couple of weeks. But she knows plumbing."

"And if I'm willing to pay and wait?"

"Then you'll get your plumbing done. We have a couple of guys who know plumbing and will do it."

"So it can be legit?"

"It is legit," said spiderman. "We can do plumbing. We have to. That's our cover. At least here."

"It's still not real evidence," said Joseph. "Where is this place?"

"It's in Jersey, in a strip mall. We own the whole place. Most of the work is done in a basement. All the businesses in the mall are just fronts to make the whole thing look legit. There's a dentist and a walk-in clinic with doctors and a dollar store. It all looks like a real strip mall."

"But all those businesses are owned by you?"

"Well, when I say that, I mean owned by the Bilderberg Consortium. Everyone works for us. The doctors, the dentist, the dollar store people. They're all part of the Bilderberg Consortium."

"And I could just rock up and go see the dentist or the plumbers? Just come in off the street?"

Spiderman nodded.

"OK. This all sounds pretty weird."

"It's not really. We've got important work to do. Creating a New World Order is not going to take care of itself. We need a lot of space. Especially IT. This way nobody is the wiser."

"Still doesn't prove you work there."

"Maybe this will," said Joseph, putting the business card back in his pocket. He rolled up the sleeve of his hoodie on his right arm. It crinkled. Joseph found out why. Spiderman rolled his sleeve carefully over a bandage of what was heavy duty tinfoil. Joseph knitted his brow again.

"Let me show you," he said.

The foil was stuck to itself with some clear tape. Spiderman picked off the tape and unwrapped his forearm. It was covered with about three or four layers of aluminum foil. Spiderman unwrapped the foil and put it aside. "Look here," he said, showing his forearm, wrist side up, to Joseph. Joseph could see what looked like a small bump just under the skin.

"Have a feel," said spiderman.

Joseph rubbed it. It felt hard as metal or stone.

"No, give it a squeeze."

Joseph squeezed it gently. Whatever it was, was hard and moved easily under the skin. It was about the size of a small capsule you might take containing antibiotics or probiotics or something like that.

"What is it?" asked Joseph.

"It's my ID. For obvious reasons we don't carry around ID badges like in most businesses. To get into my work area, the basement underneath Pipe Dreams, I have to wave his across a reader. I also have to offer my handprint and a retinal scan."

"That's pretty robust," said Joseph, playing with his now empty beer bottle.

"On a monthly basis we have to get DNA scanned."

"What does that mean?"

"They take some blood, or some cells, or a mouth swab."

"For what reason?"

"Do a profile of us. They can tell a lot by your DNA. Your current health, stress levels and more. They don't tell us. But I think it's to monitor us."

"Shit man, I wouldn't work for a company like that."

"Like I said, I thought I was working for the greater good originally. You have no idea how well they tailor their propaganda specifically to you. Anyway, this is just the beginning. We're working on nanobots that can be injected into us to do the same thing."

"Do what?"

"Identify us, take DNA readings in real time and transmit them to a central computer. Monitor our location via GPS."

"Jesus," said Joseph, "that's pretty fucked up if it's true."

Spiderman looked at him as if he'd just vomited into the back of his own throat.

"Sorry, the Jesus thing. But you've gotta admit that's pretty weird, man."

"It is. It's another reason I want this info out there. If they can perfect this, and it looks they'll be able to, then every single one of us is soon to be infected. You'll take your baby to the doctor for vaccinations and bam you're infected with nanobots. And they'll live with you as long as you do. They can take proteins, sugars, whatever they need, directly from your blood."

"So where's the hold up?"

"Transmission. How do you get this information from the bots out to a central processor or computer? You need to transmit some how. At first they were going to implant a biological motherboard into the skull. Obviously that's a bit barbaric and nobody's going to go for it. They were small, mind you, like the size of a few stamps stuck on top of one another. They might get us, their employees to sign up for it, but the general public's not gonna go for it. The big breakthrough came earlier this year when they perfected a way to interlock these nanobots and send them all to the brain like a big net using the blood vessels. The transmission was terrific, but it only worked over several meters. If they can get that into several hundred meters they're golden. Then it's gonna be implemented."

"That's a good story, Spidey, honestly it is," said Joseph. "But man, I just don't know. There's still no evidence."

"I thought you might be skeptical," said spiderman, so I brought you this to check out. He fished something out of his bag. It was a little longer than his palm and about half as wide. It too was wrapped in foil. He unwrapped it. It looked almost exactly like the new Nokia 3310. Spiderman handed it to Joseph.

"Don't push any of the buttons."

Joseph looked at it. It was the new Nokia 3310.

"Cool, I saw this at my office. We were reviewing it. Is this the 3G model that works here?"

Spiderman shook his head.

"This is not what it appears to be. I can give you a quick demo and then we're gonna have to bail outta here."

"Why?"

"Because this is a powerful piece of technology."

"And you just walked out of the Bilderberg Consortium with this in your pocket?"

"Yeah man, this is what I do. I'm in IT, I take stuff out to field test all the time. But they can track it easily and turn it off from anywhere. Also, we can melt the internals to nothing so nobody can tell what sort of technology it had. So I'm gonna show you a few things and then we're gonna have to go, because they'll know where I am."

"OK," said Joseph, "but first can I call my Mom?"

He was being facetious. Spiderman didn't catch it at first.

"I'm joking," said Joseph.

Spidey nodded.

"I see. Well, yeah, you actually could make a call from here. It works on 2G up through 5G."

"That's cool. So if it's not the Nokia 3310 then what do you guys call it?"

"T-800," said Spidey smiling.

Joseph grinned at him.

"You're not shitting me are you?"

"Nope."

"The Terminator?"

"Yup," said spiderman.

"I love it."

"Well, like I said, it's not what it appears to be, just like the Terminator."

"OK. So obviously it can make phone calls, texts I bet, and probably surf the net. Amiright?"

Spiderman nodded.

"Yeah, but so much more. Let me turn it on first."

Spiderman turned on the power button. As they waited, spiderman spoke.

"I was only joking about not pushing the buttons. They wouldn't work for you. All the buttons use fingerprint identification. Obviously, I'm the only one who can operate this phone."

The phone was on. It only took a fraction of a second to boot up.

"Let me try," said Joseph.

"Go ahead."

Joseph pushed some buttons on the phone, but nothing happened.

"I guess that's safe," he said.

Spiderman nodded.

"That's always one of the things that drove me nuts about Star Trek. Their phasers could always be taken away from them and used against the Federation. Why no biometric lock on such lethal weapons in the 24th century. I mean, c'mon."

Joseph nodded.

"Probably harder to make interesting stories that way," he offered.

"Anyway, only I can use this T-800 or whoever else is programmed to use it. That can be in the hundreds. Probably more, we haven't tested the outer limits. But for now, I'm the only one that can use it."

"So what can it do?"

"It can kill you from five meters away. Render you unconscious from fifteen meters away and spy on any connected device within fifteen meters. Or up to fifty meters if we can concentrate on that wavelength."

Joseph nodded his head.

"What does that mean exactly?"

"If we can focus the capture of radio waves into a narrow stream on this device then we can listen out further. All around us are radio waves and other waves of the electromagnetic spectrum. They start real small, like at one picometer for gamma rays. A picometer is like one trillionth of a meter. Real small."

And Spidey held his thumb and index finger about a millimeter apart.

"You could probably fit a billion of them in this space here," he said, looking at the space between his thumb and finger. "That's a billion with a b."

Joseph nodded.

"Lots," he said.

"And then we get all the way to the other end of the spectrum where the extremely long radio waves. You get ELFs or Extremely Low Frequency radio waves which have lengths in the megameter. Basically that's a thousand kilometers."

"That's cool and all, and I appreciate the tutorial, but what does it mean exactly?"

"OK, here's the TLDR. We use radio waves to communicate because the other side of the spectrum, the ionizing radiation is harmful. T-800 can pick up pretty much all radio waves except for the ELFs to ULFs, the Ultra Low Frequency radio waves…"

Spiderman noticed Joseph's eyes glazing over.

"OK, you don't care about that."

"No, I just want to see what it means in practical terms."

"It means we can listen to just about anything within about a fifty meter radius. Let me show you. We can't see it, but it's like we're in a dense wet fog of radio waves. They're all around us."

Spiderman pointed the T-800 towards the far corner of the bar where a group of Seventh Sons were sitting drinking beer and talking. You couldn't hear them from where Joseph was, you could just see their mouths moving.

"The Russians are causing us a problem in Brighton Beach and I want us to get it back. There's money there. We're gonna have to hit them hard."

"What's the plan?"

"Sunday morning we're gonna hit them hard at home. Kill them all."

Spiderman turned it off.

"Shit, who was that?" asked Joseph.

"Those bikers in the far corner of the bar. Don't look."

"There are plans to put all of these up on city light poles. Can you imagine?"

Joseph was intrigued.

"Show me more," he said.

CHAPTER SEVEN
BANG YOU'RE DEAD

"I'M gonna point this at the bartender. It doesn't even have to see him. It can recognize him by voice too."

Spidey didn't even have to turn the T-800. He just pushed a few buttons and they listened.

"The old lady's fine. Getting on me about the mistress. You know how it is?"

"I sure do. My woman doesn't complain anymore since I put her in her place."

"Yeah, but you gotta be careful about that. These chicks are quick to call the pigs if you look at them…"

Spiderman pushed some more buttons and the audio turned off.

"That's pretty amazing just by itself."

"Yeah, now we can pull up everything about him. Check this out."

Spiderman turned the T-800 parallel to the edge of the table they were sitting at. He pushed some more buttons and from the side of the phone streamed what Joseph could only imagine was a laser light. It was in color and it worked as a projector. It projected a rectangle onto the table between them. The rectangle was about 6 inches by 8 inches. It had an image of the bartender. It was a mugshot. Around his image were details about him, like his date of birth, address, social security number, arrests, time spent in jail, his family. He had 2 kids and his parents were still alive. He had 3 brothers but only 2 were still alive.

"And if you tap on anything it'll give you more information about that," said Spidey, as he tapped on the bartenders' parents names.

That pulled up info about his parents. Joseph saw similar info to what the projection had shown for the bartender. Except his parents weren't criminals. Well, there was a shoplifting beef for the old man from when he was a teenager.

"Wow, that is pretty cool. So this gives you access to the police database then?" asked Joseph.

Spiderman tilted his head to one side.

"In a way I suppose, but not directly. All this info is encrypted and coming from our servers. But we've got our tentacles into everything, including police databases."

"Can you do me?" asked Joseph.

"Sure could, but I don't think that's a good idea. There'll be a trace and all that information will be captured. It could put you in danger."

Joseph nodded.

"What else can it do?"

"Well, like I said, it's a lethal weapon. It can also look through walls using infrared. It can disable other electrical devices in its vicinity through an EMP pulse."

"Let's do that before we leave," said Joseph.

"Alright," said Spidey, and he pushed some buttons and that was it. "Done."

"What?"

"I've done it. Our phones will be OK because they're not powered on. But everyone else's is fried. Let's get going before they start to wonder what the hell's been happening, or the beer starts to get warm."

Spiderman put all his foil back into his backpack along with T-800.

"I was hoping I could keep that," said Joseph grinning.

"Wouldn't work for you anyway," said Spidey.

"Right, I forgot that part."

Spidey unwrapped their phones and put them back together. He gave Joseph his two and put his and the foil and bags into his backpack. He got up. Joseph followed him out. Music was playing in the bar as they left, but underneath it was silence. The buzz of electricity seemed to have stopped.

"Well, I'm interested," said Joseph, outside in the light snow that had started since they'd been in the bar.

"Thank you. We need to get this info out to the public. I'll text you when I get a new burner and then you go get a new one and text me back from the new one."

"OK. When?"

"Tomorrow. The longer we wait, the more I might be in trouble."

Joseph nodded, and Spiderman walked away down the sidewalk. Joseph got back into the car and started it up. It was a chilly night. He powered on both of his phones. When his iPhone was on he texted Flatter.

Me: There's actually something to this spiderman character. You won't believe it. I'll fill you in tomorrow.

Just as he'd sent it he looked up as he heard a garbage

truck screaming through the intersection. Even from here he could hear the impact it made with spiderman. He watched in horror for a moment until he came to his senses. He got out of his car and ran up the street to the intersection.

Spiderman was on the other side of the intersection. Joseph ran up to him.

"Someone call 911. Help! Call 911," he said again and again.

The Seventh Sons had heard the accident as the garbage truck had hit the light pole on the other side. They started to exit the bar.

Joseph was leaning down by spiderman. He was clearly dead. There was blood on his face and his arm and leg looked broken pretty bad by the way they lay. The driver of the garbage truck got out. Joseph looked up at him.

"Call for an ambulance. Didn't you see him?"

The driver walked calmly towards Joseph. He was dressed in a black suit which Joseph didn't acknowledge at first in his shock. Though deep in the recesses of his mind it seemed odd. Joseph didn't see the handgun with the silencer raised and pointed at the top of his head as he looked down at spiderman.

"Hey," shouted the bartender as he started to run up the sidewalk towards the man. The bartender carried a sawed-off shotgun with him, which was not an effective weapon at this distance.

Just as Joseph turned to look at the bartender starting to run up towards him, the man shot him in the head with the handgun. He then pointed towards the oncoming bikers and peeled off a couple of shots to buy himself some time. The bikers and the bartender ducked behind a car.

The man leaned down and grabbed the backpack off of

Spiderman. He looked up quickly to see the bikers running towards him. They were still about forty or fifty feet away. He ran down the street in the direction he had been driving the garbage truck. He heard a couple of shots fired his way but he wasn't worried. He was well trained. There was no way in hell even a trained marksman could hit the broadside of a barn from that distance while running with veins full of adrenaline. And he was right. The shots went very wide of him.

A black sedan was parked not far down the street. As the bikers made it up to that corner he jumped into the passenger side and the car drove off. A couple of the bikers took aim and fired a couple of shots. Then they turned back towards the carnage.

"Jesus," said the bartender when they got to Joseph's and Spiderman's bodies. "What the fuck was that about?"

CHAPTER EIGHT
WHISKEY ON RYE

I was up on Wilshire Boulevard in a little place I like to call my home away from home. It was called Sonny McLean's. Sonny McLean owned the placed. He was an old Irish lad who'd come to the land of the free, sometimes the land of the brave in his twenties. He was in his seventies now and still tended bar. It used to be a popular place with the five-o. Now not so much. Seems Chief Burton had thought Sonny was too generous. Gave away too much free food to the boys in blue. So that ended the party. I still come here because he makes the best steak. But I wasn't eating steak. I was drinking whiskey with my rye.

I was having Sonny McLean's Classic Ruari on Rye. Yeah, it was basically a Reuben Sandwich. Some corned beef with sauerkraut and Swiss and all the fixings. But who says you couldn't name it something different. Besides, Ruari meant Red King. And it was a sandwich fit for kings. And the meat was red, yeah?

It was the middle of the day and I was in fine fettle as they like to say. I'd sold a painting at Triangle. Declan had sold it for $10k. That put five crisp Clevelands in my jeans. Not really. I don't wear jeans and I'm not paid in thousand dollar bills. Still, the feeling was the same. My old buddy ol' pal, Captain John Roberts had wanted to meet for lunch. He sat across from me and we'd just been served lunch.

"You on a diet?" I asked him.

He'd ordered a chicken salad. A woman's meal. He wasn't even drinking a beer. A woman's drink. He was having a soda water. He grinned at me.

"Something like that. Gotta keep my figure for the guys at TID," he said, and there was no malice in his voice.

I'd finished my first whiskey and ordered another one from Aileen. Aileen was a looker. Her hair the color of fire and you could get burnt by her anger. She had green eyes the color of Irish emeralds. Her bosom was large and natural on a slim waist. She was one helluva gal. We'd spent time together in that corner of the night when the moon is bright, naked as peeled bananas. She was something special, but her fiery temperament took chunks from you that never healed. I watched Aileen walk away. Her bum sashayed and I knew it was teasing me. But she'd chewed on more of my soul than anyone since Racquel. Some wounds never heal. I turned to John.

"Yeah, that's a bum deal," I said, sniffing at the dregs in my whiskey tumbler. "Besides, what the hell do you know about technical investigations. Aren't you still using a dumb phone?"

John pulled out a slim black rectangular phone from out of his pocket and put it on the table next to his salad.

"Got a fancy new Android phone now," he said. "It's by Google so they tell me. Like a computer in your pocket. Shit, what do I know. I use it for texts and phone calls. Sometimes I set an alarm. You're a fine one to talk. You've got that fancy iPhone I hear."

He wasn't lying. Aibhilin had been giving me hell for over a year about my dumb phone. Told me it wasn't safe enough anymore. Artero had bought her and Racquel those fancy phones and Aibhilin wanted me to have one too. Said she was worried about me and with an iPhone she could check in on me. I spoke to Emily about it and she thought it was a good idea too. Hell, she had one.

"I was bullied into it," I said.

"Right, by your daughter and your squeeze. And you're always complaining to me. Oh, Johnny Rotten, I need some work. You gotta help a buddy out." And then he broke into song. "I'm just a poor boy whose intentions are good, oh Johnny, please don't let me be misunderstood."

We both had a laugh.

"I don't know if you were trying to sing The Animals version or the Nina Simone one. But you were shit either way," I said.

Aileen came back with my other whiskey. She made sure Sonny, who was on bar today, had been generous. She gave me a wink out of those green eyes I'd gotten lost in before. Sometimes I think she wanted another go. But hell, even if you like hamburger doesn't mean you put your own fist into the meat grinder.

"I think she still likes you," said John, when Aileen had left.

"I ain't gonna break into song John, but you know," and here's where I did break into song, "she's a man eater, watch out boy she'll chew you up." And that's about as much singing as I'm liable to do. I was in one of those moods.

"Ain't that the truth. She chewed you up real good."

We took to eating for a while.

"How you feeling about your punishment?" I asked John.

He hadn't been demoted, but he'd been put on leave with pay for a few months while IA had investigated that young girl who'd stuck herself in the neck with a pencil John had left in an interrogation room. He'd been found not responsible. Still the asshole that was Deputy Chief of West Bureau, Luano Saldana didn't want Roberts in his group anymore, so he was moved. I blame the whiny, crybaby actors and actresses who bent Saldana's ear. What a pain in the neck. Too soon?

"It's a nice change," he said, looking down at his plate.

"The hell it is," I said. "You're talking to your buddy remember. IA's finished with you."

He stopped eating and looked up at me.

"It's a fucking kick in the nuts if you want the truth, Anthony. I've been in homicide 10 years and this is how they treat you. One mistake, one little fucking mistake…"

"Well, I don't know about little, she did die right there in our custody," I said. John was worked up. He was a pretty relaxed guy most of the time. Hard to get him worked up. But he was worked up now.

"You know what I mean. I leave a pencil because she wants to draw. I'm a soft touch and she stabs herself with it. For Christ's sake. Who does that?"

I nodded and tore a hole in my Ruari. I was thinking a beer might have been nice as a sandwich chaser. But I had water and that would do. Whiskey was for savoring.

"You didn't get to choose right?"

"No I didn't get to choose. Jesus, Anthony, you think I would have chosen TID. Fuck, I'd sooner have gone with

CCD. But they new it. That cocksucker Saldana new exactly where I didn't want to go."

"So commercial crime's better than technical investigations."

"Sure it is. At least with CCD you can get some major frauds. At TID I'm conducting polygraphs and doing fingerprints and taking mugshots. C'mon Anthony, what would you rather do?"

"I'd probably have preferred Vice or Gang and Narcs," I said through a mouthful of Ruari.

"There you go. So would I. So you ask how I liked it. It sucks. I'd sooner retire."

"You're what, 42 now?"

"43."

"There you go. Seven more years and you can bail pal," I said.

"Seven years feels like a life sentence. I don't know if I can last seven years in TID."

"You're a good cop Rotten, I'd fight for getting back into homicide. I know a lot of the Hollywood A-listers like you. You should set up a petition or something."

"Yeah, but you know how Saldana likes to kiss ass to some of them. That's why he kicked me out."

"Yeah, but that was months ago now. I think people have probably settled down. I'd fight to get back in."

Roberts ate some of his chicken salad. I took a drink of my whiskey. My sandwich was almost gone. It had leaked some of its fine sauce on the plate. I picked up the last bite and mopped it up and finished it off. Sonny likes to serve his Ruaris with pickle and some chopped roasted potatoes. That keeps the Irish theme alive. I took a bite of the pickle. It was too tangy. It was gonna ruin my whiskey. So I took some potato to settle the palate.

CHAPTER NINE
POKE IN THE EYE

"MAYBE you're right," said John. "I'll speak to my Union Rep about getting back in."

"I would. IA cleared you. Hell, what they've done is downright illegal. Probably, maybe. Anyway worth a fight to have your spot back. Shit, how the hell am I gonna get any more work? Saldana hates me almost as much as Burton. And who have they got in there now?"

"Albert Anderson," said John, grinning.

"You shitting me? Fat Albert is now running homicide?"

John laughed and nodded.

"That fat twat couldn't investigate the case of the missing keys stuck up his ass crack."

John laughed heartily.

"Shit, Sid," he said, "thanks for that. I miss you, man. You always knew how to make me laugh."

"Am I not right?" I asked seriously.

Roberts nodded.

"Damn straight you're right."

"Ain't no way he's gonna give me any work. He's a yes man through and through."

I was right and John knew it.

"Please Johnny, for the love of all that's holy, you've gotta get back in. I don't want to be doing missing persons and cheating husbands just to pay the bills. I need some meat in my diet. I need something to chew on."

"You shoulda stayed in homicide then," he said, grinning at me like a rat.

"Yeah right," I said, giving him the hairy eyeball. "You know Burton had it out for me. Set me up. I'm still gonna uncover what shady shit he's up to."

"You're probably not wrong, but you gotta play the politics."

"No I don't. That's why I'm not in TID for being innocent," I said.

"Touché," he said.

Aileen came by and got our plates. She stopped for a minute to talk.

"I get off at five, Ace," she said, "if you want to take me someplace."

Where I wanted to take her was a long walk off the pier into a sea of sharks. She used to call me Ace. Got it from my initials. AC. It used to mean something. Now it grated.

"What did you have in mind?" I asked.

"Drinks. Then maybe I can show you my new digs?"

She bit her bottom lip. I knew exactly what she wanted. And what she wanted was to take another rip outta my soul. Her kinda loving took a terrible toll.

"Can't," I said. "I'm seeing someone."

"Well if you change your mind, I won't tell if you won't. We used to have fun Ace. I'd like to have more of that."

I stuck a grin on my face that felt like a grimace before a bear attack. She walked off and I looked at John.

"Why do I keep coming back here. That woman would have been the death of me Johnny."

"Because you like Sonny and his food."

That was the truth. Still, having to put up with Aileen was a kick in the groin. And she had no shame. Still, she wasn't always here serving. I lucked out more times than not.

"Something's on your mind," I said, looking at John. He'd wanted to see me and he hadn't yet told me what about. I sipped on my whiskey. I was feeling warm on this chilly December day. Which got me to thinking about The Mamas & the Papas on such a winter's day.

"I'm about to ask you for a huge favor," he said, looking at me seriously.

John wasn't the kind of fella that asked for favors often. And when he did it came from the heart. And I wasn't the kinda guy who could let a pal down.

"Shit," I said. "I guess you're buying lunch then."

Aileen came by with the check just in time. She put it down in the middle of the table.

"Let me get that," said John, reaching into his pocket for cash. He glanced at the bill.

"You know where I am," said Aileen. "My number's on the back of the receipt," she said, fluttering her eyes at me.

I felt like a schmuck. Who falls for that kinda crap nowadays? Well, this Okie from Muskogee did. I just smiled at her.

"I used to make you feel good, Ace. You remember that?"

"Sure do. More than that, I remember the price I paid."

John put two Jackson's and a Lincoln down on the receipt.

"Don't need any change, Aileen," he said.

63

"Thanks hun," she said. She took the money and then gave me a wink before she left.

"I know why I keep coming back here," I said to John.

"Yeah, and why's that."

"To remember. Lest I forget," I said. "The good thing is, I ain't even sore about it no more."

John raised his glass.

"I'll drink to that," he said. "You always had a soft spot for the damsel in distress. But sometimes, Sid, that damsel is the stress."

"You're not wrong," I said to him, and then grinning, "time for you to take your pound of flesh too."

We were seated in the booth in a back corner. That's how we usually liked it. You had a view of things when your back was in a corner. You had options, you had possibilities. What you didn't have was a chance of getting stabbed in the back. I liked that.

"Now listen, Sid," said John, leaning in from across the table, his soda water half full, because that's the kinda mood I was in. "No pressure. If you don't want to do it, that's no problem. I'm not gonna hold a grudge."

And it was true. He wasn't the kinda guy to hold a grudge. I grinned at him.

"C'mon, Rotten," I said. "I didn't come here to Waltz with you. Spit it out."

"I got this job for you, and as your friend I'm hoping you'll take it."

"Go on, I'm listening."

"You remember the Severns?" he asked.

"I think so. You've spoken about them now and then. Old family friends right? You went to school with the youngest daughter. If I remember correctly, they had two kids. Two daughters right? With a big difference in age."

"Yeah, Rebecca was my friend, her older sister was Rachel. They were fifteen years apart."

"Now you were born around these parts, right?"

"Yeah, I'm from Palmdale. Poor as dirt," said John.

I knew this. We both had a similar background. Whereas my father beat the crap out of me when he was on the sauce, John never knew his father.

"Poor as dirt, hell that's a luxury. We never had dirt. I played on a backyard of broken beer bottles."

John laughed.

"Now if I remember," I said. "They're not in Cali anymore are they?"

"No. Father moved them out to Jersey in the last year of high school. They're still there."

"Rebecca wasn't really just your friend. That's not the way I remember you telling it."

John grinned and nodded.

"Yeah, we were high school sweethearts. I coulda married her if things had been different. I ain't complaining about Jenn, she's a great woman. I've been blessed to have had two loves in my life. Her and Rebecca. But you're right. I was sweet on her. Still have a soft spot for her."

"As we all do for our first loves."

"Which is why I'm asking for a favor, Sid."

"Lay it on me, Johnny Rotten."

"Rachel's only son, Joseph, has been murdered, and the cops aren't getting anywhere."

"He's gotta be a young man right. Rachel's fifteen years older than Rebecca which puts her in her late fifties?"

Roberts nodded.

"Something like that. Anyway, Joseph's twenty-seven."

I shook my head and nodded slowly. Nothing worse than losing a child.

"I'm sorry to hear that John."

"Thanks. Rebecca's not taking it well. Rachel's in even worse shape. What's making it more difficult is that they're not getting any closure."

"I get that. What happened?"

"Joseph's a journalist with one of these Web blogs. It's called TrashCan. It's not really a tabloid, they try and do some good work. They try and uncover shady shit going on in politics or the business world."

"OK."

"From what I hear, he was helping this other guy who had been run over by a garbage truck, when he was shot, point blank in the head."

"Jesus. He must have been targeted then."

John nodded slowly.

"Thing is, nobody can figure out why. What I've heard is that this guy who was run over was just moments earlier drinking with Joseph in a bar down the street from where this happened. The bar's called 'The Rattlin' Chain'. From what I can tell, not the kinda place that Joseph would frequent."

"And this guy he was with?"

"Stanley Spencer. Early thirties, from all accounts a bit of a crackpot and from what I can tell, he's being treated for schizophrenia. He usually likes to go by his middle name, Shem. From the bible. It seems, from what I can tell, that Stanley was meeting Joseph. You know Joseph's middle name is also biblical right?"

I shook my head.

"Noah. That's his middle name, apparently Rachel gave it to him because of Noah Webster and not the biblical Noah.

Anyway, from I've heard, Stanley liked the fact they shared biblical middle names."

CHAPTER TEN
SHERIFF ON THE ARK

I finished my whiskey. This was gonna be a story. Maybe of biblical proportions. If I was gonna take it I needed to listen to John's take. He had good instincts. I smiled at him.

"So, Shem and Noah walk into a bar, and the bartender says where's the missus. Noah says she's at home making it rain."

John shook his head at me, but at least he was smiling.

"That's a pretty lame joke, Sid," he said.

"Sure is. Is Rachel pretty religious?"

John shook his head.

"No, I never knew the family to go to church. Like I said, they called him Noah because of Noah Webster, not Noah from the Ark. Now Stanley is religious. He was quoting biblical verses to Joseph before they met. On a burner that Joseph had with him. Or at least in the car he was using."

I nodded. John was still leaning on the table across from me.

"Let me boil it down. A journalist. This is Joseph, Rachel's kid, meets with a schizophrenic in a bar called 'The Rattlin' Chain' in Jersey. Shortly after they leave, the schizophrenic, Stanley, gets run down. Joseph goes to help him and he gets a bullet in the head."

John nodded.

"That's about right."

"So, arguably, Joseph's meeting this guy about a story. Maybe a big story because Joseph's carrying a burner he's been using to talk to this guy with, right?"

"Right."

"Or did he just prefer to use a burner generally because of his work as a journalist?"

John shook his head.

"No, Rachel tells me he has an iPhone. Like yours."

"OK, so maybe there's a neat story here, or maybe he just got played by a paranoid schizophrenic. What do we know about Stanley?"

"Not much. He was being treated for schizophrenia like I said. Otherwise a pretty good kid from all accounts. At least according to his parents. Gifted too with a genius IQ. He was good with computers they said."

"What did the cops find on him?"

"This is the interesting part. He had a backpack on him. The witnesses, who happen to be bikers from the Seventh Sons confirmed that. Otherwise they've been pretty uncooperative. But the backpack was not found."

"What happened to it?"

"Witnesses said it was taken by the shooter."

"And who was this shooter?"

"They aren't saying."

I crinkled my brow and thought about that for a moment.

"They won't say?"

John nodded.

"Now why wouldn't they say, Johnny?"

"Maybe because it was one of their own?"

I nodded.

"That's one option. Or maybe it was a rival gangbanger, or maybe, and this is gonna sound crazy, maybe it was one of us."

John drank from his half full glass of soda water. Now it was looking more like it was half empty. He twisted his neck and pinched the corner of his mouth.

"I don't know, Sid. You're thinking it coulda been a cop?"

"Well, we've gotta keep options open at this stage. Why won't a biker rat? I can only think of three reasons. It was one of their own. It was one of our own or it was the competition. If it was some hoodlum off the street they'd have ratted or chased him down and delivered justice themselves. If it was one of their own, why? Was Stanley into them for money or drugs? If so, why did he go into the lion's den? If it was competition, well then that's code of honor, right?"

John nodded.

"But if it was one of us, well then they aren't talking because they don't want the kind of grief it'll bring."

"Yeah, you make a point. I just can't buy it."

"No, of course not, because you're behind the blue line. You think Burton is the Chief Wizard who can do no wrong."

I was only half-joking. Burton wasn't a good cop. He was as crooked as my aunt's arthritic arm. I just didn't have anything on him. Roberts didn't say anything to that.

"OK, what do we have that's real evidence?"

"Only thing that was found on him..."

"Stanley or Joseph?"

"Stanley, was a business card and some cash."

"What was on the business card?"

"The name of a business," said Roberts, grinning. "Pipe Dreams Plumbing."

"He's not a plumber though, is he?"

"Don't think so."

"What does he do there?"

"I'm just guessing, but probably IT stuff. His folks said he was good with computers."

"And you have a number?"

"Not on me. But I can get it to you."

"And that's all that was found on him?" I asked.

John nodded.

"And we have cause of death, officially?"

"Yeah. Blunt force trauma and internal bleeding from being run over by a garbage truck. Massive contusions and broken bones. If I remember correctly the coroner counted over a dozen broken bones."

"What else did the report say. Did this seem like an accident?"

"Nope. They didn't even try to make it look like an accident. No skid marks. Stanley was hit at about fifty miles per hour."

I nodded solemnly.

"This is a hit for sure. Especially when the guy gets out of the truck and then shoots Joseph in the back of the head."

"Looks that way, Sid," said Roberts.

"Do we have anything else?"

"Flatter, Joseph's boss, the Editor of the TrashCan, said this crackpot had been calling incessantly for about a week before he handed him off to Joseph. Flatter said the guy just sounded like a kook. Thought Joseph would go and listen to him and then put it to rest. But here's the interesting part. Flatter says he got a text from Joseph just before Joseph was shot."

"And the text says?"

"The text says to the effect that this crackpot is actually onto something. There's something to the guy's story."

"That was from the burner or the iPhone?"

Roberts shrugged.

"Not sure."

"This is an intriguing case, John. When did it happen?"

"Thursday, November 23rd. Three weeks yesterday."

"Maybe they should give the cops more time," I said.

"I get where you're coming from. But I get the impression that Jersey City PD isn't putting a lot of effort into this. And what I'm getting from them is that they have no leads."

"This adds a little more credence to when I was saying it might be a cop, right?"

John looked tired. He tilted his head to the side and shrugged like a man still in chains.

"I dunno, Anthony, I don't want to go down that road of thought. They've followed the leads like they should. They spoke to the witnesses. They've spoken to his employer…"

"But you don't know what he does there," I said. "So what did they say about that?"

"I'd have to look at the notes again, but he did work at Pipe Dreams Plumbing. Nothing seemed unusual. They're thinking it's just an unfortunate wrong place at the wrong time kinda thing."

"Jesus, Rotten, you've gotta be shitting me. A guy gets run down by a garbage truck and his friend is then shot in the head. And you're telling me it's just bad luck?"

"I'm telling you what the official story is. If it is one of us, and I'm saying that's a big IF, then we're not gonna get anywhere internally with it. That's another reason I'm asking for your help. You gotta remember, Sid, you and I go way back, but I'm still behind the blue wall. I gotta play nice still. I admire you for your courage in leaving. You're the one that can get to the bottom of this."

"That's a nice sentiment, John, but I don't have an in. I can poke around, but if it's an inside job, they're gonna close up ranks and I'll get nowhere."

"You have your ways. This is the time to use those means, Sid. For a friend."

"Now you're asking a huge favor, John."

Roberts looked at me for a while and nodded.

"I know," he said.

"You're asking me to go rogue. Then I'm asking you to come clean. Why?"

"Because of young love, Anthony. Because of what Rebecca means to me. What this has done to her and her family. But because it smells real bad. There's a big part of me that's with you on this. I think this could be more than meets the eye. Could be one of us gone bad. And I want justice for Rachel and for Joseph and maybe even Stanley. Because isn't that why we signed up, Anthony? To pursue justice?"

"There're no guarantees, John. You know that. If this is some sort of conspiracy involving police corruption, then I might not get anywhere, even knocking a few heads around."

John nodded.

"I'm not expecting miracles, Anthony. If it leads you to a dead end, then so be it. But there's nobody else I can trust with this. And, God forbid, it ends up being one of us, then I want justice brought to bear. Because we should be better than that. We should be upholding the law and not skirting around it."

I looked him in the eye for a long while.

"The kind of justice you're looking for, Rotten, won't be found in a courtroom."

He nodded steadily and slowly at me.

"I know," he said. "I know."

CHAPTER ELEVEN
An Itch Begins

"Sounds like you want me to take on a case that might remain unsolved," I said.

John just stared at me.

"If it's an inside job, and I can't figure out the why for that, then they'll never rat. You know how cops are. It's why corruption gets swept under the rug."

John nodded.

"I know all that. But I can't go poking around. I can't head up to Jersey to investigate it."

"I'm not licensed in Jersey anyway."

Roberts shrugged.

"You weren't licensed in New York and you managed just fine," he said.

"The pay was good."

Roberts didn't say anything for a while. He held onto his glass with his fingertips, turning it around. Maybe trying to find a different angle to convince me. I didn't need it. I'd help a friend. I just wanted to be sure we were both on the same page.

"Rachel's gotta know that I might not get anywhere with this."

"You always say that," said John, grinning.

"No, I don't."

He got somber for a minute.

"I've told her. Hell, I've told her there's a snowball's chance in hell you'll take it and that if you do, there's a slimmer chance you'll get to the bottom of it."

"You think that highly of me, Johnny?" I grinned at him.

He smiled back.

"Nah, but the Jersey police can't seem to get to the bottom of it. Maybe because they're involved. If that's the case, how are you gonna get to it."

"And this is gonna be pro bono, right?"

Roberts looked at me.

"They're hard working folks just trying to find the money to bury their son. I'll pay you, Anthony."

Roberts fished out his wallet. It was fatter than I'd seen it before. He pulled out ten Benjamins. I knew that because he counted them out. He offered the bunched up notes to me.

"It's all I could get out at one time. You know I'm good for the rest."

"The hell you are, Rotten," I said, grinning at him. "I ain't taking your money."

"C'mon, Sid, it'll make me feel better."

"I said I ain't taking your money."

"Alright," he said, putting the notes back, "if that's how you're gonna be."

"That's how I'm gonna be. How long do we go back, JR?"

"Shit, probably twenty years. A little more."

"And in those twenty years have I ever taken your

money?"

Roberts grinned at me.

"Yeah, I remember one time you needed a couple dollars for a donut and a coffee. Before we were in homicide."

I laughed quietly.

"Alright," I said. "I'll take a couple of dollars."

"Offer's off the table."

I looked at my empty whiskey tumbler wistfully.

"Seriously, Sid,' said Roberts. "Will you take the job?"

I nodded at my whiskey glass.

"I'll take it John. I dunno if I like where it's taking me, but I'll take it. For you, old friend."

"I owe you one, Anthony," he said. "You're a good man. If you need some money, the offer stands."

I nodded at him.

"I'll leave tonight. I'm going to Jersey right?"

"I thought you might like to go home to reminisce for a day first."

I frowned at him.

"You want me going to Oklahoma?"

"That's where Stanley's folks are. In Stillwater actually."

I shrugged. I hadn't been back to Stillwater in a while. Hell, I hadn't been back to Oklahoma since my pops had died. That was in '95.

"What do they do out there?" I asked.

"The old lady works for Walmart. The old man works for a printer out there. Forgot the name."

"OK, and then on to Jersey, right?"

"Afraid not," said Roberts. "This is a bit of a tour."

"I thought you said Rachel's in Jersey?"

"Yeah, sorry. I didn't give you the full story. She moved to Jersey with the family too. Met a guy in Jersey who was from

79

Ohio. They got hitched and moved back to Ohio. That's where Joseph was born. Rachel and Paul are still in Ohio."

"So off to Ohio then."

"Yeah, Ashland, Ohio. I'll give you all the details."

"And then to Jersey?"

Roberts nodded.

"Anything else I should know?"

"I'd like you to come back to my house. I've got copies of the police file and coroner's record there. I'd like you to have them. I've also got the name of a contact I have out in Jersey. She's a good cop. I trust her."

"What's her name?"

"So-yi Park. She goes by Sue too. You'll like her. She's a firecracker."

"Sueto," I said, "or Sue, as in the Western name?"

"Smart ass," he said. "She's a detective in Vice. Black belt in Taekwondo."

"So you're saying she can be kick my ass?"

"I'm saying she could probably help you out in a pinch."

"And how do you know Sueto," I said, grinning at him.

"So-yi I've met a couple of times on conferences over the years. I think she's stalking me."

Now he was being the joker.

"I reached out to her and she's onboard with helping you out. Obviously, she doesn't think Jersey PD is involved, but you'd expect that. Still, I reckon she'll follow it wherever it leads."

I nodded and pushed my whiskey glass aside. I thought about Stillwater. I could remember some Christmases there. My mother always tried to make Christmas nice. One of the few kind memories I have of the old man is picking out Christmas trees to bring home.

You could chop down your own Christmas tree at many of these farms they had. But they want your money. Nothing was better for my old man than free. Especially free beer which he hardly ever got. But you could chop down free pine trees. Not legally. But legal was just a line my pa crossed when he felt like it. We had fun though, heading up to Lake McMurty in the middle of the week at night. Usually the week before Christmas. Most times my pops was sober that week. Saving up for Christmas when he'd get blitzed out of his mind.

We'd go up at night and skirt around the Forest Rangers and try and find a tree that wasn't too much Charlie Brown. Most times we'd get something worth having. I liked Christmas cookies too. My mother would make them as a treat. That and the Christmas tree are the only things I liked about Christmas. Nothing else worth liking about it when your pops is a violent alcoholic. I try and make Christmas fun for Aibhilin. But I still don't like it.

"You with me pal?" asked Roberts.

I looked up at him.

"Yeah, I'm here."

"You ready to go?"

I nodded and we got up and walked out of the bar. I didn't say anything to Aileen.

CHAPTER TWELVE
STILL WATERS RUN DEEP

YOU can't go direct to Stillwater from LA. Best you can do is go LAX to DFW to SWO and that's exactly what I was doing. I like red eye flights because they're quiet. Quiet and dark. You can hear yourself think, and thinking is what I was doing a lot of. I was wondering why I'd signed up for this. I didn't think it was gonna go anywhere. I was sorry for the kid's folks. But sometimes you just don't get justice.

Hamilton will get you a whiskey on most airlines, and flying American was no different. He'll even leave a couple of Washingtons behind. I got the feeling that the way Hamilton and Washington were avoiding each other that maybe they weren't friends. I didn't know my political history that well but what I do know is that time smooths out the wrinkles in men's flaws. And I wouldn't be surprised to learn that both men were pretty flawed. But that could be the whiskey talking. Angry whiskey. The price was outrageous. Back in Santa Monica I could find myself a whole bottle of golden love for less than two Hamiltons. Here I was barely getting a sniff. But they had you in a narrow tube, tied to an uncomfortable seat.

Thankfully I had the row to myself. Only lunatics and lost souls fly red eye, and I couldn't figure out which one I was.

We landed at DFW close to one in the morning. Those of us on the plane stumbled off like drunkards kicked from the bar at closing time. The Marlboro Man and me needed to chat. But DFW is one of those airports where the sanctity of the lung reigns supreme. I had to step outside. It wasn't no bother for I had a two hour layover before I had to climb back into the tin tube and tie myself down again.

I lit up outside. It was a little nippy but with my jacket and hat I was feeling fine. Cars drove by slowly with rubber necks craning to take a look. I might have been a hooker on 69 Johnny Lane. I looked back and winked at a couple of them. But that got boring fast. I hadn't looked at the folder Johnny Rotten had given me before he'd dropped me at the airport. I figured I should do some of that.

I'd wasted the three hours to Dallas watching a superhero movie that made my shoulder hurt, and my knee, and my knuckles. I was getting old. And the real tussles had started to show no remorse for an old man who shoulda known better than choose a life of hard knocks. But sometimes you're choosing between two bad choices. I figured that was more whiskey maudlin chit chat. Enough of that. If I was gonna feel sorrowful, which, incidentally I wasn't, I was gonna drown it with another whiskey.

I found a small tavern down a dark alley along the concourse. Most of that is exaggeration. Nevertheless, I walked up to the bar. This was the kinda place where you had to get it from the barkeep. Seemed like he knew I was a chained man to an airport I couldn't escape. He wanted

Hamilton for a snifter too. They way he looked at me I figured he wanted the Washingtons for himself. So I let him have them. He looked more washed up than I was.

I found a small booth uninhabited and took a seat with my little tumbler. It was such a stingy pour I coulda carried it through a marathon during an earthquake and not have spilled a drop. But I was here to work. I was on the clock and that clock was my own. I can get stingy with my own time. There were only a handful of lost souls in the bar. A guy that reminded me of Willy Loman sitting at the bar nursing a beer. A flight attendant sitting by herself drinking what looked like wine, and an old man sitting in the next booth with whiskey and sad eyes.

You can get to wondering about what lost souls are doing in an airport late at night all by themselves. But then you'll just depress yourself. And the work ahead of me was depressing enough. I took out the folder that Roberts had given me as a parting gift at LAX. I was surprised at it's lightness and thinness. For a homicide file it didn't have much to it. But maybe that's all Roberts had asked for.

I looked at it. This wasn't the whole file. Not if Jersey PD were doing even a half-assed job about it. I had no crime photos for instance. It was just detective notes and witness statements. Witness statements were light on facts. But it gave me names. Folks I could follow up on. And I had a way of speaking with difficult witnesses. I put them at ease. Made it easy for them to tell me everything. My problem was that I was not traveling with my friend Ruger. Sometimes the hassle of state firearm requirements was too much. In any event I was heading to New Jersey. That was like the Canada of the states when it came to firearms. If I wanted Ruger with me I needed to have a New Jersey permit. And I didn't have one.

Leafing through the statements I did get a little more clarity on who I might be looking for. The bikers who had been witnesses all described a smart dressed man in a black suit who got into a black car. It's not that they couldn't see a license plate on said vehicle it's that they said the vehicle didn't have a license plate.

Something else that was pretty interesting was the fact that the shooter used a silencer or suppressor. Suppressors are banned in New Jersey. So the way I'm looking at it. You've got a smart guy dressed in a black suit and his escape vehicle is a black sedan without a license plate. On top of that he's using a banned firearm device. There's a movie about men in black isn't there? Joking aside. I didn't know any criminal organization like that. But maybe the mob was on the up and up in Jersey. It's not as far fetched as you might think. They still have a presence there.

Another interesting tidbit for you. One of the witnesses, the barkeep at The Rattlin' Chain, said he barely heard the shot. And he was only about thirty or forty yards away when Joseph was shot at, point blank. Now I've been around suppressors and they're still loud. Any one that I've heard would be quite noticeable probably from even a hundred yards away. This also got me to thinking that if this was a hit it was probably by a government agency. Now before you get your knickers in a knot, this is what some of our agencies do.

You don't even have to get into whacko territory. It is a known fact that the CIA tried several times to murder Fidel Castro. And there's speculation they've been involved in dozens more. What I'm saying is that it ain't all that far fetched that our government would be in the murder business. The questions would be, why and who?

Why would two young guys be seen as such a threat they'd

be assassinated? And then who's doing it? Black suits are most commonly worn by the Secret Service. But our version of the SS is involved in protecting the President primarily, and financial crimes. I don't see them involved in the murder business. The FBI isn't known for wearing black suit but they're responsible for domestic safety. They're also not known as murderers. And in my esteemed estimation they're more Barney Fife than Andy Taylor.

There's also the NSA. But those guys aren't out in the field much. And if they are, they're technicians installing bugs on your fiber and cable connections. But who knows, it's grown to be such a Goliath that it might have clandestine activities that nobody knows about.

This is a general problem with our country. There are well over 50 Federal Law Enforcement Agencies in this country of ours. Who's watching the watchers? That's a question that no one can answer. And without getting political, it needs to be answered. Because we ain't even talking about state and local level LEOs. I shook my head. My whiskey was done and I was feeling wooly. I had to take one step at a time.

That's how it always worked. You take one lead and go with it. It shows you a new direction to follow and you take that road. Soon enough, especially if you have a little luck, you've unravelled the sweater and found your naked bosom, all tattooed with answers.

CHAPTER THIRTEEN
UNPACKING BAGGAGE

SPENCER'S parents lived in Stillwater. That's why I was here. It was the only reason I was here. I'd lost contact with friends a long time ago. Stillwater had no good memories for me. It's not the place I didn't care for, it was the ghosts that inhabited it. Ugly ghosts. But I was here.

SWO is one of those small little regional airports where you climb out of the plane on a ladder. Maybe they call it a staircase. Felt more like a ladder. They had some new tarmac down and the weather was nippy. No snow on the tarmac. I wasn't Santa Claus coming in on a ski plane. I put it at around thirty. My phone told me it was thirty-six. Same thing. I had my jacket and fedora on and walked briskly with half a dozen others to the terminal.

You can't get lost in SWO, not at around two in the morning. It didn't take long for my bag to arrive and I caught the last cabbie taking a doze in the parking lot. He was an older guy. Shoulda been retired but like much of Stillwater he needed to make a living. I needed to saw some logs. I asked him where the closest cheap hotel was. He told me the Holiday Inn Express on East Krayler wasn't bad for around eighty bucks. I was in no mood to quibble so that's where I ended up.

The hotel was clean and quiet. The room was clean and the linens were bleached white. I put my bags down and got undressed. The Sandman clubbed me to death like I was a baby seal as soon as my head hit the pillow. The next thing I knew it was 9am and I was hearing vacuuming outside my room.

Roberts had made some calls yesterday while I was in my apartment packing for the trip. He told the Spencers I'd be calling them in the morning. It was the morning. I was feeling fairly spry for a guy who'd done the red eye. I'd taken a glass of water with each of my whiskeys. This meant I had a clear head. I still needed coffee. I needed something to wash the sand outta my eyes. I put the coffee on and took a shower. By nine-thirty I was sitting at the desk drinking coffee and making phone calls.

At ten o'clock I was downstairs checking out and climbing into another cab. Stillwater stole a lot of sun from the rest of the country. I liked that. It was a sunny day. A cool day that put pep in your step and meaning to your leaning. I was heading to the 1400 block of South Husband Street. It was a poor neck of the woods. I grew up not far from it. Stillwater wasn't a booming town despite what city hall thought of itself. And I knew folks from the south side. It wasn't an easy living.

I reviewed my notes. Just to get up to speed. I had a different driver. He was a younger guy who sounded Eastern European. I asked him why he was in Stillwater. He had an uncle here. That's why. Other than that he wasn't chatty. We listened to music. That Top 40 pablum for numbing the mind and the ears.

I didn't know much about the Spencers other than they created an alliterating litter. Stanley's pop was called Saul, his mother was Sarah. I knew Saul. Saul was the first king of Israel if I remembered my bible studies. Sarah, well Sarah was such a popular name, but the biblical version had Sarah as the wife of Abraham and the mother of Isaac. A little creepy side note, Sarah was also Abraham's half-sister. Stanley also had a younger sister I was told. Her name was Shiloh. I knew nothing about Shiloh except that I was pretty sure it was probably from the bible.

The cabbie was just pulling up when I was putting my file away. I got out and paid him his fare. The house was set back on a patch of bald land. The front yard reminded me of the bald head of a kid undergoing chemo. The house itself was a small square that looked like a pig's face from the front. Some sketchy stairs led up to a low front entrance. On either side were two windows with bars across them. On the side of the house was a dirt path where an old, beat up Cadillac DeVille circa mid-nineties sat sadly. Around back I got a glimpse of an older truck. Faded blue. If I was guessing I would've said it might have been a late eighties Dodge Ram.

I hauled my rolling suitcase like a train on rickety tracks across the bald ground. There was no path and no sidewalks. Reminded me of the kinda place I grew up in. Left a bitter taste in my mouth. My shoulder bag was strapped across my shoulder. Now I was feeling like Willy Loman or some other poor traveling schmuck.

Nobody was out in their yards. Their yards weren't worth tending, and the kids were probably out exploring the woods or at a local playground if they had any sense. I got up to the front entrance and as I did so, I noticed an old wagon roll up to the curb. It was a late eighties Ford Country Squire. Same color as the Griswolds' one. The avocado was faded and sun bleached, looking more like a green-yellow.

An extremely large woman got out of the driver's side wearing black spandex and a black t-shirt. I caught a glimpse of the decal on the t-shirt. It looked like it was of Steve Perry in a power salute. "Journey" was on the top, "Don't stop believin'" was on the bottom. It was all in some sort of rock font. The front door opened. I turned to see who it was.

A slim, wiry guy with a couple of day's gray stubble that looked like dried milk was looking at me. He was a couple of inches shorter than me. He had greased back gray-white hair. He was haggard looking but his blue eyes twinkled and his smile was warm. He wore faded blue jeans and a blue checkered button-down shirt. He looked past me and waved at the fat lady hauling kids out of the station wagon like bags of groceries. He turned back towards me and extended his hand. He was wearing white tennis shoes.

"I'm Saul," he said. "You must be Anthony?"

I nodded at him. His grip was a vice so I adjusted accordingly and he let go.

"That's my daughter Shiloh," he said, nodding past me. "Come in. Come in."

It was warm inside. Almost like someone had left the oven on. Saul offered to take my bags. I gave him my rolling suitcase. The shoulder bag I kept with me to refer to if I needed it. I took off my jacket and fedora. The jacket I folded over and lay on my suitcase. The fedora on top of that. The small hall closet was bursting with clothing.

"My wife feels the cold," said Saul. "We like to keep it hot if you don't mind."

It wasn't a question but rather an explanation. Saul put out his hand towards the living room.

"Please have a seat," he said.

I went in there. It was filled with old furniture. The kind you might find in an old-age home. It was granny furniture. I took a wingback chair that looked like it might not swallow me up. Next to me was a small square glass coffee table and then a TV cabinet with what was probably a fifty or sixty inch TV on it. Underneath it was a well stocked liquor cabinet. Next to that another glass coffee table and a similar but more worn wingback chair. Opposite me was a three-seater couch. From a different family to the two wingbacks. Behind me was a wall and within arm's reach the window. Between us was a big glass coffee table with a metal frame that had been painted or something, because flecks of it had been chipped off.

The coffee table had a couple of large ashtrays almost overflowing with the cremains of dead white soldiers in their khaki pants. There were a couple of remotes on the coffee table and the TV was playing NASCAR on low volume. Above the three-seater couch was a velvet painting of a slim Elvis in white clothes holding a mic and striking a classic crooner pose. It was well painted but not my style. It was the only painting I saw.

I heard commotion at the front door. I woman came out from behind the wall, around the side, carrying a plate of fresh baked cookies. She smiled at me. I stood up and offered my hand. She placed the plate of cookies down and took my hand. She was also wearing white tennis shoes, blue jeans and button-down shirt. Her shirt was white. A thick white that you couldn't see through.

"Anthony Carrick," I said.

She smiled shyly at me. She had a hard time looking me in the eye and when she did those eyes swam in red rivers. Her smiles were weak and slippery.

"I'm Sarah," she said, and then she let go of my hand like it was an electric eel. "Let me empty these." And she picked up the ashtrays and the one next to my chair. "We smoke around here, so light up if you've got them." She disappeared around the wall again before coming back and placing the empty ashtrays back down. She went over to her daughter and gave her a kiss on the cheek. She picked up the oldest kid and carried her back into the kitchen.

I hadn't smelt the cookies for all the stale tobacco. But now they were in front of me like small moons I could get a whiff of the sweet, warm, cooked batter. I hadn't eaten. Chocolate chip cookies sounded like they could fill the void. Shiloh walked into the room. I stood up again. She was carrying an infant on her hip. The child looked less than a year old. He had wispy red hair and he was in a dirty white onesie. He wasn't an attractive child. He had bulgy eyes and snot leaking from his nose. His skin was translucent like onions, and splotchy. I shook his mother's hand.

"Anthony Carrick," I said.

"Shiloh," she said. "So you're the PI that's gonna help us?"

It sounded more like an accusation than a question. I got the sense she didn't want my help or didn't believe I wanted to help. I nodded.

"This here is Anden," she said.

I nodded again.

"And that was your daughter who went into the kitchen with Sarah?" I asked.

"Yes, she's my oldest. Her name's Anita."

I sat back down and Shiloh went and sat on the one end of the three-seater couch. Sarah came back in with Anita holding her hand. Anita was also holding a cookie. She couldn't have been more than four or five. She was dressed in a pink tutu with matching leggings and a pink top that was striped horizontally with white. Her hair was bunched up on each side into what would have been pony tails, but it was thick and curly so it stood out like soft brown curly clouds. She was a biracial girl and just about the prettiest little thing I'd seen. She smiled shyly at me as she bit her cookie. I winked at her. She climbed onto her grandmother's lap.

Sarah had gray hair that hadn't seen color since we'd seen a decent president. It was tied back into a short pony tail. She didn't wear makeup. Maybe, a long time ago when we cared about the destitute she might've been an attractive woman. Now her face was lined and weathered. She looked like a crumpled piece of paper that had been scrunched up and thrown away only to have been ironed out by time. She was as thin as a rail.

"I think coffee's ready," she said. "Will you have?"

I nodded.

"Cream and sugar," I said.

She picked up Anita and put her on the side. Sarah disappeared. Shiloh stared at me. I looked at her back.

"Something on your mind?" I asked.

"You're not really here for us are you?" she asked.

"Who else is hiding here?"

"I mean you're just more interested in that journalist. Making sure he gets justice."

"They were both killed by the same man," I said. "What difference does it make?"

"It makes a big difference. My parents are real upset about

it and I bet you don't give a shit."

I nodded.

"You're right. I don't give a shit about you. I don't give a shit about Joseph either. I'm doing this for a friend. You want me to get on my knees and sob about it? Listen sister, folks die every day. If I gave a shit about each one I'd never get my job done."

It was harsh, and mostly true. I did care. Hell, why would I be here if I didn't care? But I didn't know these people. And taking the death of Stanley or Joseph personally wasn't gonna help any.

CHAPTER FOURTEEN
THE COOKIE CRUMBLES

"STILL, it's the rich who's gonna get the justice," she said.

"You talking about Joseph, the journalist?" I asked

She nodded. Anden was grabbing her boob. It was big like the rest of her but not perky.

"What makes you think he's rich?"

"Them city folks and journalists is always rich. They's got money those educated people. Always writing lies 'bout us."

I shook my head. I knew the kind I was dealing with.

"You always been this ignorant or have you had to practice at it?"

"Don't you be callin' me ignorant. I ain't ignorant, asshole. I know who the president is."

"What about the mayor?"

Nothing.

"What about the governor?"

Still nothing.

"That's Jake Lowley and Marsha Leviant, respectively," I said.

"So?"

"It doesn't mean anything. You can be educated and still ignorant. I'm here on my own dime."

"Yeah until you go see Joseph's kin then you'll be gittin' your money."

I rubbed my forehead. This was going to be worse than I had imagined.

"Joseph's folks don't have any money. I'm doing all of this pro bono. This means the whole case I'm doing for free. In fact," I said. "Your brother Stanley has more money than both families put together I'm betting."

It was true. John had got Jersey PD to look into his bank accounts. There was a lot of money there.

Sarah came back in carrying a serving tray. Saul followed. Sarah emptied the contents of the serving tray onto the large glass coffee table. The face of the tray was another Elvis. This time in black clothes and a little chubbier than the Elvis looking down at me from a black velvet heaven. Sarah walked back into the kitchen. Saul picked up the coffee carafe and poured me a mug.

"Sarah wanted you to have that one," he said, nodding at the mug of coffee he'd just poured. It was in a white mug with Elvis' face on it. "It's her favorite."

I poured milk and stirred sugar into it and tasted it. Then I put it on the coffee table next to me.

"She likes Elvis?"

Saul nodded as he poured coffee into the remaining three mugs.

"She thinks she saw him at Walmart the other day," he said.

Sarah came in. She had overheard Saul.

"Coulda been him. The Facebook group 'Evidence Elvis

Presley is Alive' says he is. They've got evidence too. Pictures and such."

She looked at me, sad as a young boy who'd just lost his puppy.

"Stranger things have happened," I said. Saul nodded at me.

"I ain't saying I don't believe you," said Saul.

"Still, you make fun of me," she said, sitting back down next to Anita and giving the girl a juice box.

"Daddy, leave Mama alone," said Shiloh. "If she believes Elvis is alive then he's alive. That's good enough for me."

Coming from someone who didn't think I was here to help.

"You like Elvis?" I said, asking the most obvious question and hardly showing off my investigative skills.

"It was the first concert we went and seen, wasn't it?" asked Saul.

Sarah looked over at him and gave him a smile. If there was something I was sure of it was that the two of them loved each other.

"It sure was," she said. "Indianapolis in Indiana. It was at Market Square Arena. He closed it with 'Can't Help Falling in Love'."

Saul leaned over and kissed her.

"Those were good times. Managed to steal her heart with that. Sealed the deal."

I smiled, reached for my coffee and took a sip. I was surprised by the sappiness I'd witnessed so far. I was expecting wailing and gnashing of teeth. It was nice to see the feeling between the two of them. I just wasn't expecting it.

"Please have some cookies Mr. Carrick," said Sarah, "I

baked them special for you."

I couldn't refuse that offer. I picked one up and took a bite. They were damn good cookies. Crunchy outside with a soft chewy center and chocolate chunks that were still a little warm and melted.

"Great cookies," I said. "Really. Some of the finest I've had."

"Mama," said Shiloh, jutting her chin out towards the plate of cookies. Anita was still nibbling on her first. Sarah took one off the plate and offered the plate to Shiloh. Shiloh took four and put them on the edge of the coffee table. Sarah offered the plate to Saul and he took one. Then she put the plate down.

"Have as many as you like, Mr. Carrick," said Sarah. "There's another batch baking in the oven right now."

"It's Anthony. Please call me Anthony."

Shiloh pulled her black t-shirt up and over her tits, taking her bra along with it. I looked because I was astonished by it. I'd never seen something like that before in polite company. Her tits were huge but not attractive. They lay like fat pendulous bulging eyes against her chest and upper stomach. Her areoles were brown and bumpy. The breasts were rivered with blue veins. I averted my eyes lest I be blinded. She lay Anden across her lap and stuck him up against her right nipple. Her left breast squashed up against his body like some fleshy, diseased fried egg. She leaned over him and took a cookie.

I looked around casually. Nobody seemed to mind. I decided to take another cookie. I drank some coffee.

"Doesn't he look like that detective we're watching on TV the other day about that bird. That hawk or somethin'?" asked Shiloh.

Sarah looked over at her.

"The Maltese Falcon with Humphrey Bogart?" she asked her daughter.

Shiloh chewed on her cookie and nodded. She spoke with her mouth full.

"Yeah, him. Doesn't he look like Bogie?"

Sarah looked at me.

"Reminds me more of Dean Martin," said Saul.

I was flattered, but it wasn't the first time I'd been told I looked like him.

"Yes, that's right Saul. That's who I was thinking too. I just didn't remember his name."

"You ever had that before?" Saul asked.

"Some," I said. "Don't see a close resemblance myself. Closest thing we share is height."

"I'm not sayin' you're his twin, but there's a good resemblance. In the right light at the right angle I can see it."

I nodded. There was nothing for me to add. We sat in silence for a while. Shiloh munching cookies, Anden eating his mother in plain site and me feeling a little uncomfortable. After a while I figured it was time to jump right in.

"I'm sorry about your boy," I said, as a means to getting the conversation started.

Sarah got up and went to the other side of me. Where the other wingback was. She brought a box of tissues from the glass table there, and a picture frame. The picture frame looked like chunks of glass had been scooped out of it to give it a sculptured look. She took a tissue and dabbed at her eyes.

"You ain't very kind," said Shiloh.

"Shush, Shiloh," said Sarah. "Don't be rude to our guest. He's here to help."

Sarah looked at me. It looked like she was trying to find a

smile. She never found one. She dabbed at her eyes again. My cookie was finished so I reached for another one. I couldn't remember the last time this sorta thing was uncomfortable. I'd gotten real at ease with it quickly. After my first handful of death notifications.

Pain is like a dark closet. It only fits one. Best you can do is be still as a candle and offer them light when they're getting out. That always seemed best. Be a shoulder to cry on. A light to show a world that might still be worth living in and an ear to listen. I didn't know if I was any good at it. But I tried. I gave them space.

"Stanley was a good boy," she said, and the tears came. She put the picture frame on her lap and dabbed at her eyes. "Sorry."

"Nothing to apologize for," I said. "I've been here before."

Saul looked over at me and tried to break the ice. He rubbed his wife's back.

"Captain Roberts says you were a murder cop too, right? You musta done this a bunch of times."

I nodded at him.

"I was on the job for ten years. I've sat with a lot of folks going through what you're going through."

"Then you must understand?" said Saul.

I shook my head and pinched my mouth.

"I like to hope I can understand a little. But honestly, Saul," I said. "I haven't lost a child so I don't know what it's like."

"That's the first honest thing he done said," said Shiloh, with Anden still the leach on her boob. I ignored her. Sarah looked over at Shiloh and gave her daggers. I could see them glinting sharp in her eyes.

"If you don't want to respect Mr. Carrick you can go sit in

the kitchen," said Sarah, and then she turned to me. "I'm sorry Mr. Carrick. Shiloh's just upset 'bout her brother."

I nodded.

"I've been treated worse," I said. "Takes more than some sharp words to rile me up. Take your time. No need to rush it."

Sarah smiled. It evaporated from the hot stone in her throat.

"I told Shiloh you've come here to help us for no pay," she said. "She don't believe it though."

I shrugged.

"I think them rich New York folks is gonna be paying Anthony," said Shiloh stuffing her face with the last of four cookies. "Mama."

Sarah offered her the plate. Shiloh took another four cookies. It was no longer a mystery how she got that fat. A timer in the kitchen went off. The plate was empty. Sarah took it with her back into the kitchen which I figured was behind the three-seater. Saul looked over at Shiloh.

"That's enough ya hear?" he said. His voice was stern but not mean. "Mr. Carrick's here to help us whether you wanna believe it or not."

"OK, Daddy," said Shiloh.

We waited in silence until Sarah came back in. She sat back down next to Anita.

"It'll just be five minutes to let the cookies cool."

I smiled at her.

"I just want to clear something up," I said.

CHAPTER FIFTEEN
THICK AS THIEVES

SARAH took a package of cigarettes off the table and lit one. She offered one to Saul. He lit one up too. He offered one to me. I decided I'd take some payment for my troubles. He offered me the lighter and I took a puff. It was good tobacco.

"Joseph was the journalist up in New York that Stanley was meeting. His folks aren't from around there. They're up in Ohio. That's where I'm headed tonight. His old man isn't working anymore. Bust up his back in an industrial accident ten years ago. Walks with crutches. Joseph's old lady works at a local library. She gets 30 thousand a year. Joseph's old man only gets disability from the government. That's 15 thousand a year. They're poor as dirt. Poorer than you I'd bet. They couldn't pay me if they wanted to. Joseph's not much better off. Makes the same as his old lady."

I took a drag on my cigarette.

"I'm doing this for a friend," I said. "Captain Roberts who called you yesterday. He knows Joseph's folks. Now, if I'm gonna do this right I've gotta figure out who did it. One man murdered Joseph and the same man murdered Stanley. You've lost someone and they've lost someone. I find who did it and everybody's happy."

"If yous was a successful cop then how come yous left?" asked Shiloh, finishing up her last batch of cookies.

"I had issues with upper management. I will tell you this. I cleared 231 of 231 murders I investigated. But I ain't gonna lie. The chances of this happening here are slim to none and slim might've been murdered too."

Sarah got up and disappeared again.

"Why do you say that?" asked Saul.

"Let's revisit the facts as I know them when Sarah gets back and I'll tell you why."

Saul nodded. He didn't look happy. Anden had finished leaching off his mother. She put away her milk jugs. Then she burped him and he spat up what looked like half of what he'd drunk. Looked like a bird had shat on her shoulder. Shiloh grabbed a fistful of tissues and mopped up the mess. Sarah came back in with the plate of cookies now full. She offered it to me first. I took two this time. I'd seen what had happened before. She gave me a napkin and I placed my cookies on my napkin on the table beside me.

She offered Saul next and he took one. Then she gave one cookie to Anita and offered the plate to Shiloh. Shiloh took another four. I was counting. That'd made twelve just for her.

"You were saying why you don't think we'll get justice," said Saul.

"I'm gonna do my best, but I just want you to understand how it looks from where I stand."

"And how does it look over there Mr. Carrick when you ain't lost nobody?" said Sarah. She started to sob a little. Picked up a new tissue and wiped her eyes. Saul rubbed her shoulder again.

"All I can do is my best. And sometimes that isn't good enough," I said.

"Maybe if you explain it we can understand," said Saul.

I nodded.

"This is what I've got," I said. "Your son meets Joseph at a biker bar. When they're leaving, Stanley gets run down at an intersection. There is no indication that the truck tried to stop or slow down. Joseph runs up to your son to try and help. Witnesses say a man in a black suit exits the truck and comes over to Stanley and Joseph. This man puts a bullet into Joseph's skull. Then he grabs your son's backpack and runs about half a block down the street where he gets into a black sedan that has no license plate."

"That's what we're told," said Saul.

"Right. But there are no witnesses other than the bikers from the bar and they're not particularly forthcoming. I haven't seen all the evidence of the case but what I have seen seems lacking. Jersey PD don't seem to have worked that hard in following up leads. I get the feeling this is a hit and nobody seems to know why. Did Jersey PD talk to you?"

Saul nodded.

"They called to tell us our son was dead. Said they were looking into it. Never asked us nothin'."

"We still ain't got our boy back," said a teary-eyed Sarah. She picked up the picture frame and looked at it. She offered it to me. I took it. There was a skinny kid in it wearing a cap and gown. He was smiling at the camera. He had blue eyes that looked a little crazy and a freckled face. Really red hair was springing out from the sides of his cap. He wasn't ugly but he sure looked different. I smiled at Sarah and gave it back to her.

"You can keep it if you need to for the case," she said. I reached out further to her with the picture frame. She took it.

"This one looks a few years old," I said, just guessing.

Sarah nodded. Saul looked over at it.

"Yeah, musta been from his graduation about ten years ago."

"It's one of my favorite pictures of him," said Sarah. "I can look for a newer one."

"That's not necessary," I said. "The coroner would have taken a close up that will be better for identification purposes."

"You said you don't think the police have done a good job," said Paul.

"Yeah. I don't know that for a fact but I'm speculating based on the cursory nature of the notes."

I decided not to open up my shoulder bag and the file that Roberts gave me. It was likely gonna be opening up a can of worms. And I wasn't going to let them see the witness statements. Not that there was much to see.

"Why aren't they doin' their jobs Mr. Carrick?" asked Sarah.

"I've got a theory and it's another reason why this case is gonna be hard to close."

"An' what's that?" she asked.

"I think your son was purposefully murdered. I think Joseph might just have been collateral."

"What's that mean?" asked Shiloh.

"It means that Joseph was at the wrong place at the wrong time. But your brother was targeted."

"Who'd want to kill my sweet boy?" asked Sarah, looking at me with genuine astonishment.

"This is what I need to try and find out. If we figure this out we're eighty percent of the way to apprehending the killer."

She nodded, looking down at the picture frame and rubbed it.

"Do you know where your son worked?" I asked them. I knew the answer myself.

"Yeah, he worked for some plumber up in New York. Isn't that what he said?" asked Saul, looking at Sarah. Sarah nodded.

"That's right. It was called Pipe Dreams Plumbing and HVAC, I think," said Sarah. "I remember 'cos it was a funny name."

"Is he a plumber then?" I asked, straight faced. Sometimes it pays to play the country bumpkin. It was a role I was good at.

"They really ain't told you nothin' huh, Mr. Carrick," said Sarah. "He's not a plumber he works in IT."

The way she said 'IT' showed how proud she was of her son.

"He's always been good with computers. Hasn't he Saul?" she asked.

Saul nodded.

"We couldn't afford him any. But he worked two jobs one summer when he was thirteen to buy his first computer. Cost him all the money he saved."

Sarah nodded.

"But he was good with it. He got into the local college on account of his computer teacher puttin' in a good word."

"Yeah, he worked hard during summers too. Then got in free at MIT for a graduate degree they called it. Didn't finish though..."

"You and him had a big fight about it," said Sarah, looking at Saul.

Saul nodded.

"He could be stubborn sometimes…"

"Like you," she added.

Saul smiled at that.

"You wanted him to finish school?" I asked.

Saul nodded.

"He said the job at the plumbing company was better than school. I couldn't see how, but he said he couldn't learn nothing more at school. The job was what he needed he said to learn more stuff."

"And maybe he wanted to be earning proper money," said Sarah.

"Did he ever tell you what kind of work he did at this plumbing company?" I asked.

"Just IT stuff. I don't understand it much," said Sarah.

"He told me he takes care of the network and such," said Saul. "He said he got chosen by the company because he was real good at breaking things. That didn't make no sense to me."

"How did he break things?"

"He told me how he's like a burglar. That's what he said. He says that instead of trying to break into houses he breaks into computers."

Saul shrugged.

"I didn't get it. But one time he was expelled from school." He looked over at Sarah. "How old was he that time?"

"Fifteen," she said. "But we didn't understand his problems."

She offered that by way of excuse. I wasn't sure what it meant. Maybe she was talking about this mental illness.

"That's right. Fifteen. He got expelled. The police came but the charges was eventually dropped. He had to show 'em how he did it though."

"And what had he done?" I asked.

"He said he wasn't happy with his grade in math so he changed it in the computer to a A+." said Saul. "We had to move him to a new school after that. He was always good on math and computers. I don't understand why'd he risk changing an A to a A+."

"So you think he tries to break stuff at the plumbing company?" I asked.

"I asked him why a plumbing company would want to have their computers broken. He said it was different there. Said I wouldn't understand, but he was trying to make sure their stuff couldn't be broken," said Saul.

"We're not very good with computers, Mr. Carrick," said Sarah.

I nodded.

"Did he ever tell you how much he got paid?" I asked.

Sarah shook her head. She looked over at Saul. He shook his head.

"Just said it was a good paying job. But I don't know how much."

"So when did he start working there?"

"Was a ways back. Musta been seven or eight years now," said Saul. Sarah nodded.

"He seemed to like it."

"How old was your son?"

"Thirty three this past summer," said Sarah.

"What would you say if I told you that Stanley had one million dollars in the bank?"

CHAPTER SIXTEEN

1 MILLION DOLLARS

I watched their faces. They went from blank to puzzled to worried.

"Did you just say one million dollars?" asked Saul.

I nodded. He looked over at Sarah. She was still shocked. Still furrowed her brow.

"One million dollars," said Saul again, feeling it roll around on his tongue. "How?"

I shrugged.

"Don't know exactly. But he was paid well. Last year he made almost three hundred grand from what he filed with the IRS."

That was info that Roberts had gotten out of a buddy at the IRS. Nobody said anything. They were still amazed.

"That'll be yours. So keep on Jersey PD about it. Soon as the case is closed or put on ice they should release the funds. Unless he had a wife or a girlfriend or a will that says otherwise, I'm thinking that money's coming to you."

"He didn't have a girlfriend," said Sarah. "I always asked

him about that."

I ate my cookies. My stomach was complaining. I washed them down with my coffee. It was almost finished.

"Is that what they pay IT now?" she asked. She said IT like it was a specific job.

"Not any IT jobs that I know of," I said. "Unless you're really smart and work for Google or Apple."

"That plumbing company must be really doin' well," said Sarah, finally coming to terms with the amount her son had left.

"I think Anthony thinks it's not a plumbing company," said Shiloh, taking after her brother in the brains department.

Sarah looked at me. I nodded.

"You've gotta help me out. Do you really think a plumbing company is going to pay some guy almost three hundred grand to work on their computers?"

"Well," she said. "They's charge a lot of money. When was it we asked one of them for a quote?" she said looking at Saul.

"Past spring," he said. "Wanted two grand to put in a new toilet. I did it myself."

They had a point.

"Yeah, I understand. But let's do some math. An average plumbing company will charge about a hundred and fifty bucks an hour. Plus parts, but parts are only marked up ten or fifteen percent from what I've seen. If they do forty hours of work a week that's billable which is a lot, unless they have several plumbers, because don't forget they're driving around to different jobs. Well, forty times one-fifty is six thousand. That's per week. Multiply that by fifty-two weeks in a year and you've got a little over three hundred grand."

I looked at Sarah and Saul to see if they were following. They seemed to get the math.

"So you've got one plumber working full time to pay Stanley's salary. How's this plumber getting paid then? How's the van getting paid and fueled? How's the office overhead getting paid? What about Betty the receptionist who answers the phone for Pipe Dreams? Are all these folks working for free so Stanley can make three hundred grand tapping chiclets on the computer?"

I wasn't sure I was helping them. They looked more confused than enlightened.

"What are you sayin', Mr. Carrick?" asked Sarah.

"He's saying, Mama, that Stanley wasn't working for no plumbing company."

I nodded.

"But I have his card," said Sarah. She got up and went into the kitchen. She came back and handed me a simple white business card. Nothing was on the back. the front had 'Pipe Dreams Plumbing & HVAC'. Underneath that was a number: 555-444-4545.

"Have you ever called him at work?" I asked.

Sarah shook her head.

"I don't like to bug him. He's busy with IT."

I pulled out my phone. I dialed the number, adding *67 before. I put it on speaker. I put my finger to my lips to keep them quiet. A surly, grandmotherly voice answered.

"Pipe Dreams Plumbing & HVAC."

"I'm looking for Stanley Spencer," I said.

"Who?"

"Stanley Shem Spencer. S-T-A..."

"Nobody here by that name."

Then she hung up.

"That's not true," said Sarah. "Call them back and let me talk to her."

I shook my head.

"Listen," I said. "She's not exactly lying. Your son doesn't work there. At least not right now. And see how she answered? That's a plumbing company that doesn't want your business."

"I still don't understand," said Sarah, more confused than ever.

"Anthony's sayin' our son doesn't work for a plumber. I think he means something else is going on."

I nodded.

"Your son was paid very well for working with computers, and he was not in Silicon Valley. He was in Jersey. Everything I've seen so far. The police not really working hard on this. The way Joseph was shot in the head point blank. The way Stanley was run down. This seems like a hit. And I hate to say it, but my gut thinks it's a government op."

"You're sayin' the gov'ment killed my boy?"

"That's what I'm working with right now."

"But why?"

"This is what I want you to try and help me figure out. How was Stanley the last time you saw him?"

"He was fine. He was his usual self," said Sarah.

"And when was that?" I asked.

"April. He was here for Sarah's birthday which was on Good Friday, fourteenth of April. He arrived in the morning and left on Sunday 'cos he had to be back at work."

"And he was fine? There was nothing unusual about him?"

Sarah shook her head.

"Not more 'an usual," she said.

"That's not true Mama," said Shiloh, putting Anden down on the floor by the couch and taking the rest of the cookies. Nobody said anything about that. "We all thought he was off his meds."

She put the cookies on the arm of the couch and ate one in one mouthful.

"Your son was schizophrenic I understand."

Sarah looked at me as if I'd just shamed her.

"Mama," said Shiloh, still chewing the cookie, "there ain't nothin' shameful 'bout it. It's an illness. The doctor tol' us that. Ain't nothin' to be 'shamed about."

"Listen," I said. "If I'm going to help you I need to know everything about Stanley. Mental illness, like Shiloh says, is not something to be embarrassed about. You wouldn't be embarrassed if he had a broken leg would you?"

Sarah looked from me to her lap where she clutched a tissue. Saul nodded.

"That's true. It's just. Well, Stanley didn't always have it easy," said Saul. "When the doctors figured out what was wrong with 'im we kept it secret. We kept it to ourselves. Not everybody understands Anthony, specially in these here parts."

I nodded.

"I understand that. But I'm here to try and help. If you aren't going to share everything with me, I can't help."

I leaned back in my chair.

"You thought he was off his meds," I said. Getting back to where we started.

Sarah looked up at me and nodded.

"He was acting strange. Like he used ta when we started noticing his problems when he was around twelve ta thirteen," said Saul. "Stanley was what they called a

117

schizoaffective disorder."

"What does that mean?" I asked.

"As they tol' us, it means he has schizophrenia and bipolar. He could have these real up and down mood swings. One minute he's high as a kite thinking he's superman and then the next minute he wants to kill his self."

"That must have taken its toll," I said.

Saul nodded.

"Was real hard on Sarah here," he said patting her forearm. Then he looked over at Shiloh. "Wasn't easy on her neither."

"What kind of symptoms did he experience when he was off his meds?"

"He used to think people were watching him and listening to him. He said he heard these voices that told him what they were doing. How they were watching and listening. His bedroom window is still covered with foil isn't it Daddy?" asked Shiloh.

Saul nodded.

"Yeah, that's how he was. It was hard. Long time ago he used to wrap foil around his head and then around his computer. He covered his bedroom walls with it and he wouldn't turn on the lights or use the telephone. The only thing he would use that was electronic was his computer. He wouldn't use the microwave neither."

"Why would he use the computer? That's the biggest electronic device he probably had."

Saul nodded.

"Stanley said he had to because it was the only way to fight back against them. It was the only way he could break their things he said," said Sarah. "It seemed to work sometimes too didn't it?"

Saul nodded.

"I think that's why he got so good at computers. Sometimes he had success breaking into a place, like city hall and then we'd get days of pretty normal Stanley. This was all before he had his meds."

"And what happened once you got him on his meds?"

"Then we were able to take the foil off the doors and the walls and the computer. He stopped wearing it around his head. He'd even use the microwave to heat his food. It also helped even out his mood swings too," said Saul.

"Was he pretty diligent about taking his meds?"

"He sure was, Mr. Carrick," said Sarah. "Jus' like clockwork. He took them everyday. Doctor was proud of him too."

"But when he came back in April you thought he was off of them. What gave you that impression?"

"He started talking crazy again," said Shiloh.

"Shiloh!" said Saul, slightly annoyed.

"What Daddy, it's true. He was talking crazy. I don't mean nothin' bad by it."

Saul nodded slowly.

"He wasn't making sense. He was talking about people listening to him and to us. He wouldn't let us use our phones in the house. If we wanted to use them we had to step outside. We couldn't use the TV recorder. He even unplugged it. Didn't want us to use the TV neither but I drew a line there," said Saul.

"He made us put our phones in these weird bags. What did he call them, Daddy... Friday bags or somethin'," said Shiloh.

Saul shrugged.

"They were weird little bags. Felt like cloth but looked like metal or tin foil as well."

"Might have been a Faraday bag," I offered.

"Yeah, that's what he said. Faraday," said Shiloh.

CHAPTER SEVENTEEN
FRIDAY'S IN A CAGE

"DID he tell you why he wanted to put these phones in these bags?" I asked, knowing what the purpose was.

"He said it was so nobody could spy on us. He was becoming his paranoid self. I never even heard of no Farady bag," said Saul.

"Faraday," I said. "It's named after a well known scientist. Michael Faraday, who first explained how they worked and invented them. Long time ago. Almost two hundred years if I remember what my science teacher tried to teach me."

"What do they do?" asked Shiloh. "Do theys really block people from listening to you?"

"Probably not, in the sense that if you put a tape recorder in a Faraday cage it'll still record you. But, yeah, Faraday bags can block cell phones from getting a signal, so nobody can connect to your cell phone. And if they can't connect, then I suppose they can't listen in. You know why they use copper wire in appliance cords?"

I got a wall of blank faces.

"Because copper conducts electricity really well. And you need the electricity to go from the outlet to the appliance so it'll work. It's the same reason we don't put knives into sockets. Metal knives conduct electricity really well. We're not bad either. And radio waves, which is what make cell phones get calls, work like electricity that way. They need to attach to something that'll be conductive. Like the antennas in the phone. So, if you put the cell phone in a Faraday bag which probably has metal fibers in it, the radio waves will travel along the fibers in the fabric and not penetrate into the bag to reach the phone."

"I see," said Shiloh. But I didn't think they were seeing what I was trying to show them.

"What are you saying, Mr. Carrick?" asked Sarah. "I dunno how nobody can hear me on my phone if I ain't answering it."

I nodded.

"That's usually right. But you can be tricked into downloading an app or a picture or text that installs software that can remotely control your phone. In fact, with your son dead you might want to have your phones checked out."

"You sayin' that Stanley might not have been hallucinatin'?" asked Shiloh.

I shrugged.

"I'm saying he's a great candidate to use for these sorts of things. How can you ever be sure if a schizophrenic is being paranoid with reason or because of their illness? Did you ask him if he was taking his meds?"

Sarah nodded.

"He said he was."

"OK. Let's go with that then. If he was taking his meds then maybe his phone was tapped, and maybe he was worried that yours would be too."

"But the TV and the TV recorder?" asked Saul.

I nodded my head to the side and had a look at their DVR and TV. They were both new in the last few years.

"I don't know about DVRs and TVs," I said. "But it looks new to me…"

"Got it a couple of Christmases ago," said Saul.

I nodded.

"Right. So it runs software. Probably has a microphone on it, so I imagine it could be used to listen in if it had the right software installed."

"God have mercy," said Saul, his eyes getting wet. "Our boy coulda been tellin' the truth and we didn't wanta believe 'im."

Sarah nodded and she misted up. Shiloh ate the last of her cookies. Anden was crawling towards the other side of the room. Probably looking to put a finger in a socket. Test my theory.

"He might've been telling the truth," I said. "Maybe he was working for one of the three letter agencies and knew that his phone was bugged. Maybe he knew they could bug other phones just as easy. That still doesn't explain why he got killed. Wiretapping is what a lot of our three letter agencies are supposed to be doing, so long as they have the judicial oversight."

I looked around for some help. I didn't find any. Sarah and Saul and Shiloh were still trying to figure out how Stanley could've been schizophrenic and not wrong.

"What are these three letter agencies?" asked Paul.

"It's a term we usually use when talking about our spy agencies. Mostly the FBI, CIA and NSA."

Saul nodded at that. Finally getting it.

"Have you seen any strange people walking around these parts? People that don't belong? Vans that seemed to be park too long. Strangers knocking at your doors?"

They all shook their heads.

"My Stanley was killed because he knew they could bug 'is phone," said Sarah. It sounded like a statement rather than a question.

"He probably knew more than that. And maybe he didn't know what he knew," I offered, not really knowing what I was thinking he might've known. And wondering if maybe I didn't know what I thought I knew.

"There was this man at the Walmart that I thought might have been following me," said Sarah.

"When was this?" I asked.

"A month or two back."

"Why did you think he was following you?"

"I dunno. Jus' the way I caught him looking at me from time to time. And in my job there I move around a lot. And throughout the store I kept seeing him. Like the one time I was tidyin' up women's delicates and he was there by the handbags lookin' at 'em."

"Did you say anything?" I asked.

"No, 'cos by the time it started to feel real creepy he just left."

"How long was he there?"

"Musta been a couple hours."

"What did he look like?"

"Like nothin'. He was just average lookin'. I can't remember nothing sticking out 'bout him."

"Do you remember his hair color or eye color? His height?"

"His hair was brown and straight. Not like yours. Didn't

see his eyes but he give me the creeps. Jus' somethin' 'bout him that didn't sit right with me. I'd say he was maybe a little taller 'an you."

"What was he wearing?"

"Black pants, I think." She thought for a moment then nodded with herself in agreement. "Some sorta shirt and a light jacket, like a windbreaker. That mighta been dark blue or navy."

It wasn't particularly helpful. It also wasn't watertight. Not something you could take to the judge for a restraining order.

"That was the only time?"

Sarah thought for a long while. I took out my package of cigarettes and offered them around. Saul took. Sarah didn't. Saul offered the light. The dead soldier Sarah had offered earlier had burnt out in the ashtray. Saul offered me more coffee. I took it. I smoked. I drank coffee. I waited for Sarah to make up her mind.

"Can't think of nothin' else," she said.

I nodded and blew smoke up to the ceiling.

"You said Stanley didn't have any girlfriends. Did he talk to you about any friends at all?"

Saul shook his head.

"He was a loner child. Never brought home friends to the house. Sarah used to worry 'bout it. But when he got older he jus' didn't have the time. Too busy on his computer. I think he had friends online though. Like with the games he used to play."

"And what games were those?"

Saul looked at Sarah. Sarah shrugged.

"War Tyde: The Kinship of Klans," said Shiloh. "Me and him used to play it together all the time."

"War Tide. T-I-D-E?" I asked.

125

Shiloh shook her head.

"Tyde like T-Y-D-E," she said. "Kinship of Klans is with Ks. It's a MMORPG."

"A what?" I asked. Last time I'd played any games was Pac-Man. Probably when Shiloh was the age of Anden.

"Massively multiplayer online role playing game. Basically you jus' play against other people online. And there's lots."

"And you used to play with him all the time?"

"Yeah. At first he showed me and then he helped me sign up for an account. We been playin' since Kingdom's Kastle," she said. "Also with Ks. That's their thing. It Kingdom's Kastle, then Knaves' Kross, then Knight's Knives, Kalaman's Keel, Kittaman's Kord. That one wasn't very popular 'cos they put it in space. Stanley tol' me it was 'cos the developers really liked Star Trek and there was something in there 'bout a cord or somethin'. Karry on Kalaman came after that. Then there was Kinship of Klans and theys gonna release Knightsblood Killing next."

I nodded, not paying much attention to what she was saying.

"He was one of the best ever. Prolly top 10 I reckon."

She stopped talking and thought for a moment.

"You know, jus' thinkin' 'bout this now. You know when he was here in April Mama," and she looked over at Sarah. Sarah nodded. "We gots some time to playin' and he tol' me a weird thing."

"What did he say?" I asked.

"He says I could have his account if somethin' ever happened to him. He says he figured a way to store stuff online in his game account and he says it was weird, creepy stuff he found on a guy he worked with. He didn' know what to do with it 'cos this guy got away with murder practically.

That's what he says. But he says he was gonna keep it jus' in case."

"What was it?"

"He didn' say. But I know it bothered him lots. He'd sometimes get a worried look on his face when playin' and I'd ask him what's wrong and he'd say he didn' know what to do. Said this man at work was a bad guy an' he needed to pay. I tol' him to tell the police. He said the police wouldn' help. I asked why, but he wouldn' say more 'an 'at."

"Did he give you his password for his online account?"

Shiloh nodded.

"I didn't really look at it 'cos I thought he was talkin' crazy 'bout dyin'."

"That's what he said?"

"No, but he says if somethin' happen' to him I can have his account. But I knew what he meant. But he always used to say stuff about his dyin' didn't he Mama?"

Sarah nodded.

"Before his meds he used ta get real depressed sometimes."

"I'm more interested in his password. What is it?"

Shiloh got up and went to the front door where she rifled through her backpack. She came back with a small soft covered black book. I'd seen its kin in the motel I'd stayed at. She handed it to me. It was a small bible. The New Testament, Psalms, Proverbs, it said on its face. 'Placed by the Gideons' was in the bottom right corner below an old jar-style oil lamp.

I opened it up and turned the first few pages.

"It's jus' before the beginning," she said. "He wrote some verses down."

"You've never tried to get onto his account?" I asked.

She shook her head.

"Do you know his username?" I asked.

She nodded.

"FoxMulder84. It's all spelled like it's one word. The F an' the M are in big case and the 84 is numbers, not written out."

I nodded and wrote it down on the page I was looking at.

"When he gave me the book I looked at them passwords, but they don' make no sense to me. I also forgot 'till now."

I turned back a few pages until I came to the beginning. I wrote the username there too. It was the title page. Had 'The New Testament' on it. It also reminded me who it was from. But there was a lot of empty space on the page even though it was not much bigger than my phone. Wider, but not taller. I saw Stanley's chicken scratch on it. These were his passwords.

CHAPTER EIGHTEEN
OPEN SESAME

SHILOH had gone to sit back down after picking up Anden before he'd made good on his suicide mission. I turned the page to her and showed it to her.

"This is all he wrote?" She nodded.

"Yeah, that's his password is what he said."

"These bible verses?"

She nodded again.

"I didn' make sense of it at the time. But he wouldn' lie."

"You all are pretty religious?" I asked, but I didn't see any other bibles or a cross or a Jesus portrait on the walls. Saul answered.

"We used ta go to Running Deep Stillwater Church. It's 'bout five minutes from here. But they tried to cure Stanley with their prayer medicine they called it, an' when we went to the doctors they didn' approve. They said he was possessed."

Saul looked over to Sarah.

"My boy never had no devil in 'im," she said. "He's always

been a good boy. We couldn' trust no man tellin' us what God thought after that."

I nodded.

"But Stanley?"

"He didn' go to church but he read the bible cover ta cover every year," said Shiloh. "He believed but he tol' me the answers was in the book not in the buildin'. Ain't that right Mama?"

Sarah nodded.

"He could quote scripture like you couldn' believe."

I looked at the page in front of me. This is what was written in black ink.

Proverbs 3:5 1-4

Proverbs 31:10 4-5

Proverbs 30:5 7-10

Stanley's writing was worse than my doctor's, but I could make it out.

"You read these bible verses?" I asked. Shiloh nodded.

I turned to Proverbs, chapter 3, verse 5 first. This is what I found. I read it out loud.

"I might need your help with this," I said to them. "This is the first verse. It's Proverbs, chapter 3, verse 5. 'Trust in the Lord with all your heart and lean not on your own understanding.'"

I looked up at them. They looked like all congregants I'd seen in any church I'd been at, sitting in the back about to nod off. I tried the next one.

"This is Proverbs, chapter 31, verse 10. 'A wife of noble character who can find? She is worth far more than rubies.' Anything?"

Still nothing. I figured I should be writing these verses down. I took out my pen and went back to Proverbs, chapter

3, verse 5. I wrote it down on the same page Stanley had written down the passages. I did the same for the last one I'd read.

"This is the last one," I said. "Proverbs, chapter 30, verse 5. 'Every word of God is flawless; he is a shield to those who take refuge in him.'"

I wrote it down under the other two. I looked up at my rapt audience.

"Do any of these quotes mean anything to you?"

They looked around at each other. There were no shrugs. But there were blank stares.

"I know he liked Proverbs 'specially," said Shiloh, "an' Psalms."

"Do you know what these other numbers are for?" I asked, showing her the page again with my finger pointing at the 1-4 of Proverbs 3:5. Shiloh shook her head.

"I never even tried to get into his account. I'd jus' remembered 'bout this right now."

"Maybe it's an additional chapter and verse from Proverbs," I said. Not really speaking to anyone else. I turned to Proverbs, chapter 1, verse 4.

"'For giving prudence to those who are simple, knowledge and discretion to the young.'"

I looked up at them. They were staring at me. I might as well be reading the original Greek or Latin. I wrote it down underneath the others. I went to Proverbs, chapter 4, verse 5.

"'Get wisdom, get understanding; do not forget my words or turn away from them.'"

I wrote it down. I didn't bother looking at them. They could speak up if they had anything to add. Lastly, I looked at Proverbs, chapter 7, verse 10.

"'Then out came a woman to meet him, dressed like a

prostitute and with crafty intent.' Anything?" I asked.

The three of them were still ignorant. Anita tugged at her mother's shirt and whispered something in her ear. Shiloh got up and took her someplace. I figured it was the bathroom. I looked down at my page. My scratch was not much better than Stanley's. I figured I'd write them all down in the order they were presented by Stanley. Maybe I'd get some clarity that way. I had no more page to write on. I flipped it over and started fresh. I could write on the left. On the right was "The Gospel of Matthew". The first line being, "This is the genealogy of Jesus the Messiah." My eyes glazed over and I went back to the task at hand. This is what I had.

"Trust in the Lord with all your heart and lean not on your own understanding."

"For giving prudence to those who are simple, knowledge and discretion to the young."

"A wife of noble character who can find? She is worth far more than rubies."

"Get wisdom, get understanding; do not forget my words or turn away from them."

"Every word of God is flawless; he is a shield to those who take refuge in him."

"Then out came a woman to meet him, dressed like a prostitute and with crafty intent."

Shiloh came back out with Anita and they sat back down. I read all six verses to them in order. Proverbs 3:5, 1:4, 31:10, 4:5, 30:5, 7:10. I looked around and they had nothing for me.

"They don't make a lot of sense all together," I said. "Do you think Stanley would have such a long password?"

Shiloh thought for a minute.

"I don't think so. I remember him typin' it and it wasn't

that long. It seemed quite long but not that long."

I nodded.

"I'd be surprised if War Tyde allowed for such a long password." I counted the words. "Seventy six words." I shook my head. "I don't think so." I looked at what he'd written again. The second set of numbers wasn't written with a colon between them. I suddenly had an epiphany.

"What if those are not additional verses but the words in the verses," I said.

It went chapter then verse. Logically, if you wanted to drill down even further you'd get words, and then maybe characters in the words.

"Let me try it out," I said.

I looked back at my verses and wrote down words 1 to 4 inclusive of Proverbs, chapter 3, verse 5, and words 4 and 5 of Proverbs, chapter 31 verse 10 etcetera. I looked at it and nodded.

"I think this is it," I said. "I'd like to give it a try. Does he still have a computer in his room?"

Sarah stood up.

"I'll show you," she said.

CHAPTER NINETEEN
HACK ATTACK

STANLEY'S room was a time capsule. At least I liked to think of it that way. I imagined it had been left just as he'd left it when he went to university or probably MIT.

"Where did Stanley do his undergrad?" I asked. "Here at Oklahoma State?"

Sarah shook her head.

"That was 'is second choice. He got into University of Tulsa on a scholarship. It was 'is first choice. He said it 'ad the best computer program."

I nodded and looked around. The bed was small. Probably a single. Probably the same bed he'd slept in since he left the crib. The pillow case and the comforter were of The Matrix motif. On the comforter was a large picture of Keanu Reeves and Laurence Fishburne and Carrie-Anne Moss on a background of a green waterfall stream of digits and characters. The pillowcase was only of the green stream of digits and characters.

His bed was tucked into the far corner. At the foot of it

was a window neatly and carefully taped with aluminum foil. No light leaked in from the window. Opposite the window was Stanley's computer desk. A tray pulled out from under the desk which held the keyboard. The computer tower was a black Dell and sat on a shelf on the right of your right leg. Two large black Dell monitors sat on the desk. I figured they were probably about twenty inches each. They stuck over the edges of the desk like wings.

Other than that his desk was bare. The mouse was on a Matrix themed mousepad on the same tray that held the black Dell keyboard. Everything was by Dell. Next to the computer desk, away from the door we had come in, and towards the closet was a small bookshelf. It was piled high with old issues of Popular Mechanics, Popular Science, PC Gamer and PC advisor. There were also some books on there. I noticed a few that caught my eye.

"Hacking: The Art of Exploitation. The Masters of Deception. Hacking Exposed. Exposing The Bilderberg Group. The Secret Secrets of The Illuminati. The Perverse Federal Reserve."

"Your son was into conspiracy theories," I said.

Sarah shrugged.

"He used to talk 'bout it now and then. More before we gots 'im on his meds. But he still believed that stuff."

I nodded. I walked over to the closet. It was closed. I opened it up. It was mostly empty. Pushed to one side were some young man's clothes. Jeans and hoodies mostly. I took a look at them. I felt in the pockets. Nothing was to be had.

"I keep it mostly empty for guests or when he comes to visit," said Sarah by way of an explanation.

"It doesn't look like a guest's room," I said.

"I switch the sheets when we 'ave guests. But we don' have

them often."

I walked back to the desk and sat down. I reached down towards the floor on the right. I pushed the power button on the computer tower and waited for everything to start up. The monitors didn't go on. I felt for the power switch at the back of them and turned them on too.

"What's the password?" asked Sarah.

I opened the bible and ironed out the binding with the heel of my hand. I pointed it out to her.

"Trust in the Lord noble character is a shield," she said, feeling the words in her mouth. "That's from the differen' verses?"

I nodded. I got the Windows login screen. The username was already populated. The user was "Fox Mulder". The character's photo was there next to it too.

"Shit," I said. "Do you know his password?"

Sarah shrugged.

"I'm afraid I don't. Shiloh!" she yelled into my ear. "Come 'ere an' help."

I tried "X Files". That didn't work. I tried "xfiles". That also didn't work. I tried "x files". That also didn't work. I could be here all day trying wrong passwords. But I did get a password hint. It said "seek and ye shall find". I knew that was from the bible. I pulled out my phone. I typed it into the browser. I got back Matthew 7:7. I typed "Matthew 7:7". That didn't work. I tried it all in lowercase. Still didn't work. I tried it without spaces. Didn't work. Then Shiloh came in.

"D'you know Stanley's password for his machine?" she asked.

Shiloh came over and looked at the screen.

"He tol' me it was his favorite proverb," she said.

"And that is?"

She looked down trying to think.

"Do you remember Mama?"

"He never tol' me his fav'rite proverb," said Sarah.

"Ah, I remembe' it now," she said. "Proverbs, chapter 14, verse 12. That was his favorite. He said it always kept 'im on the straight and narrow."

"What does it say?" I asked.

"I don't 'member."

I typed it in as a normal person would. "Proverbs 14:12". The computer opened up. I turned to the bible in front of me on the desk. I looked up Proverbs, chapter 14, verse 12.

"There is a way that appears to be right, but in the end it leads to death," I said. "That's what the proverb is."

"What is the password for War Tyde?" asked Shiloh.

"Trust in the Lord noble character is a shield," said Sarah.

I waited a few moments until the computer had started up. I looked for a browser. I saw Chrome and doubled clicked on it.

"What is the URL for the game?" I asked.

"The website?" asked Shiloh.

I nodded. She was speaking to the back of my head.

"Wartyde.com," she said.

I typed it into the browser and hit enter. I waited. I waited some more. Nothing was happening. I pressed enter again and waited. Nothing. I took the mouse to highlight the URL but the pointer wouldn't move.

"It's frozen," I said. "Might have to hard boot it."

I pushed the power button on the computer tower. Nothing happened. Then, slowly at first, and then quicker the whole screen started to turn red. When it was done there was a black skull and crossbones on the screen at the top, in the middle. Underneath was written "Go home Mr. Carrick the case is closed". At the very bottom of the screen in smaller black lettering "This computer has now been encrypted. No point trying to take it anywhere. Only we can decrypt it."

We all stared at the screen for a while.

"How'd that happen?" asked Shiloh.

"What's happened?" asked Sarah.

"We've been hacked," I said.

I got up out of the chair and looked for the power cord. It was under the desk. I crouched up under it and pulled it out. The monitors went black and the tower turned off in a soft whirl.

"Well," I said. "That's that."

They followed me back into the living room. I sat back down. My cigarette had died of neglect. I decided not to light up a third.

"Maybe I can try to log on from my phone," offered Shiloh.

"Don't do that," I said. "If they're monitoring Stanley's home computer I wouldn't be surprised if they're monitoring your phones. I think I'll have to try logging on from a fresh computer someplace. Might have to wait until I get to Jersey."

"What happened?" asked Saul, who had been watching NASCAR while we were away.

"We got hacked," I said. "They've encrypted Stanley's computer. Bricked it. We can't get in."

"They can do that?" he asked, his eyebrows furrowed together.

"Apparently they can," I said. "If I were you I'd consider wiping and reinstalling the operating systems on all of your computers. Your phones too. I wouldn't be surprised if you're all compromised."

"Maybe he wasn't working for that plumbin' company," said Sarah, looking at her husband.

"I'd bet dollars for dimes he ain't working at no plumbing company," I said. "This goes way higher up the food chain."

"Like who?" asked Sarah.

"Like those three letter agencies I was telling you about. And the one that is the most tech savvy is the NSA. And considering your son was pretty smart with computers I'm gonna start focusing on them."

"And how they know you're 'ere?" asked Shiloh.

I shrugged. I didn't know how they knew that. They must have the place bugged or they were watching. I was pretty sure nobody was watching the Spencer residence. I would've seen a van outside up or down either street. I didn't.

"I think they've got you bugged. Probably like Stanley said. Maybe they've tapped into the TV or your phones. Maybe both. I think they're listening. That means they've gotta be NSA or FBI. CIA not so much. They're tasked with international espionage. But why Stanley? What did he know?"

They looked at me like dead wood.

"Turn up the TV. Loud," I said.

NASCAR was still on. Saul turned it up. We'd have to shout to be heard. I walked up to them all huddled on the couch.

"Give me your phones," I said, barely above a whisper. Just loud enough they could hear me. They handed over their phones. I took them all into the kitchen and put them on the table. I did the same with mine. I went back into the living room. The whine of race car engines was loud. The announcer's southern drawl annoying. I crouched down in front of the couch. They all leaned in towards me.

"You said Stanley had figured out a way to save files to the online game?"

Shiloh nodded.

"I've got to try and get on there and see what they are. They could hold the key. There's something going on here. It's bigger than Stanley. It got him killed."

"Please, Mr. Carrick," said Sarah, "find out who did this to ma boy."

"I'll do my best. Stanley wasn't crazy," I said to her. "He had found something that got him into trouble."

Her eyes misted up then.

"Don't talk about this case. Especially don't talk about it in this house or when you have your phone with you. In fact, I want you to buy a cheap burner from anywhere. Probably at Walmart where you work. Email me the number at this address." I wrote down my email address on a spare page on the bible and tore it off. I handed it to her. "Don't give anyone else that number. I'll get in touch once I've learned anything more. Any questions?"

They all looked at me eagerly but they had no questions.

"OK. I'm going to get the phones. We can talk about anything now but not the case. Understand?"

They nodded.

"You can lower the volume now," I said. It was beginning to grate on me. I went back into the kitchen and returned their phones. I rang up a cab company and asked for a ride. I was told it'd be thirty minutes. Saul and Sarah talked my ear off for those thirty minutes. About NASCAR. About Stanley and about working hard for a living.

CHAPTER TWENTY

ONCE BURNED

As it turned out, you can't fly direct from Stillwater to Ashland. Seemed you couldn't fly to Ashland at all. Not commercial anyway. Not that I could figure out. You also couldn't fly direct to Cleveland from Stillwater. I had to head back south to DFW before getting back on the tin tube for Cleveland.

My flight from Stillwater was around six that night. I had to pace DFW for a couple of hours before heading to Cleveland. Add on the one hour time difference and it was after 2am when I'd be arriving in Cleveland. I was meeting the Severns for around ten on Sunday morning. I had to rent a car. This whole case was becoming one of the most expensive I'd been on. And the guy paying my bills wasn't happy about it. I could chew through the money from my last sold painting in under a week at this rate. I cursed Roberts. I cursed friendship and loyalty. But after a few beers in DFW and a couple of whiskeys on the plane I was feeling more inclined to see it through.

I'd picked up a cheap burner at DFW. I got a gigabyte of data, 1,000 texts and 100 minutes of talk valid for the next thirty days for a hundred bucks. That included the smartphone. A cheap smartphone but it had a camera and it could record video. I was figuring I might start recording things from now on. Just in case. Just to have as backup should things go south. Sometimes if things go south it's nice to have your own evidence to fall back on.

I'd learnt that the hard way back in the day. It's a long story, but a he said, she said situation is a shit show when you're a cop. And now that I was getting into the shadowy underworld of our government's underbelly, I wanted to have something to back me up. Somebody's gotta watch the watchers. I didn't trust the government as far as I could blow smoke rings. And I couldn't blow smoke rings.

I tested the phone on my way to Cleveland Hopkins International airport. Depending on which direction I pointed the mic it was either adequate or piss poor. But it was better than nothing. It also had 8GB of storage. By the time I got it and powered it on I was left with 2.1GB for my apps and cat pictures. I didn't install any apps and thankfully the camera only recorded at 720p. I figured that would give me around twenty minutes of recording time if I was lucky. Should be enough.

You don't see much of Cleveland's downtown coming in from Dallas/Fort Worth. The airport is on the south side and that was the way we were coming in. Ahead of us was the inky black of Lake Erie. And butted up against its shores like night watchmen were the towers of Cleveland's downtown core. On the in-flight magazine I read that Cleveland is known as The Forest City. I couldn't see any forests. But it was dark and you couldn't see much. But I was pretty sure there weren't many forests around. The city got its nickname from Alexis de Tocqueville's Democracy in America.

At 1am I was feeling salty. I figured Democracy in America must have been a fictional account of a fantastical land far, far away. It sure as hell wasn't the America I knew. Just like Cleveland sure as hell didn't have a forest within a day's journey of its shores. My saltiness had only gotten worse having listened to President Troll's incessant nattering on economic issues and immigration. None of which this wart-filled silver-spoon sucking sycophant had any right to be talking about other than the fact that less than half of America had pulled the greatest political heist upon its own people in history.

Troll had divided the country deftly into two. The haves and the have-nots. The problem was the have-nots who voted for him figured they were now part of the haves. That was gonna be a long and sore lesson for them to learn.

By the time we landed at Cleveland Hopkins International, an airport named after another Hopkins who had nothing to do with both the actor or the hospital, I was in a right mood. But the airport was quiet and nothing was open. I made my way to a car rental and ordered something small and cheap. I got what I asked for. Something by Ford made for midgets or children. I put my bags in the trunk and drove south.

Not a long way south of I-80 I found a motel in a place called Strongsville off of I-71. It was cheap and I was tired. They put me at the end on the ground floor. There were only two other vehicles in the parking lot. A truck and an old American sedan. The motel manager looked neither strong nor sober. But he gave me the key with a smile on his face and didn't ask about my life. The sheets were clean and I fell onto them after having changed. I didn't set an alarm. The traffic on the I-71 sounded like distant surf and it washed over me and carried me into the arms of the sleeping dead.

CHAPTER TWENTY-ONE
STRAIGHT AND NARROW

IF there's something you can rely on from motels it's a pot of coffee in the morning. And I set it up and took a shower. When I got out the room smelled of coffee and I felt like a resurrected man. I poured some in the small white mug they give you. It's lip was chipped so I drank from the other side. I filled it up again. At that point I was out of powdered creamer and powdered sugar. There was still one cup left in the carafe. I had it black and sat on the edge of the bed smoking a cigarette while my hair dried.

Outside, an old man in an old American sedan drove away. I couldn't see the truck. I sat in silence for a while. I heard water trickling in pipes. Someplace above me housekeeping was dragging a vacuum over dirty carpet that should have been replaced when Carter left office. I looked over at my phone as I took the last swill of coffee and sucked the last breath out of my cigarette. It was nine-thirty. That meant I was gonna be late meeting the Severns.

I also had an email notification. I took a look at it. It was from Sarah Spencer. She'd used a burner email. That was smart of her. I hadn't thought of it. I had started out fucking up this job and I aimed not to finish that way. We'd spoken at length about what we knew at the Spencer home. Anyone tapped into our phones knew my plans. And I hadn't told her to email me her number from a fresh address. But she did. They were smarter than I had given them credit for. I opened the email. The subject line was "Work Invoice". The body of the text had her new burner telephone number and her initials, SS. That got me thinking about nazis. I wondered if nazis could be in on this. But I quickly brushed that aside.

I was looking at her email on my phone. I was pretty sure my phone hadn't been hacked. I hadn't downloaded any apps since Aibhilin had helped me set my phone up. And I hadn't received any suspicious texts or emails I'd opened on the phone. Still, I was gonna get Sue to have my phone checked out by her department. But for now I powered it off just to be safe. I took out my burner and decided to text Sarah an acknowledgement.

"Will be in touch, AC," is all I sent.

I opened up the file that Roberts had given me and dialed the Severns. Some people still have landlines. Some people still use typewriters. I wasn't judging. But the number Roberts had given me was called "home". It rang just a couple of times. A woman's voice answered. She sounded far away in a deep tunnel in some dark mountain. Her voice was probably an echo of her former life. It was soft and sad and folded up behind a thick curtain of loss. All of this I got from the simple word "hello".

"Hi, this is Anthony Carrick," I said. "A friend of John Roberts. I'm looking for Rachel or Chuck Severn."

The voice perked up a little then.

"Hi Anthony, thank you so much for calling. Roberts said you would. He thinks the world of you, and we're all looking forward to seeing you."

"Who am I all meeting?"

"Myself and Chuck, and Rebecca's in from New York too, for support. I hope that's OK," she said, just thinking of it now.

"Fine," I said. "I was calling just to let you know I'm leaving now, from a place called Strongsville. Should be about an hour, hour and a half."

"Drive safe Anthony. We'll see you when you get here. Thanks for calling."

I said farewell and hung up. I packed my things, donned my fedora and left the key on the bed. It was that kind of a place. No keycards, just a silver key with a large plastic rectangle attached to it that had the room number on it. The truck was still in its stall. It was the only other vehicle here. I put my bags in the trunk and hung up my jacket on the hook on the grab-handle in the back seat. I folded myself into the driver's seat in my toy car.

I was jesting now. I'm not a huge man and despite the compact nature of the car I figured someone up to about six feet could feel comfortable in there. It was amazing what a good night's sleep and a shower could do to wash the saltiness out of your mood.

I headed back out, south on the I-71. I was traveling the straight and narrow. If the straight and narrow was drawn by a five year old practicing their Js. It was a pleasant ride. The I-71 was mostly incident free and the traffic was light. The sun was watery and weak in the pale blue sky and it was a cool morning. The man on the radio was calling for highs in the high thirties which wasn't half bad for this part of the country coming up on Christmas. The roads were clear. Snow frosted some of the country here and there but there wasn't much yet. Call it climate change or global warming or just good luck but it was one helluva good day for a drive.

You pass farmland mostly. Some tree farms and some unused golf courses. Mostly unused on account that it was almost winter. Some state troopers hurried past me in the other direction about fifteen minutes out of Ashland. There was nothing about it on the radio.

I'd been playing with the dial ever since I'd left the motel. It was hard to find something I liked. And I liked jazz. I got some intermittent jazz out of a place called Elyria at 107.3 FM. But it was choppy so I eventually settled on public radio out of Kent State University at 95.7 FM. The announcers grated on me. They hadn't yet perfected their radio voice, but the music wasn't half bad. About five minutes out from Ashland I turned off the radio and gave myself some thinking space.

I wasn't sure how I was gonna approach the Severns. These were Roberts' people. Especially considering Rebecca was going to be there. Maybe it was gonna be awkward. Maybe she was just there for supporting her sister. I brushed that all aside. Hopefully they had something new for me about Joseph. Like why was he meeting Stanley at a biker bar? Why not a coffee shop? But more importantly why was he shot point blank in the head? Had Stanley told him things and made him complicit in something? Those were likely questions that they couldn't answer for me.

CHAPTER TWENTY-TWO
NICE PEOPLE

ASHLAND, Ohio is full of nice people. In fact they brag about it. Their sign says "Ashland, World Headquarters of Nice People". But that's only if you're coming up North on the I-71. I was coming south. Maybe that meant I was about to meet a bunch of assholes. Time would tell. However, everyone from Ashland had seemed real nice. But a sample size of one is hardly definitive.

I took an exit onto Route 250 which brought me onto Main Street. East Main Street to be exact. But in a small town like Ashland I didn't think I'd get lost on the long street of Main that was maybe three miles through the bustling downtown of Ashland. It's a two way street with a turning lane down the middle. Tall overhead power lines butted up against the road like shiny tin men for the first while. I passed a bank and a small, flat concrete building that called itself a mall. I carried on up to Sloan Avenue past a chicken joint. Sloan Avenue was the same as Lee depending on which way you were looking. I guess everyone needed a street named after them.

There was a dangle of traffic lights at the intersection like someone had tossed them up on on a wire like used tennis shoes. I carried on past a car wash, houses, buildings and a paint store. I took a right on Lincoln because that's where the Severns lived. Lincoln Avenue doesn't do the dead man justice. It's a tight, paved alley without sidewalks. Most of the houses show white vinyl siding. I figured the paint store I'd passed earlier didn't carry colors. Around half way up Lincoln I drove onto a dirt and grass driveway that led back to a white detached garage.

There was a white Japanese passenger van just in front on this same driveway nestled up pretty close to the house. The van must have been over ten years old. I got out of my car. I left the fedora on the passenger seat and my bags in the trunk. I put my personal phone in the glove compartment. I closed the doors and locked them. Nobody was out. There were clumps of compacted snow here and there.

I walked round the front and up some slippery steps onto the front porch. It was shallow and small, just like the house. On my right was a porch swing long faded from the sun. I squashed the round gray doorbell. The button was harder than it looked. I heard a sing-song chime inside. It wasn't long before one of the nice people of Ashland opened up the front door. I figured it was Rachel.

She looked to be in her late fifties. Her hair was dyed dirty blond. It was long and wavy. She had put makeup on her face and she was an attractive, slim woman. She was wearing indoor slippers on her feet and I looked her straight in the eye. She was a tall drink of whiskey that went down smooth. She smiled and offered me a well manicured hand. I shook it. It felt like a small, fragile bird in my hand. She was dressed in slacks, a blouse and a sweater.

"Anthony Carrick?"

I nodded.

"Rachel Severn?"

"Yes, please come in. We're so happy you're here."

She moved aside and I walked into the main entrance way which was just a part of the living room. A small closet was on my right. On the mat were scattered outdoor shoes. I got the hint and kicked off my derbys. I was wearing good socks. Brown like my shoes and without holes. Holes in socks or shoes doesn't set the right tone.

"Please come in," she said. "Chuck's in the kitchen preparing elevenses."

"Elevenses?" I said, following her into sitting room which was on my left as I came in. It was awkwardly shape. Not because it was a rectangular room, but with what they had done with it. There were two sets of chairs making an arrow head towards me with a gap between them. On the left by a small window was a recliner. On the right was a two seater sofa. Once I was in the jaws of this beast I came upon a wooden coffee table angled to align with the couch. Beyond that, on the right almost against the wall was another recliner. It was far enough away that it could recline. There was a small, round, wooden coffee table by its right arm. Parallel to the couch but on the opposite end of the room was a three-foot wooden TV stand. There was a DVR and a cable box on one of the bottom shelves and on the other shelf was a Roku and a Blu-Ray DVD player. The TV was probably fifty plus inches and slimmer than my forearm.

Rachel pointed her hand towards the far recliner. It was black. All of them were black. The tables were dark brown.

"Elevenses is a tea break. I think we got it from J.R.R.

Tolkien," she said. "We're big readers."

"I can imagine. John says you work at the library."

She nodded her head.

"I thought we were going to be drinking whiskey," I said. It was early for whiskey but I'm a trooper and a champion. I was willing to give it a go.

"Whiskey, good heavens no," she said. "We don't drink at all. Why would you think we'd be having whiskey at almost eleven in the morning?"

"Elevenses in this country gave birth to the current coffee break. We drank whiskey at eleven in the morning on our breaks at work. In fact, we seemed to have been pretty inebriated most of the week except for Sunday mornings at church. So it goes."

Rachel was grinning at me.

"Are you pulling my leg?" she asked. We were both still standing in the middle of the room. The couches and recliners huddling around us like a football scrum.

"Cross my heart," I said, crossing my heart casually. "Read it in the New York Times Magazine or something like that. Way back. That's what it said. At least that was us back in the early part of the nineteenth century. Not that it did us any good."

"I should think not."

I was just about to sit down when another, younger woman came into view. I thought she might be Rebecca. There was family resemblance and she was probably fifteen or so years younger than her sister. That would have put her at around my age. Maybe a little younger, which would have put her at the right age to be dating Roberts back in the day. Rebecca was a brunette and stunning. Time had been awful kind to her. She looked like she could have been in her thirties. She was shapely and slim and a few inches shorter than her sister. Rebecca made her way into the scrum and Rachel gave her room.

"This is my sister, Rebecca," she said.

We shook hands and I could see why Roberts still held a flower for her in his heart. She was married though. I could see that on her ring finger. A massive diamond that was probably gonna give her arthritis if she kept on carrying it. She wore clothing that made me and her sister look like homeless schlumps. It was probably haute couture if I understood that term right. Which I think I did from my time dealing with haughty rich clients in New York. But she wasn't haughty. She shook my hand and looked me in the eye and gave me a genuine smile.

"Do you like tea, Anthony?" she asked.

I looked over at the tray. There were homemade cookies on a plate. Had to be homemade because I could smell them from where I was standing. They were the size of my palm with fingernail sized chunks of brown chocolate. My mouth watered. There were also four teacups on the tray. The real, dainty kind with flowers on them and ornately curled handles with matching saucers. Next to it was a blue ceramic teapot covered with a cozy that had flowers on it. The flowers might have been roses or carnations or sunflowers even. I couldn't tell. Well, I could tell they weren't sunflowers. I ain't never seen pink and white sunflowers. I could tell the teapot was blue because I could see the base of it. In a white bowl was white sugar. In another white bowl was milk. Looked whiter than skim. Could it be cream? Could I dare dream? I looked back at Rebecca.

"Not particularly," I said.

"Ah, a coffee drinker. Just like me," she said. She picked up two teacups and matching trays. "I'll go and make us a pot."

"Not necessary," I said, but she was gone.

The house was similarly shaped to the Spencers. I figured the hallway from the front door stretched into the back where the kitchen was. On the other half of the house were the bedrooms.

"How's John?" asked Rachel. We were still standing around while the cookies taunted me with their scent.

"John's very concerned for you and Rebecca. And for Chuck of course. That's why I'm here."

Chuck started into the room. He was a big man, huddled over crutches under both arms. He was wearing slacks and a button-down shirt. He was clean shaven and had a welcoming smile. He scuttled sideways through the opening between the couch and the recliner. He came up to us and offered me a hand. I shook it. It was thick and meaty and hard. He was my height bent over in those crutches. That probably would have made him around six three, maybe more, if he could stand upright.

"Thanks for coming Anthony," he said, after we'd shaken hands. "I'm gonna sit down. Can't be up all that long without one of my legs giving out on me."

He moved over to the first recliner I'd seen and got himself settled. Rachel slid passed me and I smelled the clean fragrance of soap. She sat down by my side on the couch. I sat down on the recliner. I hadn't sat down long when Rebecca came back in. I got up again. Rebecca smiled at me, and sat down next to her sister.

"Thank you Anthony, but that's not necessary. I'm going to be up and down like a yo-yo and I'd rather you didn't. You'd make me feel awfully guilty about it."

I nodded at her.

"It is wonderful though, to meet a man with such chivalry."

I smiled at her but didn't say anything. I had been wondering over the years if it was chivalrous or stupid. Seemed it was going the way of the dinosaurs, and being the only man in a room rising for women could make you feel like a dinosaur. But women liked it. Even if they didn't always tell you like Rebecca just did.

"The coffee will be just a few minutes," she said.

Rebecca handed out napkins to everyone except me. She gave one to Rachel who gave it to me. I got the plate of cookies that same way. I took one and bit it. It was warm and soft and gooey.

"Before we get started," I said, getting out of my chair. "Do any of you have your cell phones on you?"

Chuck patted himself down.

"Think I left mine in the kitchen."

"Mine's in my purse," said Rachel, picking it up off the floor by her leg.

"Me too," said Rebecca. Her purse was on the couch next to her.

"Do you mind if I grab them and put them in the kitchen? I'll explain."

The two of them looked at me quizzically but then decided to pull out their cell phones. An inexpensive smartphone for Rachel. The most recent iPhone for Rebecca in a sparkly case. I wondered, for just a brief second, if it was encrusted in diamonds. But I dismissed it. Rebecca didn't seem that ostentatious.

I took the phones into the kitchen. The coffee was just finished brewing. The can was next to the coffee pot. It wasn't fancy coffee. Store brand but it promised itself to be dark roasted. I was grateful for that. I popped my head round the hallway again.

"Do you need room for cream?" I asked.

"Yes, please, Anthony," said Rebecca.

"Anyone else fancy coffee?"

Chuck and Rachel shook their heads at me. The second cupboard I opened had coffee mugs. I chose one with sunflowers on it for Rebecca. These flowers I was pretty certain were sunflowers. I just picked the closest one for me. It was black with white writing.

CHAPTER TWENTY-THREE
PUMPING JACK

I walked back into the sitting area. There was a generous space in the coffee mugs for cream and sugar. I handed one to Rebecca and I kept the other one for myself. Before I sat down I added cream and sugar.

"Is this milk or cream?" I asked, not really wanting to know the answer if it was milk.

"Half and half," said Rachel.

"God bless you," I said, grinning.

Rachel giggled ever so briefly. I stirred and sat down and took another bite of my cookie. I picked up my coffee cup again and pointed at it.

"Is this where you worked?" I asked Chuck.

The words on the black mug spelled out "Mathiesen Mallard Mechanical". Next to it was a drawing of a pumpjack.

"Yeah. We make small spare parts for oil rigs, mostly the small ones like that pumpjack there. But we also make some of the smaller parts for all sized rigs including the offshore ones. I busted my back there in '05. In the last few years they've gotten rid of half the guys I used to work with on account of oil taking a dump. We used to call ourselves the other 3M."

I nodded.

"I'm sorry to hear that."

"Coulda been worse. I could've broken my neck. At least I can still get around."

I turned to Rebecca.

"John tells me you're in Jersey?"

She shook her head.

"I haven't spoken to John in years. We live in Manhattan now. Have for about the last six or seven years. My husband owns a successful electrical company out there. He goes out to Jersey every day to run it."

"What kind of electrical company?"

"We service the electrical needs of homes and businesses. He has about twelve or thirteen electricians at his company."

I nodded. I was trying to figure out where she got her money from.

"Do you have kids?"

She shook her head and looked away from me. I figured there was a story there. I didn't press.

"Rebecca was always really good with Joe. She loved him like her own," said Rachel, her eyes starting to mist up.

Rebecca blinked away some hot emotion as she looked up at me.

"Joe was a really good kid," she said. Then she smiled. "Man, really. He was a really good man. He had a good moral compass. Always looking out for the underdog. That's why he wanted to be a journalist."

I nodded.

"I know this is gonna be tough, but the more I can get from you, the better my chances."

"Thanks for taking this on Anthony," said Chuck. "You know… It's a big ask. I wish we could pay you for your time."

"It's nothing," I said. "John's a good friend. I'm happy to help."

"He says you're the best," he added.

"He oversells me."

Rebecca looked over at Rachel and tapped her on the forearm.

"Is Anthony doing this for free?" she whispered, though we could hear her.

Rachel nodded cautiously. Rebecca looked at me.

"I'll pay you Anthony," she said. "send me the bill."

I shook my head.

"It's being taken care of," I said.

"By who?"

"By me. It's a favor for John. Besides, I'm traveling coach and renting bicycles."

I grinned at her.

"No, Anthony," she said. "I insist. I know you're a struggling painter who does this sort of work on the side to pay the bills. The least I can do is pay you your going rates."

"Perhaps you're the better detective," I said, noticing she had been snooping around about me, "but like I said, it's not necessary. In any event, I'm not sure I'm gonna be able to deliver the resolution everyone is hoping for. If you're happy with the service at the end of the day then a bottle of whiskey will be swell."

"That doesn't seem right," said Rebecca. "We have the means and you shouldn't have to work for free."

"I wouldn't argue with her," said Rachel, "she can be mighty insistent if she wants. Be best just to send her the bill."

"It's a kind offer," I said to Rebecca, "but I made a deal with John. This one's on me."

"And you're too proud to accept money?" asked Rebecca.

I shook my head.

"Just a stubborn fool who doesn't change his word."

"We'll see," said Rebecca.

She was smiling at me. She meant well but I ignored her. This wasn't her case to sponsor. And having spoken to the Spencers I wasn't sure anybody was gonna get their just deserts.

"I don't know if John told you I saw the Spencers yesterday?"

I looked around the room to shaking faces. I nodded.

"The trip worked out better that way," I said. "Do you know much about them?"

More shaken heads. Looked like I was in the back of a car watching bobbleheads on the front dash.

"Joe had called up just before Thanksgiving to tell us he wouldn't be coming round because he had work to do. Said he'd definitely be taking time off for Christmas though… except now he won't," said Rachel breaking into tears.

There weren't any tissues on the table. Rebecca got up. Probably to get some. I had a handkerchief in my pocket. I took it out and offered it to her. Like a white flag of peace. But there was no peace in these folks' hearts. Rachel looked up at me through wet, red-rivered eyes.

"Thank you," she said, trying to swat away her emotions. "I'm sorry… It's just still so hard."

I gave her some space and turned to my mug of coffee.

"Rachel spoke to him," said Chuck. "But how she tells me, he was working on something. He wasn't sure if it would amount to anything but he had this other big story he was working on."

Rebecca returned carrying a box of tissues. She saw my handkerchief, now wet with Rachel's tears and put the box on the coffee table.

"What was this big story he was working on?" I asked Chuck.

"He said he'd uncovered seniors' abuse by Jersey cops at some seniors' homes. He was hoping it might get him noticed by the Washington Chronicle. That was his long term goal. He wanted to go and work for them. He figured this story would help him with that goal."

"But that wasn't what prevented him from coming out here for Thanksgiving, right?" I asked.

Chuck looked over at Rachel. She seemed to have collected herself.

"That's right," she said. "His boss had forced him to take this other story. Or, perhaps it's more accurate to say his boss had forced him to meet with someone who thought they had a story."

"And this turns out to be Stanley Spencer," I said.

Rachel nodded.

"You'll forgive me for my language, Anthony," she said, "but at first Joe thought he was a crackpot."

"Did he say why?"

She nodded.

"He said this guy, Stanley, kept on with bible quotes in their texting and that he had Joe get a new, burner phone so they could text and call privately."

"Did he tell you anything else about what Stanley might

have wanted to talk about?"

Rachel shook her head and dabbed at her eyes again.

"He was going to meet him at this bar to find out in detail. Stanley wouldn't say much, but to Joe he sounded like every other conspiracy nut Joe deals with who thinks they have a story. But then that was the night he got shot…"

Her voice broke so I gave her a minute. I turned and looked at Rebecca.

"Do you know which bar they met at?"

She nodded.

"It's called 'The Rattlin' Chain'. It's not a bar I know know, but it's known to those of us from Jersey."

"How's that?"

"It's a well known biker bar. There have been police investigations there before. It's sometimes on the news. I think they've even had a homicide there before. I've heard that a biker gang called the Seventh Sons owns it or something like that."

I nodded.

"You're well informed," I said.

"It's all from the news."

"So none of you know anything about what the conversation between Joe and Stanley might have been about?"

They shook their heads.

"OK. Let me tell you what I know so far. Then maybe you can help to start filling in the gaps."

CHAPTER TWENTY-FOUR
NASTY LIZARDS

"Do you know what the Bilderberg Groups is?" I asked.

"I've heard about it," said Rebecca. "I think it's a group of world leaders who meet every so often. But from what I can tell it's pretty secretive."

Rachel nodded.

"By and large," she said, "folks who voted for Troll seem to think there's something to it, the conspiracy part that is. I think that's why they voted for him, thinking he was an outsider and not part of the Washington establishment."

"What are some of these conspiracies?" I asked, feigning some ignorance as I'd done some research on my own on the plane after seeing Spencer's books on the subject.

"There are five that seem to keep cropping up, though the first one is incongruent with more anti-semitic sentiment that seems to be the current take du jour," she said. "The first is that it is run by Nazis. You have to remember that the group was founded in 1954, not long after the end of the war. This came about due to speculation that the co-founder of the

Bilderberg Group, Prince Bernhard of the Netherlands, was a Nazi member. This is true. However, that was only in the very early days, before the war. What is not mentioned by conspiracy theorists is that Bernhard fought valiantly against the Nazis during the war and consistently detested them in speeches he gave."

This was something I was not aware of.

"He was also the founder of the World Wildlife Fund as it was called at the time. Something else that didn't help him or the Bilderberg Group was his involvement in what was called the Lockheed Bribery Scandal. It's come to light that he took a bribe in the neighborhood of around 1 million to ensure that Lockheed's plane would win out over a competitor for the Netherlands. There were some other scandals and controversies, but that one I think was the biggest. And it feeds into the conspiracy theories about the Bilderberg Group."

I sipped my coffee. Rachel obviously had done a lot more research than I had on the topic. What would have helped during this presentation was a cigarette. But I didn't see any ashtrays and I figured they didn't smoke.

"Like a lot of powerful men he was flawed. He did good things but he also made mistakes, if I can put it gently. The second big conspiracy is that the Bilderberg Group is trying to create a one-world government or New World Order. This one, of all of them, might be based in some truth."

I nodded.

"Denis Healey, another founder of the Group, and a British Labour politician at the time said to the effect that it wasn't totally inaccurate to say that they wanted to work towards a one-world government. The third conspiracy is a catchall one that started with the idea that the Bilderberg

Group were responsible for the Kosovo War. From there, other conspiracy theorists have postulated that they've been involved in every war since the Vietnam War."

"You're well informed on the topic," I said. "I was only aware of the one-world government and the starting wars conspiracies."

"As a librarian I have access to a wealth of information. Though to be honest, anyone can access it now thanks in large part to the internet."

"What are the fourth and fifth?" I asked.

"The fourth one is interesting and I think there might be some kernel of truth to this one too. But then it depends on which side you stand on regarding the Republican Party. We're Democrats. I'll say that in the interest of full disclosure."

Rachel looked up at me. I wondered if she was hoping I'd make my political affiliation clear. I didn't. Mostly because I didn't consider myself Republican or Democrat. I voted independently. I voted according to my conscience and who made the most sense to me. If anything I'd call myself an independent. I was for small government and small businesses. I wasn't for big business or for the massive wealth disparity in this country. That meant I'd voted Democrat lately more often than not. I sure as hell didn't vote for the repugnant David Troll. I smiled at Rachel.

"I don't align with any specific party," I said. "I vote my conscience every time."

She smiled and nodded at that.

"The fourth conspiracy came about by a book written by Phyllis Schlafly called 'A Choice Not an Echo'. Do you know she was?"

I shook my head.

"She wrote the book back in the early sixties I think it was. She was a staunch conservative and Republican but she had a falling out with them. Or at least an ideological falling out with them which made up most of the content of her book. In essence, it was a backlash against what she thought was the liberal influence in the Republican Party. I'd argue, and this is a sidebar, that we have her to thank for the growing conservative movement in our country which has led to the Tea Party and now David Troll. But that's an aside."

Rachel was folding and unfolding my handkerchief in her hands. She might have been trying to make origami out of it, but it wasn't very good.

"The seed of her discontent with the Republican Party comes from this idea that the Bilderberg Group had infiltrated the Party as 'kingmakers', that is to say, she believed the Bilderberg group had control of nominating the Republican leaders and they were only nominating liberals. She wanted more dyed in the wool conservatives to be leading the Party but felt that was being circumvented by the Bilderbergers."

"Wow," I said. "This is fascinating stuff. There's a large and holistic mythology around these conspiracies it seems."

Rachel nodded.

"I think the Bilderberg Group lends itself to that because of their secrecy. When you keep secrets, especially about the meetings of powerful people, ordinary folk are likely to fill in the missing pieces. And we all know how creative the human imagination can be."

"What's the last one?" I asked.

"The last one is perhaps the most out there of them all. A guy called David Icke thinks that the world leaders who are Bilderberg Group members are all part of an alien lizard species called the Babylonian Brotherhood who are here to control us by implanting chips into us and creating a one-world fascist state. He's pretty out there with his New Agey Conspiracy theories but he has a good following."

"I have heard of the name but didn't know what it was associated with," I said.

Rachel nodded.

"And from David Icke and conspiracy theorists like him, we get the Illuminati and the Rothschilds. And that leads us to the anti-semitic conspiracy theories I mentioned briefly earlier."

"So we're fucked, basically," I said.

Chuck laughed out loud. A good belly laugh and Rebecca laughed too. Rachel smiled broadly.

"Only if you believe these conspiracies," she said, "which I don't."

"They sound pretty far fetched. Did Joe mention any of this to you?"

Rachel shook her head.

"No. I started reading up on it before the last election when otherwise well informed people started suggesting they were going to vote for Troll. I'd also notice them borrowing books on these subjects too. I got talking to some of them and that's when I realized that a lot of them thought there was something to these conspiracy theories and especially the Bilderberg Group. They thought that bringing in an outsider was the answer to their problems."

Rachel poured more tea for her and Chuck. Rebecca asked if I wanted more coffee. I always want more coffee, is what I told her. She took my mug and went back into the kitchen for a refill. I started to think about things.

CHAPTER TWENTY-FIVE
UNSEEN SCENE

REBECCA came back with another steaming mug of coffee. My fingers were itchy for a cigarette. But nobody was smoking. I was now certain this was not a smoking house. And the car had no ashtray or lighter. I reached for another cookie instead.

"These are terrific," I said.

"Family recipe," said Rachel. "I've tweaked my mother's."

I nodded.

"The last time you heard from Joe," I said. "That was around Thanksgiving when he said he couldn't come out for it?"

Rachel nodded. Her eyes misted up.

"Yeah," said Chuck. "That was the last time we spoke to him. Rebecca kindly paid for me and Rachel to head up to Jersey to identify the body."

Chuck took a moment.

"He looked good," he said. He wiped his eye. "It really was him."

He looked over at his wife. Wet eyes linked through an invisible stream of pain. I gave them some time. I spoke to Rebecca.

"Did you attend?" she nodded.

"Would I be correct in assuming that no funeral for Joe has happened yet."

She nodded again.

"They haven't released him to us," she said.

"Why?"

"Because it's an ongoing investigation," she said.

"That's bullshit, sorry. It's not right. Usually within a few days or a week at the most, the coroner will release the body. An autopsy has to be done soon after death. Usually immediately. It'd be most often done within 24 to 48 hours. There is no reason why they haven't released the body," I said.

"What can we do?" asked Rachel.

I shrugged and shook my head.

"I don't know. I've never heard of this sort of thing. Maybe try getting a lawyer involved. If you can afford it."

I looked at Rebecca. She looked at Rachel.

"I'll arrange it," Rebecca said.

"I don't know how effective it'll be. If there's one thing that bureaucracies are good at, it's tying you up in red tape. I'm just trying to figure out why they won't release the body."

I chewed on my chocolate chunk cookie. I sipped on my coffee.

"Did you ask the coroner himself about getting the body?" I asked.

"Yes, but he said it was out of his hands, that I had to speak with the investigating officer. So I spoke to him too and he told me that we can't get Joe back. I asked him why. He said it wasn't up to him. So then I asked who was it up to and he said he couldn't share that with me. He said he'd be in touch when they were ready to release the body."

I shook my head and finished my cookie.

"That's the most bizarre thing I've ever heard of. And it gives some meat to my theory."

"Which is what?" asked Rebecca.

"I'll get to that in a minute. But first, did Joe give you any indication of what Stanley was going to talk to him about?"

Rachel shook her head.

"We didn't even know his name was Stanley until the cops told us who was there with him when he was murdered."

Rachel dabbed at her eyes again with my handkerchief.

"All he said when we spoke to him last was that he was going to meet a guy who seemed pretty crazy. All he knew was that maybe the guy was a religious crackpot because he kept spouting bible verses in the texts that Joe was having with him. And he called himself Spider-Man."

"There's nothing in the texts that I've seen that gave anything away. I've started to think we're dealing with a three letter agency."

"Like the FBI or CIA?" asked Chuck.

"I'm thinking more along the lines of the NSA."

"Why would our own government kill one of its own?" asked Rachel.

"It's not without precedent," I said. "Usually it doesn't happen on American soil, or when it does it's instigated to be gang related. Clearly though, in this instance, it couldn't possibly have been gang related."

"I find this extremely hard to believe," said Chuck. "Joe was a reporter on some blog. He wasn't some Pulitzer prize winning journalist in the thick of things in the Middle East."

173

"It's hard for me to think about too. But with this president we have, it makes it a little easier to go down. I think he's a narcissistic power hungry warmonger. That aside, let me lay out for you what I've got so far. Or rather, let me ask you one more question. Do you know how Joe was murdered?"

"They said it was a drive-by shooting," said Chuck, "but we've learnt different."

"What do you know?"

"It seems like he was leaving the bar with Stanley. Some time later, Stanley was hit by a hit and run driver. Joe went to help him and that's when he got shot. They don't know who did it."

"That's mostly true," I said. "Here's how it went down from what I've read in the police reports and witness statements. Seems Stanley was run down purposefully. There were no skid marks and it appears he was hit at about fifty miles per hour. The same guy who was driving the garbage truck that hit Stanley got out and put a bullet in the back of your son's head. That's pretty much all I've gotten out of the official report. And here's the thing. It's light on details and they haven't been leaning on the witnesses as hard as they should."

"Who are the witnesses?" asked Rebecca.

"Probably Seventh Sons' members."

"And they're saying they saw nothing?" she asked.

I shook my head.

"No. They're saying exactly what I told you. It's what they aren't saying that worries me."

"And what aren't they saying?"

"They're not telling who did it."

"Maybe they don't know who did it," offered Chuck.

"They know. Like I said. They described what I just told you. That means they must've been close enough to get a good description of who it was. At least in an overall sense. The reason they aren't saying can only be for one of three reasons."

"What are those reasons?" asked Rachel, not sure she wanted to know the answer.

"The first reason is that it's one of their own who did it. I don't like this reason. I don't see any connection with Joe or Stanley with the Seventh Sons. I think Stanley chose that bar because it was an unlikely place for him to be at. Assuming he was worried about being followed or spied on. The second reason is that it was one of their competitors. These outlaw groups usually won't rat out on each other unless there's a big win it for them. This is small potatoes. But I don't like this reason either. Again, for the same reasons as the first. I don't see Joe and Stanley being the outlaw types. And even if they were, you'd want to ask permission to do a hit in somebody else's back yard."

"So that leaves the last reason which is also the reason you like, and that means you think our government did it," said Rebecca.

"It's the only one of three choices that marginally makes sense. But as you asked. Why would our government want to murder a couple of civilians?"

"Why?" asked Rachel.

"Probably because Stanley knew something he shouldn't have. And in that case, sadly, Joe was collateral damage."

"But what could he possibly know?" asked Rachel.

"If we knew that, then I'd probably know who did it," I said. "What else do you know about Stanley."

I got shrugs.

"Did you know he was good with computers? Almost like a savant, so it seems."

Everybody shook their heads.

"We really knew very little about him," said Rebecca. "He wasn't one of Joe's friends. I'm up in Manhattan and I try to get together with Joe every couple of weeks. He never told me about Stan, but maybe that was because the last time I saw Joe he hadn't met Stan yet. Like Chuck and Rachel said, there was one phone call where Joe mentioned Stan as being this religious crackpot, who had a story, that Joe was going to see who called himself Spider-Man."

I nodded.

"OK. Then you probably didn't know that Stanley Spencer was a paranoid schizophrenic."

I took my mug of coffee and had a sip. I let that little bomb silently explode in their minds for a moment.

CHAPTER TWENTY-SIX
PLAYING WITH MADNESS

"I don't understand," said Rachel. "So you're saying that Stanley was mentally ill? That he was actually a crackpot then? If I can use that term."

I shook my head.

"No. I think it's beneficial for these agencies to employ someone like Stanley. I mean, if you're a three letter government agency and you're working on things that only conspiracy theorists might think of and it gets out that you're actually doing such things. Well then, being able to deny such things by pointing to a legitimate paranoid schizophrenic is an easy save."

They gave me blank stares for a while.

"Employing paranoid people basically makes it easy to deny anything if secret stuff gets out. Because after all, these people are mentally ill. Hell, they could deny that Stanley ever worked for them. For example, where do we usually keep our ID?"

"In our wallets," said Chuck.

"Right, unless you're at work. And if you work for the government surely you'll keep your ID on you at all times. You never know when it might come in handy."

"I don't understand what you're trying to say, Anthony," said Rachel.

I nodded my head.

"Yeah, I'm putting the cart before the horse. Witnesses came upon the scene almost immediately after it happened," I said. "Let me paint it for you. This G-Man runs over Stanley with a truck. By the time he gets out the witnesses are emptying out of the bar and coming up to see what's happened. That's how they know your son was shot. So, this G-Man doesn't have much time. The only thing he does is grab a backpack that Stanley had with him and he takes off. G-Man doesn't rifle through anyone's pockets."

"OK," said Rachel.

"And the only things found in Stanley's pockets was a business card and some cash. No ID. So either Stanley doesn't have ID, or he left it at his apartment for some reason. In that case, it's probably already been ransacked and taken by said agency. I'm just thinking out loud here. But if Stanley was as paranoid as it might seem, then there's a good chance he'd leave his ID at home because it might have a tracker in it. So maybe he did have something he was going to leak to Joe."

"Maybe Joe was a target then too," said Chuck. "If he'd already met with Stanley, maybe Stanley had given him the information."

I nodded my head.

"But how would they know where Stanley and Joe were?" asked Rachel. "You said they were using burner phones."

I nodded again.

"That's right. But Joe's personal phone was found at the scene. Or at least in a car he had borrowed from his friends. Dollars for dimes that's how they tracked them."

"This is getting very complicated," said Rachel. "Did Stanley have something he was going to leak or was he just a paranoid schizophrenic?"

"I believe he had something. His parents believe that he was still on his medication. And if that's the case then he was going to leak something and it wasn't just pure paranoia. But this is where things get interesting. Sarah and Saul Spencer saw their son, Stanley, in April for Sarah's birthday. At the time they thought he might have been off his medication."

"What gave them that impression?" asked Rebecca.

"He seemed paranoid. He had them put all their phones into Faraday bags to block all signals getting to them. This is how he had behaved before they had him diagnosed. There is still aluminum foil covering his window in his bedroom at their house. From what I heard, he could be pretty paranoid when off his meds."

"You did something similar when you got here," said Rebecca.

"That's right, because Stanley might have been paranoid but it wasn't without reason. And this fits my theory. Stanley's always been good with computers. He hacked into his school computer system to change a grade. Then he got a full ride to University of Tulsa. His parents are poor. They couldn't afford to send him to university but he got a scholarship from somewhere. I just don't know where from yet. He gets to go someplace else for his graduate work. I think it might be MIT. But he leaves shortly afterwards to go and work for a plumbing company."

"A plumbing company?" asked Rachel.

I nodded.

"Yeah. This is why I'm thinking we're dealing with the NSA. We've got Stanley who's real good at computers, so much so that he gets a free ride to the best state school and then he heads out to MIT. But MIT isn't good enough for him. He wants to work for a plumbing company."

"Maybe he needed money," offered Rebecca.

"Maybe, but someone with his kinds of skills doesn't need to work for a plumbing company. I mean how hard is their IT? I think it's a cover. If it's not a cover, then why is a journalist meeting with a plumber about a conspiracy that's supposed to rock the world? Makes no sense."

They all looked at me thoughtfully. Nobody had anything to offer.

"The plumbing company is called Pipe Dreams Plumbing & HVAC. I called them when I was at the Spencers. I asked to speak with Stanley. A surly woman who answered said nobody by that name worked there. I started to spell out the name and she hung up on me."

"Maybe she was having a bad day," said Rebecca.

I grinned at her. I started thinking she was having me on.

"Why do you think I'm here?" I asked.

"To help with the case."

"And if it was a simple hit and run, would any backwater sheriff's department let alone the Jersey PD need my help."

Rebecca didn't say anything.

"This isn't a simple hit and run. Your son, like Stanley, was murdered. Plain and simple. We need to find out why. If we get there, we get to the killers. So I'm pretty sure that this isn't a simple plumbing company. Not the least of which by the way they answer the phones. Stanley knew something. What he knew is what we've gotta find out. Are you with me?"

Rachel and Chuck nodded. Rebecca took longer.

"I just don't want to think of my government killing civilians. That's not the kind of world I want to live in."

"It's already the world we live in," I said. "It just usually doesn't hit so close to home."

I looked around and finished my coffee. Rachel's tea had gotten cold with a film of milk floating on the tea like pond scum.

"Now I want to tell you why I put your phones away."

I leaned in towards them on my elbows. They mirrored me.

CHAPTER TWENTY-SEVEN
Go Home

"SARAH Spencer showed me Stanley's room. It was a conspiracy theorist's haven. Lots of books on hacking and conspiracy theories from the Bilderberg Group like we've spoken about to the Federal Reserve. I had to do a bit of research on the way up here because I don't have my pulse on the heart of current conspiracy theories. Most of it sounds like crap with just a salting of legitimacy sprinkled in to help make it palatable."

"It is untrue. All of the conspiracies that I've read about," said Rachel. "From JFK to the Bilderberg Group and on. We're just good at making up stories and filling in gaps. Besides, I don't think we're really all that good at keeping secrets."

"But here's where things get interesting," I said. "Bear in mind that nobody knew I was going to see the Spencers. I only found out myself on Friday when I spoke with John. Two days ago. Yesterday I was with them. Two days ago I was with John just learning about this."

Rebecca drank the rest of her coffee.

"Stanley's room is still pretty much as it was when he lived with his parents. His computer is there. It's a pretty decent, high-end tower from what I can tell with dual monitors. Shiloh, Stanley's sister had told me that they played this online game together for years. It's called War Tyde, with a Y. Shiloh tells me that Stanley had told her he had found a way to save files within this online game, and he said if anything happened to him that she could have access to his account. He didn't give her the password but he gave her hints to it. It's a patchwork of bible verses."

I paused to look around.

"Are you with me so far?"

They all nodded their heads.

"I'm thinking that what's in this file that Stanley had saved online could be the key to why he was killed. So I boot up the computer and realize I need his computer password. I finally get it with Shiloh's help. I then start up a browser. And just as the browser opens and I type in the URL for War Tyde, the computer freezes up. Nothing I can do to unfreeze it. So I'm about to hard boot it when the screen slowly turns red. At the top is a skull and crossbones. Underneath that a message appears. 'Go home Mr. Carrick the case is closed'. That's what it said."

They all looked more concerned now. None of them spoke.

"So how did they know I was there?"

"Your cell phone," suggested Rachel.

"I thought about that. But I'm not sure that's the likely vector for them spying on me. Remember, two days ago I was in a bar having lunch with my buddy unaware I would be coming out here. The phone's pretty new. I've just had it for around a year. I haven't installed anything on it since the new year when my daughter helped me install some apps. All well known, well used apps. I don't open up attachments on it. I've never received a text from someone I didn't know."

"Then how did they know you were there?" asked Rebecca.

"They weren't spying on me. When I start a case I'm always on the lookout for that sort of thing. The road that the Spencers live on was practically empty. At least no vehicles like vans that could hide people in them. No, I think they probably overheard our conversation via one of the Spencers' phones. I think they've tapped into them somehow. And they've probably done the same with yours."

"What do we do then?" asked Rachel.

"I'd recommend you wipe your phones and do a fresh install. Best solution is probably to get a new phone, but that can be expensive. I'd start with a factory reset. I'd also ask that you get a burner to use just between us. I got one myself. I've asked Sarah Spencer to get one too. Write down my number."

I waited for a moment while Rachel and Rebecca got pen and a notepad out of their purses. Then I gave them the number and they wrote it down.

"Text me your phone numbers when you've got new burners."

"How much will it cost?" asked Rachel.

"I'll get you one," said Rebecca.

"They're not very expensive. I got one for around a hundred bucks."

"So they knew you were in the house with the Spencers," said Chuck, trying to figure out if he'd heard right. I nodded.

"That's kinda creepy," he said.

"More than that, Chuck," said Rachel, "it's down right scary."

"Yeah it is," I said. "But this is what governments can do now. We live in an Orwellian world. Like I said, it would probably be wise to wipe your phones."

I looked over at the TV. It was slim but not super slim. It was probably a plasma or maybe an LCD from some years back.

"How old is your TV?" I asked.

Chuck looked at it.

"Probably coming on ten years now," he said.

I nodded.

"That's good. It's probably not a smart TV Then. Probably not able to hook up the internet."

I looked around for reassurance.

"No, it's not hooked up to the internet," said Chuck.

"Good, because they can probably hack into TVs and things like that nowadays."

I looked around the room.

"Do you have any questions?" I asked.

"What about your safety?" asked Rebecca. "Aren't you worried that if, like you said, you're dealing with the NSA or some other government agency that they'll make you disappear too?"

I shrugged.

"Not too worried. There's a trail now with me being on this case. John Roberts knows about it. I'm going to get on the horn with him this evening and get him to buy a burner. Then I'm gonna give him updates every day. There'll be a paper trail of sorts. My biggest concern, honestly, is that I'm gonna be met with obfuscation and dead ends. That's why I want you to understand how difficult this case is. If it is the

NSA, or some entity like that, I might not be able to get you the resolution you'd like."

"We understand," said Rebecca. "It'd just be worse if something happened to you on top of everything else. Especially considering you won't let me pay for your time."

She was good. She was testing my resolve.

"I appreciate the concern. But if they start piling up too many dead bodies, it gets difficult for them to cover them up. Besides, I don't really know much at this stage other than it looks like Joe and Stan were targets of a hit. But that's as much speculation and gut feeling as anything else. No, they'll be trying to hamper me, and they can be pretty effective at it when they try."

I looked around to see if they had anything else for me.

"I'm sorry we couldn't be more helpful," said Rebecca.

"Not your fault," I said. "It's hard to figure out. It seems random and that makes solving it harder. Then you put the government behind it and it's not gonna get any easier. I'll do what I can and I'll keep you updated on your burners. Please don't talk about this to anyone, and if you talk about it amongst yourselves, please make sure your phones aren't around to listen in. The only thing I've got going for me at the moment is the element of surprise. And I need to use that to keep them off the trail so I can try and gather what evidence I can find."

I stood up. I figured it was time to get back to Cleveland. I wanted a hearty lunch and a bunch of cigarettes. I had a feeling that things from this point on were gonna get harder not easier. I went over to Chuck and shook his hand and told him not to get up. Rachel and Rebecca saw me out. Rebecca came out with me.

"I'm gonna smoke before I go," I said. She nodded. I

walked around to the driver's side of the car and opened up the back door. I got my smokes and lighter out of my jacket hanging from the grab handle. Rebecca came over to my side. I lit up the cigarette. I felt like a new man. I looked up and down the street. It was as quiet as a zombie apocalypse.

"This street doesn't do Lincoln justice," I said, trying to make conversation.

"Why is that?"

"He was a tall, great man. This street seems short and narrow."

Rebecca smiled at that. I sucked on my cigarette and blew smoke away from us. The air was crisp. I didn't want to stand out here indefinitely.

"I'd really like to pay you for your time," she said, looking up at me. "I know what it's like to struggle."

"Helping friends out ain't a struggle." ·

"Are you always this stubborn?" she asked in a friendly tone.

"Usually," I said. "It's helped me crack cases."

"But why are you so bent on not accepting money for helping us out with this case?"

I turned to look at her.

"Look," I said. "I told John this one's on me and I intend to keep it that way. It's very kind of you to want to help out. But even if you were paying, I don't think you'd be happy with the results."

"It's not the results that mean so much, Anthony, it's that you care. That you're going to give it your best."

I didn't say anything to that.

"I can just send you some cash in the mail," she said. "Or a check."

"A check won't be cashed and cash will just end up under

my mattress for the next tenant to find."

"God you're infuriating."

I smiled and smoked.

"So what are your next steps?" she asked.

"Heading up to Cleveland. From there I should be arriving at LaGuardia in the early evening. Tonight I won't be doing much. Tomorrow I'm gonna check in with a Jersey PD detective that John put me in touch with. I need somebody I can rely on when I'm there. When are you heading back?"

"Tomorrow. I'll be available if you need me. I'll text you my burner number as soon as I have it."

"Thanks. It could be helpful to have a friendly face out there."

She touched my upper arm. Her hand felt warm through my thin shirt.

"We're not expecting miracles," she said. I looked down at her. "Really, we don't. John's told us as much. We know this is a hard case. If you can't get to the bottom of it I hope you won't beat yourself up about it. You care. We can tell. And that's really what matters. The rest is just extra."

"I've solved every case I've been given. I aim to keep that record."

She took her hand away and smiled at me. I smoked my cigarette. The sky was blue. The blue of babies' hopes and dreams.

"Please keep my up to date, Anthony, and really, if there's anything you need, let me know."

"Will do," I said, and she left me and walked back into the house. I finished my cigarette and squashed it underfoot. I picked up the butt and tossed it into their black garbage cart. I got into my car and drove back to Cleveland.

CHAPTER TWENTY-EIGHT
PINK MUSTACHE

CLEVELAND to LaGuardia is practically a hop. It was the shortest trip I'd taken so far. Not counting the little puddle jumpers I'd taken back and forth from DFW to Stillwater. From tarmac to tarmac it's a little over an hour and a half. It gave me just enough time for a whiskey and some pretzels. Not the best combination. But it kept me full. LaGuardia is usually considered the crappiest airport in the whole of the United States. And that means they're trying real hard to get there. It's old and grungy and unloved, maybe like the mayor it was named after. That last part I might've made up, I have no opinion on Fiorello La Guardia. Maybe he'd be just as upset over it taking his name as you'd hope he'd be.

Coming in, it looks like you're landing on an aircraft carrier. A chatty old woman sitting next to me said the pilots call the airport the USS LaGuardia for that reason. She reminded me of my neighbor Martha, from back in Santa Monica. She was small and friendly, though she wasn't Cuban, she was Italian and lived in the Bronx. Said her name was Paloma.

Rikers is literally just a spitball away from the tip of the runway. A spitball that'd have to carry maybe a hundred yards, but that's practically a short swim. That makes me think that maybe LGA is a good place to land if you're visiting your deadbeat baby daddy with your three kids who's doing time for not being smart enough to wear a condom. Maybe Rikers is also why the cheap flights land at LaGuardia.

It was dark when we landed, sliding along gray runway next to the smooth, black body of the East River. A river likely full to overflowing with seedy secrets about this City of Broken Dreams, this Rotten Apple. But that might've just been me. The only times I'd been up here in recent memory were to clean up people's messes. Today wasn't any different.

I got my bags from the carousel and called myself a Lyft. Aibhilin had said I should try them out. Said they had pink mustaches on their cars. Said it was cheaper than a cab. I said I'd do it, just to keep her quiet. I didn't have to call anyone. It was all done in my app. I only had to wait five minutes before my ride arrived. The app told me his name was Jimmie Emerson. It had a pic of him too. When he arrived my phone turned pink. I saw a little light on his dash the same color. Maybe that was better than a pink mustache. I'd have to ask Aibhilin about that.

He helped with my bags and I got in the front seat. He was a young kid. Early twenties with a shitty mustache. It was shitty because it made him look like a pervert. It was thin and wiry. No substance to it. I didn't say anything about it.

He knew I was going to Jersey but I hadn't specified a particular place.

"Where can I take you?" he asked.

"I'm hungry and thirsty," I said. "Hungry for steak and thirsty for whiskey, Jimmie."

"Are you money?" he asked me.

"I'm not money, Jimmie, but I have some to pay for my meal."

He grinned at me.

"Nah man, I meant, like, are you a high rolla' or are you looking for something cheaper."

"The cheaper the better so long as the steak is good."

He nodded. He was driving like a gangster. He was leaning in towards me with his left wrist resting on the steering wheel.

"Lots of businessmen want something expensive. I figure they're making the company pay. So I take them to either Liberty Prime or Edward's. Both good, but you won't get out without paying forty or fifty beans for some meat. I think what you want, my man, is something different. How do you like Korean?"

I thought about that for a minute. It got me thinking. It'd be a talking point when I met So-yi tomorrow. So I figured why not.

"It's cheap?"

"Yeah, man. Ten bucks for some meat. I'd recommend the Seoul Cheesesteak or, if you're up for something a little different, but probably their best meal, it'll be their Korean Crepe. Picture this, my man, bulgogi rib eye with Monterey jack cheese, onions, mushrooms in a crazy tasty crepe with kimchi and garlic."

"What's bulgogi?"

"Nothing but tastiness, that's what," he said, grinning at me from ear to ear. I wasn't smiling. "Basically it's just their style of how they make the meat. It's thinly shaved and marinated. Trust me, my man, you'll dig it."

"Alright, take me there," I said.

It didn't change his trajectory and it didn't change my price which was gonna be around sixty bucks. I also knew the rough route he was gonna take if he was going to use the recommended one which took us through Jackson Heights, Brooklyn and across the Holland Tunnel into Jersey.

All the way, Jimmie Emerson was a chatty Kathy. He told me all about growing up in the South Bronx. How it wasn't as bad as it might have seemed. Said it was a gentrified neighborhood. Meaning it was up and coming. He liked saying he lived in the South Bronx on account of how it made him seem tough. He said people still had the wrong idea about the area. Said the Bronx had been revitalized in the 80s. He was born in '95. I asked him. He said it'd been a swell place to live. Swell wasn't the word he used. Dope, I think is what he chose.

He said he was studying journalism at Brooklyn College. It was the cheapest. In fact the only public college with a journalism program in New York. Said it cost him almost ten times less. Said Columbia University charges 55 grand. I asked him if that was for the degree.

"Nah, my man, that's just for the year."

"Jesus," I said.

I told him I'd spent four years at the California College of Arts and Crafts as it was called back then. Didn't cost me more than eight grand for my full four years, and it was a private college. Still is.

"That's dope, my man. I'm paying seven grand a year for Brooklyn College. Well, I would if I was doing it in four years, but I'm trying to stay out of debt. I figure it'll take me five years. I figure that means I've got three more semesters."

I couldn't believe how expensive school was. Not that the eight grand back in the late eighties, early nineties was chump change, but it wasn't the almost 60 grand CCAC was charging now. And that's if you roomed for free with your folks.

I asked him if he'd heard of TrashCan. He sure had. He was hoping to get an internship with them this coming summer. He wanted to write about music. He knew a lot about hip hop. Asked if he could put some on. I declined. I suggested jazz. He was cool with that so he dialed in Jazz 88. 88 on account of where you find it on the dial. It was after seven-thirty and we were listening to The Checkout. All about new and upcoming jazz. Some good stuff, but I prefer the old school cats.

We were in the tunnel before he started asking about what I was doing in town.

"I'm here to solve a murder," I said.

"Shit, you for real?"

"Real as Jessica Biel," I said. It sounded cooler in my mind. Figured I should stick with painting and not poetry.

"That was Joe Severn, right?"

I nodded. Traffic was inching along the tunnel like slow little red glow worms.

"Thought they said it was just a random drive by."

"That would make sense," I said.

He didn't say anything for a while. I figured speaking with Jimmie about it wasn't gonna screw anything up.

"So you figure it isn't a drive by?"

"Well, I'm here to try and figure out what it could be."

"Yeah, that was pretty fucked up. I don't know why anyone would kill him, for real. I mean, he was a good journalist an' all, but he wasn't exactly rocking the boat."

195

That was good for me to know. I hadn't had a chance to read any of his writing. Jimmie looked over at me.

"Yeah, my man. I can dig it. I see it now. With that fedora of yours, you do look like one of them old style PIs."

I didn't say anything to that. I was leaning back on my seat. My fedora was tilted forward on my head.

"How'd you become a PI?" he asked.

"Sorta fell into it," I said. "Left the job in '02 after ten years. I'd read all the best hardboiled stuff through college. Hammett, Chandler, Cain, McDonald and others. I drink too much and smoke too much. I've got week knees for buxom blondes and a tough chin. I figured it was a natural fit. A pal from the force got me my first gig. Been doing it every since."

"Man, I bet you've seen some stuff," he said.

"You live long enough, everyone sees some stuff. But the job puts you on the fast track."

"What's been your worst case?" he asked.

"Dealing with the Chinese gangs bringing over underaged sex slaves. Some as young as six years old."

He looked over at me with his furrowed brow.

"Dude, is that real. Here in America?"

I'd gone from being his man to his dude. Couldn't tell if that was a compliment or an insult. I nodded at him. We pulled up at Kraverie. It was a small place on the ground floor of what looked like an apartment block. It was colored green. A sort of North Korean military green. But it coulda been any kind of dark military green. I noticed because it looked odd against the red brick and the orange brown of the Spanish style apartments above it.

"I need a motel. Anywhere close?" I asked before getting out of the car.

"Your best bet if you wanna pay a hundred bucks or thereabouts is probably Hudson Plaza Motel. Up from there you've got some choices around a hundred fifty. All on the west side. Most up by the north west, the Plaza's down south west. You'll need a ride."

"Good, I'll call you."

He reached out and gave me his card which had his phone number on it.

"This is my direct he said. We can do it off the book. I get to keep a little more for myself that way."

I nodded and walked into the tiny Korean joint.

CHAPTER TWENTY-NINE
BIG BREAKFAST

I called John at work on Monday morning. I figured LAPD's landlines likely weren't tapped by a nefarious three letter agency.

"Hey, Sid, thanks for calling," he said.

"Yeah, figured it was a good way to leave a trail."

"That serious, huh?"

"Let me put it to you this way. I tried to get onto Stanley's computer he still had in Stillwater and I got a message telling me to fuck off."

"You're saying Stanley's computer was hacked?"

"Yeah. Screen went red, got the whole skull and crossbones schtick and a message telling me to go home, that the case was closed."

"So they knew you were there," he said.

"Yeah. You tell anyone?"

"Nope. This is on the DL, Sid."

"I figured they've tapped into the Spencer's personal phones and the Severn's too. Asked everyone to get burners and text me their number. I picked up one too. I want you to get one, Rotten. Then text me the number."

I gave him my number to text it to.

"So you're thinking this was a government hit."

"Looking like it. I was trying to get online onto this game that Stanley played a lot called War Tyde. His sister says he figured out a way to save stuff in this online game. I'm hoping to get access to that and see what's in it. That's probably the key right there."

"Who do you think it is then?"

"Hard to tell. These hits have been executed like it's the CIA, but the computer chops leads me to believe we're dealing with the NSA. I'm thinking the NSA has militarized some of their people for just such purposes."

"I'll look into that," he said.

"Other than that, Rachel, Chuck and Rebecca are holding up pretty good all things considered. Rebecca still thinks well of you. Can't figure out why."

Roberts laughed on the other end.

"Thanks pal, and listen, get yourself a vest or something. Just in case."

"Not gonna help me with a headshot," I said.

"Then don't give them your head to aim at," he said.

I hung up the phone and took a drag of my cigarette. Thank God some motels still had smoking rooms. Smelt like living in an ashtray, but you got over that after your first smoke. I poured the last of the coffee out of a carafe that even a midget would've found stingy. I dialed So-yi's number. I wasn't sure if she was working today or not. I got an answer on the second ring.

"This is Sue," said an all American voice. It was deep and sultry. It was the kind of voice men pay money for just to dial up and listen to. It was the kind of voice you'd want to hear next to you, naked on a pillow. I wondered if the body owned the voice. Nothing worse than a bad body that adopts a voice like that.

"Sue, this is Anthony Carrick. John Roberts from LAPD might have let you know I'd be calling."

"Yeah, Anthony, he did. You're in Jersey already?"

"I am and eager to see how we can crack open this case."

"Timing's good," she said. "I'm off for the next few days. Where are you situated?"

"I'm staying at the Hudson Plaza Motel," I said.

"Down there on West 63rd?" she asked.

"If you say so. I didn't take a good look when I arrived."

"Yeah, you're down there off of 63rd," she said. "You're not far from Route 440. Can you hear it?"

I listened for a moment.

"Sure can. Sounds like I'm being lulled by the waves."

She laughed at that.

"Are you ready?"

"Ready and eager," I said.

"OK," she said. "I did some snooping around. I was able to get some stuff from the case file. Not much in here considering it's a homicide."

"Not surprised," I said.

"I'll see you in about an hour. I'll come to your motel."

"See you then."

I looked at the time. It was coming on ten-thirty. There was a McDonald's about a quarter mile down the street, heading east. I figured that was a way to pass the hour while I waited. I looked out my window and saw that it was snowing softly. The weatherman was calling for the snow to continue into the evening with highs in the forties. I should've brought a warmer coat. But when you live in LA and get asked to travel to New York last minute, those kinds of things aren't top of mind.

I figured an undershirt, button-down shirt and my jacket would do well enough for a five minute walk. And on my head I put my hat. I made the walk brisk and the weather wasn't all that bad. On my way over I was figuring I was gonna have a burger. But by the time I stepped in I'd settled on breakfast.

I chose what McDonald's optimistically calls the Big Breakfast. It might be considered a big breakfast for a petite woman watching her figure. For me it was a decent sized snack. But I took a large coffee with it and that helped plug the remaining holes in my hunger. The one thing you can rely on with the big chains like McDonald's, is the consistency of their product. It was tasty and satisfying. If you've never had the Big Breakfast it consists of scrambled eggs, a sausage patty, hash browns and a biscuit. It's not gonna win any awards but you'll be happy and satisfied with the money you paid.

Which got me thinking about the crepe I had at the Korean joint last night. That was surprisingly good. I was thinking maybe I'd take So-yi there for dinner. That might gain me some points.

I picked a table that had the local paper left on it. It was The Jersey Journal. It was the same kind of paper you'd find anywhere across these States of ours. Bright colored photos on the front page with big headlines that the kids call clickbait.

I leafed through it to see if I could find anything interesting about Joseph or Stanley. There wasn't anything. There was plenty of petty crime to go around but nothing about my two victims. I ate the rest of my meal in silence and took my coffee to go. The place was mostly empty when I left and by the time I arrived back at the motel I only had around ten minutes to wait for So-yi. I put on The Price is Right and watched the worst of us get excited about the least interesting things. But that got me to thinking about government hits. I wanted to see what files Stanley might have hidden in his online game. But I figured I should see his boss first.

CHAPTER THIRTY
LIGHT ON EVIDENCE

I met So-yi Park down in the lobby and walked her back up to my room. It didn't make anyone uncomfortable. First of all, if she was going to be a hooker, she'd be a high priced one and not seen in a joint like this. Secondly it's eleven-thirty in the morning. An odd time to be knocking boots with hookers. Thirdly, she wasn't dressed to impress.

She was a looker though. Full red lips helped along by lipstick and nice big brown eyes. Her hair was black and shiny and shoulder length. She wore blue jeans, runners and a winter jacket over a long-sleeved t-shirt. The t-shirt had a logo of some sort of K-pop band that I hadn't heard of. So-yi told me they were called the Wonder Girls. Their name was written in Korean and they looked like anime dolls. Maybe 'cos that was how they'd been stylized in the logo as a cartoon.

So-yi was a slim woman with curves in all the right places. Her hourglass figure stopped time and I lost myself for a moment in admiration. Her bosom was ample and if I was a younger man I might have tried my luck. I put her in her late twenties to early thirties. She was about five-four and friendly.

"Are you carrying a phone?" I asked.

She nodded.

"Do you mind if I have it for a minute?"

She took it out of her handbag. I noticed a compact Sig Sauer P229 in there too. She gave me her phone. It was a fancy new smartphone.

"Is that 9mm or 40 Smith and Wesson?"

"9mm. We moved to them about a year ago. I like it much better."

I took the phones over to the small bar fridge and put them inside. I figured it would do well enough. At least against eavesdropping. So-yi looked at me funny, but she didn't say anything.

"Maybe we should put what we have on the bed," she said, looking around and finding the table wanting. I agreed.

So-yi took out a folder from her shoulder bag and spread the contents out on the bed.

"These are copies I had made on the way here," she said. "Not being primary I didn't want to risk a trail by signing out the files. I took photos of them with my phone."

"Makes sense," I said. "I've seen the witness statements from the bikers and the officer notes. It hasn't been very helpful."

She arranged everything neatly and then looked up at me.

"Yeah, you're right. This is not going to alleviate that concern," she said.

We spent a moment looking over what we had. There were the officer notes. Those didn't tell me much I didn't know. They described the scene and what they found. They also alluded to who they'd interviewed. Maybe I was being unkind but there wasn't much to go on. What I did find out is that the primaries on this case were Detectives Wilson Wast and Devon Schirru.

"Have you spoken to either of these guys?" I asked.

"Yeah, they said there's nothing to go on. It's probably gonna end up a cold case."

"How many homicides you get in Jersey City each year?"

"We had twenty-four last year."

"That's not a lot," I said.

"No. Not a ton. Thank God. But still, we've got city hall and the mayor on our backs to try and get higher closure figures."

"Do you think Wast and Schirru followed through?" I asked.

So-yi looked down at the array of paper on the bed and nodded slowly.

"I think so. I mean, I got the impression they had done the best they could. But everything runs cold here. This is still an open case. But honestly, I can't think of much else they could do. Can you?"

Maybe I was being a little hard on them. They'd spoken to the families but gotten nothing of note. Much like I had. They hadn't visited them, but then that wasn't surprising. Homicide detectives very rarely made out of state visits, and if they needed to, a local LEA would help out.

The two detectives had interviewed the families. They'd interviewed the bikers best they could. They'd interviewed colleagues of both Stan and Joe, including Joe's boss who I wanted to see today. I took down the names of those colleagues just in case.

The receptionist at Pipe Dreams Plumbing was Marni

Coxley. Two plumbers there had also given brief statements. They were Alexander Granary and Rudolph Hodgkin. Everyone had pretty much said the same thing about Stan. He was a quiet, hard worker who kept to himself and didn't socialize much with the others. He kept their computer systems and network working. Nobody knew he struggled with mental illness. It all seemed above board.

At the TrashCan they'd spoken to Joe's Editor, Rufin Flatter and a colleague of Joe's named Reed Soakes. Wasn't much there I didn't know either. Reed said Joe was cagey about meeting a guy that he called spiderman. Said the guy seemed a little whacko and had given a name of "Shem" at one point. Joe hadn't said much about it because Reed got the impression he didn't know much about what the story was going to be about. The only thing Reed or Rufin knew was that this "spiderman" was supposed to have a story that would rock the US to the core.

There wasn't anyone else to speak to. The Rattlin' Chain was in an area that was made up of businesses, most of which were closed at the time of the murders. There was a kebab place down the road, but that was in the opposite direction of the accident and they hadn't seen anything. Hadn't actually heard anything either. But then the notes had suggested the place was loud with Arab music when the officers entered to speak with the owner.

So-yi was right. There wasn't a lot to go on. I wanted to speak with Wast and Schirru just for my own clarification, but they'd probably run the case cold.

The only other items on the bed were a couple of photographs of both victims and the coroner's report. The report suggested severe blunt force trauma as the cause of death for Stanley and a gunshot wound to the head as the cause for Joe. This was pretty obvious. What was interesting, however, about Joe's death was that he looked fairly good for a man shot in the back of the head with a bullet at close range. What I meant by that was that there was no exit wound. That was a small mercy. At least for Rebecca, Rachel and Chuck.

The entry wound was at the back of the head near the crown. The bullet had gone in at an angle and finally got stopped at the rear right shoulder. The coroner had found the bullet behind the scapula. It must've bounced around a bit on bone and gristle. The bullet was a 9mm. That explained why it likely didn't exit. Well, that and the angle of the bullet's trajectory. The coroner's report gave no indication of what type of handgun it was. Could've been a whole bunch of different ones.

The FBI carries Glocks. And those Glocks are recently shooting 9mm. The CIA uses whatever the hell it wants. But often you'll find Glocks there too. Most LEAs will follow the FBI's lead because they're the ones doing most of the research on the best bang for ballistics. Without seeing the gun or testing it, it's hard as hell to tell which handgun was used to shoot Joe. It could be anything taking 9mm, from Astra to Zastava and all the letters in between. I looked back at So-yi.

"I guess they've done about as good as they could," I offered.

"Were you expecting less?"

"Do you know Wast and Schirru?"

"Casually," she said. "They seem like decent hard working cops from what I've seen. But looking at what we've got. What else could they have done? If you can think of something, let me know, because I'm just not seeing it. You know how hard these cases are to solve. These are pretty much all the people involved and the witnesses are few and far between. I'd like to interview them myself. But other than that. We don't have much to go on."

I looked around at the sheets of paper on the bed. There wasn't a lot. It looked like we were trying to put a collage together. A morbid one, but one nonetheless.

"You're right. I guess I'm just a bit jaded about this case. I'm doing it as a favor for a friend."

"Me too," she said. I looked at her. She was right. She was doing me and John a favor. "I want to catch these guys. But you know it's going to be a challenge."

I looked around at the bed again. She was right. We needed something to crack open this case and I was hoping whatever it was that Stan had saved on War Tyde's servers was our missing piece.

"I'm glad you're here," I said. "I know John's appreciative too."

"I'm happy to help," she said. "I just get the impression you're cagey about all of us. Do you think some of us might be corrupt?"

She was direct. I liked that. I shrugged.

"I don't know," I said. "You're the first Jersey cop I've met."

"Well then, let me be the first to reassure you that Jersey cops are just like LA cops and New York cops. Most of us are trying to do the best we can. We joined to make a difference in our communities. Yeah, there's gonna be some bad apples but we try to weed them out and get rid of them."

"Fair enough," I said. Then I took a few minutes to bring her up to speed with my meetings with the Spencers and the Severns. The Severns weren't able to offer much input. You know that. But what had happened at the Spencers with Stan's computer was something. There was obviously something greater going on here than just a simple hit or drive-by shooting.

"So that's why you've put our phones in the fridge?"

I nodded.

"I'm getting paranoid. My phone is new from last year," I said. "I haven't added any apps in several months. I don't get messages from anyone I don't know and I don't open up attachments on it that I'm not expecting."

"I use the same precaution. I got my iPhone just a few weeks ago. It's practically brand new. I've only installed popular apps and the ones I need. I doubt they'd have hijacked me yet."

"This is the thing. I'm not an expert. But clearly they hacked into the Spencers. I mean the only way they knew I was there was probably from listening in live while I was there or the day before when John called to let them know I was on my way. Still, that's a helluva fast turn around to hack into a computer. Unless it was set up weeks before."

I shook my head and looked back down at the bed again. I hadn't told So-yi what Shiloh had told me about War Tyde.

"Stan's sister, Shiloh, told me that she and he used to play this online game a lot over the past several years. It's called War Tyde. I didn't tell you that I was trying to access it when the computer was hacked. Shiloh tells me that Stan had told her he'd found a way to store files on War Tyde's servers. He said if anything happened to him she could access his account and find these files. I got the impression there was some damning information on them but I have no details what it's about."

"I just got a new laptop a couple of weeks ago. It's an

early Christmas present from my parents. We can try to access the account on that."

I nodded.

"There's a few things I want to do first before we get to that stage. I want to try and gather as much information as possible. I want to reinterview friends and colleagues of Joe's. I want to speak to the bikers, and I want to call in a plumber before we tip them off with trying to get back online."

"But they probably already know you're trying to get onto the online game," she said.

I shook my head.

"I don't think so. The computer froze before a connection to War Tyde was set. All it looked like to them was that someone was accessing Stan's computer. And they probably saw me sitting at it, or assumed it was me."

"So, Captain," said So-yi, smiling. "What do you want to do first?"

"I want to head on over to the Bronx and visit the offices of the TrashCan. Did you drive here?"

So-yi nodded. She cleaned up the papers from the bed while I got our phones. They were cold and frosty like a nice cold beer. But that wasn't what I was thirsty for. I was thirsty for justice.

CHAPTER THIRTY-ONE
FIFTH FLOOR

So-yi had parked right out front. It was still snowing. A light carpet of which lay upon her silver car like a blanket. It was the new Honda Civic Type R. She got the snow brush out from the trunk and I took it from her. I wiped it down and put it back in the trunk. I climbed in. The front seats were roomier than I was expecting.

"You've got all the newest toys," I said.

She turned to me with a serious face.

"I'm on the take," she said.

I squinted at her. She punched me softly on the shoulder.

"Relax, Anthony. I'm a single woman who likes to spend money on some of the finer things. It's not like I'm driving a Porsche."

I nodded. She was a detective and probably had ten or so years on the job. I decided to be bold.

"How much do you make?"

"Not as much as a New York detective. But I pulled in a little over 100k last year with some overtime."

I nodded. That sounded about right. For a single woman, she could have a nice car and a nice apartment and still eat out all the time. I needed to get my head in the game. Roberts wouldn't have set me up with someone shady.

"Didn't mean anything by it," I said.

So-yi spun out of her parking spot, sliding the front wheels on the wet snow.

"Think nothing of it. John told me you were jaded and salty. But he said you had your reasons."

I didn't say anything to that. So-yi was a fast driver. I got the sense she liked to drive fast. She should've moved out into the country. It didn't take long for traffic to slow us down. I don't think she got past fifty before we headed onto the I-95. Traffic picked up quicker there through North Bergen. The needle crept past seventy but not much further. We slowed down again coming onto the George Washington Bridge and from there we didn't get above thirty. I didn't have my eyes fixed on the dial the whole time.

The ride was comfy. But if you're gonna be in a big city you might as well have a comfortable ride. 'Cos there ain't no way in hell you're gonna be able to enjoy a sports car as much as you'd like. My LeSabre was exactly the kind of car that offered that ride. But it was old. Older than me it seemed like sometimes.

The TrashCan is not far from the zoo. It was down in Port Morris on the border with Hunts Point. I got all of this from So-yi. She was giving me the ten dollar tour as we drove through the Bronx. Hunts Point and Port Morris, she said, were sort of being diversified. Mixed use, is what she called it. And you could tell. There were homes and businesses all over the place without much sense of order to it. Though it looked like that was trying to change.

We pulled up to a low, five story building, that looked like it could've been an apartment at one point. The bottom level was full of small businesses including a coffee shop. So-yi suggested a coffee and I wasn't about to argue. It was a fancy place. Independently owned. Bean Scene is what they called it. The prices were high and the coffee was dark. One out of two ain't bad. The barista told us we had to go around the side to the main entrance to get into the TrashCan. All four of the upper floors were owned by Webswum.

So-yi got something fancy with milk and syrup and whipped cream. I wasn't paying attention. I got a large dark roast. Used ample cream and sugar to make it worth So-yi's money she'd spent.

The building was a salmon colored brick building not trying to look fancy.

"They're going to mess this place up just like they've done elsewhere," she said.

I didn't know what she meant.

"There're permits already in place for at least two luxury high rise towers. Right now, this place is pretty affordable. It's sort of artsy and bohemian. Pretty safe now that it's being gentrified. But you wait, in a couple of years when the first of those luxury apartment towers goes up, this place is going to push all these middle-income folks out."

"Happening everywhere," I said, trying to add to the conversation.

We walked into the large lobby of the building. It had a glass face and marble or tile floors. I wasn't a contractor and I couldn't tell. There were some uncomfortable looking couches dotted around amongst some trees. The back was a barricade of security desks and a body scanner. We walked up to the security desk. They were dressed in the same

215

uniform you see everywhere in large cities. Navy jacket and gray pants. Not meant to be intimidating but it means the same thing.

A large black guy looked up at us from behind a bank of monitors. Next to him was a similarly sized white guy. I started singing the first couple of lines of Ebony and Ivory in my head. I didn't think offering them a rendition was gonna help. Though my intentions were pure.

"We're here to see Rufin Flatter and Reed Soakes of TrashCan," said So-yi.

"Are they expecting you ma'am?" asked the black guy. He was friendly and very cordial.

"No," she said.

"I'm sorry, you'll have to make an appointment," he said, his friendliness unwavering. "We've had incidents here before and I'm afraid this is how we do things now."

So-yi put her hand into her purse. The black guy watched her very carefully. He looked like he might have had some training. But I figured if push came to shove I could lead him in a dance. The white guy seemed unperturbed. So-yi pulled out her police ID.

"We have further questions about the Severn homicide," she said.

"Of course," he said, standing up. "You should have led with that."

His smile was consistent and his tone still friendly.

"Are you carrying?" he asked her.

"Yes, in my purse," she said, "and it'll be coming with me."

"Of course," he answered good-naturedly. "Please step on through the scanner."

We both walked through. It didn't beep when So-yi

walked through it. It didn't beep with me either. But I wasn't packing. Maybe the bell was broken.

"Just head to the fifth floor and reception will help you out," he said.

We got into the elevator and rode the short distance to the top floor. The elevator panel was digital and gave us a rundown of the news of the day according to Webswum Incorporated.

CHAPTER THIRTY-TWO
NOT A RUFFIAN

THE doors opened up to a large waiting area. There was a young woman waiting on a couch reading a woman's magazine. She was dressed casually in jeans and a sweatshirt and a black parka. The parka was open. Most likely because it was too hot to keep it closed indoors. She had a nose ring and a couple of earrings. Her hair was short in a boyish cut and dyed jet black. There was another couch on the other side of us that was empty. There was a young woman behind a tall desk who wore a discreet mic and earphone combo. The logo of TrashCan was on the front of her desk. Behind her was a floor to ceiling frosted glass wall with an electronically controlled door. I spotted two cameras pointing towards the elevators at about eight feet high.

On the main reception desk was a potted plant in an ornately colored mosaic tile pot. I figured there was probably another camera hidden in that pot. I was right, though it took me a while to notice the lens hidden amongst the multifaceted and multi-colored tiles that made up the pot.

You wouldn't find it on a casual look.

Emily had a name tag that told us that. She looked up at us as we walked over to her behind her desk. She was young and blonde and hip. She wore faded jeans and sweatshirt over a t-shirt. The sweatshirt had the same TrashCan logo on it. It was a stylized trashcan with the lid coming open and letters floating out of it. The name was underneath it all. It was in a dark gray and the letters in a dark, almost maroon red. That was pretty much the color and decor around the reception area. The walls attached to the glass back wall weren't painted this dark red and gray in totality, rather they gave the impression of those colors.

"Hi, and welcome to TrashCan. How can I help you?"

Emily was friendly. Friendlier than the guard downstairs. I decided to let So-yi lead. She pulled out her ID and showed it to Emily.

"We'd like to speak with Rufin Flatter, the Editor-in-Chief. It's regarding the Severn homicide."

So-yi spoke low enough so that the woman sitting on the couch by the elevator wouldn't be able to hear.

"Certainly," she said. "He pronounces it Raff-in." She punched a couple of numbers on her computer keyboard. "The police are here to see Mr. Flatter about Joe's murder," she said. She nodded at nothing in particularly and then tapped another key on her keyboard. She looked up at us.

"His assistant will be right out to take you to him. Please have a seat." She noticed our coffees. "Would you like anything else besides what you have?"

We shook our heads and went and sat down in the available couch. There wasn't a lot of available sitting room. But then from the effort you needed to maintain to get up here, it wasn't surprising. Only those who were invited needed a place to sit it seemed. We didn't have to wait long. The frosted glass door in front of us opened up from behind in under a couple of minutes. A slim young man, also in his mid-twenties walked towards us. He wore glasses and his hair was styled in what I called the surprised wave. Short on the sides and tuft up front on top. He was clean shaven and wore light blue pants that ended above his ankles. On his feet he wore brown loafers without socks. Over top a pink dress shirt he wore a slightly darker blue jacket. Around his neck was a red and gray bowtie. It might have been a haphazard look on anyone else, but he pulled it off. In my mind I figured he was gay. He walked up to us offering a well manicured hand.

"Adam Sizzle," he said, without a smirk or any sense of irony. "Assistant to Rufin Flatter."

His voice was effeminate. He was most certainly gay. I tried to hold back a smirk of my own. On account of his name. He was certainly a handsome man, but I couldn't believe that was his birth name. Though truth can be stranger than fiction.

"Detective So-yi Park," she said, shaking his hand, and then looking at me. "My associate Anthony Carrick."

We shook hands and it seemed to me that Adam took a little longer both holding my hand and sizing me up than what was likely to have been deemed appropriate for a first meeting.

"Please come with me."

He showed us through the frosted glass door. The back of this floor was large and open. It also had similar gray and red decor but it was bright and light in tone. There must have been over two or three dozen clumps of desks in groups of two, and four and perhaps as many as eight. It looked like a tech startup. If you can rely on movies as your resource. I didn't see anyone who looked older than forty.

"Is Reed Soakes around, Adam?" I asked. "We'd like to see him before we go."

"He's over there," said Adam, pointing in the far right corner, amongst a group of four desks. Three clearly had owners, one of them was vacant, but only Reed occupied a chair.

We continued to walk down towards the back of this large open area. There were four offices at the back. They had similarly styled floor to wall frosted glass walls like we had just walked through, with one difference. At around the five foot mark was a band of clear glass a couple of feet in width. As we get closer we saw placards on the sides of the doors to each office. The door on the far right was "Rufin Flatter" and underneath that was "Editor-in-Chief". I didn't care about the other three. Though I did catch "Publisher" on one of them.

Adam knocked on the glass door and walked in. We followed him. Behind a large white desk with a computer monitor on it and a bunch of magazines and newspapers sat a man of average build. I don't have to describe him. He looked like a living, breathing version of Spider-Man's boss. The Editor at the Daily Bugle. I didn't know his name. He was missing the toothbrush mustache but carried a full one instead. And he didn't have a stogie. Though in a clean, never used ashtray sat a chocolate cigar. I'd put him in his early fifties. He looked up at us as we walked in and stood up.

"Sir, this is Detective So-yi Park and her associate Anthony Carrick. They're here to see you about Joseph Severn," said Adam.

Flatter nodded at him. Adam turned and looked at me. He put his hand on my shoulder.

"I'll let Reed know you're expecting to see him when you're finished with Mr. Flatter."

I nodded and with that Adam left. Flatter reached out across the desk and shook our hands. He gave us his name. I got the feeling everyone wanted to make sure we knew how to pronounce Rufin. We sat down and in front of us, towards our side of the desk was a wooden box of cigars. There were about three-quarters of them left. They were clearly of the chocolate variety. Wrapped in gold foil with a blue band around the one end.

Flatter leaned over, picked up the box and offered me one. I'm always up for a gag. And a chocolate gag is pretty fun. I took one. So-yi declined. He grabbed his and bit off the end.

"So you know who you look like?" I asked him.

He nodded, chewing on his chocolate.

"Not at first. But Joe eventually had the courage to tell me. In his honor I've been buying these chocolate cigars these past couple of weeks and offering them to anyone who comes into the office. J. Jonah Jameson, Publisher and Editor-in-Chief of the Daily Bugle."

I nodded at him and unwrapped the top end of my cigar.

"I'm grateful for the full mustache," I said.

"This style is called the chevron. Not that you care. But ever since Hitler took to using the toothbrush, well, let's just say it's gone out of fashion."

He laughed and bit some more off his cigar. He patted his stomach.

"I might have to put an end to these. At my age the extra calories aren't helpful."

"You have pretty tight security here," I said. "Anything to do with Joe?"

I bit the top off my cigar. It was creamy and smooth

chocolate. Not the cheap flavored chalk you get at the dollar store.

"No. We've had the odd problem for a few years now. We write on some pretty controversial topics, especially here at the TrashCan. All sorts of weirdos come by wanting to sell us odd stories or we get patriots threatening to blow up the building if we write something unfavorable about David Troll for example. We've also had the odd incident of violent boyfriends trying to get up here to engage with their exes. It's a security measure."

"So what sorts of things do you write about here?"

"Well, Webswum has a variety of properties. We write about politics and malfeasance of all sorts. Mostly government. Local, state, federal. On other floors other properties write about vehicles, tech, entertainment. Here at TrashCan we seem to get the ire of the public by and large."

"Which I suppose, brings us to why we're here," I said. "What was Joe working on last?"

I reached for my coffee and drank a good mouthful.

"I'd put him onto somebody who I thought was a crackpot at first. Still not sure about the veracity of what he had to say. He only went by the name Spider-Man. Ironic, isn't it."

"I don't understand," said So-yi.

"Well, what with me looking like I do."

So-yi nodded.

"Like Spider-Man's boss?"

Flatter nodded.

"So you spoke to this spiderman?" I asked.

"Yeah, a few times. I told him we weren't interested without some sort of proof to back up his claims."

"And what claims were those?"

"He said he had information that would literally rock the

world to its very foundation. I asked him what sorts of things. He said it was about things that only conspiracy buffs wouldn't be shocked by. At that point I knew we were dealing with a conspiracy theorist or worse, a crackpot."

Flatter ate more of his cigar. It was now half the size it had originally been. It had started out at about six inches long and as thick as my thumb.

"But he kept calling. Said he wanted to speak with a real journalist. I finally relented and put Joe onto him."

"Why Joe?"

"In hindsight I shouldn't have. Obviously. But Joe was one of my best investigative reporters. A real up and comer. He was working on a real interesting piece about police brutality and seniors."

"What's happened to this story?" I asked.

"It's been given over to Reed Soakes. It's a good story. In a nutshell, there are a handful of police officers in this city who are abusing their parents at the senior homes they're in and it appears like the staff is turning a blind eye to it. It's going to be very damaging to the NYPD."

"Any chance it's related to what happened to Joe?"

Flatter shook his head slowly as if he was worried about hurting it. I drank more coffee and ate more cigar.

"I don't see how. This Spider-Man wanted to meet Joe out in Jersey. As far as I can tell, there's no connection. But getting back to why I chose Joe. Like I said, he's my best investigative reporter. And when you've been a pressman for as long as I have, you never fully discount a potential story without investigating it. That's why I wanted Joe to take a look."

"Was he able to uncover anything before he died?" I asked.

Flatter shook his head slowly again.

"No. This Spider-Man was pretty cagey. Kept quoting bible verses though. That made me think we were probably going to get nowhere with him. But then, the very last text I got from Joe intrigued me. It's in the police report. I've kept it too."

Flatter reached for his cell which was on the right side of his desk. He tapped away at it for a short while. Then he showed it to us.

"There's actually something to this spiderman character. You won't believe it. I'll fill you in tomorrow."

Flatter took it back and put his phone back down.

"Don't know why he spells Spider-Man the wrong way," he said.

CHAPTER THIRTY-THREE
BACK UP

"THAT'S how he wanted it spelled," I said. "I read it in the notes someplace."

Flatter shrugged.

"In the newspaper business we get a little prickly about things like that," he said.

"What time was it again when you received that text?" I asked.

Flatter picked up his phone and tapped away.

"It's says it was at 11:03pm."

"Just before he went to help," I said. "Minutes before he was dead."

I ate more chocolate and cut it with the last few sips of my coffee.

"There's nothing that Joe shared with you about this spiderman, whose name is Stanley, that you forgot to share with the police?" I asked.

Flatter looked over at me. Looked like he was taking a moment to consider where I was coming from. Was I genuinely just asking an innocent question or had I layered in a thick slab of sub-text about how I didn't trust Flatter, that he was hiding something, 'cos maybe the NSA or other agency had pics of him prancing around his living room in women's underwear. I was coming at him from the former position. He didn't strike me as the kinda man that wears women's underwear. In fairness to me, I didn't know what kinda man did that anyway.

"I'm not a fan of texting. At least not at work," said Flatter. "If there's something I need to know related to a story my cubs are working on, then there's only two ways to tell me about it. Come and see me and talk about it or send me an email. I never got any emails from Joe about this because it wasn't anything. I asked him once where he was at with it. We got the call from this Stanley in late October. I can get the exact date if you want?"

I shook my head.

"Middle of November I asked Joe where he was at with it. Said he was building rapport. That this guy, Stanley, seemed a little whacko, but he was going to follow through with it. Joe was good like that. He was thorough. About a week before he had his meeting with Stanley, which as you know was on the 23rd of November, Joe told me he was going to meet him."

"What did he say then? Was he excited, or was he just trying to get it over with?" asked So-yi.

"I would say he was just trying to get it over with. Though I think he was interested in meeting this Stanley. As you know, he texted using a lot of biblical quotes. I think Joe was intrigued about what kind of a person he was meeting. Especially at a biker's bar."

"And that didn't give you any concern?"

Flatter shook his head. More vigorously this time. He must have ironed out the kink.

"Not in this line of work. You generally meet your sources where they feel comfortable. Back in the mid-eighties when I was starting out I did a story on the crack epidemic in this city. I met with people in all sorts of odd and dangerous spots. A biker bar is relatively mundane to be honest. Especially if you're not interviewing the bikers who patronize it. So no, I wasn't worried and neither was Joe."

"So you got nothing from him?" I asked.

Flatter shook his head.

"No, and I remember the last conversation I had with Joe. It was a little after six when he left on that Thursday. He popped his head in and this is what he said. 'I'm heading out now boss. I'll be seeing spiderman at nine at that bar, and I'll fill you in tomorrow.' I wished him good luck, and he said 'good night', and that was the last I heard from him, other than the text that came in about five hours later."

I ate the last of my chocolate cigar and I looked at the box. Flatter didn't take the hint. I rolled up my gold foil and threw it into my coffee cup on the edge of his desk. An easy three pointer.

"Look," said Flatter. "I'm sorry I don't have anything else to offer. But from what I've heard, it sounds like this Stanley was a little ill. My sources tell me that he was a schizophrenic and that he worked at a plumbing company. From what I've heard it was a terrible accident that he got hit by a drunk driver. And worse, is that this drunk driver shot Joe when he went to help. There are some really screwed up people out there. I don't know what else to tell you."

"These are inside sources?" asked So-yi.

"We have folks inside the NJPD and the NYPD who are

willing to talk to us under the cover of anonymity."

"Or to get you to stop snooping?" said So-yi.

Flatter stared at her for a while. So-yi met him until he backed down and leaned back in his chair.

"You have half the story," I said. "Stan was a schizophrenic. And he was on medication. Toxicology report found that he was taking his meds. He also had a small amount of alcohol in his blood. Maybe a beer's worth. Joe wasn't found to have any illicit drugs in his system. He too had some alcohol in his blood. Maybe a couple of beer's worth. Neither of them seemed impaired. But answer me this."

I looked at Flatter steadily for a moment to make sure he was paying attention.

"Who drives a garbage truck at eleven pm impaired while wearing a black suit? More than that. Who is this guy driving a garbage truck while impaired who runs down a young man at an intersection and doesn't even try to stop until after he's run down that man? And then he gets out and casually shoots Joe in the back of the head whilst bikers are making their way towards him carrying, and this isn't in the police statements, a sundry of weapons. What's more, this impaired hit and run driver is also using an incredibly quiet silencer, the likes of which a civilian is unlikely to obtain."

"How do you know this?" asked Flatter.

"Sources," I said. "But not from the NJPD. The bikers didn't say much, but they gave enough to fill in the blanks. We know for a fact he was wearing a suit and he used a gun with a silencer before he ran off, after stealing Stan's backpack. That gun incidentally is a 9mm. A favorite amongst the gaggle of three letter agencies."

"So you're saying it's murder? Murder by our

government?" asked Flatter a little incredulously.

"Or a couple of rogue agents. But why they killed Stan and Joe, though Stan's the obvious target, is what we've got to figure out. That's why I'm asking if there was anything you got from Joe."

I looked at Flatter for a while. Then my eyes drifted down to the box of chocolate cigars. A love unrequited.

"I'm sorry. I don't know what to say. There's nothing more. Nothing of consequence. I suppose I'd ask if you've interviewed the parents? What about the detectives? I don't know what else to suggest."

I nodded.

"We're just trying to uncover any crumb that might help. Have you heard of the Bilderberg Group?"

Flatter smiled and leaned back in this chair. He steepled his fingers together.

"Of course I know of the Bilderberg Group. It wouldn't be an exaggeration to say that we get 'insiders'," and he air quoted the word with his fingers before steepling them again, "calling at least once a year with a hot story about the latest conspiracy related to the Bilderberg Group that we should expose. But what's that got to do with anything?"

He looked at So-yi, but I hadn't filled her in with what I had gleaned. She shrugged at him.

"I've visited both Joe's and Stan's family. Stan's an interesting guy. There's tinfoil on his bedroom window still. His bookshelf is filled with conspiracy based books on the Bilderbergers, the Illuminati, David Icke and the Federal Reserve. His parents acknowledge his mental illness but he was medicated for it."

Flatter chuckled.

"David Icke is a real lunatic if you ask me. Alien lizards?

Come on. And as for the Bilderbergers. It's all make believe by imaginative, creative minds. Next you're going to tell me that you have 'real',” and there went the air quotes again, “evidence to prove that the The Protocols of the Elders of Zion are not actually fake.”

“Hadn't heard of those,” I said.

“It's a piece of fabricated antisemitic text purported to describe the Jewish goal of taking over the world. It was fabricated and first published in Russia in 1903. The Russians!” Flatter was getting boisterous. “The same people who it seems hacked our election recently and tried to do the same in Europe. I'm sorry Mr. Carrick, but you're beginning to sound a little antisemitic.”

Flatter stopped and picked up a mug of coffee, water, tea, it could have been anything. I noticed his hand was shaking slightly. He was clearly passionate about this.

“You've misread me, Rufin, all I said was that I visited Stan's childhood home and I noticed he was a conspiracy buff. I only asked if you had heard about the Bilderberg Group.”

So-yi was watching us both.

“Yes, Anthony, but anytime anyone says to me have I heard about the Bilderberg Group they're about to try and get us both stuck in some conspiracy laced rabbit hole. And that inevitably leads towards antisemitism in my experience.”

He took another sip from his mug.

“And the problem with that, is that the Jews have been unfairly prosecuted for centuries. More than that,” said Flatter, “I would argue that the Jewish people have probably done more to help society in the sciences, economics, philosophy, music, art and literature than any other group given their relatively small number in the global sphere.”

"I'm just asking about the Bilderberg Group," I said. "And frankly I resent your tone which seems to suggest that I might have even the smallest hint of antisemitism in my blood at all. I do not. Everyone gets a fair shake with me unless they prove otherwise."

"In fairness to my associate," said So-yi, "nobody knows what takes place at these meetings. Do you?" She waited while Flatter shook his head. "If any minutes are kept, nobody's seen them or released them publicly."

Flatter was shaking his head.

"Look, I'm sorry, Anthony. It's been a bad few weeks. And this conspiracy bullshit rubs me the wrong way. And mostly because it's not just innocent mythology. Like I said, it generally starts as a roadmap towards antisemitism."

I nodded.

"OK, but we're dealing with someone who was clearly mentally ill and drawn to conspiracies. What if there is something to that? Can you not admit that at the very least none of us knows what goes on at these meetings?" I asked.

Flatter looked at me for a long while before speaking.

"Admitting that we don't know what happens behind closed door meetings does not mean there is some great conspiracy taking place," said Flatter.

"Of course not, but in our line of work, we have to be open to all sorts of unpleasant and perhaps even unlikely motives and means."

"Are you saying that there is a big conspiracy amongst the most powerful in the world to rule us all?" asked Flatter.

I nodded my head.

"I am open to that possibility. Not that I believe it. But it is possible. It is more likely than the possibility that Stan was run down by someone impaired who uses a garbage truck as his daily driver, wears a suit out of Men In Black and uses a silencer that's probably not available for public purchase."

Flatter looked down at his lap.

"And what's more," I said. "As soon as I tried to get onto Stan's computer, it was hacked, and a personal message addressed to me, told me to go home."

CHAPTER THIRTY-FOUR
TRASH TALKING

"So what are you actually saying then?" asked Flatter. "Because that sounds to me like something the NSA could do."

I nodded my head.

"Right, and we know that Stan was good with computers. I'm saying that the most likely scenario is that Stan was killed over something he knew or found out. And who would likely do that? Either a government agency or an NGO that doesn't want any secrets leaking out, and unfortunately, whether you like it or not, the Bilderberg Group fits that description."

"I'd focus on the NSA or FBI then," said Flatter. "I don't believe the Bilderberg Group is all that interested in world domination. From what we know, it's a loose affiliation of world governmental and economic leaders. It's a long reach to go from there to a large, multi-tentacled organization that has the money and resources to conduct murders. I'm sorry, I just don't see it."

"I know it sounds remote. But I'm open to the idea. I have to be."

"I don't," said Flatter. "What does he have that would be reason enough to kill him?"

"That's what I aim to find out. On another note," I said. "If I came across a real story related to this. Perhaps even something that seems conspiratorial to you, but was verified. Would you run it for me, or at least hold onto it just in case?"

"I thought you were hunting for the killers. Why not take them to the police to have them dealt with that way?"

"What if I found some documents that proved something else, and that what I found was enough to kill over? If you had them to publish, if anything happened to me, that would help. I'd rest easier."

"I would do that. If it seemed legitimate."

"There's also Wikileaks," said So-yi.

I looked at her and smiled.

"I prefer to deal with people I know."

I stood up. It was time to see Reed Soakes. I leaned over the desk and shook Flatter's hand. He had a firm grip. He stood up and shook hands with So-yi too. He grabbed the box of cigars and shoved them at me.

"Take one for the road," he said. "God knows I shouldn't be eating them all."

I'm a gentleman. So I obliged. We turned to leave.

"If this is murder, Anthony," he said. "I hope you get the bastard who did it."

I nodded at him.

"I plan to," I said.

Reed was just in front of us at the grouping of desks which were open to each other. No one else was with him still. His back was towards us and as we came up to him I could see that he was surfing the web. It looked like he was looking at a car website called Horse & Buggy. I moved over to the side so he could see me. He looked up and then he stood up. He was about my height with brown curly hair and brown skin. He had green eyes that caught your attention. I figured he was bi-racial but his hair had softer curls than you'd expect. The best way to describe him was Brazilian. An attractive and slim young man in his late twenties. But he was not Brazilian.

"Reed Soakes?" I asked, offering my hand. He nodded and took it. "Anthony Carrick. We want to talk with you about Joe Severn."

He nodded at that, then turned and did the same with So-yi. He took one of the chairs from the other desks and offered it to So-yi. I took another one for myself. We sat elbow to ribs at his desk, in a small triangle.

"You from around here?" I asked.

"Born and bred in the Bronx," he said.

I looked over at his screen. The Horse & Buggy was reviewing the new Tesla Model 3.

"Is that site part of Webswum?" I asked, taking a shot in the dark, just trying to start a conversation.

"Yeah," he said.

"And what do they think about that car?"

"It's the future, man. It's the best electric car you can buy at the price range. This is where things are going. I bet by 2025 over one quarter of all cars on the road will be either electric and/or self-driving."

Not if I still had my LeSabre going by then. Which was asking a lot of it. I liked driving, but I could see the appeal of automated cars. Accident rate would fall and so would road rage.

"But you write for TrashCan right?" I asked.

Reed nodded.

"Yeah, but ever since what happened to my buddy, I'm thinking of making a change to Horse & Buggy."

"You're worried writing for TrashCan is too dangerous?"

Reed smiled at me and shook his head.

"Nah, man. I just like cars a lot better than politics and other bullshit like that. But this was the only gig they had available at the time. And I kinda stuck with it on account of Joe and me becoming buddies."

"How long have you been buddies?"

"A little over a year. I started in the fall of last year."

"But now you've been given Joe's senior story, right?" I asked.

Reed nodded.

"Yeah, but when that's put to bed, Flatter says he'll get me into the Horse & Buggy. There's an opportunity there now."

"Do you think that has anything to do with why Joe was murdered?" I asked. Sometimes I just like to come out bold. Like a picante salsa. I've softened the guy up with idle chit chat, then wham. A tough question. How they react tells you more than what they might say. Reed grinned at me.

"I don't think so, man. I mean, it's a story about police brutality. Those are literally, like, shooting fish in a barrel."

I looked at So-yi. So-yi shrugged. Reed looked at both of us.

"It's true. Am I lying? You're from Jersey PD, right?" he asked, looking at So-yi. She nodded.

"Last week one of your guys was in the news for shooting an unarmed black man in a drug bust."

"And before that?" she asked.

Reed looked at his computer for a while before answering.

"None this year," he said.

"Not true," said So-yi. "There've been thirty-one intentional police shootings this year. And only one you know about because it might be suspicious."

"Word," I said. Not sure why I said it. But it felt appropriate. Reed frowned at me. I grinned at him.

"You give enough assholes a gun," I said, "and you're bound to have a bad shooting."

"You know how many homicides were attributed to guns last year?" asked So-yi. Reed shook his head. "Fifty-six thousand. Only about two thousand were unintentional. Only two thousand were by police. Seems to me that the problem isn't so much reckless police brutality but civilian trigger fingers."

Reed shrugged.

"Yeah, but I bet that on a per-capita basis the cops are shooting more people."

"Maybe, but every cop has a gun. Not every civilian has a gun. And every day a cop is put in the line of fire. That's not the same for civilians."

"So you're saying we should just give the cops free range to mow down civilians left and right?" asked Reed.

I shook my head.

"I think we're getting stuck in the weeds. It's important that we hold the police accountable. But I want to get back to this cops-bashing-grannies story. Are you familiar with it?"

Reed nodded.

"Did you come across the names of Detectives Devon Schirru or Wilson Wast?"

Reed shook his head. Then he played with his computer, bringing up some documents.

"No, I don't think so, but let me check the notes."

He tapped away at the black chiclets on a tray that slid out from under the desk. He shook his head.

"No, man, nobody by that name. Most of the stuff I saw was mostly for officers. I don't remember seeing any detectives in Joe's notes. Who are these guys?"

"Not important," I said. "I'm trying to see if Joe's death or meeting with spiderman was related somehow to this other story he was involved with."

Reed looked at me.

"I don't think so. He never mentioned anything about them being related."

"Did he mention anything about this guy he was meeting?" asked So-yi.

Reed shook his head.

"Nah. But there wasn't much to say. He said the guy sounded like a lunatic. Said he had some big story that was going to shake the world to it's foundation. I asked him what it was about. He didn't know. All he said was that the guy called himself Spider-Man, but he didn't spell it properly. He spelled it all in lower caps. Spider-Man is…"

"We know how it's spelled," said So-yi.

"The guy made him get a burner phone before they could text. I think that's all they did. I don't remember him making a phone call on it, but maybe he did. I do remember him showing me some of these texts. Man, this Spider-Man seemed like a real religious lunatic if you asked me. Kept quoting bible verses and shit. Joe thought it was a waste of his time, but he had promised to meet with the guy, so he kept his promise. He was like that. But I kept asking Joe, why, if the guy had such a big story didn't he just go to the police?"

I loved the irony. Everybody's always ragging on the five-oh until they need them.

"And what did he say?" asked So-yi.

"He agreed with me. Said this is why he figured the guy was a nut job. But he was gonna follow up just in case. You see, Joe was always looking for that big story that would get him into the Fourth Estate."

"Fourth Estate?" asked So-yi.

"It's a term that's used for the press, or media," said Reed. "Goes way back."

"To the seventeen-hundreds," I offered. "It's based on the even older estates of the realm which were three. The clergy, the nobility and then the lowly commoners."

Reed was looking at me and nodding.

"Cool," he said, "I didn't know that. Us social media writers, bloggers, journalists and pundits are known as the Fifth Estate. Joe was looking to get into the Fourth Estate. He was trying to get a job with the Washington Chronicle. He was hoping this senior's story would do it. I have my doubts."

"Why is that?" asked So-yi.

"I think it's too pedestrian for them. Too provincial. They like the bigger stories. Federal political intrigue or world centered events. That sort of thing. Anyway, Joe was a great writer, and he was always looking for the next story. He just hadn't found it. Maybe this was it."

Reed looked at us hopefully. Like maybe he'd asked a question. If it was a question, I didn't have an answer.

CHAPTER THIRTY-FIVE
STRIKE OUT

A young man and a young woman walked down towards us. When they got close they saw their chairs were occupied. They left again towards a foosball table off to one side. They started playing and didn't pay us any more attention. Reed turned to me and tried a direct question.

"Do you know what happened? I mean, like, why he was really killed?"

I looked at him for a short while.

"What do you know of it?" I asked back.

Reed shrugged.

"Not much. Nobody tells us anything. From what I've gleaned from the police and from Flatter, they're saying it was a hit and run and drive-by shooting. But that sounds like bullshit to me."

"What do you think it could've been then?" I asked. "You're a journalist, maybe even an investigative journalist."

Reed shook his head slowly, like I'd tweaked it and turned his mouth upside down.

"I dunno, man. But c'mon. Joe was meeting a guy who seemed sketchy. Maybe this guy had enemies, or maybe, and this might be a stretch, the guy wasn't a lunatic. Maybe he knew stuff that people didn't want him telling journalists or leaking to the press. I don't know. This is all speculation. But something's weird about it. One thing I know for certain is that I doubt it was a hit and run."

"What makes you so sure?"

"C'mon, man. A hit and run in a garbage truck, by a guy who was apparently wearing a suit who calmly walked up to my buddy Joe and shot him in the back of the head. That ain't no hit and run I ever heard about."

So-yi smiled at me. I smiled back.

"You should be a cop," I said. "I like how you're thinking. It isn't any kind of hit and run I've come across. I think they were both murdered. Probably because spiderman knew something that people didn't want leaked. Like you said. Between you and me, I think it's a three letter agency. My best bet is the NSA."

"Shit," said Reed, looking at me like I'd just slapped him in the face. "This is big."

"Yeah, and it's gonna be tough cracking it open to prove who did what. Folks like we're dealing with are used to cleaning up behind them and leaving little to go on. That's why I'm talking to you. I'm searching for any little crumb. Have you found any?"

Reed was still digesting the little bombshell I'd dropped into his neat and tidy little worldview.

"No, man. I've told you everything I know. One thing Joe did tell me, was that the guy had dropped his name. This spiderman had called himself... what was it again..."

Reed took a moment to think about it.

244

"I think it started with an S too…"

"Shem," I offered.

Reed smiled. "Yeah, that's it. I guess it made him feel more comfortable with Joe, seeing as how Joe's middle name is…"

"Noah."

I'd taken to finishing sentences now.

"Guess you knew that too."

I nodded. Reed sounded like I'd broken open his piñata and stolen all his candies.

"Don't feel bad," I said. "This ain't an easy one. Seems like spiderman never spoke to anyone about much. I figure that's what the meeting was about."

Reed nodded. I looked at the empty chair across from us. I thrust my chin at it.

"Was that Joe's desk over there?" I asked.

Reed nodded.

"Can you sign onto his computer?"

Reed shook his head.

"I mean, I can sign onto that computer, because it's just a dummy terminal. It hasn't been assigned to anyone yet. About a week ago or so, IT came by and wiped the drive and did a fresh install."

"What about all his notes for this stories and things like that?"

"Well, that's all been archived. I'd have to get Flatter's permission to pull them from storage, and then I'd have to send that authorized request to the IT department. It's not stored locally or even on the intranet anymore. His current story, this seniors' one is now on my machine. The only other basic stuff we have is the log notes. And those don't tell you much."

"What about any notes related to this spiderman story?" I asked.

"First of all, it's not a story. It only becomes a story once one of us thinks there's something to it. Then again, we have to run it up the pole to Flatter to see if he wants us to pursue it."

"But you keep notes of calls you receive and things like that, right?" asked So-yi.

Reed turned to look at her, and nodded.

"Yeah, we do. But you're not gonna like it."

"Why not?" she asked.

"Because, like I said, it's not a story. So it's just the log notes we have, and they're minimal."

Reed tapped away at his computer keys. He brought up some kind of tracking software. Then he pulled up a folder in there that was titled "2017-10-27-P-spiderman".

"What does that all mean?" So-yi asked.

"That's the date the file was created," said Reed. "Then we put a letter to it. The acronym is PIE. All files start with P. P is for preliminary, it's just the very beginning of a story to see if there's anything there. Then if we take it further we change the file's letter from P to I. I means it's under investigation. Usually, that means there's something to the story but obviously we can't write about everything that's interesting. So we take these 'I' sorts of stories to our editor and if we get the go ahead then it becomes a story that'll be written. We change the I to an E which means that it's got editorial approval. However, not all 'E' stories will get published."

Inside the spiderman folder was a file called "Logs". Reed opened it up.

"Here you go, this is all we have. All that Joe wrote down."

The first entry was for the 27th of October when Joe took the first call from Stan. There were maybe a couple of dozen lines of notes from different dates. Nothing that I didn't know about. Joe wrote about getting the burner. That maybe the guy's name was Shem but wanted to be called spiderman. Joe was a careful and cautious guy. There was very little to no opinion. So as much as Joe might have thought he was meeting a crackpot, he wrote nothing suggesting such an opinion. It was all factual. But the facts painted a picture of someone either crazy or deeply overcome by conspiracy theories.

The last entry was on the day that Joe was going to meet Stan. All it said was that he was meeting spiderman at The Rattlin' Chain. That was it.

"You didn't lie," I said, looking at Reed.

"About what?"

"There's nothing here."

"Like I said, man, it was the very early stages of what sounded like a crackpot with a story. We get a lot of these. I'd say that ninety-nine times out of a hundred they go nowhere. So there's nothing to put in the notes in the beginning. Besides, we're trained to be cautious with this stuff. It can be subpoenaed and has been on occasion."

"If that's the case, then how do you protect confidential sources?" I asked.

"By not writing anything down about where or when or who we're meeting with. But that's not the case here."

I nodded. I felt like a blind man traveling in a forest feeling his way around tree trunks and hoping for elephants. I looked over at So-yi.

"Anything else?" I asked her. She shook her head. We were on a very short Möbius strip that felt like a leash. I stood up and shook hands with Reed. He stood up and wished us well.

"Hope you get the asshole who did this," he said. I was getting that a lot lately. It was meant as encouragement. But all it did was twist my stomach. If the NSA didn't want to be found out, I probably wasn't going to find out who did it.

So-yi and I walked ourselves out. We didn't say anything to each other or to anyone else until we were outside.

CHAPTER THIRTY-SIX
HOPE IN SMOKE

OUTSIDE had remembered my mood. It was gray and snowing slightly. Just like it had been when we entered. We huddled against the building under an overhang. I pulled out my cigarettes. I offered one to So-yi knowing her answer. So I smoked alone.

"This is going to be a hard one," she said.

No shit Sherlock, I thought. Instead, I said, "yeah."

I blew smoke rings at the gray static of the sky. My mood was sour. I was hungry and thirsty. And I couldn't figure out what I was more thirsty for. Whiskey or justice. Both had wet my lips and both tasted like winning.

"Have you ever had a case like this?" she asked.

I shook my head.

"Never had to deal with the government murdering civilians on home soil."

"Maybe it's not the government."

I turned to look at her. I turned the back of my collar up. It was cold enough that I was feeling it. I wanted to solve crime in Puerto Rico or Barbados, hell Hawaii or Florida sounded nice about now. I'd even take California over New York at this time of the year.

"You now think it's the Bilderberg Group?" I asked.

She shook her head but held my gaze.

"No, I don't believe in that nonsense. But we know there're shadowy organizations that help the government out when the government doesn't want to get its hands dirty. You remember Blackwater from oh-seven, right?"

I nodded. They'd come to the world's attention for killing civilians in Iraq.

"How many of these sorts of organizations are there?" she asked.

I didn't say anything.

"Probably more than just that one. Probably at least a handful. And probably some of them are going to work for whoever pays the best. The Russians, the Chinese, maybe even the Cubans."

"It's a good thought," I said. "Leaves us with the same problem."

"Which is?"

"How do we figure out who they are?"

"Probably by asking a lot of questions to a lot of generals," she said. "But I know of one. Started by an ex-South African Special Forces guy, Hans Marais. He started Assegai. A special ops NGO that helps out and delivers results."

"You sound like you're reciting their brochure."

"He gave us some self defense training a couple of years ago. That's one of the things he does with his organization."

"And he'll remember you?"

So-yi shrugged.

"He's a friendly guy. I get the impression he prides himself in remembering people."

"Did you make yourself memorable?"

She smiled at me.

"He's not my type."

"No?"

She shook her head.

"What's your type?" I asked.

"You're kind of my type."

I grinned at her. I was already starting to feel better. I sucked on my cigarette. It never tasted so good.

"Do you know how to get a hold of him?"

"I'll just call the Assegai main number. They'll be able to find him."

I nodded.

"Are you getting hungry?"

"I could eat something," she said.

"Good. How about this little Korean joint called Kraverie? Not far from my motel and not far from The Rattlin' Chain."

"How do you know about Kraverie?" she asked.

"What? I don't look like a guy who could enjoy Korean food?" I said, grinning.

"Well, no, not especially."

"My Lyft driver recommended it last night when I came in. I had the crepes. They were better than I thought."

"You continue to surprise me, Mr. Carrick," she said.

She was flirting with me. I could feel it in my gut. It felt warm and soft as jelly, and my spirit was weakening.

"That's a yes then?"

"It's a yes."

"Good," I said. "Because after that I want to rattle some

chains. We aren't getting anywhere, So-yi, and I know those bikers saw more than what they're telling. And I want them telling what they saw."

"Shouldn't we get some backup before we do that?" she asked.

"You are my backup," I said. "But listen, if you're a little unsure, I'll go in myself. Keep the car running."

I grinned at her, she looked up at me and shook her head like a friendly but frustrated school marm.

"You always this reckless."

"I try not to be."

"You don't even have a gun," she said.

"But you do."

She shook her head some more.

"When this is done, the very least you'll do for me is start wearing a vest."

"I always wear a vest under my shirt," I said.

She put her hand on my stomach and rubbed it up and down gently. It was warm and soft. I wandered what it would feel like skin to skin. But I brushed that aside. Because then she slapped me on the belly.

"You're not wearing a vest," she said, smiling.

"Am too," I said, unbuttoning a few more of the top buttons to my dress shirt and showing her my undershirt.

She laughed and shook her head.

"You're calling your undershirt a vest?"

"That's what the Brits call it."

"You know that's not what I meant."

I nodded. I took the last drag on my cigarette and walked over to the tall cylindrical ashtray not far from the main doors. I put my cigarette out in the sand and then tossed it into the opening underneath.

"I have a spare at my apartment," she said. "It'll probably be a little small but it'll work. Better than nothing."

"If you insist," I said.

"I insist."

We walked back to her car. I held her door open as she climbed in. That's just the way I am. She liked it. I could tell. If I was looking for it I could get lucky tonight. But I wasn't looking for it. I was looking for trouble. And she always finds me.

CHAPTER THIRTY-SEVEN
ON A DIFFERENT DAY

THE Kraverie was better at lunch the day after the dinner I had. Probably had something to do with the company. This time I had the Seoul Cheesesteak and So-yi had the Korean Crepe. She ordered for both of us. In Korean. Meant I had to trust her. She didn't let me down. They didn't have a liquor license so I had coffee. So-yi had green tea.

At the end of it we were pleasantly full but not stuffed. That was a good feeling to have in my belly. The way I figured it, I was going to be dancing this afternoon. I was either gonna be offering dance lessons or being shown how to dance at The Rattlin' Chain. If I knew bikers, and I had known some in my life, pretty-please-with-a-cherry-on-top wasn't gonna get me what I wanted. But they understood sign language. The sweet science of sign language.

We headed back to my place and reviewed the files we had. So-yi made herself comfortable. She took off her jacket and her figure gave me longings. She flirted with me the whole time. I pretended to be a dense dummy. Finally she put her hand on my lap and leaned in. I pulled away from her and stood up beside the bed. If I was a weaker man I would've scooped her up in my arms and had my way. I wasn't a weaker man and I wasn't drunk, which mighta helped. Depending on which side of morality you're standing on.

"You're a very attractive woman, So-yi," I said.

She looked like I'd slapped her across the face.

"But I'm not your type," she said, disheartened.

"You're my kinda type I whispered in God's ears that he'd never offered before."

"Then what… are you gay?"

Sometimes women will say that out of spite. To get you riled up. Like a verbal slap in the face. Doesn't work on me. Firstly because I don't care how people find love. And secondly because I'm not gay and I don't need to prove it. But So-yi wasn't like that. I got the impression she was really just trying to figure me out.

"No, I'm not gay. I'm seeing someone out in LA," I said.

"Oh," she said.

She was breaking my heart. That 'oh' sounded like I'd just burst into her birthday party and popped every one of her balloons.

"I'm also not from around these parts. I live on the other side of the country. It wouldn't work."

She wasn't looking at me. She was looking down at her lap.

"That we could've figured out," she said.

"Yeah, but I'd have wanted you to know up front."

"What's her name?" she asked.

"Emily," I said. "She's the coroner out in LA."

"She's lucky," she said.

"You're kind. I'm the one that's lucky."

We didn't say anything for a while. I sat back down on the bed next to her and put my arm around her. I kissed her on the side of the head and whispered in her ear.

"Any other day, and twice on holy Sundays," I said. "If things were different. My honor won't let me. I hope you understand."

She looked at me and patted me on the knee. She nodded her head.

"I wouldn't want it any other way."

We stared at the paper on the bed some more. It didn't tell us anything else it hadn't said before. Four o'clock rolled round. I figured it was time to start making our way towards the biker joint. I wanted to get there before too many of them were crawling around like roaches in the place. I wanted to try and even out my chances if I had any.

Four thirty we packed everything away and headed out the door.

CHAPTER THIRTY-EIGHT
CHAIN GANG

A little after five we arrived outside The Rattlin' Chain. We sat in the car for a minute to get our bearings. I imagined Joe sitting here just before he was shot. That's what I figured had happened. He'd left Stan and come back to his car. He texted Flatter when he heard a large crash. He must've looked up to see the garbage truck coming to a stop just on the other side of the intersection. That's when he got out and ran over to his friend. Maybe they were friends by that time?

The street was quieting down. It was mostly small little businesses up and down both sides of the street. I saw the kebab place on the corner opposite from where the accident occurred. I didn't figure it was worth revisiting. I didn't see any cameras about either. It was in the more downtrodden part of town. The kind of place where bad things happen and nobody to witness them.

"Listen, Anthony," said So-yi as I was about to get out of the car. I turned towards her. "I'm a real cop here. I'm not a cowboy. We've got to do this right. By the book."

"What does that mean?" I asked.

"Let me lead. I don't want to have to use my weapon. There's too much paperwork. It's not like it is in the movies."

"Yeah, I know. I was a cop for ten years in LA. I know how it is."

"OK, good," she said. "Then let's do this right."

I nodded and grinned at her.

"'Cept I'm not a cop anymore."

I got out of the car before she could protest and waited for her to come round to my side.

"I'm serious," she said. "I don't need any aggravation in my life."

"I don't need any either," I said. "Don't worry, Sue, I won't let anything happen to you."

"I'm not worried," she said. "I'm a fifth dan taekwondo martial artist. I just don't want to have to rescue you. That'd be embarrassing."

She grinned at me.

"Then let's go knock some heads."

I opened the door for her and let her lead. Just like she wanted. It was dark inside, but it was dark outside too. Our eyes had already adjusted. We walked up to the bar. As we did, I counted four. Four waiting for the dance floor. One of them was big. He was the guy behind the bar. That was helpful. It gave us space between each other. The biggest problem with big guys is they sometimes have a longer reach. But a lot of the time, big guys haven't had to learn how to use it on account of their size. They've found that intimidation has worked more times than not. This gives you the advantage if you've actually had to fight. And I had.

We walked up to the bar. Behind him I could see a whole array of fancy liquor bottles. The one I wanted was labeled

Jack Daniels Old No. 7. Jackie D Black, as I like to call it. I was looking for something Irish, but there was none on the shelf. The bartender tossed his head back at us. He had big forearms that looked like they'd grown out of the polished wood of the bar like branches of the same tree. I gave him four or five inches on me. That put him at six-two, maybe six-three. I also gave him sixty, maybe seventy pounds on me. That meant his fist would hurt. It also meant I could use his momentum against him.

"Give me a double Jack Black," I said.

I looked at So-yi. She shook her head.

"We don't serve bacon," he said.

He wasn't starting off on the right footing. I was thirsty. And I was now thirsty for both whiskey and justice, and he was getting in the way of both. I saw So-yi put her purse on the chair and blade herself towards the other three. We were about to party.

"I'm not a cop," I said. "I'll now take a triple."

He looked at me and grinned. It was the kinda grin that I wanted to wipe off his smug face. He leaned in towards me so that we were now the same height. I thought about offering an Irish kiss but his positioning was awkward. I put my hands on the bar, mirroring him.

"Well, we don't serve no slant eye around here. Take your chink and get the fuck outta here."

He was one of those big guys who hadn't had to fight much. I know this because of what I did next which took him way too easily by surprise. His first mistake was leaning in towards me. That gave me access to the back of his head. His second mistake was not moving his hands forward to brace himself. His hands were still back at his end of the bar. That meant his head was top heavy. I thrust my hands up real quick around the back of his neck and brought his head hard into the bar. I wasn't taking any chances. I used as much of my weight and strength as I could. His face made a dull, sickening sound when it hit the bar. There was also the crack of his nose breaking. Maybe his cheekbones had cracked too. I couldn't say for certain and I didn't care. The result was that he was out cold and slid off his end of the bar when I let go.

I spun around to punch more holes in my dance card. So-yi was way ahead of me. She had moved right towards the other three who were only now figuring out what was playing. So-yi was on to the guy on the far right. She gave a high spinning kick to the side of his face that knocked him out cold. I was impressed. The guy on the left was reaching for something in his pocket. That something was going to be sharp and metal and I hadn't prepared for a knife fight.

The nice thing about him rummaging in his pocket for a knife was that it left his face open for a knuckle sandwich. And I gave him one with all the fixings. The movies lie to you. They show guys beating the shit out of each other and barely leaving a scratch. That's not how real life works. The head is a sensitive and fragile cage for consciousness. One good punch can knock out the biggest guy. Especially if he isn't expecting it.

I had landed my fist right on the guy's chin. I had probably dislocated his jaw. I had also probably dislodged a couple of teeth. More importantly, the follow through meant that his head had spun towards his right shoulder faster than his brain could move. This flicked the switch on his internal lights. He dropped like a stone, and I felt the pain in my hand. Bare knuckle fighting is not all it's cracked up to be. I turned towards the man in the middle but he had already given up the fight. He had held a pool cue which now clattered against the floor. His hands were partially up.

So-yi went back to the bar and took out her handgun and trained it on the one conscious biker. I patted down the two guys on the floor. I found two knives, one from each, to add to my collection. I went back round the bar and dragged the big guy out towards the front where his mates were. He wasn't wearing anything, though I noticed a sawed-off under the counter on his side.

I went back round to the far side of the bar and took Jackie D Black off the shelf. I found myself a tumbler and poured a couple of fingers into it. I put the bottle down close by. My right hand was hurting like hell. Like I'd just put it into a meat grinder. The middle finger knuckle was split and bleeding. I hadn't dislocated my joint, but it hurt almost as bad as if I had. And I had done that once or twice before. Now I was better trained. Still, fighting ain't as glamorous as the movies will have ya believe.

I sipped my Tennessee whiskey and watched the guys on the floor start to come to their senses. Big guy's nose was still bleeding but it had started to slow. You could see the red smear from where I'd dragged him from around the bar. He slowly stood himself up and took a moment to reconsider what had happened.

"It's gook asshole," said So-yi, "you should know your racial slurs. I'm not Chinese. I'm Korean, dick fucker."

I looked at So-yi and grinned at her. She was riled up. She looked at me all serious at first before starting to laugh.

"Dick fucker?"

She nodded.

"Yeah, that's the best I could come up with at the time."

I nodded.

"I like it," I said.

"What do you fuckers want?" asked the big guy.

So-yi ignored him. She turned to me.

"That was your idea of letting me lead?" she asked.

"I opened the door for you," I said. "You were the first one in. You lead the charge."

I winked at her and she grinned at me.

"Maybe lock the front," I said. "My dance card is full."

"I asked what the fuck do you guys want?" said the big guy again.

CHAPTER THIRTY-NINE
TELLING TALES

"WE'RE having a moment here," I said, looking the big guy in the eye. I raised my glass at him. He didn't say anything. He kept staring at me.

"I'll find out where you live and come and beat the living shit out of you and your dog."

"I'm a cat person," I said.

So-yi returned to the front of the bar where I was. She had trained her gun on the floor close to their feet.

"Take a seat," I said, shoving my glass of whiskey towards the small table with four chairs around it. It was getting hot in here. Or maybe it was on account of my workout. Whatever it was, I took off my hat and lay it down on the bar.

"If you know what's good for you," said So-yi, "you'll behave and answer our questions. Otherwise, I'm gonna come back here with my buddies in blue and turn this place upside down. Maybe I'll bring some cockroaches too and the health department."

"Thought you said you weren't a cop," said the big guy.

"He isn't," said So-yi.

"Alright, then what the fuck do you want?" he asked.

"Well," I said, being a dick, but not the private kind. "I'd like you to use the kind of language you'd use in front of your mother. We have a lady present."

"I'm using the kind of language I use with my ma," he said.

I nodded.

"Of course you are. That's why you're the kind of asshole you are. OK. Let's try and use the sort of language you'd use when speaking with, let's say, I don't know, the Pope. Let's use clean language."

I'd noticed a door to the back room. I kept one ear to the ground for any noise coming from it. More than that, I took a moment to see if the sawed-off was full of shot. It was. I put it up on the bar pointing towards the direction of the backroom.

"Anyone else here?" I asked.

The big guy gave me his shit kicker's grin.

"No," he said.

"Doesn't matter to me," I said. "I'll as soon put lead into one of your friends as look at them. You want to answer again?"

He stared at me for a long while before replying.

"There's nobody else here. We ain't open yet."

I believed him. But I still kept two barreled Barry pointing in the direction of the backroom just in case.

"Can we get to business. There's not much cash here and not as much liquor as you'd like."

"I can see that," I said. "About the liquor I mean. You'd attract a higher-end client if you offered a nice Irish whiskey."

"That's not our demographic," he said, grinning.

"We're not here for your whores or drugs. Besides, an outfit like you have, you probably have that shit elsewhere."

Big guy didn't say anything for a while.

"Then why are you here?"

"I want you to tell me everything you didn't tell the cops about that double homicide a few weeks back."

"Which homicide was that?" he asked.

"You get a couple every week here?" I asked. He didn't say anything. "I can stay here all night. And the longer I stay the more pissed I'm gonna get. And the more pissed I get, the worse your place is gonna look by the time I'm done. And maybe the worse you're gonna look too. There were two kids came in here on Thursday November 23rd at around nine pm. Didn't look like they belonged. The one was run down after leaving here. The other was shot point blank in the back of the head. You were witnesses to it."

The big guy shrugged.

"Seems to me you know all about it."

"OK," I said.

I grabbed the sawed-off and turned around. I looked at the rows of liquor bottles on all the shelves. I picked a row I figured cost the most. Must have had a couple of hundred bucks worth of bottles. Easy. I took Barry and busted them all up. The aroma of the different liquors mingled and wafted over to us. It wasn't unpleasant. I turned back around to see how he liked them apples. He shrugged at me.

I turned back around and destroyed all of the liquor bottles on all of the shelves. Then I opened up the taps on the beer kegs. Soon this place would be flooded. I turned back around.

"Tell him Big Mike," said the uninjured guy amongst the bunch. "Frank's not gonna be happy if this place floods and we gotta be out of business for a couple of weeks."

"Flooding's the least of your problems," I said. "I'm about to light this place up and make you watch it burn to the ground from inside."

I took out my lighter and flicked it on for effect. Big Mike looked over at the uninjured guy. Then he looked at me.

"Alright," he said. "Turn off the taps."

I turned off the taps and filled up my whiskey glass.

"What do you want to know?"

"Everything you didn't tell the cops."

"Well, it's like you said. This guy comes in at around nine. He goes and sits in a booth, like this is some sort of fancy table service joint. I tell him if he wants to drink he's gotta come and see me. So he does. He orders a couple of beers and then goes and sits back down."

I come around the bar, crunching on glass as I do, and show him a couple of photos on my phone.

"Which guy?" I ask.

He points to Joe.

"Then maybe five minutes later that other guy comes in. He's wearing a hoodie and a backpack. He takes a moment to look around and the guy in the booth raises his bottle to him. So this new guy goes and sits with his buddy."

"I'm gonna make this easier," I said. "The first guy who came in and ordered beers is Joe. The second guy is Stan. So what do they do?"

Now that my lighter was out it felt lonely. I took out my smokes and lit one up.

"I didn't pay much attention to them on account of them being a pair of nobodies. Not sure why they were here.

They're not the kinda people we have drinking here. But so long as they're drinking and paying they're welcome. Like I said, I'm not staring at them. I'm not watching them carefully because they're nobodies. Probably college kids thinking it's cool to drink at a biker bar. A story to tell their frat buddies."

"OK," I said. "But what did you see when you did glance over at them?"

"The second guy…" he said.

"Stan," I said.

"Yeah. The first thing he does is ask for Joe's phones. Joe's got one of them fancy new iPhones and another one. Also a smartphone. Stan takes the battery out of the other phone. He wraps them all up in thick aluminum foil and puts them in plastic baggies."

I looked over at So-yi. She was looking at the group of bikers. That got me to thinking about what a group of bikers should actually be called. We had a murder of crows. There was an unkindness of ravens. An intrusion of cockroaches. A gang of buffalo. But none of those collective names did these dirtbags any justice. Then it came to me. A group of bikers was a trash. A trash of bikers. Yeah, that's what they looked like too.

"…weird."

I looked up. I had been lost in thought.

"What was that?"

"I said it was weird how he was pulling apart his phones and putting them in foil."

"He was making a Faraday bag," I said. "To keep the phones from connecting to any signals."

Big Mike stared at me with a long blank stare. The kind of stare that puts his eyes on hiatus while his mouse of a brain tries to figure out what I just said. I didn't help him.

"What else did you see them do?"

CHAPTER FORTY
SELECTRICK

THAT made him blink and he readjusted himself in his seat. The ash on my cigarette was starting to grow long. I thought about tapping it out on the floor. But I wasn't feeling as much of an asshole as I had five minutes earlier. I grabbed another whiskey tumbler and dumped ash into it.

"They sat around and talked for a while. Joe got up and got more drinks. Stan peeled the label from his bottles. Didn't seem to be drinking too much. Then Stan pulls up the sleeve to his right arm and it's wrapped in foil. He takes the foil off and shows Joe something on his forearm."

"What was it?" I asked.

"Couldn't see from where I was. Joe squeezes at something on Stan's arm though. But like I said, it was either non-existent or it was small. I couldn't see it. But he wraps his arm up again in that foil. He also gives Joe a small card. Maybe like a business card. The last thing I seem him do is pull out a small object, like a turd. This turd is wrapped in foil too. Seems this guy might have been wearing foil underwear."

"Just give me a second," I said. I turned to look at So-yi. "Did the coroner say anything about something in Stan's arm?"

She looked back at me before returning her gaze at the trash of bikers.

"Yeah, it's in there. Not much to say about it. Said he pulled out a small RFID chip but it wasn't working. Didn't speculate about what it could have been used for."

"Why you so interested in a couple of kids?" Big Mike asked.

I looked at him. Figured sharing my reasons might soften him up.

"I'm doing a pal a favor. These kids were murdered and I want to find out why and by whom."

"And what do you think?"

"I think I'm asking the questions and you're answering them. But if there's a small chance you actually give a shit, I think it's the government for some reason."

Got that blank stare again.

"Hell friend, you should have led with that. I'm all about giving it to the government."

"You didn't give me a chance," I said. "I asked for a whiskey and you got all redneck racist on me."

Big Mike grinned.

"Yeah, sorry about that. I was in a bad mood. I'm not really racist," he said. That last part was for So-yi.

"You can prove it by helping us out then," she said.

I kept thinking about how every racist I'd ever met was adamant they weren't.

"So you're saying how Stan pulled out this small object," I said.

"Yeah. Inside the foil was another phone. Like one of them old small brick phones. Like that old Nokia they used to have."

"Like a candy bar phone?" asked So-yi.

"Yeah, I guess it might have been about that size."

"What color was it?"

Big Mike shrugged.

"Hard to tell. Maybe gray, blue. The light in here is not the best for that kind of thing."

"What did he do with it?" asked So-yi.

"Not much. He placed it on the table so the top of it was pointing towards us. They pushed some buttons on it. At one point I saw what sorta looked like a projected screen on the table that came out of the side of the phone."

"What size was it?"

Big Mike shrugged.

"A little bigger than the phone."

He showed us the size with his big hands. Looked about twice the area of a standard letter envelope.

"What was on this projected screen?" asked So-yi.

"Couldn't say. Looked like pictures and writing. I wasn't staring and I was way over there where you are." He meant me and not So-yi.

"What kind of pictures?" I asked.

"Pictures of faces I think."

I nodded.

"Then he eventually puts it away. He takes the phones back out of their foil and gives Joe his phones back and they leave. That's when I notice something weird. The whole place has gone quiet. We weren't playing any music at the time. But there's still sound made by stuff. You know, like the bar fridge, the lights and things like that. The place got real quiet just as they left. I noticed the register wasn't working. It's all computerized now, and the fridge had turned off. Seemed like everything running on electricity stopped working. 'Cept the lights. For some reason the lights were still on. I figured it must have been those kids."

"How'd you figure that?" I asked.

I put my cigarette out in the whiskey tumbler. I finished up my whiskey. I looked longingly at the bottle of Jack Black. Figured I'd be taking him with me when I left. A small payment for my troubles and split knuckle.

"I knew everyone else in here. Besides, that phone they were playing with. I figured that must have been what did it. So I grab my sawed-off and head out the front door. The guys follow me."

"You were going to shoot a kid over what was maybe a prank?" asked So-yi.

"No. I was gonna intimidate him and get him to hand over his prank tool and fix what he done."

I nodded at Big Mike to continue.

"Well, I reckon by the time I figured out what had happened with the electricity and got my shotgun, must've been a couple of minutes later. Just before we leave we hear this crash. Must've been the garbage truck hitting the light pole on the other side. We get outside and look around. Up at the top of the street here is the intersection with Woodacres."

He looked at us. I pointed with my right hand. I was facing the outside.

"Up the street," I said.

Big Mike nodded.

"Yeah. Well we get out here and when we figure where the sound come from we see this guy getting out of a garbage truck. He's wearing a black suit with a black tie. Just like in that movie, Men In Black."

I nod in encouragement.

"In his hand he's got a pistol. Weirdest pistol I've ever seen."

"Describe it to me," I said.

"The handle looks the same as other pistols. But from there it just blows up into what kinda looks like a huge Taser. The barrel is distorted and sorta round but sorta like a stop sign but with way more angles. Other than the handle, the pistol is huge. Probably as big around as my fist."

Big Mike shows us his big meaty fist. It's about one and a half times the size of mine.

"You told the police it was a silencer," I said.

"Yeah, well you're asking me what I didn't tell them. I can't tell them that shit. They wouldn't believe me and it'd just cause more headaches. You gotta treat the cops simple."

"Alright," I said.

"I reckon it's about a foot long but it doesn't seem to be top heavy. This guy walks up to Joe who's now by Stan calling for help. We start up towards them. This man in black sees us and points this gun at us. We duck down by a parked car, but I don't think he shoots at us."

"How do you know?" asked So-yi.

"We didn't hear nothing. I wait just a couple of seconds and then poke my head up and I see this man in black pointing his gun at the back of Joe's head. Joe's looking down the street towards us. The gun makes a soft popping sound. I ain't never heard such a soft gunshot in my life."

"What did it sound like?" I ask.

"Like a soft pop," he says. He pinches his lips together and then quickly and forcefully blows them open with a quick blast of air, making a popping sound. I look at So-yi. She looks at me. I look back at Big Mike.

"Was it about that loud?"

He nods.

"Yeah, maybe a little softer. We start running up towards this guy. We're all armed. But he grabs the backpack that Stan was carrying and runs off down Woodacres. I notice as we get closer, as the guy's running, that the barrel or whatever it is is spinning inside this big cylinder of a gun he has."

"Maybe that's part of how it suppresses the sound," I say, looking at So-yi. "Dissipating the noise as momentum."

She nods thoughtfully. I look back at Big Mike.

"We get up to where Joe and Stan are. The man in black is about a hundred feet away and just getting into a black sedan. I unload my shotgun, but I ain't hitting nothing that far out with a sawed-off. Slimmy Jimmy here, might have hit the car with his .45."

I've now been told the name of the guy who didn't get punched or kicked in the face. I look at him. He kinks his neck to the side and back.

"Maybe. I like to think I placed lead on target. Hard to tell though."

I nod and look back at Big Mike.

"Then what?"

"Then we check on Joe and Stan. They're both dead. Slimmy Jimmy collects our weapons and I call 911."

CHAPTER FORTY-ONE
NO CLARITY

"AND that's all?" I ask.

"Yeah, that's exactly what happened," said Big Mike.

"Since then have you had any other strange guests or visitors? Any strange events like the electricity not working?"

Big Mike thinks for a minute. Shakes his head.

"No. Been business as usual since then."

"What about the cops. They been back since?"

"Yeah. Couple of detectives came by. Told them the same story. We told them we heard the accident and came to investigate. Just found these two kids here dead."

"So they don't know that they were drinking in here?"

"Yeah. We told them that. But we don't like to entertain the five-oh here. As you can imagine."

I nodded. I looked over at So-yi. She shook her head.

"Listen," said Big Mike. "If you're going up against the G-man you'll need some hardware. We have the kind of stuff that could help. You let me know and I'll get you a good price. Won't be traceable if you understand what I'm saying."

"We're going by the book," said So-yi.

Big Mike laughed and slapped his knee.

"Yeah right. So if I go to IA and tell them about you breaking in here and beating us up. Wrecking our place. They're gonna tell me that you were following protocol?"

So-yi didn't say anything.

"Alright," I said. "If I need something like what you're offering I'll be back."

"Alone," said Big Mike.

"Alone," I repeated. "But like my colleague said, we're gonna try and do this by the book."

Big Mike grinned and nodded his head up and down slowly.

"Good luck with that. If this is a government job you're not gonna get anywhere that way."

I didn't say anything. So-yi didn't say anything. Outside, a couple more bikers were starting to mill around. It was coming on six. So-yi had shooed them away with her gun and badge at first. Now they were just being rubber necks. I took a dead president out of my wallet. His name was Franklin. I made a show of it putting it on the bar.

"Thanks for the drink," I said, grabbing Jack Black and raising it at them. "If we get any grief leaving here, we'll be coming back with a whole army of the blue man group if you get my meaning."

Big Mike nodded.

"Nobody'll stop you leaving."

I nodded and So-yi and I left. We got a lot of hairy eyeballs but nobody bothered us. Just like Big Mike said.

"Let's walk up to Woodacres," I said.

We did that. The road we were on, Foist Avenue, led up

towards Woodacres at a slight incline. The Rattlin' Chain was about in the middle of the block. The light pole and the stop sign the garbage truck had crashed into had been fixed. This part of town was quiet at this time of night. Most businesses along Foist had closed up by five. The traffic at the four way was almost non-existent. It had stopped snowing and the snow on the road had melted. You could see black tire skid marks halfway through the intersection. After he'd hit Stan.

I stood on the corner of Foist and Woodacres and replayed the scene in my mind. I was looking down Woodacres to where the black sedan was parked. City blocks are most often rectangular in shape. This was true of Woodacres and Foist. Woodacres was the short side. Foist the long side. Even on the short side, that black sedan was only about a third of the way down the block. There was an old white Japanese import at about thirty-three yards or a hundred feet down the block. About where the sedan should have been. I was a competent shooter and I could take out the back windows easily at this distance.

Still, I wasn't sure if bikers practiced at the range all that often. Probably not. And just coming up from running up this hill. The two, maybe three hundred yards, they'd be breathing heavy. They were drawing quickly on the car. Slimmy Jimmy with his .45 might have hit it. But under pressure like that. Controlling your breath and the kickback and the car taking off within a second or two. Yeah, he might have hit it. Still wouldn't help though. Doubt he hit the shooter and the car would've been patched by now. That's assuming it was government men.

I turned towards So-yi.

"Could you make that shot," I asked, pointing to the white

car.

She looked at me.

"You joking?"

I shook my head.

"Don't know about the LAPD but if you couldn't hit a target that large from this distance you aren't graduating police academy," she said. "I could probably hit the brake lights. On purpose."

She looked down Woodacres at the car. She put her hands up as if she were aiming a gun.

"Yeah, that's probably what, about a hundred feet. Same as the black sedan was supposed to be parked at."

I nodded.

"You don't think Slimmy Jimmy could've hit it?"

She looked back at me. I was looking down the road. It was wet and black, lit with nicotine yellow street lamps. I shrugged.

"Yeah, I think he could've hit it. But I doubt he's trained like you and me. And he's just come from running up this hill, having ducked earlier because they thought they were being shot at. He's got maybe a second or two to acquire his target and control his breath. The adrenaline is going in his veins. It's possible, but it's probably a lucky shot for them."

"Good points," she said. "In that case, I could probably hit it. But probably not make my brake light shot. Does it matter?"

I turned to look at her. She looked like a dark angel in the street lamps. They accentuated her bone structure and gave her a waxy glow. It was very attractive. I looked back down the street.

"Doesn't matter," I said. "Just goes to show you how brazen that assassination was."

In my mind I watched the black sedan take off down the road. I looked at Joe and Stan in the middle of the intersection, already dead. I needed to get the bastards who did this. And there were two of them. That guy driving the getaway car might as well have pulled the trigger himself.

"Listen Anthony," said So-yi, putting her hand on my upper arm. I looked down at her. "I think you should stay at my place. And before you get all weird. I heard what you said earlier. I just think it'll be easier for us to both be in the same place to make greater strides on this. I have two-bedrooms."

She took her hand off my arm. I nodded.

"OK," I said. "Let's go."

She looked at me puzzled for a moment.

"What?" I asked.

"I thought you'd protest."

"I've taken you at your word So-yi. It's better for this case that we have a combined base of operations. I want to get these guys bad. Worse than letting a little awkwardness get in the way."

CHAPTER FORTY-TWO
THE WATERFRONT

So-yi lived in an area of Jersey City called The Waterfront. It's not imaginative. You don't have to guess at what kind of a place it is. It's on the waterfront. You'd think that folks buying apartments here for half a mill for a closet could come up with a more creative name. But I guess all the money's been spent buying a place to live and not on naming your little slice of suburbia.

The Oracle is an apartment building on the waterfront in The Waterfront. That's where So-yi lives. It's a blue glass building the kind you see everywhere. She's on the thirty-third floor and looks out over the Hudson River towards Lower Manhattan. The views are spectacular.

We'd picked up my suitcase from the motel I'd stayed at. I felt like Charles Dickens' Oliver Twist who'd just been given a whole lot more. From the underground parking to the elevator to her apartment couldn't have taken more than three minutes.

"I know you're wondering how I afford this," she said, in

the elevator. "My parents helped my brother and me get started when we graduated from university. They paid for half of this place and some of the mortgage until I got on my feet. Now I pay the mortgage by myself."

"That's very generous of them," I said.

She nodded.

"It was, but back then, this is in oh-nine, this place was only eight hundred thousand. So my mortgage is only around four hundred now."

I smiled at her. She was lucky and I didn't begrudge her any of it. Having spent the day with her I didn't doubt her sincerity.

"Your parents obviously have money," I said. "Why did you decide to become a cop?"

We walked down the hall to her apartment and she opened it. It led into a hallway that led towards a large bank of windows that overlooked the river and then the lighted buildings of New York. It was a million dollar view. The kitchen was behind us. An open and spacious kitchen that led out into the living room and off of it to the dining room. To my right were the bedrooms and bathrooms.

So-yi showed me to mine. It was the first bedroom down that wing of the apartment. Opposite was a large modern bathroom with the shower separate from the bath. She showed me the rest of the place. Her bedroom was larger than the spare and had an ensuite larger than the other bathroom.

We came back out into the living room. I sat down on a couch.

"I think I only have wine," she said. "We should have stopped for some beers."

"I'll drink beers if there's nothing else. I'll drink wine

before beers. But what I really like is whiskey. I'll have some of that."

I had placed Jack Black on the kitchen island when we'd walked in. I got up to help. She had me sit.

"Tonight you're my guest, Anthony. Tomorrow mi casa es tu casa. I'm getting hungry. How about you?"

I was. So-yi made us up a beef stir fry that was as good as any restaurant's I'd tasted. We had red wine with it and afterwards I had another whiskey. We were sitting together on the couch after dinner. So-yi had another glass of red wine. I wanted a cigarette but there weren't any balconies around here. I'd have to wait until tomorrow.

"You were asking why I became a cop," she said.

I nodded.

"It's a bone of contention with my parents. They wanted me to become a doctor or a lawyer. I took my undergraduate degree in social work. I thought they'd disown me. But my brother really helped them see what I was trying to accomplish."

"Which is?"

"Make this city a better place for everyone. Especially immigrants. My parents came from Korea almost forty years ago now. Before my brother and I were born. They started from nothing and built up a successful business."

"What kind of business?"

"They own a handful of dry cleaning stores in Jersey City," she said. "But for me, it's always been the case that you can't have a successful business without the law. My sense of justice has always been keen. Especially having been an outsider myself. I thought of social work, but I sort of changed my mind and decided that law enforcement would be better. What about you?"

"I kinda fell into it. I have a BFA from the California College of Arts. I majored in painting."

"No way," said So-yi, taking a sip of her wine. "You're a dark horse aren't you."

I smiled at her.

"Do you show anywhere?"

"At Triangle Gallery in LA," I said.

"Wow. I would never have known. Law and art," she said, weighing them up in her hands as if she was balancing a scale. "I don't get how you got into law enforcement from that."

"I met a woman and had a kid and she didn't think art was any way to make a living. Back in the nineties the LAPD was on a big hiring push. I figured it wouldn't be that bad. Driving around, arresting bad guys. Little did I know."

"What didn't you know?"

"You're buried alive under paperwork. Policing is more like babysitting now. You even look at a suspect wrong and they'll have you in front of IA. The job's become too political. The hours suck as you get older. I could go on."

"But you were in homicide, John said."

"Yeah. The hours still suck. Murderers aren't all that considerate about killing people during bankers' hours."

So-yi giggled at that. She was almost finished her second glass of wine. She was small and slim and I bet she was feeling it.

"What about your brother. What does he do?"

"He works at New York-Presbyterian Children's Hospital. He's a pediatric oncologist."

"Doing God's work," I said.

She smiled at that.

"It's hard. Most times they lose the kids. Every once in

awhile they're able to cure a child. I think he lives for those moments."

We sat and chatted for a while longer. I found out her brother is married and has two kids. A boy and a girl. Her brother's name is Jae-joon though he goes by Jay or JJ at work. I learnt her parents were married the year before they came to the States. She spoke with admiration and pride about her parents and brother. I had the impression they were a close family.

I asked about why she wasn't married. It came down to not finding the right one. Her parents were constantly trying to set her up with what she called "nice Korean guys". By all accounts they were successful. Guys in medicine, banking and business. But she said they were all too bland. Not interesting.

I got the impression that she'd been in love before. I had to tease it out of her. His name was Jarrod. They'd been on the job together not long out of the academy. He was in a different district to her. She told me he was black. She told me he was black, not because his skin color was important but that it had been a huge issue with her parents. They hadn't wanted to meet him. They never did. They were together three years before he was killed on the job. It had been a drug bust gone bad.

She told me she'd never really connected with anyone since then. At least not until now. She looked at me then with her seductive bedroom eyes. Eyes that looked sleepy but didn't want to lie in bed sleeping. My tongue had been loosened by the whiskey, but I quickly lassoed it down. I told her I was flattered and that I hoped she'd find love again. Then I said, "we should call your guy."

"What guy?" she asked.

"The guy you know from Assegai," I said.

"Oh yeah, him. You're a poet and you don't even know it."

I winked and grinned at her.

"Is that your way of diverting the conversation?" she asked.

The wine had taken hold of her tongue and probably her inhibitions.

"I'm flattered. But your saying it ain't gonna make it so. We need to get back to business."

She turned her bottom lip upside down. It was cute and I wanted a bite. But I wasn't hungry enough. I grinned at her and raised my eyebrows. She finally got up and got her phone. She came back to the couch and tapped away at it.

"I need to find their main number," she said.

"You instill me with confidence," I said.

She looked up at me and grinned.

"Listen, you," she said. "He personally told me that if I needed anything he'd be happy to help. All I had to do was call."

"How long ago was this?"

"Four or five years ago. I'm telling you, he'll remember me. He said he has a good memory like that."

"And why did he take a particular interest in you?"

So-yi shrugged. She was looking down at her phone. She put it to her ear and looked back at me.

"I wasn't the only one he took under his wing," she said. "He offered the same to a few of us. I guess he took to us. Saw potential or something. There was nothing awkward about it."

She put her hand up and looked away. I looked at her sitting there. She'd be hard to forget. I was counting on that.

"Hi, yes, Assegai? Great. I was hoping to speak with Hans Marais. I understand. Can you tell him that Detective So-yi Park from Jersey City Police Department called. I need his help on a case if he doesn't mind. Yes. My number is 201-555-9599. OK. I understand. Thank you."

She turned and looked back at me and grinned.

"You didn't take my number down," she said, still grinning.

"I have an eidetic memory," I said.

"Really?"

"Uh, sorry, I meant idiotic memory."

She giggled at that. A small little giggle that came up from inside her and spilled out like champagne. She was a hard woman to turn down. So I moved on to other things.

CHAPTER FORTY-THREE
PMG

"WHAT did reception say?" I asked.

"They were pretty noncommittal," she said. "She took down my info like you heard and she said she'd pass it along. She said if he wasn't on a mission he'd call back within twenty-four hours. If he was in the field then someone would call back and let me know when I might hear from him."

"And if he doesn't want to call you back?"

"That didn't sound like it was an option. You've got the wrong idea about this guy. He's really nice and friendly. Seems he's pretty sincere in calling people back I guess. Time will tell."

And it did. The wine and whiskey had made us hungry. So-yi pulled out a container of chocolate mousse. It wasn't fancy but it was good. She put two big dollops in martini glasses and we fed ourselves. I got the feeling she wanted us to feed each other. I was on a slippery road as it was and my feet were giving way. Spooning chocolate into her mouth wasn't going to help. I was saved by the bell, or the ring, really. Her phone had a default ring like telephones used to have. Like mine used to have. It had been about a half hour since So-yi had spoken with Assegai.

So-yi stuck her tongue out at me.

"See," she said.

She answered the phone and put it on speaker.

"So-yi Park," said the voice on the other end. It was deep and thick with an Afrikaans accent that dragged and flattened out the vowels as if hitting them with a hammer under a heavy woolen blanket. "How's my favorite New Jersey cop?"

"Hans?" she asked. Sounded like she didn't recognize his voice all that well. Yet it was a voice that seemed unforgettable.

"Who else, doll," he said. To my ears the "doll" sounded like "dull" in his accent. "I heard you called."

"Yes, I did. I'm just surprised you called back so quickly," she said.

"Only for my favorite pupils," he said. "You caught me at a good time. How can I help you?"

"I'm here with a friend of mine. His name's Anthony Carrick…"

"Where's here?"

"Jersey City."

"OK."

"He's up here trying to help a friend from the LAPD. There were a couple of murders a few weeks ago. You might have heard about it. The one kid was run down and the other was shot at close range."

"Ja, that was terrible. Stanley Spencer and Joe Severn if I recall."

"Yeah, that's exactly right. How did you know?"

"I've been here since the beginning of November. Helping out the FBI and some local LEOs. You know how it is."

"Right. Well Joe was a friend of Anthony's buddy. Actually, his mother was. Anyway, Anthony's here trying to figure out who did it and why."

"It's not going anywhere hey?"

"No it's not, and it seems like we're not getting anywhere either."

"The cops aren't being helpful?"

"No, it's not that," she said. "It's my department investigating. It's just that there are no leads. Anthony thinks it might be a US three letter agency. I think maybe a private military group has been hired. Maybe by a three letter agency, maybe by an NGO. You heard about the Bilderberg Group."

"We do some security for them," said Hans. "I'll tell you right now, this is not the kind of thing they do. Honestly, Sue, despite all the conspiracy theorists out there, the Bilderberg Group is a big circle jerk of the rich and powerful trying to see how they can become more rich and powerful."

"Yeah, that's what I figured. But we've gotta keep an open mind. I mean, you've never actually been inside the closed door meetings have you?"

"No, but listen, I've been in this business a long time. These guys aren't interested in that sort of stuff. Yeah, they might push for an intervention in the Middle East or elsewhere but they use diplomatic channels to get their message across. They don't do shadow ops. They use Assegai mostly, and of the other's they've used in the past, well, we all talk. The Bilderberg Group is not calling for assassinations or dictating world affairs other than through the businesses or political positions its members already have."

293

"What about a three letter agency?" asked So-yi.

"I don't know, Sue, I mean all of this sounds pretty crazy. No disrespect to your friend Anthony. It would be highly unusual for the government to be murdering its own citizens on home turf. Not saying it's never been done, but they'd probably do something like that themselves."

"Could you ask around? See if any of your guys know anything. Maybe they hired a PMG to carry it out?"

"Like I said, we don't do those kinds of black ops in the free world. I can tell you it wouldn't be any legit PMG either. But I'll ask around."

"Thanks so much, Hans. We could use all the help we can get."

"Ja, I can understand that. If it is government, you're gonna have a hell of a time getting to the bottom of it. You be careful, Sue. I don't want to have to go looking for you if you know what I mean. Do you need backup?"

"No, that's OK, thanks. Anthony's a big help."

"OK. That's good to hear. I'll touch base with you tomorrow night if I have anything. Worst case I'll call on Wednesday."

"Thanks so much, Hans."

"It's nothing," he said, and hung up.

"That's a thick accent he's got," I said. "Like a tractor dragging a chain down a back country road."

"Yeah, but you understood him, right?"

I nodded.

"He was speaking English. So yes, I do understand my mother tongue." I winked at her.

"He told us, when he had us for training, that he grew up on a farm not far from Bloemfontein. He's an Afrikaner through and through."

"Sounds like a likable guy," I said.

"He is. You'll like him when you meet him. He's a big guy. Solid like an oak tree too. I like to think of him as an African lion."

"PMG?"

"Oh, that's the acronym for private military group. Like Assegai and others like it."

There wasn't much left to say. Turned out I'd underestimated So-yi's contact. If nothing else he could help us rule out PMGs or maybe rule them in. It'd be something.

CHAPTER FORTY-FOUR
OVER HARD

THE next morning I was up at eight. I could hear So-yi showering in her bathroom. I went and did the same. My morning rituals. By the time I was out of the shower, shaved and dressed, So-yi was in the kitchen making breakfast. Ain't domestic life grand.

"Good morning," she said, with a big smile on her face.

"Morning," I said.

"I took the liberty of choosing what kinds of eggs you like. I thought that sunny side up wasn't your style. But over easy might not cut the mustard for you either. I was going to chicken out and cook yours over medium. That's the safe way. Instead I took a risk and cooked them over hard. If you don't like them like that, I'll just make you more."

She had lived with me for a hundred years it seemed.

"You're spot on. Over hard is just how I like them," I said, and I wasn't lying. "How did you know?"

"Well, you seem like a tough guy. I think you've got some hard edges. I figured, runny yolks weren't your style. It was probably just a guess at the end of the day."

"How are you having yours?"

"I prefer mine poached."

"No need to have gone to the trouble to cook them two ways," I said. "I'd have eaten poached eggs."

"It was no trouble at all."

I had smelt the bacon when I'd gotten out of the bathroom. She was cooking a lot of it. I went over and took a closer look.

"I don't have sausages, so I figured bacon would do?"

I nodded.

"Crispy, if you don't mind."

"Just how I like it," I said. "Listen, I'm just gonna call John quick and give him an update. We should also get you a burner."

"A burner?"

"I'll explain later."

I walked off to the far side of the living room and stood looking out over the Hudson River at an overcast Manhattan. It wasn't snowing today. I took out my phone and dialed Roberts. I filled him in. He encouraged me to get a vest to wear. He thought it was safer, especially since I wasn't carrying. I humored him and then hung up. Breakfast was ready. We sat down to eat. So-yi had given me more bacon than I usually ate. Eight rashers, but I ate them all. I was polite that way.

"I'm gonna have to run down stairs for a cigarette soon," I said.

She nodded with her last bite of food in her mouth.

"You thought we should get a burner?"

"I do. I've had everyone get one so far. Whoever we're dealing with thinks nothing of spying on anyone associated with this case, and they have the chops to do it."

"But they don't know I'm on the case," she said.

"Maybe not originally, but they're probably keeping tabs on me. Which means they do know now."

"OK. I'll tell you what. We can go and get a burner if you promise to wear my spare vest."

"It'll probably be too small."

"It'll be better than nothing. You don't have a gun and we're dealing with ruthless killers."

"But I have you."

"Anthony, I'm serious. If anything happened to you, John would kill me. I'm not getting a burner unless you're wearing a vest."

I nodded, and sipped on my coffee.

"OK then, my Captain, a vest it is."

I was actually hoping that the thing wouldn't fit. In fact I was counting on it.

"So," she said. "What are we up to today?"

"Well, I figure you should call Pipe Dreams Plumbing about that toilet leak in your spare bathroom," I said.

"My toilet's not leaking," she said, before thinking a little bit more about what I'd just said. Then she grinned. "Oh, OK, I see what you did there."

I nodded at her.

"Then, while we're waiting for them to show up we'll go and get you a burner and we'll get a couple of USB flash drives."

"What for?"

"You have a computer?"

She nodded.

"I'd like to try and access this mysterious file that Stan apparently has stored on his online game account on War

Tyde."

"Oh right, I'd forgotten about that."

"Yeah, well, I reckon that's about the only lead that we have left. I'm hoping it holds the key to the kingdom."

So-yi nodded and drank the last of her coffee.

"I'm hoping that Hans will find something for us too. I mean, I just can't come around to this being the work of our government."

"Why not?"

"Because it would rock my world to the foundation. I mean, really, if the government is killing its own citizens on their own soil then nothing is sacred."

"What if it's a PMG acting on behalf of our government. I see that as no better."

"True, and I hope that's not the case either."

"Then you've gotta give some credit to it being the Bilderberg Group or some other nefarious NGO."

"I'm starting to come around to your position on that. But from what we've heard, BG doesn't seem to act that way."

"According to your guy," I said.

"Yes, according to my guy, who I happen to believe. Maybe it's some other nefarious NGO."

I shrugged.

"I'll take some other nefarious NGO for two-thousand dollars, Alex."

So-yi giggled.

"Seriously, that's the problem. I don't know of any other nefarious NGOs."

"Maybe Hans will enlighten us," she said.

I drank my coffee and thought about smoking a cigarette. I was starting to get a little antsy.

"Call Pipe Dreams," I said.

She took out her phone.

"Wait," I said. "Here, use my burner."

I gave it to her and gave her their number. She put the phone to her ear.

"Be persistent," I said. "They'll likely try to put you off."

"Hi there, I need a plumber. My toilet's leaking. Wow, you're expensive. No, that's OK. I've heard you're the best. Can he not come sooner. No, I really want to use you guys. That's OK. I know I can find a cheaper plumbing company. Yes, but you've got good reviews on the Business Bureau. Oh, you're not. I still want you to come around. Yes, I insist. I suppose that will have to do then. Bye..."

So-yi looked over at me.

"God, that woman is so rude," she said.

"What did she say?"

"She didn't want to send anyone out. My God they're expensive. It's gonna be five hundred bucks minimum, and they can only come out this afternoon around two. They're also not in the Business Bureau."

She grinned at me.

"At least you got them to come," I said.

"Yeah, but why them specifically?"

"I want to see who we're dealing with. That was the company that Stan worked for as you know. They don't sound like any sort of plumbing outfit I've heard of. I mean you practically have to beat them into coming out on a call. What kind of legit plumbing company, hell, any company, isn't eager for business?"

"So you think his colleagues at work killed him?"

I shrugged.

"Maybe. They could be working on something really secret that maybe they didn't want Stan leaking. That's if this

301

plumbing company is actually a front for the NSA or somebody like it, which is what I'm inclined to believe."

"Well, why don't we just get the file downloaded from that online game first?"

"Because if my suspicions are correct, then all hell will break loose as soon as we try. Remember what happened when I tried to access it at Stan's place?"

So-yi nodded.

"They're probably monitoring that online game. If it is the NSA or some other government agency, they'll be crawling all over us and confiscate everything, and we'll be no better off. I want to get a feel for how this company works. Put some faces to the corporation."

So-yi nodded.

"You want to meet this guy," she said. "Are you hoping he's the killer?"

"Not necessarily. But I'll be able to tell if he's a real plumber or not by his body language. Meeting him will tell me a lot. If he is the killer that's a bonus. But we won't know that at the time will we?"

"I guess not."

We sat and drank more coffee for a while. I ended up needing to go back to the washroom. So did So-yi. I waited for her in the living room. I sat on a nice blue couch. It wasn't leather but I bet it cost more than my current salary. That wasn't hard. I wasn't earning any money on this job. She had a nice distressed metal coffee table in front of the couch. It was a dull gray and looked like a grinder had been taken to it. The wall on my right held a large bookshelf in the same style as the coffee table, though the shelves were made of wood. The frame was distressed metal. The wood looked like it had been found in a barn a hundred years ago.

I think they call it "reclaimed" now. And for that they tack on thousands of dollars.

It looked good. It looked good in So-yi's place but it wasn't my style. And not just on account of me not being able to afford it. So-yi came out of her bedroom. I got up to go.

"Not so fast Mr. Gumshoe," she said. In her hand she had a white vest. "We're not going anywhere until you put this on."

She tossed the vest to me. It didn't look bigger than a hand towel. I was wearing a white shirt over a white undershirt with dark gray slacks. I took off my shirt and put the vest over my head. The shoulder straps were slightly elasticized but not adjustable.

"You're in great shape," she said. "I've been wanting to see what was underneath your shirt."

"Another shirt," I said.

"You can take that off too if you'd like."

She was flirting with me.

"Seriously though," she said. "How do you keep in such good shape with all that smoking and drinking you do?"

"Good genes," I said. "And decades of boxing I guess."

"You still box?"

I nodded.

"When I can, just for fitness."

The straps on each side of the vest were velcro and attached the back part to the front. I attached the straps to each other. The vest was small on me, but thanks to the adjustable, elasticized straps I could make it fit. I spread out my arms and spun around like some awkward fashion model.

"Happy?" I asked.

So-yi nodded. "Very happy. Now we can go."

The front of the vest barely covered my nipples in width

and ended just above my belly button. My lungs and heart were protected but a gut shot would still have me bleeding to death slowly like an uncorked barrel of fine wine. I put on my shirt and grabbed my jacket and fedora and we headed out. I took my time and smoked a cigarette outside the main entrance while So-yi went and got her car.

CHAPTER FORTY-FIVE
EAST NEWARK

WE drove around in the late morning finding a burner for So-yi. She was pretty particular about the kind she wanted. For a burner I thought that was nuts. But the lady wanted what she wanted. We finally found something that suited her at the third store we tried. It was a mom and pop type of electronic joint. Sal's Electronics Superstore is what it called itself. There was nothing super about it. It was jam packed with product display cases and stands in a jumble that made no sense to me. But Sal, if that was his name, was friendly despite his looks.

I pegged him at around five-seven or eight. He was a big fat man in his sixties. He had a combover that seemed flattened over his bald head with mechanic's grease. A stubble that was at least a week old wasn't helping him out in the looks department. On the end of his nose was a librarian's pair of glasses. They looked old fashioned and hung around his neck with a purple beaded chain. He was smartly dressed with a waistcoat, bow tie and dress pants. But above the neckline was a car wreck. He was some sort of character alright. He had what So-yi wanted and he had the USB sticks.

"I want to head out to Pipe Dreams Plumbing. Just check them out," I said, once we were back in the car. "Before we do that. Just send me a quick text so I get your number."

She did. It was two emojis. A winking face and a kissing face. I hadn't worn a vest in years. Sometimes I put one on for a particular job, but I didn't like them. Felt like you were wearing a cardboard shirt. They were uncomfortable as hell. Especially the kind the police departments issued.

"OK," she said. "Where are they?"

"East Newark," I said. I gave her the address and she drove us out there.

"This is going to be a bit of a hike for them," she said.

"Maybe that's why they didn't want to come out and serve you," I said. "They're not in the Yellow Pages and they don't have a website."

The trip only took us about thirty minutes. We parked in a parking stall far away from any of the businesses. It was your usual mix of strip mall offerings. Dentist, walk-in clinic, dollar store, small grocery, the plumbers, a small electronics store, an independent gym and the like.

"You don't have binoculars do you?" I asked.

We were far enough away that it'd be hard to make out who was coming and going from Pipe Dreams Plumbing.

"Actually, I do," she said. "I keep a small pair in the glovebox. They come in handy as a detective."

I opened the glove box and took out the binoculars. They were a black pair in a soft plastic pouch. I opened them up and they were a compact pair about six inches by five inches. The bridge of the binoculars told me that they were 10x42.

That meant I was getting ten times closer to my subject with a front lens that was 42 millimeters in diameter. In bright conditions like today it didn't make much of a difference.

I put them up to my eyes and focused in on the far corner of the mall. That's where Pipe Dreams Plumbing was. It was clear they weren't looking for business. Their sign was plain, light gray cursive on a white background. It didn't jump out at you. The windows were frosted the first halfway up from the ground. I looked around at the other businesses in the mall. It was fairly busy for a late morning on a Tuesday the week before Christmas.

"Let me take a look," said So-yi.

I was already bored. I handed them over to her. She put them to her eyes and took a look.

"Not much is happening there," she said.

"Yeah."

She stared at them for a few minutes longer. I was looking in that direction too. Nobody had come in or out in the five minutes we had been there. She took the binoculars away from her eyes. She offered them to me. I took them and put them up on the dash.

"What did you see?" I asked.

"A business that doesn't seem all that busy," she said.

"Yeah, on purpose."

"What do you mean?"

"Take a look at their sign for one thing. Light gray on a white background. Letters in cursive, a thin cursive at that. Really? I can barely read it from out here. And yet, if you look at all the other businesses, their signs are practically jumping out at you."

So-yi nodded slowly, looking in the direction of Pipe Dreams.

"Yeah, you're right. It looks like an old-fashioned sign from a sixties business."

"Even back then they would have used at least black paint with a thicker line on the letters. They don't want business."

"You have a point."

I picked up the binoculars and looked through them again. Then I handed them to So-yi.

"Take another look at the front of Pipe Dreams. Take a look around the door and the windows."

She put them up to her eyes and took another look.

"What do you see?"

"Nothing," she said.

"Exactly. There's no placard telling customers what time the business is open. No credit card stickers or industry stickers to give you some reassurance that this is a business you can trust with your money."

So-yi looked a while longer.

"You're right. There is absolutely nothing on there."

She looked some more.

"And yet the dry cleaner right next to them has a whole bunch of stickers about their environmental footprint, the types of payment they accept, their hours. They also have some nice posters in the window."

"Right. Everyone here is hustling for your dollar. They're all trying to stand out and tempt you to do business with them. Pipe Dreams is like the opposite. It's very sketchy."

We watched the front of Pipe Dreams for another ten minutes. In the first fifteen minutes we were there nobody came in or out of that office in the corner. That was unlike most of the others we could see. Most of the other businesses in this strip mall saw at least a couple if not more customers in that time period.

"I'm gonna take a closer look," I said, getting out of the car.

"Do you think that's wise?"

"What?" I said. "I'm just gonna do some shopping."

I grinned at her. I put my hat back on my head and a cigarette in my mouth. The wind was calm and the day was cool and cloudy. I lit my cigarette and walked towards the first block of businesses that made up the L shape of this mall. The parking lot was spottily covered in clumps of crusted, gray, dirty snow and melting ice. I didn't look back at So-yi. I browsed the fronts of the store windows while enjoying my cigarette.

Nothing caught my eye but I made a good impression of someone looking for something. That something was justice. And a bagel from the bakery wasn't gonna cut it. But I played the role of customer very well. By the time I got to the corner of the L shaped mall my cigarette was finished. I squashed it underfoot.

As I approached the front door I could see over the frosted half of the glass. Inside was sparse. There was a chest high desk and behind it an older woman who looked like she'd lived rolled up in a wet newspaper most of her life. I could see she was smoking. I wasn't sure that was legal. I walked in with my best aw-shucks smile on my face.

CHAPTER FORTY-SIX
DREAMS UP IN SMOKE

SHE looked up at me over silver, wire-rimmed glasses perched halfway down her nose. They were around her neck on a silver chain. She was already pulling the look off better than Sal at his electronic emporium.

The air was cold and charged. I couldn't smell any smoke on it, but she was definitely smoking. I could see the cigarette in an ashtray as I approached the desk. The air inside caused the hairs on the back of my neck to stick up like pins. I started to feel like I'd made a mistake. There were cameras all around here. I was sure of that, but I couldn't see any of them.

There was nobody in this place. There were no chairs to sit on. A fake plant stood awkwardly in a corner. Clearly not welcome or wanted. But its leaves weren't covered with dust. That meant either the air in here, which was as crisp as a lightning strike, never carried dust, or the plant was tended to. The carpet was a thin gray scab over the concrete. Probably just stuck on. I felt like I was walking on iron. I felt shin splints developing just standing there.

That was it. There was nothing else here. No tables for magazines. No water stand or coffee maker. The receptionist was behind a chest high, white counter that captured her in a cubic prison. Behind her was a door. To my right as I stood in front of her was another door. I walked up and leaned on the counter. She took a long drag on her cigarette. She was probably mid-fifties with dyed brunette hair in curls. Makeup was thick. It looked like you'd imagine putting lipstick on a pig.

She was not an attractive woman. She was fat but not obese and wore a cream colored cardigan over a pale yellow blouse. The bottom bit of her, at least from the waist area that I could see was gray slacks. She put her cigarette back down in the ashtray. She took her glasses off her nose.

"What can I do you for?" she asked.

"I need to speak to a plumber," I said.

"We don't have any available."

"Maybe you can help me."

"Maybe," she said.

"I need someone to install a dishwasher for me in my apartment."

"Where's that?"

"The Waterfront," I said.

"There're plumbers closer to you that should do."

"Yeah, well I was here and figured I'd ask you guys about it. How much would you charge?"

"If it's a simple job, it'll be twelve-hundred. But only one of our plumbers can give a reliable quote. If you want someone to come over it's gonna be two-fifty but that'll be put against the job if you use us."

"Jesus, twelve-hundred. That seems like a lot. And two-fifty just to come out and take a look. Man, you guys don't want much business."

"We're busy enough."

"You don't look real busy."

"Like I said before, we ain't got no plumbers here for you to talk to. Besides, if you're at The Waterfront how come you care so much about price?"

"Because I saved up to live there. That's how."

"Sorry I can't help you. Those are our prices."

"I'm gonna go speak to one of your guys. I think you're mistaken."

"There's nobody here at the moment. Give me your name and number and I'll get someone to call you."

I could tell that was bullshit, because she'd gone back to perching her glasses down at the end of her nose and she was no longer listening or looking at me. She was typing away at her computer. A computer that looked like a high end unit of the sort I'd never seen before.

I walked towards the door that I could access. It looked like a cheap white, flushed, hollow core door covered in a laminate. I figured a gentle kick would knock it down. But I wasn't gonna be kicking down doors. Not this early in the game anyway. The door had a cheap, round silver handle to it. I knocked on the door. Not so much to be polite but to test out my theory on the door. I was wrong. It made a solid thud. I figured I was knocking against a solid steel door. That's what it felt like.

"I have to ask you to leave now," said her voice from behind me.

I figured I was in no danger from a woman in her mid-fifties who looked like she was a good ten years older. I ignored her. That was my mistake. I reached for the doorknob and then that's when I felt it. It was the last thing I felt. My last thought was "lightning". That's what it felt like. I've never been hit by lightning so I wouldn't know. But what this was I imagined was akin to lightning.

It knocked me on my ass. It felt like someone had hollowed me out and attached electrodes to my insides and turned up the voltage. I felt the tingling in my teeth. It came at me from everywhere at once. I couldn't be certain if I'd been electrocuted from the door handle, from something coming down from the ceiling or from the floor. When I came too though, I was pretty sure I had been electrocuted.

I don't know how long I'd been out. But the jolt had been extremely unpleasant. Felt like someone had somehow got a knife inside of me and then sliced me into ribbons from the inside out. I took a moment to get my bearings. I reached for my chest and patted it. My heart felt OK. I felt surprisingly OK considering I had just moments before felt like I was dying. It only took a few seconds for me to remember where I was. I was on my back looking up at two new faces I'd never seen before. They were large and black. They were helping me to my feet.

The receptionist was still typing away at her computer behind her desk.

"You OK, sir?" one of the big black guys asked me.

I looked from one to the other. They were dressed in security uniforms and carried Sig Sauer P226s shooting 9mm from what I could tell. I found all of this disconcerting. Not because of the electric shock but because I'd never seen such heavily armed mall security. Especially in a small strip mall like I was at. And their uniforms were unlike mall security uniforms I had seen. They weren't black and white. They were dressed in steel blue uniforms, top and bottom. It almost looked like a onesie, only it wasn't. The pants were cargo type and the shirt a thick button down number with a zip underneath the buttons.

"You OK, sir?" the same guy asked me.

I looked at him, and I felt surprisingly good for a man who'd just had a cattle prod shoved up his ass. Or so it felt like. I nodded. The two of them had me under the armpits. I felt steady on my feet. I looked over at the receptionist still typing away.

"That was unnecessary," I said.

She took her time to take her glasses off her nose and swivel in her chair to look at me. The exasperation on her face was like a waterfall. Making her look drowned out in impatience.

"I asked you to leave. You didn't and then you passed out. Looked to me like you fainted. Maybe you had a heart attack or stroke. I called security to check on you. And here you are, about to get escorted out."

I looked from the one security guard to the other. They were big black guys but pleasant looking. Their demeanor was friendly but their eyes told me that wild animals were waiting to be let out. They were both a little taller than me. At least six feet.

"How long was I out?"

"At least a few minutes," she said. "Five, seven. I wasn't counting. I have work to do."

"So you electrocute a man in your place of business and you don't tend to him. I'm gonna have my lawyers all over this place. I'll sue you out of business."

I was trying my best to be the affronted and insulted customer. I was neither.

"You were not electrocuted. You walked over to that door,

and I asked you to leave and then you dropped. I assume you had a fainting spell. Security doesn't seem to think you had a heart attack."

And I started to wonder if I had been electrocuted. My memory of these last several minutes were becoming a little more blurry. It was like trying to grab at a strand of mist. It disappeared as soon as you thought you had it. Like a dream that's burned up by the waking minutes.

"I don't believe you. I felt great pain," I said.

"Are you in pain now, sir?" asked one of the security guys.

I thought for a moment. And no, I wasn't in pain. I felt as right as rain upon a western plain. He handed me my hat.

"No, but, uh, but I'm pretty sure I was electrocuted."

I was saying it because that's what I believed, even though my memory had now started playing tricks on me.

"Show me," I said. "I know you must have cameras here."

"Alright, then you're leaving, and you're banned from coming back," she said.

"That seems a little harsh for just asking some questions," I said.

She ignored that and I walked over to her desk after security had loosened their grip on me. They walked with me like shadows and stood behind me on either side. She swiveled a monitor towards me so that I could see her screen. She started playing a recording of me that started just before I left her desk to walk towards the door. It was in color and it was sharp. That seemed strange. I'd never seen video surveillance footage that sharp or clear, and in color. I figured you could blow this up onto the side of the building and count my individual hairs under my fedora. The individual threads in my jacket. It was amazingly sharp.

I watched as I saw the back of me walking towards the

door. I knocked on it. Nothing happened. I heard her ask me to leave. Her voice sounded as if she had said it right now in front of me, in person. At least I knew there was audio. I reached for the door handle. From this angle I couldn't see if I made contact with it. I assumed not. Then I just dropped like a stone. I could see no sparks, no electrical discharge from anything. There were no sounds. Just me buckling at the knees and falling down. I looked at her. She swiveled the screen back towards her.

"Like I said, you fainted," she said.

I looked behind me from the angle that the camera should have been at. I couldn't see anything. It was likely someplace in the corner of the front and the right wall. But I couldn't see anything.

"Please escort him out now," she said. She looked at me. "Don't come back. You're not welcome."

"Wouldn't give you my business if you were the last plumbing company on earth," I said.

The security guards gestured towards the front door. I picked up my hat off the counter and put it on my head. I walked out followed by my two security guards.

"You guys work for Pipe Dreams don't you?" I asked, turning to look at them once we were outside.

"No, sir, we're mall security. We work for Muspell Logistics which is hired by the mall for their security needs."

I nodded. A mish mashed bundle of bullshit if I'd ever heard any.

"We need to see you leave," said one of them.

I fished a cigarette out of my jacket and lit it. God knew when the next time I'd have the chance to smoke. I turned and wandered down the mall. I walked into the bakery. I was getting hungry and I figured they'd be watching. Might as well do the consumer schtick.

CHAPTER FORTY-SEVEN
SLIPPERY MEMORIES

I came out of the bakery with half a dozen bagels and a loaf of sourdough. I turned left, pretending I'd missed another store. That left turn was to see if the security were still there waiting outside Pipe Dreams to watch me go. They'd disappeared. I looked up and down for them. I didn't see them anywhere. I looked across the parking lot. They were gone. So I walked back towards So-yi and her parked car. I climbed in and grinned at her, offering my kill as a prize.

"Bagels and bread," I said.

"You were gone a long time, Anthony," she said.

"I know, I was out for five or so minutes."

"It's been thirty minutes," she said. "I was about to come in and see what was going on."

I looked at her and understood her frustration.

"Thirty minutes?" I asked.

She nodded. I did the math. No more than five minutes to get there and five minutes back. Maybe five minutes chatting with the unhelpful receptionist. That meant I was on my ass for fifteen minutes at least. Two to three times longer than she'd told me. But she was full of lies. I wasn't as surprised as maybe I should have been.

"What happened?" asked So-yi, losing the prickly edge to her voice.

I patted my pockets down. I started to wonder what they'd done with me in those fifteen minutes. Fifteen minutes was a long time to go through a man's pockets. My pockets were empty except for some cash and now coins. I remembered I'd purposefully left my wallet at So-yi's place. Clever boy, Anthony, clever boy.

"You OK?" she asked again.

I looked up at her and nodded.

"Yeah. Tell me what happened from your end?"

She frowned at me.

"Well, you left here and walked down that side of the mall," she said, nodding in that direction with her head, "smoking a cigarette. You stopped to look at a couple of stores and then you finished your cigarette, put it out underfoot and walked into Pipe Dreams."

"I remember that," I said. "How long do you reckon it took?"

"I don't know. Maybe five minutes."

"And how long was I inside the plumbing office?"

"At least twenty minutes. Maybe a little more. That's when I started to get a little worried. I was just about to get out of the car when you walked out with two big black guys."

"You saw them?"

She nodded.

"How did they get in?"

"They weren't in there when you were inside?"

I shook my head.

"Then I don't know. I just saw them escort you out. I didn't see them go in. What happened in there Anthony?"

"I'm not exactly sure," I said. "I walked in like you said. I pretended I needed help with installing a dishwasher. She asked me where I lived. I told her The Waterfront. She said there were other plumbing companies that could help that were closer. I asked her what they'd charge. She said at least twelve-hundred. I told her that was a lot. She said it was two-fifty to come out which would be applied to the bill."

"That's what I was told too," said So-yi.

"Twelve-hundred or two-fifty?"

"Two-fifty for the call out. That's the minimum we'll be paying for this toilet leak you created."

I didn't say anything to that.

"So I told her that I wanted to speak to one of the plumbers," I continued. "She said there weren't any in. I said I was gonna speak to someone. Their prices were outrageous, yada yada. I went to the only door I could see that looked like it went into their back area. I knocked on it 'cos I figured it was hollow-core. But it felt like a solid steel door. She told me to leave. I didn't. I went to reach for the door handle and the next thing I know, I was knocked on my ass. Felt excruciating pain like maybe I was electrocuted before I lost consciousness."

"Good God, Anthony," she said.

"Nope. It wasn't good and God wasn't there," I grinned. "I woke up what seemed like moments later with those two big black guys looking down at me. So it's weird that you said I was in there for a good twenty minutes."

"You could've died," she said.

"I don't think so. I mean I lost consciousness for fifteen minutes. For a split second I'd felt the worst pain in my life.

321

Now I feel as if nothing had happened. And the weird thing is, I'm starting to second guess what actually happened in there. The memory of it seems unreliable. They did something to me So-yi, either through that jolt or while I was out cold in those fifteen minutes. Because the harder I try to remember the further it seems to slip away."

"But it did happen to you right?" she asked.

"Now you don't believe me," I said.

"I do, but I wasn't there."

"She showed me the footage. That place was teeming with cameras, and yet I couldn't see any of them. The footage was clear and crisp and in color with full audio. It showed what I just described but there was no evidence of me being electrocuted or anything like that. I don't know how they did it. All it showed was me falling to the floor."

"All I know was you were gone a long time."

"I'll tell you one thing. They're not a plumbing company. And those guys who escorted me out were not mall security. They told me they were hired by Muspell Logistics which was hired by the mall. But you never saw them come from outside."

I looked at her. She shook her head.

"And what happened after I started to make my way here?"

"Shortly after you went into the bakery they went back inside Pipe Dreams," she said.

"Really?"

So-yi nodded.

"And I haven't seen them since," I said. "Something else that was strange with this place was the environment inside. It felt charged. Like the air is, after a heavy thundershower with lots of lightning. I could feel it on my skin. It felt almost prickly and sharp. Clean and exceptionally dry. Almost as if the air in the room could be sucked out in a split second. I dunno. It just gave me a weird feeling."

So-yi didn't say anything.

"These people aren't what they seem. That's something I'm pretty sure of now."

We sat and watched for a while longer. After about five minutes So-yi turned to me.

"What do you want to do?"

"Let's head back and prepare for the plumbers. But before we do that. Just drive round back, or see if we can't get a view of what's behind Pipe Dreams. Maybe that'll give us something."

CHAPTER FORTY-EIGHT
GOOD NEIGHBORS

WE couldn't drive round back of the mall. We had to get onto the side road and drive parallel to it. But there was a tall wooden fence that was built up as an enclosure on that length of the mall. From behind the first shop, which was a beauty salon, all the way up to the end where Pipe Dreams was. The wooden fence enclosed a large square jutting out from behind that line of shops, taking up just about the same amount of space as the whole of the mall.

I got out of the car to take a closer look. I crossed the street and walked up towards the fence. I could see that on the other side of the wooden slats was a chain link fence. Both were probably about eight feet tall. The chain link fence ended in angled barbed wire that jutted out overhead about two feet. It was thick and the barbed part of it looked as sharp as razors. There were signs on the fence at about five feet up from the ground and spaced about twenty feet apart. They warned that the fence was electrified, and they forbid trespasses.

I knew the wood wasn't electrified. Wood isn't a good conductor. I touched it gingerly nevertheless. I could feel the buzzing and I could hear the humming of the chain link emanating from behind it. I looked around. This neighborhood looked like a fine middle-class neighborhood. The streets were clean and there was no graffiti around. So why would you electrify a fence?

The slats of wood were tight up against each other. You couldn't see between them. I pushed on them. They were solid. Secured in really good footings. This was a great fence. Looked nice and kept people out. Kept prying eyes out too. I scanned up and down the fence. I finally found what I was looking for. A small knot in one of the slats had popped out. I could put my index finger in it but no more.

It was a little higher than eye level. I had to get on the tip of my toes to see in. It didn't give me a good view but it gave me a taste of what might be behind that fence. It was a parking lot full of cars. Private cars, the kinds employees might drive to work. It was jam packed. Towards the far side from me was the exit. It was manned by two similar looking jackboots that had called themselves mall security in the plumbing office. They carried FN P90s and sidearms. I couldn't tell what kind of sidearms because of the distance between them and me. But I figured they were probably the Sigs my friends at Pipe Dreams had been carrying. They had a concrete hut they could use, about the size of a bedroom. Both were outside smoking.

The P90s were a nice touch. Small and easy to conceal and hardly intimidating. Yet they were devastating at close range. And I figured these guys were only worried about close range problems.

Just inside this parking lot, away from the mall was a ramp

that went down into what I assumed was underground parking. This parking lot was pretty quiet at the moment. Nobody coming or going. I scanned around some more and found a gift. Up against the wall of the mall were a line of half a dozen or so black sedans. The kind that G-men are always using. They were a mix of Chevy Impalas and Ford Taurus and Chrysler 300s. I counted six of them in a row. The second one closest to me had what looked like a bullet hole in the trunk, just off from the license plate. I couldn't read it.

I turned around and jogged back over to the other side of the street where So-yi was waiting. I opened up her door.

"I need your help," I said.

"What is it?"

"I think I've found the car that was used as the getaway in the Joe and Stan shooting."

"Really?"

"Yeah, but I can't be sure. Grab the binoculars. I'm gonna give you a boost."

She got the binoculars which I'd left on my seat. She climbed out. We looked left and right before crossing. This was a quiet street. Most of the mall traffic came in and out from the cross street. It was more to see if anyone was watching the watchers. We were the watchers.

On the other side of the street we walked to the corner furthest away from the beauty salon. I pointed diagonally towards the back of the mall. Cutting a line with my hand through the fence. Metaphorically of course. I ain't a superhero or one of Odin's kids.

"Against that wall, about in line with where I'm pointing is the black sedan I was talking of. Confirm if it's got a bullet hole in the trunk and if so, grab the license plate if you can."

327

"Didn't witnesses say they didn't see a license plate?"

I nodded.

"Yeah, that's right. I guess they've put one on since."

So-yi nodded. I leaned down by a tree and she used it to climb onto my shoulders. I walked her to the fence. Not too close on account of the barbed wire that was getting into her grill.

"Try and keep steady," she said to me.

"I'm trying," I said. "You're heavier than you look."

She kicked a heel into my ribs.

"Are you calling me fat, Anthony?" she asked.

"With a P H," I said.

She giggled.

"Get to work," I said. "There're guards up in that parking lot too with P90s. Don't let them see you."

"Oh, yeah, I see them."

I gave her a few moments.

"Do you see the car?"

"Yeah, I see it. Just give me a sec, I'm trying to read the license plate."

I waited patiently a couple more seconds.

"Oh shit," she said.

"What?"

"Let me down, they've seen me."

I let her down and she almost broke my back trying to dismount. She ran across the street to her car. I followed. We got in and she drove off. As she did her u-turn I saw a drone coming towards us. It was just on the parking lot side of the fence. It had a camera and what I assumed was some sort of weapon on it but I didn't see a barrel. Maybe it was an electrocution device. Or an EMP weapon. I didn't want to find out. I'd had enough with the first taste I'd been given of their capabilities.

So-yi was driving fast. Weaving in and out of traffic.

"We can go back to your place if you're asking," I said. "And the drone's not following us anymore."

I figured they might have gotten her license plate number. That was enough. But I didn't say it to her.

"What did you see?" I asked, after she'd slowed down and merged into the thick of traffic. She turned to look at me briefly as she drove.

"I saw the sedan like you said. An older model Chevy Impala. I'm not so good with my cars, but I'd say it was probably around ten years or more old."

"It had the bullet hole right?"

She nodded.

"It did. In the back of the trunk like you said. It's weird though."

"What is?"

"Well, you'd think they'd have gotten it fixed by now."

I didn't say anything to that at first. It was a valid comment.

"Maybe they didn't realize it," I said, not buying it myself.

So-yi didn't say anything for a while.

"Who are these people?" she asked.

"That's a good question. I want to see if Roberts can find anything out about Muspell Logistics. Maybe that's a front for a PMG."

She looked over at me again.

"I'm starting to come around to your view," she said. "Not that it's a three letter government agency. I mean, when was the last time you heard of a government agency working out of a strip mall."

"Never," I said. "But that would be one way to keep it

secret. I mean if this had never happened. If we'd never found that business card on Stan, would we know to look here?"

So-yi didn't say anything.

"But I'm starting to think this could maybe be more NGO or PMG. Maybe your friend Hans will find something. He said he'd call today or tomorrow right?"

So-yi nodded.

"Yes. I'm having a hard time thinking this is government. But PMG or some other third party I can get behind."

"Did you get the license plate number by the way?"

So-yi nodded and she gave it to me. It was a standard non-commercial, non-governmental plate and I repeated it over and over again to make sure I didn't forget it.

"What else did you see up there?" I asked.

"Just a parking lot full of cars. Regular cars, plus that handful of black sedans you pointed out."

"Did it look like there was an underground parking lot accessible?"

So-yi nodded.

"Yes, just off to the right side of the guard's hut as we looked at it. I counted two guards, but there must have been a third."

"Why do you think that?"

"Well, the one guard pointed his weapon at me. Then he started gesticulating with it in his hand. Sort of like he was trying to tell me to get down. That's when I asked you to let me down. The other guard then turned around and they both started running towards us. But a drone came at me too. Seemed to come up and out of the roof of the hut. It came fast. Faster than the guards."

I thought for a moment.

"It probably got your license number," I said.

"Oh well, the plumber's coming around this afternoon anyway. It was only a matter of time before they figured out who I was."

CHAPTER FORTY-NINE
SPY CAM

WE stopped on our drive back to So-yi's place to get buns, roast beef, tomatoes and lettuce for lunch. So-yi promised a roast beef bun of the likes I'd never enjoyed before. She didn't want to use the bagels I'd gotten. I figured it was a good thing we weren't a couple. I'd be getting fatter and fatter as each meal time rolled around.

It was just coming on one when we arrived back in her underground parking stall. We took the elevator up to her apartment.

"Pipe Dreams said they'd send someone around two, right?" I asked her.

She nodded as she unpacked the groceries, leaving the meats and buns for our sandwiches on the cutting board.

"We don't have a long time to prepare," I said. "I'm going to check out the bathroom again and see if I can't place my phone there surreptitiously to take pictures of our plumber."

"Why do you want to do that?"

"Because I'm betting he won't let me take his picture

standing in the hallway," I said.

"Yes, I know that, but for what purpose."

"To send to John. See if he can figure out who one of these guys is at least. We have a friend at the FBI who can do that sort of thing."

"Cool. Then we can check it against the ID he gives us when he gets here."

I nodded.

"If that's worth anything."

"OK. Well, you be quick. I'm the fastest sandwich maker in the east," she said.

I grinned and walked into her spare bathroom. There was a cupboard above the toilet which I'd told her was leaking. It was working just fine. The cupboard had glass doors in a wooden frame. Inside were soaps, perfumes and other toiletries including toothpaste and an extra toothbrush. There was also a box of antacids. I took it out. The box was wider than my burner phone and almost as long.

I took out the blister packs of antacids and tried my burner phone. It fit, but it's chin pushed out the other side. I put it back in and rearranged the toothpaste to stand on its head. That was enough to hide my phone sticking out the other side. I aligned the toothbrush alongside the box, and angling it just right, the handle of the packaging would frame my phone's lens perfectly.

At least that's what I thought. But my phone was inside the box and I couldn't see it. I took the blade out of my safety razor and put it on the edge of the sink. I took So-yi's fingernail clippers and with the attached nail board with hook I twisted a hole into the box. That was after I had measured it twice against my phone. Then I took my blade and cleaned up the hole so that if I was in kindergarten my teacher might say it was a circle. I put my phone back inside the box. The hole was in the right place. Time for a test.

I took the phone out. Opened up the camera app and begun recording video. I put the phone back inside the box and put the box inside the cupboard and arranged everything just so. I looked at the box and made some goofy selfie poses. Then I moved around the toilet a bit. I squatted and moved off to the left and then to the right. This was on account of me trying to play being a real plumber trying to fix a real toilet leak.

Then I took out the box and my phone. I stopped the recording and played it back. It worked like a charm. There was a nice big three foot by four foot rectangle area of recording just in front of the toilet that was captured. I was pleased with my work. I deleted the recording. I wanted all the memory I could get from my phone to capture this plumber. Maybe he wasn't the one. But if I had him and his ID then I could start working on associates.

I put the box back into the cupboard and arranged everything the way I wanted again. I looked at it all. I could see the hole but then I knew what I was looking at. I walked out and came back into the toilet and looked around like I was just a stranger, casually visiting this place. The hole wasn't that obvious. At least that was my hope.

I walked back into the kitchen area. So-yi had prepared a place for me at the island. There was a white bun with roast beef, lettuce, tomato, mayo and mustard on a plate. A cold beer in a bottle was next to it, blistering. It was an IPA. A nice, crisp, dry ale. At least that's my take on it. It was by a local brewing company. For a thirsty man it was good. But then very few beers aren't. Though it ain't no whiskey.

"Some people think a roast beef sandwich shouldn't be

served with lettuce or tomatoes."

"Some people are wrong," I said, through a mouthful of food. "This is really good."

So-yi smiled at me. She was nibbling at hers and sipping a glass of white wine.

"I'll make you another if you'd like."

"I would like, but that would be too much."

"I suppose we should keep an appetite for tonight."

"What's happening tonight?" I asked.

"I want to take you to my favorite Korean restaurant. It's called Kimchi's Korean BBQ. It's a bit of a drive, but you'll love it."

I nodded my head slowly.

"I'd like that," I said. "My first impressions of Korean food in Jersey have been pretty good so far."

It was one-thirty by the time we finished lunch. It was time to call John. He'd be at the office, or maybe at a homicide, so I called him on his cell.

"Sid, buddy," he said, "nice to hear from you again."

"Snarky morning to you to," I said.

"Just having a go, Sid, like you like to say. You know I'm always happy to hear from my pally ol' pal. What's up?"

"You got a minute?"

"Yeah, nothing much going down in TID."

"Shit," I said, under my breath. I'd forgotten he'd been kicked out of homicide. That was how wrapped up I was in the case.

"What's that?"

"Nothing, just sorry to hear you're still there."

"Well, we both knew it wasn't gonna change over the weekend. By the way, I've reached out to my union rep like you suggested."

"And what did he say?"

"Said I've got a case. But it'll take a bit of time."

"Good," I said, "that's great news."

"Yeah, but you're calling about Joe's case and that's what I'm more interested in"

"We went out to the mall today."

"I'm not interested in your vacation and shopping experiences in Jersey."

I laughed.

"Very funny, I went to the mall where Pipe Dreams is to take a looky-loo, Rotten."

Roberts didn't say anything to that so I decided to continue.

"It's obviously a front. But a front for what, is what we're gonna try and figure out. Plain storefront that's not trying to attract business. We must have been there around half an hour with nobody coming or going, and the mall was quite busy."

"Yeah, but who visits a plumber's office. They call for service," he said.

"True, but I went into the devil's den. There's something weird about the place. The air was sharp and dry. It felt like it coulda been sucked out of that office at a moment's notice. The receptionist wasn't helpful. They wanted twelve-hundred bucks to replace a dishwasher and suggested I try someone else. I told her that was way too expensive and that I wanted to speak to a plumber. She said there were no plumbers. Anyway, I didn't believe her. There was a door to the back, probably where the plumbers and tools and supplies were, so I figured I'd walk into the back to speak with a plumber. Or barring that, check the place out a little more."

337

"You've got cojones, Sid, I'll give you that."

"Like I said, there was nobody there except this receptionist. She must have been in her sixties, or at least she looked like it. I wasn't worried. That was my first mistake."

"Shit, what happened?" he asked.

"I knocked on the door expecting it to be one of those hollow core types. It wasn't. Felt like solid steel or lead. So I reached for the doorknob. I didn't make it. Next I knew, I was in excruciating and debilitating pain throughout my body and knocked on my ass."

"Jesus, Anthony, you need to be more careful. These people aren't playing. They killed two kids already. I'd assume they'd be just as quick to do you in and bury you out back. Especially if there's nobody in there."

"Pretty sure there were cameras by the dozen in there. Not that I could see any."

I knew John was getting serious when he used my real name.

"Anthony, seriously. You've gotta step gentle into this. We don't know who we're dealing with. It's bad enough Rachel lost a son. But man, if anything happens to you. Well, that wouldn't be cool. I've got enough mouths to feed. I don't want to have start feeding Aibhilin."

Roberts was Aibhilin's godfather. I appreciated the sentiment he was trying to share.

"Don't worry about it," I said. "She'd still have her mother and that dipshit, Artero, to live with."

"Asshole," said Roberts, joking, "I was trying to have a sincere moment, Sid."

"Do you want to hear the rest of my story or are we going to hold hands and sing kumbaya all afternoon?"

"Carry on with your story."

"So, I was knocked out on my ass. When I woke up, these two big security guards were looking over me. The receptionist told me I was out for around five minutes. I figured it must have been closer to fifteen, maybe twenty minutes."

"How do you know that?"

"So-yi was in the car in the parking lot waiting for me. She told me how long I was gone. I was gone thirty minutes. And what's more, every time I tell this story it feels a little stranger to me. Like it was a dream or a long forgotten memory. I'm starting to wonder if I'm making it up."

"And how do you feel now?"

"Like nothing happened."

"That's good news."

"Yeah. But there're a couple other things I wanted to share. Those security guards were not mall security as much as they tried to convince me otherwise. They came from inside Pipe Dreams office. So-yi never saw them enter or exit. They said they work for Muspell Logistics. I was hoping you could check that organization out."

"Will do. But you know as well as me, that if they told you that, it probably means jack."

"You never know," I said. "Loose lips sink ships. And maybe we're dealing with drunk sailors with loose lips."

"I'll check it out. Anything else?"

"Only the crown jewel, Rotten. I found the black sedan that was the getaway vehicle at the scene."

"How can you be sure?"

"I can't, but how many other black sedans are gonna have a bullet hole in the trunk, and is associated with Pipe Dreams. Behind Pipe Dreams, all along that one row of businesses at the mall, on the back side, is a fenced in parking lot. That's where I found it."

"Maybe it's a public lot."

"How many fenced in public parking lots do you know attached to a mall have an electrified fence and are patrolled by armed guards carrying FN P90s and drones?"

"Valid point."

"So, do me a favor and run the license plate and see if we can't get a name."

I gave him the license plate.

"Thanks, Sid. That's some good work you're doing out there. But please. Take care. And are you wearing a vest?"

"Yeah, So-yi gave me one."

"Good."

"Last thing," I said. "We're waiting for a plumber from Pipe Dreams for a fake leaking toilet. Should be here in fifteen, twenty minutes. I'll try and grab his mugshot and send it to you later. See if you can't get our FBI guy to run facial recognition on it. I've got a feeling the name he's gonna give will be fake."

"Sure thing."

"That's it. I'll talk to you later."

"Thanks, Sid. And for God's sake, take it easy out there."

"No problem, I've got a five foot four, fifth-dan taekwondo bodyguard."

Roberts laughed on the other end and I hung up.

CHAPTER FIFTY
NO LEAKS

IT was two-thirty when the plumber decided to show up. I guess a half-hour wait ain't too bad on a plumber's schedule. So-yi answered the intercom.

"Pipe Dreams Plumbing, ma'am, we're here about a leaking toilet."

"Yes, thank you. Please come up," she said.

She hung up and walked over towards me. I was sitting on her couch in front of her coffee table. I was drinking a coffee and reading the paper. I wanted a cigarette, but I guess a plumber would have to do.

"They're here."

"Great, let me go set up my spy cam," I said, grinning.

She followed me into the bathroom. I took out the box of antacids and I put them under a pile of towels in a wicker shelf next to the bath. I unlocked the phone and started the video app. 720p would have to do. I put my phone back inside and placed everything just so.

"Are you sure it's gonna work?" she asked.

I nodded.

"I practiced earlier, remember. There's a good three by four feet of recording area in front of the toilet so I'm pretty sure we're good."

I looked at it one last time and gave it a wink. Then we walked out and back into the kitchen to wait for the plumber. We didn't have to wait long. A minute later there was a knock at the door. So-yi went to answer. I went with her.

There were two guys standing at the door. Both of them were dressed the same and both of them held large rectangular tool boxes, or plumber's bags. They were filled with tools of the trade. Tools that looked like they had been well used and some that had perhaps been passed down. They also wore steel blue plumbing coverall with what looked like a white undershirt. If it had been a two piece I might have mistaken them for the Muspell security guards I had met in their office.

They walked into the hallway and introduced themselves. Their first names were embroidered on their coveralls. Their last names were not.

"Alex Granary from Pipe Dreams Plumbing and this is my apprentice Rudy Hodgkin. I hope that's OK?"

"Not if I'm going to be charged twice," said So-yi.

"No, ma'am," said Alex.

"Then it's OK."

They shook hands with both So-yi and me. They were rough, meaty hands that did work. I just wasn't sure what kind of work they did. The embroidered names matched the man wearing it. They were both around six feet and in their mid-thirties. I found that strange. Not for Alex, 'cos he was probably a journeyman. But a mid-thirties apprentice plumber needed some explanation.

Alex was the more handsome of the two. They both had military style haircuts. Short on the sides and back and not much longer on the top. That sorta gave them away. They were selling everything else well. Alex had dirty brown hair and brown eyes. Rudy had black hair and grey eyes. He also had a busted up nose and a scar above his lip.

Alex didn't look like he'd seen violence. Or if he had, he was just that good. Their demeanor was friendly but I could see them both giving me the once over.

"You in the middle of a career change?" I asked Rudy as they knelt to take off their boots.

"Yes, sir," he said. "Came out of the army a few years ago and needed something different. I figured a trade was as good as any."

"So where's this leak?" asked Alex, not wanting idle chit-chat.

"This way," said So-yi.

She led them into the bathroom and I followed. She pointed at the toilet.

"It's been leaking on and off for a while now. I don't know why. But I used some food dye to check and it sure is leaking. Maybe you can fix it?"

Alex took off the tank's lid and then flushed the toilet and watched it refill.

"I called you guys up earlier about replacing my dishwasher. I was quoted twelve-hundred bucks. Does that sound about right?"

Alex nodded, not taking his eye off the filling tank.

"That must include the new dishwasher, am I right?" I asked, grinning.

Alex shook his head.

"No, sir, just the installation. Depending on the job. Could

343

be more."

"Jesus, that's highway robbery."

Still no reaction. He was cool as a cucumber just watching the toilet tank fill back up with water.

"I don't make the prices," he said. "There are cheaper companies out there. But we have a twelve month warranty on parts and labor."

"I see," I said.

The tank was full again.

"You take a look," Alex said to Rudy.

They switched places and Rudy did the same thing as Alex had done. So-yi and I watched. And we waited as Alex and Rudy seemed mesmerized by a filling toilet tank.

"What do you think?" asked So-yi.

Alex looked at Rudy. Rudy shrugged. Alex looked at So-yi.

"I don't think your toilet's leaking," he said. "It seems in pretty good condition. How long have you been here?"

"Since two-thousand and nine," she said.

Alex nodded like he knew that.

"Yeah, these places were built in oh-five if I remember. And this is original right?"

So-yi nodded.

"Yeah, I'm not gonna lie, but I don't think this toilet is leaking."

"Maybe not right now. But it's like I said. It does it every so often. Can you replace some of the stuff in there to make sure it doesn't leak at all?"

Alex nodded.

"Yeah, we'll replace the fill valve and flapper. That should do it. You said it's leaking into the bowl, right, not onto the floor?"

So-yi nodded.

"Yes, that's right. Just into the bowl."

"OK. Ma'am, before we start work I've gotta get you to sign off on the invoice. It's so you know how much it's gonna cost. If you choose not to have us do it then there's the two-fifty call out fee. Otherwise that fee is included in the job."

So-yi nodded. Rudy and Alex switched places again. I took a quick glance at the cupboard above the toilet. It was like these two were auditioning for my hidden camera. I was getting great exposure.

"Rudy's gonna do up the job."

So-yi nodded again. Alex just stood around not doing anything. It was like they were real plumbers. And I started to believe them. I started to think that maybe these two guys were just part of the cover story. The killers practicing in a gun range some place else. A guy could get a bust up nose a bunch of ways. He could fall of a bike. He could play hockey or football. Hell, he could even box. Didn't make him a killer.

Rudy pulled out an iPad from the side of his tool box. It was covered in a solid rubber case. He tapped away at it and finally offered So-yi the tablet.

"It's all self-explanatory," he said.

So-yi looked at it. She started frowning.

"You want five-hundred and fifty dollars just to replace some rubber?"

"That's right ma'am," said Alex. "We aren't the cheapest, but we like to think we're the best. You don't have to go with us. Of course, that's your choice, but you did agree to the call out fee of two-fifty."

She passed the tablet to me. I raised my eyebrows. I figured it would be around this considering how much their call out fee is.

"Well," I said. "They're here. May as well have them do

it."

I handed it back to her.

"So if you agree ma'am, just use your finger to sign there," said Rudy, pointing at the spot.

So-yi reluctantly signed it.

"I don't know how you guys are still in business with these kinds of prices."

They didn't say anything to that. Rudy put away the iPad and rummaged in his tool box before coming out with some flappers and an intake valve.

"You okay to watch, make sure we get our money's worth?" I asked So-yi.

She nodded. Her arms were crossed over themselves and she was playing the pissed off homeowner very well. Maybe she really was pissed off. I would be too if I was paying five hundred bucks just to have my intake valve and flapper replaced.

I walked back out into the living room to finish my coffee and paper. About a half-hour later they all came out of the bathroom. They thanked us for our business and left. They didn't leave business cards or ask us to recommend them. I was still pretty sure they were a fishy outfit. We walked back into the living room together.

"Well, that was damned expensive," she said.

"I can maybe try to get you reimbursed," I said, thinking of Rebecca.

"No, that's okay. Just complaining."

"You have a right to. We just got genuinely ripped off. Especially considering there's no leak."

She laughed.

"But they did seem like real plumbers to me," said So-yi.

I nodded. I hated to agree with her.

"Doesn't mean you can't be a plumber and a killer. In this economy I hear you've gotta diversify your skills."

I was only half being facetious. So-yi liked it and laughed at me. It was nice to see her laughing.

"You're funny, Anthony. But seriously, didn't they really seem like plumbers. Discounting the company itself, couldn't they just be part of the front?"

I looked out the large windows and across the Hudson to Lower Manhattan. I could see Pier 25. So-yi had pointed that out earlier. It was a view I could get used to. But the price was too high. Nothing was happening at the pier. I bet in summer it was vibrant. I bet more people would be dead by then and I hadn't yet solved this one. I nodded. So-yi could be right. I don't know why I was expecting the killer to show up and introduce themselves to me. Especially knowing I was on the case. I was pretty sure they knew about that by now. I turned around and sighed.

"Yeah, I think you're right. Guess I was being too optimistic. I mean, why would they show themselves to me face to face knowing I was on the case?"

"And they probably do know, right?" said So-yi. "I mean, they've been tapping the folks you've been interviewing."

I nodded.

"Yeah. Well, looking on the bright side. I'm pretty sure I got them on candid camera. Hopefully ID'ing them will get us something to work on."

"Speaking of candid camera," said So-yi. "Do you want to get it now?"

I shook my head.

"No, first I want to see if we can't get into War Tyde and find out what Stan had uploaded there. Maybe that's the break we'll need."

347

CHAPTER FIFTY-ONE
X-FILES

So-yi got her laptop out of her room. It was a sleek and slim little Windows machine. She also brought out the couple of USB flash drives we brought from Sal, our pal at the electronics store. I got my notebook out and reviewed my notes. So-yi started up her laptop. She used her fingerprint to unlock it.

"What's his password?" she asked, not looking at me, but bringing up a browser.

"I think it's 'Trust in the Lord noble character is a shield'," I said.

Now she looked up at me.

"Seriously?"

"Yeah, I think so. I never had a chance to try it. Stan was pretty religious from all accounts. His sister Shiloh gave me his bible that she'd been given by him. She said he told her that it contained his password to War Tyde and that if anything happened to him she could have access to his account. He told her he had stored files up there that were important."

"So he wrote out 'Trust in the Lord noble character is a shield'?"

"Not in so many words," I said. "He wrote down his favorite Proverbs. I deduced the rest. If you want I can get you the bible and go through it, but I'd just as soon try it. I feel pretty confident."

"OK, OK. Just asking," said So-yi, feeling my frustration.

I was frustrated. I was hoping to have met the killers, and now I wasn't so sure. That was a disappointment. And I didn't think we had a lot of time.

"We need to work quickly," I said. "I've got a feeling these guys are probably tracking anyone who signs up to War Tyde under Stan's username. And I wouldn't be surprised if they're able to piggyback us into the game. Hopefully we'll get two copies done, but we might only get one."

So-yi nodded.

"You think they're that good?"

"I'm not an IT expert. But they were tracking me logging in to Stan's computer at home and they shut me out, so yeah, I wouldn't be surprised if something like that was possible for them."

"I guess it's possible," she said.

"Oh ye of little faith. If you've seen what I've seen. These guys hacked into Stan's computer remotely right when I was trying to get on. That seems pretty clever to me."

So-yi nodded.

"OK, let's give this a go. Username and password again."

I put down my notes where I had written the one below the other. So-yi typed in the War Tyde URL into the browser address bar. I held my breath. I didn't have to hold it long. I guess living in The Waterfront gets you blazing fast internet.

A colorful home page populated the screen. It was filled with animated characters of men, women, wolves, other animals that seemed made up, elves, goblins, pirates. Just a whole mishmash. The characters were dressed in a combination that looked like old pirate, fantasy and viking type clothes.

So-yi found the login button and hit it. Then she typed in the username followed by the password.

"Huh," she said.

"What?"

"He's pretty religious, but then his username is FoxMulder84. A show that believed in alien conspiracy theories."

"You could argue that Jesus might have been an alien," I said, half seriously.

So-yi laughed.

"Yes, I suppose it is all fantasy and make believe," she said.

"The 84 is his year of birth from what I gather."

The login screen opened up to us and Stan's main character who looked a lot like Fox Mulder from the X-Files show was ready to go.

"Shit, can we hurry?" I said. "Where the hell would you find documents?"

"Let me see," said So-yi. "I've played a couple of games like this before, a long time ago. Usually you'll find all sorts of things under 'settings' or 'your account'."

She seemed more technologically savvy than I was so I let her drive. Settings menu didn't have what we wanted so she went into the "Your Account" menu. She played around in there until she found what she thought were the documents.

"This is very clever," she said. "It looks like he's created another menu heading that probably isn't on any other player's' account tab."

"Yeah, and that is?"

"Look," she said, moving the cursor all over the menu heading so I could see. To be fair to me, I wasn't sure what I was looking for so I hadn't been looking at the smaller details.

"X-Files," I said. "That is clever."

"Exactly. It doesn't match any of the other menu items and it's in a slightly different font."

"Well, let's step to it."

So-yi had already put one of the USB flash drives into the laptop port. They were small little drives. Easy to lose. In hindsight I was thinking we shoulda got bigger ones. These were the size of the first joint of my thumb and not as thick.

I kept waiting for the hack. For Pipe Dreams, or whoever the hell they were, to shut us out. It hadn't happened yet, but I was expecting it at any moment. So-yi double clicked on the X-Files link. It opened up to a black screen. There were only two options on it. "Secure Erase" or "Download".

"Download," I said.

"I'm going as fast as I can."

She hit download and Windows asked her where to save it. She saved it to the USB drive. There was just over a gigabyte of content to download. It only took half a minute or so.

"Done," she said.

"Great, give me that one for safekeeping."

"Cool your jets cowboy, I'm going as fast as I can. At least we've got one already."

She ejected the USB drive and then pulled it out and gave it to me. I took it and put it in my sock. Right up against my shoe and the arch in my foot. She looked at me.

"Really?"

"Where else that's safe?"

"Your pocket," she said.

"Things can fall out of pockets. I want this on my person at all times. Safe and secure."

"OK, Mr. Paranoid," she said.

"Just do the next one, and you can keep that lying around if you want."

"There's nobody here but you and me," she said, popping in the second USB drive which was a clone of the first. She hit the "Download" link again and had it save to the USB drive.

I heard a clicking noise. So did So-yi. I looked at the computer. It wasn't coming from there. I stood up fully and listened some more. There it was again. It was coming from her front door. She looked at me. I looked at her.

"Go get your gun," I said.

She went off to the bedroom and I made my way to the hallway.

CHAPTER FIFTY-TWO
SNAKE IN A BAG

I was close. I made it halfway down the hallway when the front door opened. I was only half surprised by who I saw greeting me. It was Alex, and right behind him was Rudy. Dressed just like they had been maybe five or ten minutes ago. Only this time they weren't carrying tool boxes. But they were carrying something else. In Alex's hand I saw what looked like a gun or a taser or something like that. But not exactly like anything I'd seen. It was smaller. All black and he held it at me differently than you would a gun.

I lunged at them for the last six or so feet. If I could just get one good punch to the mouth I'd have a chance. The hallway was narrow and Rudy wouldn't be able to get around Alex. I could take them one at a time. And that would buy enough time for So-yi to get out here with her gun. That was my intention.

You know what they say about good intentions. It's the pavement upon which the road to hell is laid. And I was on the road to hell. The next thing I knew I was falling on my ass again with excruciating pain. This shocking treatment at the hands of Pipe Dreams was becoming tiresome.

I didn't know how long I was out. When I came to, I was zip-tied behind my back and propped up against the bookshelf in So-yi's living room. So-yi was naked and spread prostrate over her steel coffee table. Her ass was just off the end and her thighs were parallel with the table legs. They were tied to the those legs and her arms, at the wrists, were tied to the opposite table legs. They were stretched out and looked uncomfortable. She had a gag in her mouth. She looked scared. Her eyes were wide like hardboiled eggs. They were looking at me. Looking for help.

I couldn't tell how long I'd been out. Was it fifteen, maybe twenty minutes like the last time. I couldn't tell. It was at least five minutes. I figured that's how long it would've taken the two of them to tie me and So-yi up like they had.

Rudy was playing with So-yi's computer. Alex was yanking on his cock with a condom nearby on the top of So-yi's ass.

"I told you one of us should have stayed behind," said Alex, getting himself halfway to hard.

Rudy didn't look at him.

"I wanted to see the asshole we're dealing with. Besides, it doesn't matter. We've got the files and I'm deleting them. I'm also going through her computer and reformatting the whole thing. Once these two are dead there's nothing on us anymore."

"You sure about that?"

"Yeah," said Rudy. "Sure as sunshine."

Alex had a half ass boner and he put on the condom. Then he started fucking So-yi. My blood was boiling. So-yi was making awful guttural sounds from behind her gag. All this time I'd been playing with the zip ties, but these fuckers had tied them real tight. Too tight. I could feel my hands turning purple.

They were gonna kill us. That was clear. Rudy had said as much. I needed a way not to make that happen. I looked at both of them. Rudy was still tapping away at his computer, Alex was tapping away at So-yi.

"How do you like that, bitch, huh?" said Alex, and he punched her on the lower back around the kidneys. He punched her with effort. I heard her muffled scream and that was enough. To hell with plans.

I slowly tried to get up. That wasn't working so good. I got up quickly and forcefully, and launched myself towards Alex. He didn't see me until the last minute. He looked at me with surprise on his face. Perhaps he was expecting me to still be out cold. I gave him a headbutt like I'd been saving them all up my whole life for this one chance. I knew his nose would break by the way it felt when my head hit it. Now the pretty boy wouldn't look so pretty anymore. I hit him hard enough he landed on the couch.

Rudy spun around and he wasn't waiting to figure out what had happened. He was up by the kitchen island. I had to be aggressive. I needed to put them under pressure. I ran to him and we met halfway between the couch and the island. He swung at me and I swayed back, the blow just missing. I could feel the wind of it. I could tell he had boxed. He was agile and quick with his feet and hands. I'd probably get one freebie like I'd just received, but he'd figure me out real quick. With my hands behind my back I'd be a punching bag. Before he could go for another swing I kicked him as hard as I could in the kneecap. He went down onto that knee. A genuflection at my wrath. That brought his face closer to me. I kicked it again as hard as I could. My shoe caught him on the cheek. Hard enough to break his cheekbone. That kick lay him out cold on the kitchen floor.

I turned to address Alex. I was too late. Out of the corner of my eye I saw two unpleasant things. His shriveled up prick in a bag, and that goddamn taser or whatever it was. Then it was lights out to excruciating pain again.

When I woke up I was up against the bookshelf again. My face was hurting. I tasted blood on my lip. I figured they'd laid into me when I was out cold. Fucking cowards. My hands felt the size of swollen hams and my ankles were now zip tied together. Alex was slapping me on the face. He had two tissues in his nose. One for each nostril. Already his nose was swollen up. He was dressed again in his blue steel coverall. On his hands he had surgical gloves.

"Now you're gonna sit there and watch like a good asshole," he said to me.

He had pulled a chair around so that he could sit and keep an eye on me. He had a gun pointed at me too. It looked like it could have been So-yi's Glock I'd seen in her purse. I looked passed him and saw Rudy. Rudy had now taken to raping So-yi. So much for his broken cheek. He was also wearing surgical gloves now. It must've been hurting though. He too was wearing a condom. I looked back at Alex.

"Who do you guys work for?" I asked.

"Pipe Dreams Plumbing," he said. "We're laying pipe."

They both thought that was fucking hilarious. So-yi and I were not laughing. I licked my lip. It was swollen and I tasted the metallic of blood. I wanted to kill these assholes so bad. I wanted to tell them that's what I was going to do. But I was hardly in a position to be doing much about anything.

"Muspell Logistics," I said.

I saw the flicker behind the eyes that told me I was right.

Alex didn't say anything.

"So you guys probably do contract work for the NSA."

I didn't get the flicker I wanted there.

"Or the DOD, I bet."

That was a bingo. Rudy finished raping So-yi. She'd stopped sobbing. I looked at her. She looked like she'd turtled. Gone someplace real deep inside. Someplace so deep that maybe nobody would find her again. I vowed to myself then, that if I got out of this alive I would hunt down these motherfuckers and kill them, even if it took the rest of my life.

"You know she's a cop. You can't kill a cop," I said, "and get away with it. You'll have the whole of the NYPD and Jersey PD hunting you down."

"We're above the law asshole. How'd you think we found you?" said Alex. Then he turned to Rudy who was getting dressed. "This place been looked over?"

CHAPTER FIFTY-THREE
DOUBLE TAP

"YEAH, I've looked it over," said Rudy.

"What if they made another copy of the files on another stick?" said Alex.

"I don't think they had time. Ask the asshole."

Alex turned to me. I could feel the flash drive in my sock. It was now up against the sole of my foot.

"You download any files before we got here?" he asked me.

"What files?" I said.

That got me a punch in the nose. It was a half-hearted effort on account of him using his left hand while holding the gun in his right. It still hurt. My eyes still watered, and it started bleeding. Dripping onto my nice clean shirt.

"I said, did you download any other files, asshole?"

Alex was pointing the gun at me menacingly. That was the least of my concerns. I figured if this lasted more than another fifteen or twenty minutes I might end up losing my hands. They'd gone numb. That wasn't a good sign.

"You didn't say," I said, "you asked."

This time he changed hands and slapped me across the face. I have no idea why he slapped me across the face, perhaps he'll die.

"Say again?"

He was snarling at me. He was right up in my grill. I might have managed another headbutt but I didn't have any room for back swing.

"No, we didn't have time. What's in those files anyway?"

He ignored me. He looked over at Rudy.

"Did you go through his pockets?"

"Yes, I told you this shit already. When he was out cold the first time. He just had some money in there. His wallet and shit we found in the bedroom. It's over by the island. His name's Anthony Carrick. Some private dick asshole out of California."

"OK, then we're gonna play it like we had discussed," said Alex. "Make sure all evidence of us is gone. Wipe it down and check everything out again."

Rudy left and scoured the rest of the apartment for around ten minutes. Alex never said anything to me. We sat and waited and watched each other.

"Why'd you kill those kids from The Rattlin' Chain?" I asked.

"Why do you care?"

"Because I'm investigating their murder."

"You'll never find anything. Even the cops couldn't."

"So you're not denying it?"

"I took pleasure in it."

He snarled at me again. After a while he got bored. He went up to So-yi and grabbed her ass, hard and violently.

"Isn't she a piece of work," he said. "I bet you've been

tapping that? Don't blame you. She's wet and tight. Wish I had more time."

He grinned at me. He could tell I was getting angry. He walked back up to me and taunted me with So-yi's gun.

"And you've just got to sit there and take it like a pussy," he said.

"Unzip me and I'll give you a lesson in manners," I said. My voice was hoarse and dry and full of broken glass.

"Man, I wish I could. But we're running out of time. We're gonna be missed back at the office. I'll tell you one thing though. I'd fuck you up so bad you'd wish you were dead."

"If wishes were horses, beggars would ride," I said.

Rudy came back into the room carrying a couple of items.

"That bitch has got this huge black dildo in her drawer, and check out what I found."

He showed Alex his spoils. In his one hand he had her police flashlight. It was a black 3-cell Maglite. In the other he had some lube.

"This here's an even bigger black cock," said Rudy, putting it down by his crotch.

"Just make it quick," said Alex, obviously of the same mind as Rudy.

Rudy went over to So-yi and squirted lube on her ass. Then he sodomized her with the flashlight. I heard her sobbing. I was apoplectic. I tried to get up. I'd fight these assholes with my knees and elbows and teeth if that was all I had. I got up to kneeling when Alex kicked me in the ribs. He might have cracked one. It took the wind out of me. By the time I had collected myself, Rudy was finished.

He pulled the flashlight out of So-yi. She had gone real quiet now. He came over to me. Alex turned me onto my front. Rudy did something with the flashlight on my dead hands. Then he turned me back up against the bookshelf.

"Now your fingerprints are on this, asshole. Looks like you sodomized this poor bitch," said Rudy.

"That's enough," said Alex, "let's go."

Rudy took the flashlight and put it back inside So-yi. Alex went up to her and shot her in the back of the head. I wasn't expecting it. The sound barked like a demon dog inside the apartment. Then Alex turned around and pointed the gun at my head.

"Two shots in the gut, like we said," said Rudy. "If he makes it, he'll be the prime suspect and he'll have to live with what we've done to this sweet ass. If he dies, well, fuck yeah, good riddance."

Alex nodded. He pulled the trigger and the demon dog barked twice more. For one of the very few times in my life I was glad to be wearing a vest. I was also glad to have bled from my nose onto my shirt. It'd make it look authentic. Something was wrong though. It felt like an icicle had stuck me in the lower gut. It hurt like hell. I'd been shot. One of the bullets had missed the vest.

I was complaining and hyperventilating to sell it. But also because it hurt like hell. Alex came over to me. Same smirk. Same asshole he'd been since the second time I'd met him. He cocked me with the butt of the gun and I went out cold. I came to, to the soft, distant sound of a door closing.

I was on my stomach. It hurt real bad. My head throbbed. My hands were free and tingling with a fiery sensation. I touched my head. It was wet. I looked at it. It was red. I tried to get myself up to kneeling. I grimaced in pain. Each movement was like a knife digging deeper into my belly. Blood dripped from my head, down my cheek onto the carpet. I leaned back onto my feet. I gingerly touched my side. It was warm and wet. I looked down. I was bleeding pretty good. There was a small round circle of my blood on the carpet where I'd been laying.

I remembered what had happened. I looked over at the coffee table. So-yi was there, her eyes open but dead. The back of her head matted and wet. My eyes welled up. I took the cuff of my sleeve and dabbed at them. I crawled over to her in searing pain. She'd been cut loose. There was no sign of the ropes used to tie her down. I pulled the flashlight out of her. I checked her carotid for a pulse.

"If wishes were horses," I said, under my breath. She was long gone. I sobbed. But that didn't last long. The pain was overwhelming in my heaving. I was weak and losing blood. I had to get help. I used the table to stand up. I looked around. Her clothes were on the couch. I went over to them and grabbed her cell phone. I couldn't unlock it. I gingerly took her thumbprint and used it. It opened up the phone. I went into the settings and disabled fingerprints and passwords.

Her gun was lying on the floor, close to where I'd been shot. I picked it up and took it and her phone to the kitchen island and put them next to the laptop and my wallet. The laptop had gone to sleep. I woke it up. Rudy must have disabled the password. I went into the spare bedroom and shoved my things into my suitcase. Thank God it was on wheels. All of this was taking five times as long as it should on account of the searing and debilitating pain in my side. I went into the bathroom and looked for bandages and tape. I didn't find any. Not any for a gunshot wound at least. I grabbed my burner out of the cupboard. It was still recording. I stopped it.

I grabbed a hand towel and then went and looked in the

hallway linen closet. I found an extra sheet. I grabbed it and brought it out into the living room. I was smearing my blood all up and down the walls, leaning on them for support. I almost passed out a couple of times. I didn't know how long I had. I figured if those assholes were smart they'd have called the police. At this moment I didn't give a shit.

I closed So-yi's eyes.

"I'm sorry," I said, as my eyes welled up again. My tears were hot and stung like acid. My throat felt like a hot poker had been shoved down it. I dabbed at them with the hand towel. "I swear to you, I will avenge you. They will pay for what they've done."

I covered her with the sheet. I went back into the hallway and brought my suitcase into the kitchen. I rifled through the kitchen drawers. I figured the bullet was still inside me. I found some duct tape. I used it to tape the hand towel over my wound. Then I put So-yi's phone and laptop and my wallet and phones into my suitcase. The gun I put down the front of my pants. I cleaned up my hands and face best I could, and I put on my jacket and hat with great difficulty. I buttoned up the jacket. I looked halfway decent. I hobbled out of the apartment. I'd left my fingerprints and DNA all over the place. Any half-assed cop would figure I'd done it. Any decent cop would have their work cut out figuring I hadn't.

I had to stop every so often to catch my breath. I could feel my blood leaking through the towel, and I was feeling the worse for it. On the main level, with grit and determination I managed to limp through the foyer and out into the cold air, barely raising an eyebrow. Outside it felt incredibly cold. I heard sirens from off in the distance. I walked round the side of the building into the back alley. I was finished. I slid down by a dumpster breathing like I'd gone ten rounds with Lennox Lewis.

I could tell time was running out for me. I had to get help. Hospitals wouldn't be the right place though. The police would be swarming them. I fished out my phone from my suitcase and dialed a number.

CHAPTER FIFTY-FOUR
SOS

REBECCA answered on the third ring.

"Hi Anthony, I was just doing some laundry," she said in her chipper, happy voice.

"I need your help," I said, breathing like I was running out of air.

"What's wrong, you sound horrible?"

"I've been shot," I said.

"Good God, Anthony, where are you and I'll call an ambulance."

"No," I said forcefully, though my voice sounded like it was coming up from a clogged sewer. "No tri-services. I can't explain now. I need you to come and get me. Back alley of The Oracle."

I passed out briefly. I came to when my phone clattered against the pavement. I picked it up and put it to my ear. The line was dead. Hopefully she was coming for me. If not, here was where I was gonna die. I needed to get a handle on my breathing. Slow and steady. I started practicing. I figured if Rebecca was coming for me she was only coming from Manhattan. That was probably only fifteen minutes away. I hoped.

The funny thing about gunshot wounds is their randomness. You can get shot half a dozen times and survive. Or you can get shot once and die. It all depends on what the lead finds inside of you.

Take me for example. I'd been shot twice. Only the one which counted. The one that was in my lower gut. I felt ice in my veins. I'd never been shot before but I figured the bullet had nicked something and I was bleeding. The towel was almost soaked through. I knew the body carried a lot of blood. I'd seen how much could be spilled at a crime scene and people live to tell about it. But there comes a point when you've lost too much. I didn't know what that point was. I just focused on my breathing.

Rebecca had heard the call. I was starting to think I was seeing things when I saw her face looking down at me. Her eyes were wet.

"Oh my God, Anthony, what happened."

I struggled to get up. She helped me.

"I'll explain later. Can you help me with my bags. Get me the pink iPhone from out of it."

She took my bags and put them in the trunk. She opened the passenger door and I climbed in slowly like an old, arthritic man. She passed me So-yi's phone. She got in the other side. I was worried about leaking out onto the nice beige leather interior of her S-Class Mercedes. But that worry soon evaporated.

"Where am I going to take you if I can't take you to the hospital. You really need a hospital," she said.

"Your place, please. I've got a plan."

She didn't argue. I was grateful for that. She started off down the alleyway.

"Watch for cops if you can."

I fumbled around with So-yi's phone. There were a couple of voicemail messages. I listened to them.

"It's Hans. This is for Anthony, if you get it. I just saw the news. Tell me what happened."

Then the second one.

"Hans again. Call me."

And he left his number. It was different to the number that had left the message. I dialed it. Maybe he could help. I was grateful for his concern. He was the guy I was gonna call in any event. Maybe he knew a paramedic or someone who could help. I dialed the number. My hands were shaky.

"Let me put that on bluetooth," said Rebecca. She pressed a couple of buttons on her steering wheel and the ringtone came to life inside the car. I lay the phone on my lap. Hans picked up quickly.

"Anthony?" he said, in his thick, deep accent. I was calling from So-yi's phone, but he must have known what had happened.

"You know?" I said.

"Ja, it's on the news. What happened?"

"Hi, it's Rebecca. He's in really bad shape," she said. "I'm taking him to my place. He really needs a hospital, but he won't let me take him to one."

"What's happened to him?"

"Looks like he's been beaten up pretty badly and he says he's been shot. There's a lot of blood around his stomach."

"OK," said Hans. "I thought this might be worst case. Where do you live?"

Rebecca gave him her address.

"I've got a doctor with me who can help. Anthony, what's your blood type?"

"AB positive," I said.

"That's good. OK, Rebecca. Listen to me. Take him back to your place. Get him naked and tape a bandage or towel to the wound with as much pressure as you can. He's probably in shock. Try and give him some warmed extra sweet gatorade for fluids and electrolytes. Not much. One cup at the most. And don't let him sleep or go unconscious. Do whatever you can to keep him awake. Even if you have to slap him or pour cold water on his face. He needs to stay conscious. We can get there in thirty minutes."

"OK, thank you," said Rebecca.

Hans hung up and I felt like I was hanging by a thread.

CHAPTER FIFTY-FIVE
BLOOD OATH

I don't remember much after the phone call with Hans until we got into Rebecca's apartment. It was the penthouse suite. I leaned on her as she got me into her place and onto a bed. She took off my shoes and pants and jacket and hat and shirts. Including the vest. They were tossed into a corner in a pile. She let me keep my dignity and left me with my boxers on. For some reason I was wearing a gag pair I'd bought at the spur of the moment. The boxers had happy, yellow smiley faces on them with a bullet hole in the forehead and a drop of blood dripping down. Even in my dazed state, the irony was not lost on me.

Rebecca tried gingerly to take off the duct tape and the towel which was wet with blood. She exclaimed when it came off and she saw the wound.

"Oh God," she said, "this looks bad."

"'Tis but a scratch," I said. That didn't help. She didn't laugh or even smile. Perhaps she was focused on putting another bandage on the wound. And she had a proper bandage this time. She did her best to put pressure on it. It was better than nothing, and any pressure there hurt like a punch to the gut. But the bleeding had slowed down. Maybe because I'd stopped moving.

Rebecca got me a gatorade or something that tasted like it. It was warm and disgustingly sweet. But she made me take some sips. My mouth was dry and felt filled with sand. She tenderly wiped a wet cloth at the wounds on my face. I kept wanting to go to sleep. She wouldn't let me. At one point she splashed cold water on my face. That woke me up for about five minutes.

I lost track of time. I lost my grip on reality. Sometimes I thought I was back in Santa Monica with Racquel taking care of me. Sometimes I mistook Rebecca for Emily. A couple of times I forgot that I'd been shot and I tried to get out of bed. Thankfully, Rebecca didn't let me.

Then Rebecca just left me and I heard a couple of other voices. Then the three of them just reappeared. I heard Hans looking over at Rebecca and agreeing with her that I looked bad. He dwarfed her. He looked like a big human oak tree, wide as the room.

"He was six-foot-four and full of muscles, down from under and vegemite sandwich," I slurred. Even in my delirious state I was pretty sure I was fucking up the lyrics.

"Six-foot-six actually," said the big oak man, grinning from ear to ear but carrying no sandwiches.

They picked me up like light laundry and put me on a table so I was waist high. The other guy who I thought was the doctor looked small. But everyone looked small next to Hans. They rolled me onto my side. The doctor was saying something about an epidural and nerve blocker. I kept thinking that I wasn't pregnant.

Hans said something to Rebecca about arriving just in time. I felt tugging and pulling at my lower abdomen. I tried to look but I couldn't lift my head real good. The doctor said something about trying to get the bullet out. Said it had nicked a vein which was good. Something about if it'd been an artery I wouldn't have made it. Rebecca left, probably not being able to stomach the view. Pun intended.

The pulling and tugging at my belly seemed to last a while, but it was a sensation and not a feeling. My head was wet with sweat and I was looking out of eyes that seemed to have been smeared with vaseline. There were also rubber snakes coming out of a bag full of blood and dripping it into my arm. I could feel that. It felt cold.

The last thing I remembered was the doctor looking at Hans and saying something about it being a good thing the bullet hadn't broken up. Hans nodded and looked at me. Then it was lights out.

The first thing I noticed when I woke up was the pain. Felt like somebody had opened me up, taken out my guts, punched them to smithereens and then put them back inside. I did a roll call on my body. I found out that the side of my head was tender. I went to touch it and felt stiff hair up by by hairline. Only my hair didn't feel that coarse.

"They stitched you up, Anthony," said Rebecca. I looked over at her and smiled.

My lip and eye on the left side by the head wound were swollen and tender too. In fact, I couldn't quite see out of my left eye. It was swollen shut. Then I felt a rib that seemed pretty bruised and breathing reminded it to give me hell. Then there were the main citizens of complaint gathered around my lower belly. I gingerly touched the bandaging. It seemed fresh and dry. I looked around some more. I was in a hospital bed but I wasn't in a hospital.

"Where am I?" I asked.

"You're still here at my home," said Rebecca. "Do you remember calling me?"

I nodded.

"Yeah, I remember arriving here and then things start to get blurry. Two men were here with you? One of them was a doctor?"

"That's right. You called Hans Marais. He said he's a friend. He came over with a doctor he knows. Dr. Van Niekirk. He patched you up. They gave you two pints of blood. They said you were really lucky, Anthony, that I got to you when I did and that they were able to get here when they did."

"This bed?"

"I had this brought in from a medical services company. We put you in it just after your operation."

I felt urine leaking out of me. I checked myself. I hoped I wasn't losing control of my bladder, even though it didn't feel full. I felt a rubber hose coming out of my penis. They'd put me on a catheter. Rebecca noticed.

"Dr. Van Niekirk doesn't want you getting out of bed until he's seen you. He's coming this evening."

Rebecca came around to the other side.

"You're on a drip with painkillers," she said, pointing at the bag hanging by a metal arm attached to the bed above my head.

"Doesn't feel like it's working," I said.

"Well, you can give yourself an extra boost if you want by clicking this button," and she showed the button which was attached to a different small machine which fed another host into the main rubber hose of my drip.

"As you know, it'll only work so many times and only so often."

I winced.

"I think I'll give it a try now," I said. I pushed the button and a few moments later it felt like someone had doused the fire in my belly with soothing, cool water.

"Where am I?"

"You're in my living room. I thought you might like the view better when you woke up."

I adjusted my bed so that my head and upper body inclined to about forty-five degrees. And what a view it was. I could see the long end of Central Park. It was a clear day and the sky was blue.

"How long was I out for?"

"Almost twenty-four hours," she said. "The operation lasted about an hour yesterday afternoon. Dr. Van Niekirk was here until seven-thirty when I wheeled you out here. He wanted someone with you until you woke up."

"Thank you," I said.

"I'm just glad you're doing much better," she said. "You gave me a real scare yesterday. I've never seen anyone in such bad shape."

"Well, you saved my life."

"I couldn't bear to give John any other bad news," she said. "In fact, I told him I'd call him when you were awake."

"Can it wait," I said. "I'm just not quite ready to talk to him right now."

Rebecca nodded.

"Are you hungry? Dr. Van Niekirk said you might be hungry when you woke up."

"I'm starving," I said.

"John says you like steak. I had Mike, my husband, pick

one up. He brought it home just a couple of hours ago at lunchtime. How about some steak and eggs. I make a really good black pepper sauce."

"I'm salivating already."

"OK," she said.

"Listen, have you told anyone else I'm here or what happened?" I asked.

She shook her head.

"No, only John, and obviously my husband knows, but he's discreet."

"Good," I said. "Let's keep it that way for now."

I noticed I no longer had my socks on.

"What happened to my socks?"

"I washed your clothes," she said.

"Shit," I said, under my breath.

"Don't worry, I noticed your flash drive. It's in your bag with everything else. It didn't go through the washing machine."

"Thank God. That's the only bit of evidence I have on the assholes who did this to me. Did you look at it?"

"No, Anthony, I don't go snooping through other people's things. Especially in situations like this."

"Sorry," I said. "This case has just made me a little paranoid."

"Maybe some food will help."

CHAPTER FIFTY-SIX
Placebo Affect

I was enjoying the steak and eggs about a half hour later. Rebecca hadn't asked me how I liked my eggs. They were sunny side up. That got me to thinking about yesterday morning. I think it was yesterday morning, when So-yi had made me eggs and bacon. She just intuitively knew how I liked them, over hard. My throat got a lump in it and my eyes prickled. I shook my head and went back to eating my lunch. I figured it was somewhere around lunch time.

"So it's Wednesday then, right?" I asked Rebecca.

She nodded, sipping on a tea of some sort.

"Yes."

"What time?"

She looked at her watch.

"Ten after three."

I took a drink of my beer. I had wanted whiskey but I hadn't asked. Under the circumstances Rebecca was reluctant to give me a beer, but I'd charmed her into it. The steak was perfect. The eggs, well, I'm not gonna get into the eggs again. But I ate it all. I was hungry and I was grateful.

"Is Hans coming over with the doctor?" I asked.

Rebecca nodded.

"I think so, but he didn't say for certain."

She got up and took my plate away. The beer wasn't finished. I was feeling good after the lunch but the pain had returned and it seemed he'd brought some friends. I didn't realize I was such a baby when it came to surgical pain. Maybe I wasn't, maybe it was just a real bad pain. I clicked on the button. Nothing happened. I clicked it again. Nothing. Goddamn rations. I tried breathing through it. Rebecca came back. I guess she could see the pain on my face.

"Are you in discomfort?"

"Just a whinge," I said.

"Try the button."

"It's a fake button," I said, grinning at her.

"It's not working."

I nodded.

"I have Tylenol with codeine, but I'm not sure we should be mixing your medications."

"Don't worry about it. I'll breathe through it. Then I'll try the fake button again in a while. It worked the first time. What time did the doctor say he'd be here?"

"He didn't say. He just said this evening. How do you know Hans?"

"I don't actually. You probably know him better than I do. Yesterday was the first time I'd laid eyes on him."

"Really?"

"Yeah. So-yi knew him. She called him a couple of days ago."

I paused to think for a minute. My time had gone out of

whack.

"It's Wednesday, so she called him on Monday evening. We're trying to figure out who might have killed your nephew and Stan. I was thinking one of our three letter agencies. So-yi wasn't so sure. She thought maybe it was a PMG or NGO."

"PMG?"

"Yeah, a Private Military Group. Anyway, she'd met Hans some years back when he'd been in to train the Jersey PD on tactics or something. She thought highly of him. Figured he'd remember her and that he might have some knowledge of other PMGs we should be investigating. The kind who might be up for murder for hire. He was gonna call us yesterday or today. So I took a gamble he'd be willing to help on account he thought highly of So-yi."

"So he's with a PMG?"

I nodded.

"You didn't talk to him much?"

She shook her head and sipped on her tea. I drank some beer.

"Not about that sort of thing. I was concerned about you and about what I should do and things like that. He was very nice, very calm and very friendly, but he didn't tell me anything about what he did."

"From what So-yi tells me he owns a PMG. They're called Assegai. He's from South Africa originally. I guess you figured that out by his accent. That's about all I know, other than So-yi vouched for him. And that's good enough for me."

"Assegai, that's a spear," said Rebecca.

"If you say so."

"Yes it is. I took some wine classes earlier this year and

381

each month would be about different regions. We had a whole month on South African wines. Anyway, part of the course was also a bit of history. And the Zulus came up. A warrior tribe in South Africa who were well known with their expertise in the use of this spear or assegai."

I nodded. I looked outside over Central Park. We were high up and you could see the whole park. Looked like it'd make a nice bed from this vantage point.

"The good news is, I've found the assholes who killed Stan and Joe," I said.

"The ones who did this to you?"

I nodded.

"How do you know it was them?"

"He said as much to me in between the fisticuffs."

"I'm sorry it cost you so much."

"Hasn't been too much," I said.

"You still won't let me pay?"

She looked at me sincerely.

"You've done too much already," I said.

"I've hardly done anything."

"You came for me. You're taking care of me. You'll probably let me stay here as long as I need."

"Of course."

"You've already paid it ten times over."

I turned to her and looked at her steadily for a while. She got worried.

"What?" she said, breaking eye contact.

"I will get justice for Joe and for Stan and for So-yi," I said.

"I believe you."

"It's probably not gonna be the kind of justice that society dishes out," I said.

"What do you mean?"

"I'm saying, that sometimes justice can only be sought through the barrel of a gun."

She didn't say anything for a while.

"John said you'd do what you could. That you'd do what was right. I trust you to do what's right, Anthony."

I nodded slowly. I looked back over Central Park. I finished my beer. I pushed on the fake button. The fire was roaring in my belly. The goddamn button was still broken.

"Sometimes what's right ain't legal."

She didn't say anything. I didn't need her to. I wasn't looking for permission I was offering advice.

"You know..." she said.

I looked over at her.

"What?"

She was quiet for a bit.

"The police are looking for you."

I nodded.

"That's not surprising."

"They said you did it."

I looked at her and she looked at me. We held each other's gaze for a while.

"You think that's true?" I asked.

She shook her head.

"They said So-yi was sexually assaulted and tortured."

I nodded my head.

"They're sick fu... They're sick assholes," I said. "What they did."

"What did they do?" she asked, and I sensed she immediately regretted asking the question.

"You don't want to know," I said. "They were sick, twisted assholes. They have no sense of decency and they'll get what's coming to them."

I picked up the beer to finish it. Putting it to my lips I realized I'd already finished it. I put it back down. Rebecca drank her tea.

"What's on the flash drive?" she asked.

I shrugged.

"I haven't looked at it yet. But now's a pretty good time as ever. Would you mind getting me the pink iPhone and the laptop. I didn't get cables. Do you have any for the phone or laptop?"

"What kind of a laptop is it?"

"A Windows machine."

Rebecca nodded.

"I think I probably have something for it. Give me a minute."

She left me in my bed and I looked out through the windows. Over Central Park with New York within my grasp and there wasn't a goddamn thing I could grab.

CHAPTER FIFTY-SEVEN
MONSTERS OF MEN

I spent the first while downloading the recording from my burner. I figured I had about twenty minutes, or something like that, of recording time available on the space that was left on this shitty phone. But boy was I talking out of my ass. The phone had recorded the whole event. From the time those mother fuckers from Pipe Dreams had arrived to fix the leaking toilet to the time they left after having murdered So-yi. There was an hour and fifty-three minutes of video. The little burner had managed some magic. I didn't know how. I didn't understand video recording or compression. I was just glad to have it.

Rebecca sat with me and watched. I took a couple of screen grabs of the best headshots I could grab of Alex and Rudy or whatever their real names were and I emailed them to John. I figured I owed him a call too. So I called him. He picked up pretty quick.

"Jesus Christ, Sid, what the fuck did you get yourself into this time?" he asked.

His bravado was as thin as a blushing bride's lingerie on her wedding night. I could feel the concern in his tone.

"I found those mother fuc...," I remembered Rebecca was sitting right next to me. I covered the phone and apologized. She waved me off. "I found those cock suckers who killed Joe and Stan and Sue."

"What happened?"

"They told me they did it. I'm sorry John," I said, almost choking on the words. "It's my fucking fault So-yi's dead."

"No it's not," he said.

"It was my idiotic idea to have Pipe Dreams plumbing come and have a look at a bullshit toilet leak at her place. I was hoping I might get a look at the assholes who murdered Joe and Stan, or maybe worst case, just get something to go on."

"And did So-yi complain?"

"No."

"Then it's not your fault, Anthony. You couldn't have known."

"I should have been more careful. I knew we were dealing with bastards who didn't give a shit."

"But we've got them, Sid. You said so yourself."

"Yeah, I know who they are. Now I've gotta find them again."

"What you've gotta do is take some time to rest. Let me help you out from this end while you recuperate."

"Well," I said. "I just emailed you some mugshots I grabbed of these assholes. They're pretty good. Maybe our guy with the FBI can run them through facial recognition or something. I gave you their names too. At least the names they gave us."

"Leave it with me."

"Also, there's this company I want you to look into. Muspell Logistics. See if there's anything to it. Is it a shell? Is it an umbrella group? Anything you can find on them."

"Sure thing, Sid, don't worry. I've got this. By the way, that plate you gave me yesterday."

"Yeah."

"Nothing. At least not from our end. I've kicked it over to our buddy at the FBI, maybe he'll have better luck."

"That's weird."

"Yeah, it is. Makes me think you might be onto something with your feelings about this being an agency of ours or some other clandestine group. Otherwise, we should have seen the plates on our system."

"Right."

"You have enough resources out there? Want me to reach out to NYPD or Jersey PD again?"

"No, Johnny, I'm gonna take a different tack on these guys. They think they're above the law, so I'm gonna go above the law to get justice."

"You know I can't condone that."

"Do you want justice?"

"Yeah."

"Do you want me to do what's right?"

"I want you to be safe, Anthony. Maybe let Jersey PD take it from here."

"You're not listening. These assholes have framed me for Sue's murder. We've got nothing to tie them to Joe and Stan's murder. They're gonna walk on this unless we go outside the system. I'm gonna do what's right John."

"OK, Anthony. I owe you big time on this one. I've got your back. Just be sure. Are you comfortable with what you want to do?"

"Very comfy, John. I'll keep you posted. Let me know what you find out."

"Listen, before you go. How are you doing?"

"Hurt like hell. Got shot in the gut. But thank God I was wearing the vest. It caught the other slug. Got beat up pretty good too, but I'll be right as rain in a couple of weeks. Then we get back to business."

"Good. Listen, Sid, don't give me another fucking surprise like this, OK?"

"Sure thing, Dad."

We hung up and I looked over at Rebecca.

"He sends his best wishes."

She smiled and looked back down at the still images of asshole one and asshole two.

"They don't exactly look like monsters," she said.

"If they did, it'd be easy to avoid them. When monsters look like men, which they often do, it's easier for them to screw me and you."

I pressed play and we continued to listen and watch. I got the impression they didn't have a clue they were being recorded. They were real natural in the bathroom, selling their schtick as plumbers. You saw me leave but So-yi was only ever briefly in the frame at the beginning. All told they were with us about thirty-one minutes the first time.

Outside in the hallway you could only hear muffled voices. I figured that wasn't bad considering it was a cheap burner phone I'd bought. Audio in the bathroom was crystal clear. I could hear the front door close and all I could see was the off-white color of the bathroom wall opposite the toilet. There was also a small painting there. Or rather a print of a painting. It must have been around one-foot by two-feet, or thereabouts. I knew the painting well. It was one of Georges

Seurat's works. A lesser well known one. At least to the public. Painted before his pointillism period.

It was Bathers at Asnières. Asnières was a working class suburb in Paris. The painting showed a young man, maybe a teenager sitting at the water's edge. Two other older boys are in the water. A man lounges on the grassy bank with a small brown dog curled up by his back. Clothes are piled up on the bank and a couple more men sit on the grassy shore. There are a couple of sailboats on the water. The water being the River Seine. In the background is a bridge and beyond that smokestacks.

Nobody is looking at the viewer. Everyone except for a man is looking at the river. A boy looks like he is trying to call to a bird off canvas. I find it a desperately bleak painting. There is no happiness in what should be a happy scene. The real painting is large. If I recall correctly it's about six-feet by ten-feet. Seurat's first major work by all accounts. You can find it hanging in London's National Gallery. I've never been, so I've never seen the real one.

I know it, because it's a painting studied in first year art history class at the California College of Arts. It's renowned for it's use of color theory as well as other bullshit that art theorists try and put on a painting after the fact.

As an example. Seurat's more well known follow up painting is A Sunday Afternoon on the Island of La Grande Jatte. This one showed the bourgeoisie allegedly on the opposite bank facing the boys from the Bathers painting. We've all seen A Sunday Afternoon. It's the one where a woman with an umbrella and a big ass, and her husband in a top hat take up much of the right of the painting and the woman has a monkey on a leash. It's probably the most famous painting when you think of pointillism.

Anyway, art theorists have suggested this is the mirror painting of the Bathers, and that in fact the one boy in the water in the Bathers is shouting out to these bourgeoisie on the other bank. But that just can't be true. For one thing, if you look at the shadows, they're scenes painted at different times of the day. For another thing, the Bathers are further away from the bridge than the folks from A Sunday Afternoon.

But this isn't an art theory class. I was just thinking all of this as I watched the seconds and minutes roll by on the video. I felt like those bathers. Stuck in time, not able to do anything.

Shortly after we closed the door on the soon-to-be murderers you could hear me say something to So-yi. She replied, but none of it was clear enough to make out. It was I believe, when I asked her to grab the laptop so we could download the files.

A few short minutes after that and you could hear some struggles. This was So-yi and I getting electrocuted and tied up no doubt. Shortly after that, Rudy enters the bathroom. He looks around. He leans down off camera. He's in there under a minute. He doesn't see my camera, though he looks at the contents of the cupboard through the glass doors. Then he leaves.

"What's he doing?" asked Rebecca.

"I think they're going through the apartment looking for anything of note. Making sure that we don't have any other flash drives or damning evidence. In a little while I'm gonna wake up. They've tasered or shocked both of us somehow and we're out cold. Last time it happened I was at their offices and I was out cold for around fifteen to twenty minutes I figure."

"What sort of taser can do that?"

"None that I know of," I said.

After that, there's more talking. I'm getting asked questions and So-yi is getting raped. You can't make out any of it real well, but the memory is burned into my mind like a branding. There's a few more loud words.

"This is where I try to take them on," I said to Rebecca. "I headbutted the one asshole and then went after the other. I got a couple of shots in, even though my hands were zip tied behind me. But asshole one got his taser back and knocked me out on my ass again."

Louder voices now, but just a couple. Here they're probably beating the shit out of me as I lay unconscious. Time rolled by again. Fewer voices and lower volume. This must have been when they were talking amongst themselves while I was out cold. My mind started to wonder if So-yi was raped again during this time, or close to it. Because when I come to, Rudy was giving it to her.

"Things get nasty here," I said.

There were more muffled voices as I looked at the Bathers and the Bathers looked across the river bank at nothing. Or maybe the boy on the edge by the water was actually shouting at the assholes to stop. Maybe he could see what shit they were up to.

"What's happening?" asked Rebecca.

"Around this time, I'm coming to. Asshole one is asking me about any other flash drives we might have."

"What are their names?"

"Alex is who I've been calling asshole one. Rudy is his partner."

Rebecca nodded. I don't tell her about the raping and sodomizing. She knows about the rape anyway, on account of it having been on the news that an Anthony Carrick is wanted for questioning in the murder and rape of Jersey PD Detective So-yi Park. Rebecca showed me the news on the crime.

"I try to get up here and take another go at them. This time both my hands and feet are zip tied. Alex is waiting, so I get clocked again and kicked in the ribs. The he starts asking me about any other flash drives we've got. I lie to him that we didn't have a chance to make any others. Rudy goes around the apartment looking for any evidence to the contrary."

"You have your flash drive in your sock already? Before any of this happens?"

I nod.

"That's right. It was the first thing I did. Not because I was expecting this but because I didn't want to lose it or have it fall out any pockets."

You can hear his voice now. It's a little louder but still unclear. I remember this was when he came back with lube and a flashlight. Voices continue for a while. I know what's going on but I'm not telling Rebecca.

"In a little while they're going to kill So-yi. Alex just walks up to her and shoots her in the back of the head. I wasn't expecting it."

"Where is she all this time?" asked Rebecca.

"Pretty close to me. We're both tied up. Then there's a couple more gunshots. That's when they shoot me. I get cold cocked with the gun too."

"That's why your forehead was bleeding so much?"

I nod. It doesn't take long and the first gunshot sounds loud on the recording on So-yi's laptop. I turn the volume down. We wait several seconds and then there's a couple more in quick succession.

"Have they left?"

"Yeah, they leave pretty quickly. We might be able to hear the door close."

And we do, though it's soft, like it might've been a neighbor leaving early for work and trying not to disturb his neighbors.

"I slowly start to gain consciousness. I'm assessing the situation. I realize that it looks like I might have done this, so I figure I have to try and get out as soon as I can."

A couple of minutes go by and then a zombie appears in the camera frame in the bathroom. Rebecca gasps.

"My God, Anthony, they really did a number on you," she said.

I nod. I'm watching myself fumble around the bathroom for a towel and tape. I don't find any. My face is looking pulpy and bits of blood are congealed here and there. Blood is dripping from my head wound and across the side of my face. I don't look pretty. I look like a wild man. My eyes are big as saucers and I'm grimacing. I remember the pain well. I'm smearing my bloody prints all over the cupboard as I'm trying to get my phone out.

I don't turn it off but I must've put it in my pocket. Then awhile later it's on the kitchen counter filming the kitchen ceiling. Shortly after that you see my zombie face hovering over it as I pick it up and power off the phone.

"I'm leaving the apartment now and the rest you pretty much know."

CHAPTER FIFTY-EIGHT
FILTH

I figure it's time to look at the files I've downloaded onto the flash drive. I ask Rebecca if she can get it for me. She does. She offers me something to drink. I ask for whiskey. She says no. I ask for a beer. She says yes. A beer'll have to do. She brings the beer at the same time as she brings the flash drive. She's not drinking anything.

"Are you hungry?"

"No, thanks," I said.

And I'm not. The eggs and steak are sitting in my gut like a big stone. I take a drink of beer. It tastes like cool nectar. My gut is flaring up. I figure I'll give the fake button one more try just to see. It works this time. I'm grateful for that. It means I can get some work done. I put the flash drive in one of the ports.

"Do you know what's on this flash drive?" Rebecca asked.

I shake my head.

"We just downloaded the files onto it and I took it from So-yi and stuffed it in my sock. I was worried we were going to get hacked as we were trying to do this. I figured time was of the essence. You'll remember they hacked me at Stan's place. I was expecting a repeat. Anyway, you know that didn't happen. We had just started on the second flash drive when Alex and Rudy barged in."

Rebecca nodded. I opened up the flash drive. A window popped open with the contents inside. There were a couple of PDFs and around a dozen video files. I started at the beginning. I'd heard that was a very good place to start. The video player started up and the video started playing right away. Didn't take long to realize what sort of smut we were watching.

It was high quality video. It had some editing done to it. It was in color and the sound was clear. It showed Alex raping a couple of young girls. They couldn't have been older than around twelve or so. They were naked and the room was a concrete shit hole with a bed and not much else. The girls looked hollow. Their eyes were vacant and they were probably high on something.

I bladed the laptop away from Rebecca.

"You probably don't want to watch this," I said.

She was wiping her eyes of tears.

"What is this God awful filth?" she asked.

"Exactly what you said," I answered. "That's Alex incidentally. Asshole one."

I put the video on fast forward. I didn't want to watch the rape of young girls, but I needed to know what these files were. I needed to know what was on each one. My stomach was turning as I watched. At one point I had to pause the video and breathe deep for a while. Out of anger and also out of a sense I was about to puke up my guts.

All the videos, except for the last one showed the same

thing. Alex and Rudy, raping and sodomizing young girls. None of whom I'd put over the age of twelve or thirteen. That was my daughter's age. I was incensed. Hatred and anger burned in my stomach like hot bile. I would kill Alex and Rudy and I was gonna do it as soon as I could. There was no doubt in my mind. Rebecca left shortly after I started the second video of the same filth.

There must have been over a dozen different girls in all the videos. I made a copy of the files. I was going to send this to my guy at the FBI. Hopefully they'd be able to match many of the girls with missing children. He was gonna have a lot of work from John and me.

The last video was interesting. It showed the murder of Stan and Joe. And it looked to me like it was filmed from the back of the getaway car. It obviously had a pretty big zoom on it because it looked like you were standing just on the other side of the intersection. The one problem with the video was that you never saw the killer's face. He must have known he was being filmed. And the killer of Joe and Stan, the same guy driving the garbage truck, looked to me to be Alex.

The reason I say that was the way his body language spoke to me. The way he moved was the way I'd seen Alex move, more so than Rudy. The video cut off just after he'd shot Joe in the back of the head and before he turned to run towards the parked car.

The last couple of files in the folder were of two PDFs. The one was a detailed schematic of the gun used to shoot Joe in the back of the head. At least I surmised it was the gun from what the bikers had told me. The other was a schematic of what looked like a small candy bar styled phone. It reminded me of those old Nokia phones that were all the rage before smartphones became a thing.

Only this was a little different. From what I could tell from the schematic it could do all sorts of things. Mostly through electrical and other magnetic radiation. It looked like a neat device. Looked like it could fry circuits within a pretty large area. Apparently it could also do live facial recognition and voice recognition. It was also a lethal weapon. There was enough here to get Stan in a lot of trouble. The smut was enough to have him killed by Alex and Rudy. As for the schematics, leaking those would be a huge headache for the corporation that was working on them. And that corporation was not Pipe Dreams. At least not the Pipe Dreams I had visited. This was military weaponry.

On each page of each PDF was a small trademark and copyright symbol next to the words Nifilheim Advanced Weaponry (NAW). I'd get John to look into that too.

That was all there was. But what it was had gotten Stan and Joe killed. It was gonna get Alex and Rudy killed too. I had never seen such filth in my life. Never come across anything so vile in my years on the job. What Alex and Rudy were was a black mark against anything that was good. And with evil that vile the only thing you can do is rub it out.

Rebecca came back and sat near me. I closed the laptop.

"Sorry," she said. "I couldn't stomach it."

I looked at her a long while. I took a long drink on my beer.

"In all my years," I said. "I've never seen such filth. But I will make it right."

She didn't say anything to that. We both looked outside and down onto the green and white that was Central Park. We sat in silence for a long time. Our own thoughts were our company. And my thoughts were raping each other and giving birth to little bastards called hate and revenge. And we sat like that until Rebecca's husband, Mike, got home.

CHAPTER FIFTY-NINE
GROOT OU

MIKE was a nice guy. I had prejudged the poor bastard on account of him having stolen John's sweetheart from back in the day. But that was juvenile. Mike hadn't actually stolen Rebecca from John. Rebecca had left to come out east long before she met Mike. They did meet in high school though. So I guess in that way you could call them high school sweethearts. And John had a lovely wife now. And two great kids. And I was being a shit. But sometimes I'm like that.

But Mike never took my snide remarks personally. He was handsome and he was tall. Tall in the appropriate sense of the word, which means in polite society he's six feet. He was also kind and generous. Telling me I could stay as long as I wanted. He never asked questions about the case that I couldn't answer. He was erudite and clued in. Which meant he knew when to back off. He wished me well and hoped that I got justice for his nephew.

If there was anything he could do he'd happily oblige. You've met these kinds of people before. The kind that have worked hard to earn their success. They know where they've come from. Mike came from the wrong side of the tracks. He knew it. He knew every man carries a struggle within. And if he could help, he would.

By the time the dinner of wild salmon was over, I got to figuring Mike and I coulda been best friends if I was gonna stick around. But I wasn't gonna stick around. Because Dr. Van Niekirk told Rebecca I couldn't get out of bed until he saw me that evening, Rebecca and Mike ate dinner with me around my hospital bed.

It was right on eight o'clock when Hans and Dr. Van Niekirk showed up again. Rebecca let them in. It was the first time Mike had met them. They all made small talk for a few minutes before they came over to see me. Mike and Rebecca left for the TV room as they called it.

Hans towered over me and offered his hand. I took it. His grip was firm but gentle. It felt like I was shaking a soft leather baseball mitt.

"How you doing Mr. Cool?" he asked.

"Other than your doctor giving me a fake button to push for the pain meds, I've never felt better."

Hans laughed. I had a feeling he had an easy laugh.

"Listen," said Hans. "I'm glad you called. You were in bad shape. Those guys did a number on you."

I nodded slowly.

"Yeah, I got a couple of licks in."

"Ja, I figured you would Mr. Cool."

"Mr. Cool?"

"Ja, I give everyone a nickname. Yours is easy. Your initials are A.C., ja? AC is air conditioning. And from how Rebecca tells it, when you called and carried yourself, you're a pretty cool bloke. So I figured Mr. Cool would suit you."

Hans looked at Dr. Van Niekirk.

"Dr. Johann Van Niekirk here is Needles. On account of his always giving us needles for some shit reason when we head to a new place."

Van Niekirk grinned at us.

"And what do they call you?" I asked

"Oom," he said. "It's a term of endearment. Literally, it means uncle."

"Oom," I said, trying the word on for size.

It felt like my mouth was taking a long ride on the ooh you'd say in excitement. Then you added a whim on the end and you squashed them together pretty quick.

Hans put his big hand on my shoulder and leaned in towards me.

"I'm gonna let Needles here check you over. Then I'll come back and we'll talk business."

I nodded. Hans left the living room and went looking for Rebecca and Mike. I watched him leave. Heading down the hallway he almost had to turn sideways on account of his width. He was a big, tall man full of muscles and he carried it with the ease of a leopard.

Needles must have seen me looking after Hans.

"Interesting story," he said. "That man saved my life in the mid-eighties in Mozambique. Carried me out of a shit storm while also carrying six slugs. One in his shoulder, three in his torso, one in his thigh and one in his ass. Don't ask him about the one in his ass," said Needles laughing.

"He's lucky to have survived," I said.

Needles nodded.

"Yeah, luck was involved. Plus he's full of muscle which helped."

"How big is he?"

"Six-six, two-eighty in his prime. Carried me like I was a toy."

"And you're about what, five-nine?"

"Five-eight. One-fifty. You?"

"Five-ten on a good day. Sometimes I feel like six-feet. But that's when I'm lying to myself. One-sixty last I checked."

Needles smiled at that.

"He's the best of men," said Needles, looking down the empty hallway that Hans had been swallowed up in. "Loyal to a fucking fault and hell bent on justice for the vulnerable. You're gonna have to convince him to let the law man take Sue's death on, unless you want a couple more homicides."

I grinned. Needles had just whispered the sweetest words in my ear. He looked at me and grinned too.

"That also works," he said. "But let's see how you're doing."

"You a real doctor?"

Needles nodded.

"I am. Been working with Hans ever since the Mozambique massacre as we like to call it."

"What happened?"

"Long story. The short end of it is that we were up in Mozambique stirring up shit against the Marxists. We being the South African Special Forces Brigade, colloquially known as the Recces. Our intel was bad and we got squeezed by a surprise attack. Lost half our guys that time."

"They were all Recces?"

"No. Only Hans and I were operators in that unit at the time. We usually supplement regular forces. Hardly ever just a squad of us by ourselves. You ever in the military?"

I shook my head.

"Just the regular police."

Needles nodded and put a warmed stethoscope chestpiece over my heart. He asked me to breath. Breathing deep was a little bit like tearing open my wound in my lower belly. He asked me to lean forward. I had to help myself with that by pushing against the back of my bed with my hand. I had to gingerly. The wound snapped at me angrily. I breathed through it.

"OK, you can lie back down. How does the wound feel?"

Needles untaped the bandage and looked at it. He nodded.

"Feels better than it was a day ago when I first got it," I said.

"I've seen a helluva lot worse," he said. "Now that second slug. If that one had found it's mark, I think you would've been a gonner."

"That's comforting," I said.

Needles looked up at me and grinned.

"I'm just saying, you're no Hans. You don't have enough meat on your bones to take a bunch of slugs and keep them from the vitals."

I looked down at my belly. The coarse hair of the stitches was poking out.

"How many did you have to do?"

"You've got seven here and five on the side of your face. It was this one down here I was worried about. It didn't go too deep. It hit the vest first and that absorbed a lot of the momentum. But it mushroomed out and a sharp bit nicked a vein."

"What did you do to stop the bleeding?"

"I used this self-healing tape that's only available for the DOD. But we've got some too. It's great for wounds of all sorts, but especially bleeders. It seals the wound and lets the

405

blood start to clot and heal. It'll be absorbed by the body within a couple of weeks. The stitches too are dissolving."

Needles went and looked over my head wounds.

"I wasn't so worried about this," he said, poking around at the side of my head. "It was a nasty gash, but you just look at a scrape on the head and it bleeds like a crybaby. Your eye is another thing. They really gave it to you. I figure you must have been kicked close by it. If they'd been more accurate, that eye would've had to come out. And I'm surprised with all of that they didn't manage to bust up your nose."

"Not much left to bust."

"You used to box?"

I nodded.

"Ja, I thought so."

"How'd you know?"

"Old scars around the eyebrows, busted nose. I'm not saying you're not a handsome man, but your face tells me about it's troubles. You think you're ready to stand up?"

"I've been wanting to get out of bed all day," I said. "But Rebecca wouldn't let me."

"Ja, she's good peoples. I asked her not to let you. I wanted to check you out first. Here, let me help you."

Needles came round to the other side of the bed and I used him as a brace and a crutch to get out and stand on my own two feet. I was naked now except for those ridiculous blue hospital gowns open at the back.

"You good?"

"I'm OK," I said.

Needles went round to the other side of the bed and came back holding my bag of electrolytes and the pump that gave me fake pain meds.

"How about we walk out there and back again just as a

test?"

He nodded his head towards the kitchen island. It looked miles away. I started stepping towards it.

"If you get tired let me know and I'll grab you a chair, or just lean on me."

I nodded at him and we walked. One step at a time. When we got to the island I had to rest. I was breathing heavy. Felt like I'd done a couple of rounds of sparring. Needles grinned at me.

"This is good. This is great. You're doing better than I was expecting."

We turned around and went back. Probably took three to five minutes to walk fifty feet. I got myself back into bed and lay there and breathed hard for a while. Needles reattached my pump and bag to their arms. He looked at my exposed belly.

"This is good. The wound is not bleeding or weeping, even after that exertion."

I nodded.

"How old are you, Anthony?"

"Forty-four."

"Now's the time to quit smoking," he said.

I looked at him. I thought of something snarky to say but I swallowed it instead.

"How do you know I smoke?"

"I smelled it on your clothes. Listen, I'm gonna be harsh with you. The truth is, smokers don't heal as well as non-smokers. More than that, it's starting to kill you from the inside. Now's the time when you have the best chance of walking away from that filth with very little long term damage."

"I feel fine. I can quit anytime I want to."

"Fuck me, man. You can lie to your mother, but you can't lie to your doctor. If you think you can quit anytime, why not do it right now. I'm going to call you on it. I don't think you can. You know why? Because you're pussy whipped by that cigarette. That's why. You can't."

"Fuck you, who even asked for your opinion anyway."

Needles nodded.

"I knew it. Another fucking addict who's in denial. You can't do it, and instead of admitting that you're a pussy when it comes to tobacco you want to blame me. It's your death, man. It's your death. I just figured a tough guy like you could lick a little tobacco addiction. Guess I was wrong."

"Why the fuck do you even care?"

I didn't know where this was all coming from. I mean, yeah, we know smoking is no good. But this guy was taking my smoking personally.

"My grandfather died from emphysema when he was sixty. My father died from throat cancer when he was fifty-seven. Had to talk through a hole in his fucking neck for the last few years of his life. It's not a fucking joke, Anthony. Smoking will kill you inch by inch and make those left suffer while they can do nothing about it. If you've got kids, you'd have stopped years ago."

"OK," I said. "Fuck it. I'll quit right now. Throw my smokes away."

Needles nodded.

"So you've got kids," he said.

"Yeah, a daughter."

"Then you'll thank me later. I threw your smokes out yesterday."

I looked at him and shook my head.

"Why'd you start smoking anyway?"

"All the tough guys in the westerns were smoking. Humphrey Bogart as Sam Spade was smoking. You know how it goes."

He nodded.

"Yeah, you look a little like Bogie," he said.

"I've been said I look more like Dean Martin."

"I can see that too. Well, you've made the right choice. You're lucky you're also healing from these wounds. That means you'll not notice the physical withdrawal which usually peaks at about seventy-two hours. You'll probably be on pain meds for the first week or so, and they'll take care of the physical aspects. The psychological craving can last months. You're gonna have to remain vigilant."

"What do you suggest then, doc?"

"Get into an exercise program. You used to box, and I can't really recommend boxing on account of the head trauma but maybe try and find something you like doing to keep you active. Figure out your triggers. Like why you smoke. There're no simple answers. I'm gonna be honest with you, you're gonna have to remain vigilant and self-police. But a tough guy like you, I'm sure you can do it."

"Really, though, why do you give a shit?"

Needles was taping up my wound again.

"I told you why."

"That doesn't explain your exuberance about it," I said. "You don't know me from a hole in a ground."

"And that's it. A hole in the ground is not where I want to put you." He stopped what he was doing and looked me straight in the eye. "I've seen a lot of shit happen on the battlefield. That's one thing. But when you're trying to kill yourself with booze and cigarettes that's another. I get to asking myself, why am I even trying to help, if the asshole just wants to die anyway. And you know what, the way tobacco kills you, taking little pieces here and there, that ain't no way anyone wants to die."

I watched him work and I thought about smoking a cigarette. Now I wanted one. And like an ass I'd told this guy I hardly knew I was gonna quit. Now I had to follow up with that. Goddamn, Anthony, shooting your mouth off just to get the doc to shut up. And he got me at a vulnerable moment on top of that.

"I'm gonna take out the catheter" he said.

"You just want to give it a yank then," I said, grinning.

"I see what you did there," said Needles. "But no, that's not how it works. When we put it in, we've gotta make sure it doesn't come out. So we fill a little balloon with water once it's inside the bladder so it won't come out. I watched him take a syringe and siphon off an amount of clear liquid that almost filled the syringe from a branch off of the main tube.

"Now it should come out easily. I'll just pull slow to see how you like it," he grinned at me. I was no longer enjoying the joke. "Might sting a bit."

And it did, but it also didn't take too long. He put all of it with the bag still three quarters full of piss into a yellow, rectangular bio-hazard box along with the syringe and old bandages.

"I'm gonna put my stuff away and let you and Hans talk for a while. I'll be back in a while."

CHAPTER SIXTY
Plan for Stan

I didn't have to wait longer than around five minutes for Hans to come back in. I figured Needles had given him the 411 on my situation. He walked into the kitchen which turned into a open dining room and then living room where I was propped up in my bed. He stopped in the kitchen first and took a couple of bottles of beer out of the fridge. He opened them and brought them with him. He grinned at me and handed me a bottle. We clinked.

"Cheers,"

"Sláinte," I said, taking a sip.

"So-yi liked you," he said.

"I liked her too."

"What happened?" he asked.

He brought a dining room table chair close to the bed and sat down on it. He looked like a man sitting on a kid's chair. I told him what happened. I started from the beginning of the day when we went to the mall Pipe Dreams was at. I told him about the flash drives and my camera recording. I told them how Alex and Rudy broke in and fucked me up and raped and sodomized So-yi and then murdered her. My eyes stung and they got wet, but I choked the emotion down. Hans just listened and watched. He drank beer and he said nothing. His face was a blank slate. At one point I wondered if he had tuned me out. He just drank beer and watched me tell it.

"Show me what you've got on your recording," he said, when I was finished telling it.

I played the recording from my burner phone. I paused it at the moment when I took screen grabs to send to Roberts. I told him that. I told him we'd find out who the assholes were. I told him I thought the names were bogus. I continued the recording, offering voiceover highlights when all we could see were the Bathers at Asnières. Hans watched the recording. He looked at me and he sipped on his beer. He said nothing.

"Let me see the files you downloaded from War Tyde," he said.

The man was a stone. To this point he had given no sign of any emotion.

"There's some real shit on there," I said. He nodded. I played the videos sped up. I told him who was who in each video, though he could have figured that out from the earlier images of asshole one and asshole two taken by my burner. After I'd shown him everything he got up and put his empty beer bottle on the dining room table. Then he came back to my bed and stood next to it looking down at me. He was a giant of a man. Looked like I was picnicking under a large oak tree.

"What are you gonna do?" he asked.

"I'm gonna kill those mother fuckers," I said, and my voice was calm and serene.

"That's a feeling," he said, "not a plan."

"I've got a plan," I said. "Just as soon as I can, I'm gonna get a line on their day to day. Then I'm gonna pick them up one by one, take them back to So-yi's place and shoot them in the fucking head."

He grinned at me and put a large hand the size of a baseball mitt on my shoulder and patted it.

"That's a plan," he said. "I was hoping you'd say something like that. Let me help you."

I looked at him for a long while. I prefer to operate alone. But having been shot and giving up tobacco I felt that maybe a little help would be nice.

"Why do you want to help?" I asked.

"I know these assholes," he said, and he sat back down in the chair that looked like a child's. "Remember I said I was gonna look into a couple of PMGs for So-yi. See if there were any that might do this kind of black ops."

I nodded. So-yi had told me that.

"I came up with two names. T.N.T. and Red Blade."

"T.N.T., really?"

He nodded, grinning.

"Those are the founders' initials. Taylor, Nillingham and Truchant. At first I thought it might be them. They're hungry, they're new to the game and they're genuine assholes. Three ex-Rangers who were kicked out for some serious shit. Given dishonorable discharges for murdering civilians. As you can imagine, the US government won't hire them, but they'll work for anyone. It's only a matter of time before they either end up dead or in jail."

"No court martial?"

"No, they had a colonel who pulled in a favor for them. It was a black ops in Afghanistan a few years ago. If you look at the situation at the right angle, a lawyer might say those dead civilians were accidental. It'd be a stretch but with the Colonel's help they got quick dishonorable discharges without court martial, and they'll never get work from the US. But it's not them, now that I've seen your recording. Which was a helluva of a thing. Good job on that by the way."

I nodded.

"So T.N.T. isn't who you're looking for. This brings me to Red Blade. Which is odd, because Red Blade generally works for the good guys. And when I say good guys, I mean they work mostly for the Five Eyes, sometimes others, but pretty much always democracies. Real democracies. I've never heard them do black ops. Especially here in the States."

"But," I said. "You know these guys."

Hans nodded.

"Assegai and Red Blade worked together a couple of years ago in Central America looking for leads on El Chapo. Those two assholes you showed me were with Red Blade. And real assholes they were. I eventually pulled my team out of the hunt and told my contact at Red Blade about these two."

"What did you tell?"

"They were fucking whores. Didn't give a shit about age or trying to work with the locals. Used intimidation, used drugs, liquor and almost murdered a fifteen year old boy because they thought he was lying to them. My guys had to step in and fuck those two up. That was when I pulled out."

"And who's your contact at Red Blade?"

"The guy in charge," grinned Hans. "Names aren't important. I'll be speaking with him again about why those assholes are still kicking around. Thankfully, they're now our problem."

"And their names?"

"The names they gave you. Alexander Granary and Rudolph Hodgkin."

"Ballsy assholes," I said. "What's their background?"

"Nothing special," said Hans. "Just marines who think they're tougher than special forces. They might have done some courses, but they're no MARSOC."

"MARSOC?"

"Ja, that's the marines special forces unit. Maybe they overcompensate because a lot of the guys come from special forces' units in our line of work. Whatever it is, these guys are just assholes."

"And I'm gonna kill them. I don't see getting justice any other way."

CHAPTER SIXTY-ONE
TESTING METAL

HANS got up and took my empty bottle to stand with his dead soldier on the dining room table. He came back and sat back down.

"You sure about that?" he asked.

I nodded.

"You ever killed a man before?"

I nodded again.

"OK then," he said. "I see you're serious."

"Yeah, I'm serious. Didn't I just tell you what those cock suckers did to me and So-yi. What would you do?"

Hans grinned.

"I would do the same. So-yi was a special woman. She had a good heart and she was a good cop. If you wanted to get the police involved, I'd have let you. But there wouldn't be any bodies to find."

"I want the bodies to be found. That's why I want to do it at So-yi's place. Come full circle."

Hans nodded.

"You'll need to get the evidence you have then to the police afterwards. You're public enemy number one on this right now."

"Yeah, I've seen the news."

We didn't say anything for awhile.

"Were you and So-yi close?" I asked him. "She said she hadn't seen you in some time."

Hans nodded.

"Not the kinda close you're thinking. There's always a student or two that I meet when training local LEOs. I'm good at remembering people, and I tell them that. I guess So-yi remembered me too. I just didn't think I'd be getting a call like this."

Hans looked away, out over the dark night in New York. Maybe he was looking at ghosts swimming through memories. Whatever it was, he didn't say anything for awhile. When he turned back to look at me his face was as composed as ever. But I had the feeling that old demons swam and tormented him deep inside his soul.

"This is what we're gonna do. I'm gonna get my people on these assholes. We're gonna follow them around for the next couple of weeks while you're recuperating. See if we can't find some routine to their behavior. Then once you're up to it, we'll put you in play."

I nodded.

"I like you, Anthony, but I'm happy to take this one if you want to leave it in my court."

I looked at him hard and I nodded slowly.

"I like you too, Hans," I said. "But this one's on me. It happened on my watch and I'll be damned if I don't clean up my own mess."

Hans stood up and patted me on the shoulder.

"You're good peoples. I'll let you drive."

Needles walked into the room and came towards us. Hans turned to look at him when he reached the bed.

"He's doing alright?"

Needles nodded.

"He's doing real good for a smoker, surprisingly," he said.

"Ex-smoker," I said.

Hans laughed.

"Shit man, did he get you to quit as well?"

"He wouldn't give up on it," I said.

"You should have told him to fuck off," said Hans.

"Like you did?" asked Needles.

Hans laughed again. A deep belly laugh that came up through gravel and glass in the pit of his stomach and erupted out of his mouth like heavy chains.

"Ja, Needles here got me to quit twenty-two years ago. You've gotta honor your agreement with him now, Mr. Cool. He won't let you alone about it unless you do."

"My word is my honor," I said.

"Then you'll thank him for it later," said Hans. "Just like I did."

He slapped Needles on the back.

"We're out of here now. I'm going to put a line in the water. I'll see you in about a week and let you know what's what," said Hans.

"I'll be back tomorrow to see how you're doing and probably take out your IV. Try to start eating and drinking like normal," said Needles.

I nodded.

"Thanks for your help," I said.

"This is nothing," said Hans. "It's for So-yi. But now you're family. It's hard to get in and you can't ever escape," said Hans, grinning.

"True," said Needles.

I watched them walk out and down the hallway where they disappeared. I heard distant voices as Rebecca and Mike said goodbye. A short time later, Rebecca came back in with my clothes. Clean and washed and ironed. She gave me space to change. That was a helluva job. Took me almost ten minutes just putting on my clothes. Then we all went into the TV room and watched Goodfellas. I didn't find a lot of good in most of them fellas on the big screen.

CHAPTER SIXTY-TWO
HARD LABOR

Two weeks is a long time. Or it isn't. Depends on your perspective. Einstein explained relativity well using time. He said something along the lines that sitting with a pretty girl for two hours felt like one minute, but sitting on a hot stove for one minute felt like two hours.

I guess it's the same with my two weeks. Two weeks cruising around Barbados might have felt like just a couple of days, but my two weeks in captivity felt like two months.

And I ain't complaining. It's just that I had a lot going on in those two weeks. I was healing from a bullet to the belly. I was quitting smoking and there were days that was all I could think about. I cursed Needles a blue streak. But mostly I cursed myself for having been played like a patsy. I shoulda known he was trying to pull a fast one on me.

But the worst of those two weeks was stuck in a penthouse overlooking Central Park. There was a warrant out for my arrest, so I couldn't go outside. Mike worked all day. Mostly he was gone before I got up and back late at night. He only took Christmas Day and New Year's Day off. Rebecca was swell to hang around with, but she had a life too. I learned that a socialite's life is busy.

Sleep was hell the first few days. I blamed the nicotine withdrawal. Needles wouldn't give me anything for it. I didn't experience headaches but my mood turned foul really quick. The headaches, if I had any, were probably taken care of by the pain meds I was still on for that first week. I quit them on the Monday after I got shot.

My mood was worse that first week. They say you can experience that from nicotine withdrawal. I blamed being stuck in a hole. I watched too much TV and surfed too much internet. I even tried playing War Tyde, but that's not an old man's game. It's for the young kids. And lying in bed or on the couch flipping through channels, I felt like an old man for my forty-four years.

I got real angsty and fidgety. I tried eating shelled sunflower seeds, but the shells started to drive me nuts after a few days. I tried pistachios and had the same problem. I thought of trying to chew on unlit cigars like Columbo but Needles didn't think that was a good idea. I didn't either. I tried lollipops like Kojak, but that wasn't a look I liked. Then it was onto bubblegum. But bubblegum made my jaw ache.

I drank too much coffee. Six mugs a day, and that helped. But it made me piss like a fire hydrant on a summer's day in the Bronx. Hans came by like he said he would on the Wednesday after he'd seen me. He suggested I try meditation. For fifteen minutes we sat there like he'd told me and counted breaths or focused on my breathing. My mind was a monkey playing on an infinite field of trampolines. Hans said that was to be expected.

More importantly, he said he'd gotten a line on what

asshole one and asshole two were up to. He didn't want to share much more, but he figured they were brazen, arrogant dicks who thought they could get away with anything. They were gonna find out just how wrong they were.

I found some other tutorials on meditation. Some were guided, where you listen to a voice talk you through it, others just explained what to do. They all suggested focusing on the breath or the rise and fall of the belly. I chose the latter on account of I could still feel the twinge in my belly going into the second week.

I started meditating every time I started thinking about taking a smoke. That meant I was meditating fifteen to twenty times a day at first. I set a timer for fifteen minutes each time and my eyes stayed closed the whole time. I was meditating for three and a half to five hours a day at times. And it started to work. I started to feel a little more relaxed. A little more focused and a little more calm.

Christmas came and went. Rebecca and Mike bought me some new clothes. A whole outfit. Shoes, socks, pants, underwear, shirt, jacket and new fedora. Must have cost them around a thousand bucks or somewhere around there. They were fancy threads. I got them nothing on account of not being able to leave the apartment. They insisted I'd done more than enough in trying to solve the case. In fact, Rebecca tried paying me again. I put a stop to that. I was saving money by not having to rent a motel room.

I got shot on the nineteenth of December. On the twenty-ninth, the stitches started to fall off and get absorbed by my body. By that time my eye was pretty much fully healed which meant I could open it. In fact it looked like the other eye except for the purple and dark grey bruising around the bottom and side of it. My fractured rib wasn't bitching at me much either. I was pretty much walking around as if I'd never been injured at all. The belly wound was a bit whiny but nothing that needed pain meds anymore. The only telltale signs of violence to my person were the leftover bruising around my eye.

By that time I'd spoken to Johnny Rotten a couple of times. He'd called me on Christmas Day too. Our families had hung out on Christmas Day in years past. But not for a while. He wanted to tell the guys out here that I was innocent. Innocent I tell ya! But I wouldn't let him leak anything we'd shared. I told him I'd get Jersey PD the tapes and other evidence when the time was right.

He asked how I was doing. I was doing great. I was feeling my oats. I wanted to step back into the game. He told me to take my time. That I needed to wait. Be patient. I was getting a lot of that, and there's only so much meditating and navel gazing an ex-smoker with murder on his mind can do. I'd broken down and cleaned and oiled So-yi's gun about a dozen times by then. I could do it blindfolded. And I did. Just to prove I could.

JR had some interesting info for me. Nothing that changed my process, but it gave me some more insight into asshole one and asshole two. Muspell Logistics, I learned, was a holding company. Pipe Dreams was one of the companies they owned. They owned a security company that had a couple of contracts with some malls on the East Coast. The mall that Pipe Dreams was in was one of them. I found that weird on account that the security guards said they worked for Muspell, when in fact they probably worked for the security firm under Muspell which was called Surtir Security Services.

That was an aside. The more important item that Roberts

shared was with the car I'd given him the license to from the parking lot behind Pipe Dreams. It came back registered to Red Blade Incorporated. That put everything neatly into a nice package wrapped with a bow. Red Blade, Roberts informed me, and which I'd figured out as soon as he'd told me, was under Muspell Logistics.

Muspell, Roberts had found out, was actually the fire realm of the nine worlds in Norse mythology. Interestingly, it was ruled by the fire giant called Surtr. In other words, we had vikings playing devil's dice here in Jersey and getting away with it. I didn't know my Norse mythology from horse mythology, and I didn't care. What it gave me was more reason to believe the thesis. Alex and Rudy were carrying out homicides and whether that was on behalf of Red Blade or as a side gig I didn't care. Though if push came to shove my feeling was that they were off book.

I told Roberts I was getting help from 'Oom'. A giant of the South African realm. He got that. I also said that Oom had got a line on my guys and that in the next week or so we were gonna see if we couldn't get justice. I'd told him this on his burner which I'd called from my burner.

I hadn't spoken to Rachel and Chuck or Sarah and Saul. I wanted to have good news for them. And the news I had was just that I knew who did it. I asked Rebecca to hold back on telling her sister too. And she did. But she did tell Rachel that I had good information on who the killers were and that I was likely going to get justice soon. This was all through burners of course.

New Years Eve I spent alone. Rebecca was upset about it. I wasn't. She and Mike had plans to attend some function with dignitaries. I didn't want to stand in the way. I called Aibhilin and we spoke for a while. I wished her a merry

Christmas. I watched a bunch of old movies. It started with It's a Wonderful Life and then I went on to binge Bogart. It started with Casablanca, then went through to The Maltese Falcon which I'd always loved. I continued on with The Treasure of the Sierra Madre and ended the evening with The Big Sleep. Those were probably the best Bogart movies. But you could argue with me if you wanted.

Between The Treasure of the Sierra Madre and The Big Sleep I took a break to watch the fireworks coming out of Central Park. There's one thing I'll say about Empire City, there's always something to do. And it was a grand show they put on for me sitting on the top of the world all by myself.

Mike and Rebecca made it home just as The Big Sleep was ending and I was feeling one coming over me. Rebecca brought me back some fancy chocolates they'd been given at the banquet. Said she'd been thinking about me and wishing me well as the new year rolled around. They're good people, Rebecca and Mike. The chocolate was creamy and sweet but it did nothing for me as I lay my head down in The City of Broken Dreams.

CHAPTER SIXTY-THREE
Two For The Show

I was sitting in an old panel van with Hans and Needles. We had a driver and we'd been following Alex and Rudy. Every Monday, Wednesday and Friday, they drove out to East Orange. And in a boarded up part of town on the outskirts they parked their car and got out. They'd done this six times already. Today was the seventh. They'd probably done this dozens of times before. But Hans had only got a bead on them a couple of weeks before. The day we'd spoken which was a Wednesday. Wednesday the twentieth of December. Today was Wednesday. Wednesday the third of January.

I was watching the assholes get out of their car.

"What's going on inside?" I asked.

"Something nefarious," said Hans. "We haven't taken a look yet. I first wanted to get their routine down. Next, I thought we'd let you be here for the first look."

Alex and Rudy looked around and walked up to the steel door of an old abandoned warehouse. We saw them knock. We were too far away to hear. Rudy looked nervous. He kept looking around, but we were a block away, watching on tech that zoomed in real nice and close. It was night vision and incredibly crisp and clear, though still tinged in green.

A large, stocky man with a bald head and around Alex's height let them into the building and closed the steel door behind them.

"Time to get a close look," said Hans. "Get me the drone in the air, Bird."

The fourth guy with us in the van was Bird. He could generally fly anything. That's what Hans had said. And that's what gave him his nickname. Hans had a drone stored in a dome compartment on the top of the van. Bird was an average sized guy, trim with thick black hair and bright blue eyes. He opened up a laptop and launched the drone.

We watched it go with an aerial view of the warehouse. It was an advanced DOD drone, the kind you can't hear unless it's right up on top of you. The aerial camera was also showing a night vision view. There were still street lights out in this dead part of East Orange, but it seemed every other one was knocked out or broken. And those that were on, leaked a stingy orange light.

As the drone came up on the building it changed to an IR camera. This camera was also sharp. You could make out detailed images of anything that was emanating heat. It appeared that the warehouse was divided into rooms. You could tell that by the way the people moved around the place. Also, the wood beams were cooler than the surrounding so you could make them out faintly too.

There seemed to be six adult males in the warehouse including Alex and Rudy. Beyond that, it seemed like there were about a dozen young kids in half a dozen rooms. The kids looked to be female from all accounts. This seemed to be the case from the longer hair we could make out.

Bird flew the camera around much of this half of the warehouse. The upper half of it didn't seem to carry much of anything except large pieces of machinery.

"This used to be a steel sheet manufacturing facility," said Needles.

After we'd had a good long look at the building from all angles, the drone was delivered back to it's pad on top of the van. I didn't hear it or feel it land. Bird had soft hands. Hans looked at me.

"Are you thinking what I'm thinking?" he asked.

I nodded.

"If what you're thinking is this is the pedophilia palace."

Hans nodded.

"It's a glorious day," he said. "We get to close down a pedophile ring and get justice for So-yi."

"And for Stan and Joe," I said.

"And for Stan and Joe," repeated Hans. "Alright, you leave everything to us now. We've got this under control."

Hans got on his radio and called in his backup. We watched two large, black SUVs roll slowly into view and park on the dark side of the warehouse. A couple of motorcycles were unloaded off of a trailer from one of them. Hans was gonna leave two guys here until just before the police showed up. The bikes were their getaway vehicles. Hans was pretty sure his guys could escape on them. They were electric and thus extremely quiet. I thought it was quite the gamble. Hans didn't.

Eight guys had gotten out of the two SUVs and made their way towards the upper end of the warehouse. The part where no people were. There was a window they were going to detach and get one of the guys to climb inside and open up a door from inside. All of Hans' guys were dressed in black, or a dark blue. Looked like they could've easily been SWAT. They wore balaclavas over their faces.

One of the lead guys had a camera attached to his night vision goggles that fed us his feed. We were right there with them. It carried audio as well. These guys were quiet like ninjas. I couldn't hear them breath. Only occasionally did we hear footfalls.

These old warehouses had windows stuck in with putty. One guy put a suction on the outside of one of the windows and with a little manual manipulation and use of a tool the window popped out in under a minute. It was large enough that I might even have been able to climb through the hole. We watched one of the guys get hoisted in and swallowed up by the hole. This was the loudest part so far, but even then, I doubt you could have heard anything from more than ten feet away.

One of the guys was also feeding us IR video. Alex and his guys seemed oblivious. They were small little colored images far away down the warehouse. In fact, all six guys, including Alex and Rudy, seemed to be huddled together. Nobody had gone into any of the rooms yet where the girls were.

The door opened from the inside out. It creaked a little but was otherwise fairly noiseless. Our guy entered the warehouse in front of the others and they all fanned out.

"Infiltration and engagement has become much easier," said Hans. "You can basically kill a man from the sky without ever having to get near him."

"With drones," I said, nodding. This was not news to me.

"You can also kill him without him ever knowing who you are."

"That's what snipers are for," I said.

Hans shook his head. He pulled out a rifle round from a case he had at his feet. It mostly looked like a rifle round except most of it was bullet and only about a third was shell. The end of the bullet was a needle about a quarter of an inch long.

"This round is self guided," he said. "Our guy is gonna use it on those six assholes up in there. He'll aim and lock in the target. He'll do this six times for each of his targets. Then he'll squeeze the trigger. Shortly after our targets hear the shot they'll drop like flies. Watch."

And indeed, from the cover of darkness and bout a hundred yards away, the sniper locked onto his targets and fired. A second later, all six men had fallen.

"That's cool, but what if there were walls or things of that nature in the way?"

"You generally need to be able to see your target. DARPA's working on self-guided bullets that should be able to overcome those sorts of obstacles, but that's a ways away. This however is part of Project EXACTO. Extreme Accuracy Tasked Ordnance. These ones here though, are subsonic. Super slow and filled with non-lethal high potency soporifics and anesthetics. It's more like a dart than a bullet. The cartridge gives the dart its first push. Then fins eject out of the side for it to maneuver and a propeller to propel it to its target. They're good to about half a mile depending on wind and environment."

I nodded.

"So they're not dead?"

"No, I thought something like this might be going on by the way they kept coming out here. So I figured the police might like to lay some charges on these assholes, and secondly you wanted Alex and Rudy alive, right?"

I grinned. I did indeed.

"Now I've got you your live bait. We're gonna grab these guys and bring them to you. But you've gotta get prepared first, right?"

"I wouldn't want to get on your bad side," I said.

Hans laughed and slapped me on the shoulder.

"I'm one of the good guys. Just like you," he said.

I thought about that as we drove back to So-yi's place. Killing in self-defense was one thing, but I was about to do it premeditated. Did that make me one of the bad guys? Then I remembered what these guys had done to So-yi. What I'd seen them do to those young girls on the tape. And I was okay with my decision. I couldn't see how we'd get justice any other way.

CHAPTER SIXTY-FOUR
PATIENCE

'KEYS' helped me into So-yi's apartment. In fact, he helped all of us into the whole building. His name was self explanatory. Seemed like he could get into and out of anything. He was a thin wiry guy with a shaved head and freckled face. His teeth seemed to have been stuck into his gums by a toddler but he was a friendly guy.

We were in So-yi's apartment first. He then left to help bring in Alex and Rudy and Hans' team who were carrying them. I hadn't been back to So-yi's place since I'd left, bleeding like a pricked balloon. It had been just over two weeks. The police had long left. There was no tape up on the front door anymore and it looked like a cleaning crew had come by. It was probably gonna go up for sale in the near future.

It looked just like I remembered it from the first time I'd seen it. In my mind I saw So-yi sitting on the couch sipping from a glass of wine. I almost smelled steak and eggs. All this reminiscing made my eyes sting so I put a stop to it. I rubbed my belly. It was tender to the touch, the scar felt like a small finger of hard rubber.

I started to doubt myself. I'd never murdered anyone before. Not in cold blood. I wondered if I was starting to slip down a hill into hell, or maybe it was the road paved with good intentions. I'd killed a couple of men before. But that was on the job. That was under extenuating circumstances. That was them or me. Maybe this was them or me. I'd never come face to face with such evil in men before. I took a minute to think about how many ways this could go. And I didn't see anyway through this forest to a just outcome if left to the courts. These two men had murdered three innocent people. They had to pay.

I was gonna have them set up at the end of the living room, perpendicular to the large windows. That way they were across from the bookshelf, looking right at it. I placed my burner phone up there and tested the video recording. You could get a good view of them.

Hans had given me black tactical, slash-resistant gloves before we had left for the evening. I was still wearing them. They gave me comfort. Reminded me of when I was on patrol in LA. I'd wiped So-yi's gun down a couple of times already. My prints weren't on it.

I walked out of the living room towards the kitchen. There was a kitchen table and four chairs there. This is where I'd sat to eat breakfast with So-yi. Where the eggs were sunny and the bacon crisp. I took three chairs one at a time. I placed two in the middle of the living room. There was ample space for them side by side with a bit of room between them and the coffee table where So-yi had died.

I put the third chair halfway between them and the bookshelf, right up against the coffee table. I was gonna sit there. It was angled towards them and out of the way of the burner phone which would record everything.

I sat down and tried it on to see how it looked. The blinds were open. I closed them. Now nobody could look in at us from across the Hudson. I brought a desk lamp out from the spare bedroom and put it just in front of the coffee table. It had an articulated neck and I angled it towards the two chairs. It would illuminate them nicely without letting them see much of the bookshelf.

There was a knock at the door and then it opened. Hans walked in with four of his guys followed by Keys. His guys were rolling in what looked like refrigerator boxes on dollies. They brought them into the living room and kitchen and laid them flat. They opened them and carried Alex and Rudy out into the living room where they sat them in the chairs and tied their hands behind them and their legs to each other.

These guys also brought out what looked like large pop up displays. They were huge, almost floor to ceiling. They enclosed the living room in a square of these displays.

"I've got a camera there," I said to Hans as they were putting one in front of the bookshelf.

"Not necessary," he said, "I've got something better."

I grabbed my phone and put it back in my pocket. Hans' guy put up a tripod with a small video recorder on it.

"This will record visual and audio and also dynamically change your voice so that it's unrecognizable."

"I get the feeling you've done this before."

He smiled at me and nodded.

"What's all the displays for?"

"Well, some folks in here might be sleeping and if you're gonna go off shooting that gun you're gonna wake them up. We can't have that. These are acoustic dampening shields.

They'll halve the sound that can be heard outside of them. Quite remarkable actually. Anyone walking by will just think we're popping champagne in here."

I nodded. Hans had thought of everything.

"A couple of my guys will stay with me to help clean this all up afterwards," he said.

I noticed that behind Alex and Rudy was another plastic sheet before the acoustic dampening shields. That was gonna be for splatter. Behind that was a plate of glass or hard plastic on a stand. That was to catch exiting bullets I reckon. I watched Alex and Rudy. They were still unconscious.

"How long?" I asked nodding towards Alex and Rudy.

"Five, maybe ten minutes," said Hans. "Do you want me in here with you or just outside."

"Outside," I said. I wasn't sure what that meant. Was that outside the apartment or just outside the acoustic shields. I figured it was outside the acoustic shields. Didn't matter to me. This was my rodeo.

I waited patiently for almost ten minutes with So-yi's gun on my lap. Alex was the first to come to, followed shortly thereafter by Rudy.

CHAPTER SIXTY-FIVE
FULL CIRCLE

"WHAT the fuck," said Alex as he started to get his bearings.

I gave him another minute to figure things out.

"Your days of raping children are over," I said.

He looked at me and squinted, trying to see past the bright light in his face.

"Fuck, you again?"

"Me again."

"What do you want?"

He was testing the ties on his hands and feet. He was pretty secure. And if he wasn't, he was gonna die all the quicker.

"I want to know why you did it?"

"Did what?"

"All of it. Raping children. Murdering Joe Severn and Stan Spencer and of course So-yi Park the cop you killed right in this room."

Alex shrugged.

"Because we could," he said. "Never been a problem

before."

"Which part?"

"All of it."

"Does Red Blade know about this shit you pull?"

Alex didn't say anything for a while. I looked over at Rudy. Rudy looked like the one that might crack. I stared at him. He shook his head.

"No," he said.

Alex looked at him. Rudy shrugged.

"We knew we might get caught one day," said Rudy. "I fucking told you we should cool it."

"Did you know Stan was going to speak to a reporter?" I asked.

Rudy nodded.

"And that's why you killed him?"

Rudy shook his head.

"No, man. I, we didn't give a shit about any military weapons he was gonna leak. Our bosses were gonna approach him about it and either get him to come clean or fire him and have him jailed. A lot of the shit they do in that basement…"

"Goddamn it," said Alex, "don't you ever know when to shut the fuck up."

"I know all about it," I said, lying.

"It's too late now," said Rudy.

"That's right, it is," I said. "You guys are working on some crazy weaponry in the basement of Pipe Dreams. Probably got defense contract work. I don't care about that. I want to know why you killed a couple of kids, especially if Pipe Dreams knew about it and was gonna have Stan put in jail."

"Because of the girls," said Rudy.

"Because he had footage of you pedophiles raping

children," I said.

Rudy nodded.

"Yeah, he hacked into that warehouse where the girls are kept and got the footage."

"How did you know?"

"He left logs. He might have been a great computer hacker, but he left logs. He was lazy sometimes. I asked him about it. Told him he better delete them. You know what that mother fucker said?"

I shrugged.

"He told me he was gonna use it as leverage. Said that either we shut that down and turn the girls over to social services or he was gonna leak it to the police."

"So you killed him," I said.

"No. I told Alex about it, and he decided we had to kill him. The journalist was just collateral."

"Shut the fuck up," said Alex.

"So you're the mastermind," I said, looking at Alex.

"When I get out of here, you are so fucked," he said to me, grinning. "You have no idea the capabilities we have at our disposal."

"Except you're running off book. How are you gonna access those capabilities?"

"I don't need nobody else. Just you and me and some of my favorite tools."

This idle bravado was getting tiresome.

"So I understand why you killed Stan and Joe. Why come after me and Detective So-yi Park?"

"You were getting too close," said Rudy. "We tried to give you a way out when you were at Stan's people's place. You wouldn't listen. That Asian bitch was just collateral. And a fine piece of ass."

Rudy laughed at that. So did Alex.

"She was some of the best full grown tail I've had in a long time," said Alex.

I wanted to bust up their faces with the butt of my gun. Instead, I took a moment to focus on my breath. I found my calm center. This meditation was doing wonders for my composure.

"You were a mistake," said Alex. "I realize that now. We should have killed you too instead of just letting you live with it."

"You have no remorse at all, about any of what you've done?" I asked.

Alex grinned and looked over at Rudy.

"My psych evals at the Marines showed psychopathic tendencies. Sometimes that makes for good soldiers. Rudy is the same. That's how we're made."

I looked over at Rudy. He nodded.

"Yeah. Psychopathic tendencies they said."

"So no," said Alex, "we ain't sorry. It's in our nature. We like fucking young girls. And they like it too. We have no problem ending somebody if that's what's gotta be done. But I'll tell you what. You let us out of here and we'll give you a pass. We'll pretend this never happened. Evens Stevens."

Alex looked over at Rudy.

"Agreed," said Rudy.

"This is all recorded on tape," I said. "Maybe I should let you go. Have you put in jail for the rest of your lives."

"Except you know that's not how it works," said Alex.

"Pretty sure it does," I said.

"You've figured out nothing yet. That tape, it can go missing. Plus, looks like you've got our feet to the fire. What do they call that. Coercion. Yeah, this is a coerced confession.

Doubt it'll get into court."

"You're right," I said. "You've helped smooth out the wrinkles on my conscience."

I'd heard enough. I raised So-yi's gun and shot them both in the forehead. They hardly had a chance to figure out what was going on. The gunshot was muffled. I felt like I'd put earplugs in my ears. But I hadn't. I hadn't stood up or moved. I'd just raised my gun, taken aim and fired. I rested the gun back on my lap in my hands. I took a moment and looked at them. I could see the two small red holes just above their right eyebrows. I'd always been a good shot. Had been invited to join SWAT as a sniper. But I went with homicide. There was no back splatter. The bullets hadn't exited their heads. I was grateful for that.

I didn't feel much of anything. So-yi was dead. This hadn't brought her back. But at least two assholes wouldn't bother anyone else again. I felt no remorse, but neither was there any pleasure. I felt like a man who'd worked a hard day. Who wanted to just come home, put his feet up on the ottoman. Scratch his dog's ears. Pour himself a scotch and read the paper. I was tired and ready to put this behind me. Hans stepped back into the space.

"How are you doing?" he asked.

"I'm alright," I said. "Glad to be finished."

I stood up and placed the gun on the coffee table.

"I'll help you pack up."

"Not necessary," he said. "It'll be quicker if you let us do it. Great questions. We got everything we needed. I can't send you a copy on account of it being traced, but you can take a look at it before we erase it from our end. The only copy will be the one on the flash drive. You okay with that."

I nodded.

441

"I don't need to see it."

"OK. Let us take it from here. You've done a good thing."

I went into the kitchen and leaned against the kitchen island and watched them pack everything back into those refrigerator boxes. I'd done a thing. Whether it was a good thing wasn't for me to say. Maybe it was. Maybe it wasn't. But I wasn't bent up about it. One thing I knew for sure. A bunch of young girls were safe and these assholes weren't gonna hurt anyone else. So yeah, maybe I'd done a good turn.

They were done in less than five minutes. Hans took a moment to feel for a pulse on both of them. He also held up a mirror to their faces. They were dead as wine bottles at an alcoholics' revival.

We all left together. It was after midnight and nobody was in the hallways. Keys locked up after us. We didn't want anyone getting in before the police did. We loaded up the vans and headed on out. I was in the same van I was in earlier when we'd done reconnaissance on Alex and Rudy. Hans called up the police and told them he'd heard gunshots coming from So-yi's apartment. Said he was the neighbor across the way. Somebody was about to get woken up. A small price to pay for justice.

CHAPTER SIXTY-SIX
PIPE DREAM KILLERS

I stayed with Rebecca and Mike for several more days. The Thursday, the day after I'd murdered Alex and Rudy, I called Rachel and Chuck and Sarah and Saul. I told them I'd found out who had murdered their sons. I told them their names were Alexander Granary and Rudolph Hodgkin. I told them they were two of the vilest men I'd come across in my years on or off the job.

They asked what happened. I told them the men had been murdered. I did all of this over the phone. My burner to theirs. They asked me who had murdered these men. I told them I had. Said I hadn't figured a way around that in order to get justice. Sarah wept on the phone on hearing that. Thanked me for taking justice into my own hands. Rachel was grateful too, but she wasn't a weeper. I told them to check out the news. Alex and Rudy had confessed. I told them not to believe everything they heard on the news. I told them to toss out their burner phones. I said I'd have a couple of guys come by to check out their homes for bugs.

Well, that wasn't actually gonna be me. Roberts had taken that on himself. I told him what had happened. He was thankful. He was also sorry it had cost me a pound of flesh. Sorry that I'd had to take justice into my own hands. The thing of it was, I wasn't sorry. I'd slept like a baby. My meditation that morning, the day after, was blissful. I hardly ever thought of cigarettes anymore. Though I had a bit of a phlegmy cough.

The news media were calling me a vigilante. Not me personally. The guy who had taken a confession from Alex Granary and Rudy Hodgkin. They had called them the Pipe Dream Killers. There was no longer a warrant out for my arrest. Coincidentally, a pedophile ring was also unearthed that day. Six girls had been found at a warehouse according to news reports. They sent cops to a beaten up house where another six were found. Seven men in all were arrested. That was just gonna be the start. I figured if Stan had accessed tapes from them the police would too. A lot of families were probably gonna find out daddy was a pedophile. I wasn't sorry.

It was funny how the media had spun the Pipe Dream Killers' story. Two rogue plumbers who had killed a couple of young men during a road rage incident. That was the story that had been leaked to the press. They didn't have the confession. The police had that, but that's what had been shared with them. Muspell Logistics had spun that story pretty quickly and pretty good. I didn't know how they did it. I also didn't care.

So-yi's funeral was on the Sunday. Sunday the seventh. I attended it. So did a couple of dozen police and some friends and family. I watched the family. The mother was a wreck. The father held himself stoic as did her brother. I didn't approach them and I didn't say anything to them. What do you say to a man who's lost his daughter? There's nothing you could tell me that would help if I ever lost Aibhilin. Nothing at all.

Detective Devon Schirru approached me after the ceremony. I was standing not far off, looking at the casket.

"You were looking into those Pipe Dream Killers with Soyi," he said.

I nodded.

"She said you were good police."

He was looking at me hard. Like maybe if he looked hard enough he could peel off some layers with his eyeballs. But I was a tougher nut than that.

"And yet, you were at the scene when she died in her own apartment. First you were the primary suspect. Your blood was all over the place. Then a couple of weeks later those assholes confess to three murders. How does that work?"

I shrugged. Devon was trying to push my buttons. Meditation was my shield. He was hardly getting me to increase my heart rate.

"Did you kill her?" he asked. "I want to know."

I looked him steady in the eyes for a while.

"No wonder you fuck ups in homicide couldn't solve this case. It had to take an outside gumshoe and one of your own from major crimes. Because you couldn't see the fucking strings that tied this case together that were right in front of you. And then you ask me a question like did I kill her. Fuck you asshole."

He didn't say anything. He stood with me and we watched the casket and we watched the congregation melt away into the cold day. Then he turned to face me again.

"No," he said. "I don't think you killed her. I think you

445

killed Alex and Rudy on account of what they did to Sue. But that's not how the law works…"

"Law doesn't seem to work around these parts," I said.

"Sometimes things slip through the cracks," he said. "Nevertheless, don't come back here thinking you can pull this kinda shit a second time."

"From your lips to God's ears."

He left me then and I stayed and watched over the casket for a long while. Long after everyone had left. Long after the cold became a numbing nothingness. Then I turned and walked out of the cemetery and hailed a cab. I had a flight to catch.

CHAPTER SIXTY-SEVEN
INVINCIBLE SUMMER

I was sitting at the bar at Sonny McLean's. It was Monday. The day after So-yi's funeral. They day after I left the Big Apple with its rotten core. I was on my third or ninth whiskey. I wasn't counting. But I was reminiscing. I hadn't called anyone since I'd come back. I needed a few days to get my bearings straight.

Sonny had asked me how New York was. I told him it was cold. It was like a different world to LA. A different country. I looked at the whiskey. It was the color of burned sand. Or caramel drizzle on vanilla ice cream on a hot summer's day.

Summer was a lady you knew once. Back in your childhood when you had your first kiss. Maybe she was a desert apparition. You weren't sure you'd see her again. Not now. Not in January. Not in the dead of winter. You had to wander the cemetery of broken dreams and lost souls first. You had a long way to go before the heaving bosom of spring burst forth with a scent of green. A long way indeed. Even the other side of the country wasn't far away enough from dead bodies. So-yi's in particular. I still slept like a baby. I wasn't bent about Alex and Rudy. I'd done a good turn.

But winter was the no-man's land between death and birth. A purgatory. A waiting room for the living. Where the lost souls mark time and wipe away grime from the highway of broken dreams. But maybe that was just the whiskey talking.

Monday nights at Sonny's were lonely. A couple of alcoholics and me in the place. Not much else going on. It was early still. Not quite eight and I was gonna make a night of it. I hadn't eaten and I wasn't hungry. There was a leak in my soul I couldn't quite plug. And it wasn't just these recent events. Maybe it's a leak my old man had sprung the first time he beat me. Or maybe it was the first time he beat my ma. Maybe we all have it. Maybe it's just the slings and arrows of outrageous fortune we all must bear. Whatever it was, sometimes I noticed the leak. I was taking on water, and whiskey seemed to be helping.

My phone rang. I'd tossed the burner at the airport in New York. This was on my fancy phone. It was Declan Dawson the gallery owner at Triangle Gallery. Usually, his calls are pleasant. He wants to give me some money, and money was something I could use right now.

"Hello," I said.

"Anthony, it's Declan."

"How are you Declan."

"Terrific. Just terrific," he said. "How about you."

Declan was a charming man with a slight English accent. He'd been this side of the pond long enough he could speak either way. His natural tone was ever so slightly British. He could charm Scrooge out of his last ten dollars.

"I'm fine, Declan, thanks. What brings the call?"

"Great news Anthony. You've sold the remaining five paintings. Time to get back to work on more."

"Is that right," I said, somewhat surprised. The show had been in November and it was unusual to sell so many at once so long after a showing.

"Quite right. A wonderful woman from New York bought all of them, sight unseen. Said she'd seen them online and wanted them all."

"Really? What's her name?"

"One moment, let me check that again," he said.

I waited on the line for a moment.

"Here it is. Her name is Rebecca England. Do you know her?"

"Yeah," I said. "Casually. I just got back from New York helping her with something."

"You must have made quite an impression. I'll cut the check in a couple of weeks once we've packaged off the paintings."

"What did she pay?"

"Full price. You'll be getting five grand of the ten as per our agreement."

"Thanks Declan. Always good to hear from you."

"My pleasure. Stay well, Anthony."

I hung up. Twenty five grand would be coming my way soon. Ain't life grand. Rebecca ended up paying anyway. I'd have to send a personally signed letter of thanks as I did to all my patrons. I dialed her up.

"Anthony," she said. Might have been me, but there seemed to be a mischievous tone in her voice.

"I just got a call from my gallery," I said.

"Yes, I bought them all. You never told me you were so talented."

"I never told you I painted."

"Of course you didn't. But you're not the only one who can do a bit of investigation."

"Well, I guess thanks is in order."

"No, no. The gratitude is all mine. I was looking for art to put up at our Hampton's home. This will do just the trick. I'm also going to bring a gallery owner around to have a look at them once I have them. I think you should show out here on the East coast too."

"Listen," I said. "There's really no need. I was just happy to help."

"And we're all terribly grateful. This has got nothing to do with that. I'm a collector," she said. "Didn't you appreciate the art we had when you were here?"

"I did, though perhaps not as much as I might have done otherwise."

I remember seeing original Jasper Johns, Andy Warhol and Christopher Wool's work amongst others.

"Then please rest easy, Anthony, I look forward to finding new artists to buy. And your work is now my favorite."

"That's kind of you to say."

"How are you doing now that you're back in your neck of the woods."

"Slowly getting drunk at my favorite bar."

"But still not smoking."

"No, not smoking."

"Good, Anthony. Very good. Well, it's getting late out here. Stay well, and we'll talk soon. Send my love to John."

"Will do."

She hung up and I put my phone back down on the counter next to an empty tumbler. Sonny came by and filled it up. I thought about buying a round for the bar. But that meant spending money I didn't have. I decided against it. I also didn't need friends right now either. My thoughts and my whiskey was all I needed.

My phone rang again. I didn't recognize the number. But I figured, what the hell, I was on a streak.

"Hello."

"This Anthony Carrick?"

"Who's asking?"

"Albert Camus."

He said it like it really was his name. Like he might even have been French, or knew a bit of French. El bear kamoo is what I heard.

"That's absurd," I said.

I got a laugh on the other end.

"I wanted to apologize for Alex and Rudy," said Albert.

"Why?"

"They were under my employ. It saddens me that you had to fix my problems. Though in fairness, I wasn't aware of what was going on. I'm taking a keener interest now."

"Alright."

"Wanted you to know I don't run my businesses like that."

"What's it to me?"

"Not much. Just want you to feel good about what you did. There'll be no consequences from this end."

"Wasn't expecting any."

"There are always consequences, Anthony. Every action causes a reaction. But you've done me a solid. All I ask is that you not release those blueprints you've got. That'll make things more complicated for me."

"Wasn't planning on it."

"Terrific. Then I'll wish you well. Like I said. You did me a favor and I'm grateful. If I can ever return it, call this number and ask for Albert Camus. Tell them you're The First Man."

"Will do."

Albert Camus hung up the phone. I didn't know what to take from the call. I knew enough about Camus to know he was a philosopher and novelist. I also knew that The First Man was an autobiographical novel he didn't complete on account of his premature death.

The guy I'd just gotten off the phone with wasn't Camus. Obviously. He'd died in 1960. The guy I'd spoken with was probably the owner of Muspell Logistics. It was the softest threat I'd been lobbed my whole life. And it didn't bother me. I wasn't planning on doing anything with the blueprints on the flash drive. In fact, I'd erased it and reformatted it. After sending the video footage to Jersey PD anonymously.

But more than that, as I sat here nursing a whiskey and meditating on my angst, Albert Camus spoke to me. A truth I had long forgotten, but one that seemed so poignant right at this moment. In a bar in LA in the middle of winter.

"In the depth of winter I finally learned that there was in me an invincible summer."

ENJOYED THE BOOK?

Reviews are my bread and butter. That is, they help get other readers interested in my books and when readers are interested, they buy. When they buy, I get the monies, and with the monies, I can eat… groan, I know, Al Pacino would be laughing at my feeble attempt at misquoting Scarface!

Seriously though, an honest review would be exceptionally helpful.

I don't have the backing of a big publisher to help sell my books. But what I do have is a million times better. AWESOME READERS - like you. Please consider reviewing any/all of my books you've read. Thank you so much.

Also, are you a subscriber? If not, hop on over to JasonBlacker.com and sign up for FREE books, character interviews, swag, other news and fun stuff, and to join the very exclusive D.A.R.T. Group.

What is the D.A.R.T. Group you say? You'll have to join my awesome readers' list to find out :)

SOME OF MY OTHER BOOKS

I write two mystery series. A cozy mystery series and a hardboiled detective mystery series.

Lady Marmalade Mysteries:

The charming and warm Lady Marmalade is the Baroness of Sandown. But don't let that full you, she also loves solving crime and crafting the best ever marmalade jam you'll taste.

Check her out for some cozy, warm mysteries set between the two World Wars. You'll find cameos by some of history's greatest characters like Gandhi and Lord Mountbatten!

Anthony Carrick Mysteries:

The tough drinking, hard talking Anthony Carrick is an ex-LAPD homicide cop with a conflicted past. From the same mold of Sam Spade and Mike Hammer, he enjoys seeking justice for the downtrodden. Sometimes that means using his fists.

He's a painter in his spare time and lives with a one-eyed rescued cat called Pirate. For fans of noir and hardboiled fiction, this is your stiff, tall drink of fun.